*N*o one knew the real reason she couldn't marry. Yes, she didn't know how to be a wife. True, she didn't know how to live as society expected. But the truth was, it was too late to learn. Learning wouldn't change what happened the night she went to Grayson's cramped garret in Cambridge, needing him. But her plans had gone awry.

"I always wondered why you didn't say good-bye."

His words surprised her since she hadn't gone there intending to say good-bye. At the time she didn't know how wrong things were about to go. But she didn't tell him that.

"I knew I couldn't have been so wrong about you," he said.

His joy was contagious. And the late-night visit was suddenly in the past. She felt his joy, felt that old bond as if they were connected. Before she knew what she was doing, she pelted him with another handful of snow.

This time he wasn't surprised. He grabbed some up himself, and when she tried to scramble away, he held her with his free hand. But he didn't pelt her. He pinned her in the snow. His smile faded, that deep intensity filling his features.

She could only stare back. Then he tossed the snow aside and lowered himself until they lay face-to-face.

"I'm going to kiss you, Sophie. . . ."

By Linda Francis Lee
Published by Ivy Books:

DOVE'S WAY
SWAN'S GRACE

SWAN'S GRACE

Linda Francis Lee

IVY BOOKS • NEW YORK

Lee

An Ivy Book
Published by The Ballantine Publishing Group
Copyright © 2000 by Linda Francis Lee
Excerpt from *Nightingale's Gate* by Linda Francis Lee copyright © 2000 by Linda Francis Lee

www.randomhouse.com/BB/

Library of Congress Catalog Card Number: 00-103280

ISBN 0-449-00206-3

Manufactured in the United States of America

First Edition: September 2000

10 9 8 7 6 5 4 3 2 1

I would like to express my deepest gratitude to Stephanie Vial, DMA and Fred Raimi, MM, Duke University, and Gloria Dale Skinner, who read *Swan's Grace* in its early stages and offered invaluable insight.

And, as always, to Michael.

Prologue

Boston 1892

No one who met Sophie Wentworth could forget her, though Grayson Hawthorne had tried his damnedest.

Leaning back in the chair behind the massive desk of his Boylston Street office, Grayson steepled his strong hands in front of him and thought of Sophie.

When the two of them were young, she had followed him around with the tenacity of a bulldog. Always awkward, she never quite fit in—her knees scraped, her curls wild and unruly, her three-quarter-size cello never far from her side. A prodigy, they had called her. Not what proper Boston Brahmins wanted their daughters to be.

But as an adult, she was captivating. More alluring than simply beautiful.

Grayson glanced at the magazine that lay open on his desk. *The Century* was one of the new weekly publications that had become so popular with the masses. Each issue was filled with different stories of famous people and carefully copied sepia photographs.

Upper-crust Bostonians wouldn't be caught dead reading such a thing. But somehow the feature article on Sophie was the main topic of conversation at every social event since it hit the newsstands.

Boston's prodigal daughter had grown up and become

famous. Grayson nearly smiled at the thought of Sophie causing such a stir. Though thankfully, if she had to be famous, it was as a classical musician and not as some provocative singing star or flamboyant stage actress.

He had a flicker of thought that he had never seen her perform as an adult. In fact, he didn't think anyone in Boston had. But how many ways were there to play the cello?

Until a year ago, Grayson hadn't seen Sophie in ages. But at a party for her father she had sailed into town, arriving late in a whirlwind of velvet cape and shimmering gown, jewels at her ears and neck. No longer the awkward child.

She had kissed cheeks and held her father's arm, teasingly setting too-forward men in their place. Laughing. Always laughing.

He had thought that his heart had hardened long ago, leaving no room for sentiment. But at the sight of Sophie he had felt something shift inside him, something undeniable, elemental and raw, drawing him in.

Grayson hadn't been able to forget about her since.

In truth, he knew he shouldn't be surprised. Glancing across his office, he caught sight of a polished wooden box, its brass funnel attached at the top reflecting the morning sun. A gramophone, or a talking machine, as it was commonly called. He'd had the box for years—saw it every day, sometimes hated the sentiment it represented.

Regardless, he had never been able to get rid of it—all because of the words imbedded in the tin cylinder. Sophie's words from so long ago, words he couldn't forget. And staring at the talking machine now, Grayson finally conceded that he never would.

Turning away, he picked up a file that lay on the walnut desk. Sophie's father, Conrad Wentworth, had discreetly set out to sell the Wentworth family home, Swan's Grace.

Grayson wanted the redbrick-and-limestone house on Commonwealth Avenue, had for some time. Glancing out into the busy, carriage-lined street, he conceded that he also wanted Conrad's daughter.

He wanted her passion; he wanted her fearless charging through life.

A wry smile pulled at his lips. She also would never bore him.

Picking up the document, Grayson read each line with an attention to detail that belied the fact that he had drafted the agreement himself only days before.

Everything was in order.

But when he came to the end he hesitated. If he put his name to the pages he would change his life forever.

Then he remembered Sophie. The feel of her in his arms as he danced her across the floor. The sound of her laughter.

With that, he took the pen from its holder and signed.

There was no turning back. In a matter of months, Sophie Wentworth would return to Boston and become his bride.

Chapter One

The lights went down.

Voices in the opulent gilt hall quieted to a buzz of anticipation. Standing behind the long velvet curtain, Sophie Wentworth could feel their desire. Unrelenting, intense.

With a slow, sensual pull, like strong male hands to a woman's velvet gown, the draperies slid back. Sophie stood onstage, but she stood in darkness, waiting, her heart pounding in her chest, excitement and anticipation swirling together in a heady mix. She could sense the sea of faces in the dark, sense the hundreds of people who filled the concert hall, waiting for her.

Then it happened, that one piercing stream of light, capturing her, tangling in her upswept hair, reflecting off the black satin cape she wore around her shoulders, and the crowd erupted in a roar of applause.

She smiled into the light, her head tilting back as if she were soaking up the sun, her throat tight with exhilarating joy.

This was the moment she lived for—the wave of excitement that swept through an audience when she appeared.

It was the end of her first tour, and over the past months she had taken Paris by storm. Stockholm and Salzburg.

4

Geneva. Even London, with its strict Victorian ways, had adored her.

Only Vienna, the crowning jewel of the music world, remained. It was the city where the greatest had composed and played. Bach and Beethoven, Mozart and Mendelssohn.

And now she would play there, too.

She stood without moving in the Grand Hall of Vienna's Musikverein, the deafening applause feeding her soul. It hadn't started out this way six months ago when she first began the tour. In the beginning she had played as she was taught, proper and decorous—played as she should. And critics had dismissed her as yet another former child prodigy who played the cello with a small, quaint sound.

But she had changed all that, had changed her show. And she had surprised herself by reveling in the change. She loved the extravagant gowns and the glittering jewels. The drama. The deep, throbbing pulse of excitement.

Boston would no doubt keel over from shock if they saw her perform now. She started to cringe, but determinedly held it at bay. Boston was the past. Europe was her future.

Pushing back whatever remnants of inhibition she felt, Sophie let the satin cape drop from her shoulders. A gasp rose from the rows of velvet-cushioned seats up through the ornate tiers of elegant boxes at the sight of her creamy white skin revealed from her low-cut, crimson gown.

And Sophie could feel the instant that they started wanting her even more.

Confidence filled her like wine poured into a glass, and she took her cello from its stand, then gave a discreet nod for the pianist to join her onstage. The excited buzz ceased abruptly, encapsulating the concert hall in silence, complete and clear—not even a whisper was heard.

She could feel the audience, feel their anticipation like a touch as she sat down with the grace of a perfect lady, then slowly pulled the instrument between her legs in the manner one of her more persistent admirers had called a provocative mix of bold abandon and startling titillation.

No one seemed to breathe. Sophie savored the moment, closing her eyes in that crystalline space of perfect quiet while the audience waited, her bow poised. Then she began with a flourish, the faces and adoration forgotten, the world set back as she brought the bow to the strings and pulled a dazzling G major from a lively, popular tune that ensnared every man and woman there. She drew out the music with such passion and beauty that no one in the audience gave a thought to the fact that the piece she played wasn't technically difficult—so different from the pieces she had played when the world had considered her a prodigy. There was no more Beethoven. No more of her beloved Bach.

After that she flew through a repertoire of favorite operatic pieces that had been adapted for the cello, mixing in a few heart-stirring waltzes, and captured the one remaining citadel of Europe with her dazzling up-bow staccato that wowed the crowd.

The night was exhilarating. She could feel their desire—for her music, for her. But toward the end of the show, during a piece that was different from the rest, a more complicated composition she had thrown in because she couldn't help it, she started to savor a note, shaping it. For one unexpected second she tumbled back in time to Boston and long hours of devoted study. Playing and practicing. Striving to be perfect.

But then she remembered where she was, and what her audience was there for. Flourish and vibrato. Spectacle and show. And she leaped into a Danzi duet with a flutist who joined her onstage.

Then it was over, the repertoire complete, two encores played. And Sophie found herself in a dressing room backstage filled with flowers from admirers and compliments from her entourage, who traveled with her everywhere she went.

"You were spectacular!"

"You were beyond spectacular!"

Sophie smiled euphorically, adrenaline pulsing through her veins as Henry Chambers kissed her extravagantly on both cheeks. He was a slight man with dark brown eyes and sandy blond hair. And he was devoted to Sophie.

Deandra Edwards lounged on a sofa, her auburn hair artfully arranged, a glass of champagne between her long, manicured fingers. "Yes, you were fabulous. But you'd best freshen up, *chérie*. The crème de la crème are here. Powerful politicians. Wealthy industrialists. An assortment of men."

Indeed within minutes the suite was filled with dignitaries and important politicians sipping the finest of wines and vying to get closer to Sophie.

"Miss Wentworth," the mayor of Vienna called out in a grand and courtly manner when she entered, quieting the room. "You were divine."

"Thank you, sir." Her voice wrapped around the guests like honeyed velvet. "Your city is a jewel, and I am thrilled to have been given the chance to play here."

"Of course we want you! And now with the article in *The Century* magazine, all the more people are becoming aware of your talent. We could not let you end your spectacular first tour without playing for our city."

Deandra had arranged for the article, saying that publicity would be just the thing to catapult her career from moderately successful to wildly triumphant. Deandra was a genius at garnering attention. She was also right. The magazine had run the glowing article highlighted with printed woodcut impressions of Sophie, making her the musician everyone had to see.

Only Sophie seemed to notice that there was not one

mention of the specifics of her playing, no review of her skill—only a broad sweeping statement that she was a talent that one could not miss. Deandra and Henry had been ecstatic over such complimentary sentiments.

Sophie, however, understood the hidden meaning. She was something to see, but she was little more than spectacle and show. Put her up against a cellist the caliber of Pablo Casals, who had made his debut only a year before her and already was lauded as a genius musician, and she wouldn't stand a chance.

She pushed the thought away. The fact was, she couldn't please everyone. She had made her decision to play this way six months ago after her disappointing first concert, and there was no turning back. She needed this. She needed to perform, and Europe had given her the chance.

An older man stepped forward, his manners old-world and charming as he took her fingers in his white-gloved hand and pressed a kiss to the air just above her knuckles. "Miss Wentworth. You leave me breathless."

"Thank you," she said, her smile seductive.

"You must not remember me."

Sophie tilted her head in surprise, the light catching in her ruby earrings.

"I see you don't. I am Herr Wilhelm," he explained in a heavy German accent. "We met once before. In Boston."

She went still.

The man gave a slight bow of his head. "It was years ago, of course. You were perhaps sixteen or seventeen. I saw you play for a small group in the governor's home."

The memory of that night leaped out in her mind. It was all she could do not to close her eyes, to hug herself tight like the foolish, naive child she had been.

"As I recall," he continued, his light eyes boring into her, "you played quite differently back then. You played Johann Sebastian Bach. His third suite for cello in C major.

The andante was superb. I remember your performance distinctly."

As did she. She had been born to play Bach, and she had that night. It had been a night of triumph and glory, a night that was to have been one of the first intimate concerts she was to give leading up to her eighteenth birthday and her performance in the Grand Debut.

The Grand Debut was a much-anticipated concert created to introduce Boston's finest talent. Only one student a year was awarded the coveted solo position.

The conductor of Boston's prestigious Music Hall had promised her mother that he would ask Sophie to perform the solo—an event she had dreamed of her whole life. But the recital never happened.

Glancing away, she focused on the crystal glasses and sparkling wines. She didn't want to think about Boston, not tonight of all nights when crowds of people loved her. But Boston was relentless, leading her as always to Grayson.

Grayson Hawthorne, the oldest of the well-known Hawthorne brothers. The powerful man whom all of Boston either feared or greatly respected.

He was also the object of her most devoted childhood infatuation.

She couldn't remember a time she hadn't known Grayson. Just the thought of him made her smile, made her heart settle in a way only he had the ability to do. Where was he now? she wondered. What was he doing?

Some months ago while she and her entourage had been in Paris, Margaret Brimley, the woman who kept Sophie and her entourage together, on time, and on schedule, had received word from her cousin in Boston that Grayson had finally turned his attentions to choosing a wife. For half a second, Sophie had felt a young girl's wish that he would choose her. But she had just as quickly stamped out the thought. She would be no man's wife. Not even Grayson Hawthorne's. Or perhaps especially not Grayson Hawthorne's. The past had ensured that.

She felt the familiar flare of guilt and despair, followed quickly by anger. But she turned away from the feelings. It was futile to feel anything about the past. And the fact was, she didn't want to return to Boston, she told herself forcefully.

As to Grayson, it was rumored that the lady he chose had to be of unquestioned virtue, impeccable lineage, and high-minded principles. In short, the woman had to be as dull as the waters in Boston Harbor.

Sophie shuddered at the thought of what he would think of her now if he ever saw her perform. Grayson Hawthorne might have smiled indulgently at her childhood antics, but she had learned the night of her father's birthday party that he had become a man who would not find outrageous behavior from a wife tolerable—much less charming. He would expect her to do as he wished, when he wished it, and without question.

Shaking her head ruefully, she wondered who the poor woman was whom Grayson had chosen to be his bride.

"Why don't you include Bach in the pieces you play now?"

With a start, she forced a laugh and stepped closer in a rustle of satin and lace. "Bach is so boring, Herr Wilhelm. A waltz is much more provocative, and sometimes it is nice to hear a passionate minuet. But the cello suites? Everyone plays Bach." Which, of course, wasn't true, since the pieces were undeniably difficult.

She placed her hand boldly on his forearm and smiled. "Don't you agree?"

She could tell the second he forgot about Bach.

"You have a point," he said, his eyes drifting low to her

décolletage. "Perhaps we could talk more about that over a glass of cognac at my hotel."

"Perhaps," she teased, knowing she never would. "First, however, I must see to my other guests."

But just when she stepped away in a sweep of satin and shimmering lace, the door pushed open and in raced the primly dressed Margaret.

"You've received a letter," she said, her eyes brimming with excitement. "From Boston."

Sophie's smile froze on her lips.

"Look," Margaret said, showing the return address, "there's no mistake."

With her heart in her throat, but a casual laugh for the crowd, Sophie took the letter, then walked out the door into the narrow backstage hallway. The dignitaries were left behind, but her entourage followed.

Forcing her hands not to tremble as she broke the seal, Sophie read once, then twice.

"Who is it from?" Margaret finally demanded.

"My father," she whispered.

"Good Lord. What does he want?" Deandra demanded.

"He wants me to come home." She looked up.

That was the surprise. The minute she stopped waiting for him to ask her to return, he did.

Deandra raised a brow. "Did he tell that new wife of his he was writing?"

"She is not *new*, Deandra," Henry drawled. "They've been married five years, for God's sake. Regardless, we can't go." He rubbed his hands together and licked his lips. "Now that the tour is finally over, we are going to have a grand time in Monaco. Gambling. Sea bathing. People watching." He looked directly at Sophie. "We discussed this."

They had, but no promises had been made. And suddenly the thought of late nights and endless parties lost its appeal. Besides, what her entourage didn't know was that just then she couldn't afford the expense of staying in Monaco. She had put every penny she had earned into her new concerts. The gowns. The trains and hotels for four adults.

She shuddered to think that she had borrowed money to pay for the jewels. But flash was important. And it had all paid off. She was booked for the next season—this time with concert halls paying her exorbitant fees, not to mention her expenses. But she had to survive until then. And the new concert season didn't start for months. Her father's invitation to come home couldn't have been better timed.

When she didn't answer, the little man grew childlike. "Sophie," he stated, his tone petulant.

"I know, I know."

She started down the dimly lit hallway, the swish of her long gown echoing against the barren walls. The entourage followed.

"Don't tell me you are considering it?" Deandra demanded as they walked.

Sophie didn't answer. She searched for the back door, needing some air, needing to be alone. Had her father seen the article?

Even though there had been no mention of how provocatively she played, she still knew that to be written about at all was scandalous by Boston's standards. If he had read it, was he dismayed? Or was he the tiniest bit proud?

But more than that, did she care?

Margaret hurried a few steps to catch up. "I think we should go to Boston. I've been to Monaco. You would hate it, Sophie. It is so boring there."

"Maybe for a plain little mouse like you," Henry said with a huff.

Margaret gasped.

"Henry." Sophie shot him a censorious glare.

He glared back. "It's true."

"Enough!"

They continued on, their footsteps echoing as they took a left, then another quick right down a long hall that led to the stagehands' exit.

"Don't even consider it, Sophie," Deandra instructed. "How many times have you told me how much you hate Boston?"

Sophie stopped abruptly at the back door and whirled around to face them. "But my father has asked me to come home." She looked at the three people who had come into her life and become a family in place of her own. "He has never asked before," she whispered, more to herself than to the others.

Henry cursed; Deandra sighed and shook her head.

"You go to Monaco," she offered, searching her mind for a way to pay for their trip. She took care of them. They stayed with her because of money. She understood that, but as far as she was concerned, it was a fair trade. She hated the thought of being alone. "You will have a grand time. Then we will meet up again in May to prepare for the summer tour." She hesitated, her mind racing. Was she crazy to be considering Boston? Surely she could find a place to stay in Europe until spring, when money started coming in again.

But then she thought of her father. Money concerns or not, she loved him, had desperately wanted to be a part of his new life. But there hadn't been a place for her. Until now.

"I am going to Boston." To her father and to her home, Swan's Grace. And perhaps, she thought with a rush of anticipation, just once she would see Grayson before he married.

"This is grand, simply grand," Margaret practically sang, pulling out a tablet from her pocket to start making lists. Then she stopped and glanced up. "In fact, to make it even better, why don't we arrange for a concert at the Music Hall?"

Deandra laughed harshly. "Our dear Sophie, play for Boston's old guard? She'd curl their hair with her show. Those pilgrims would be shocked silly."

Sophie forced a smile, hating the sting the words caused. "It hardly matters. I won't be playing there."

"Why not?" Margaret demanded. "You could buy new gowns. Play different music. You could—"

"No, Margaret. It's not going to happen. I'm not going to change my concert."

She turned away and pushed open the door, breathing in the cold, biting air. "Besides, even if I wanted to, the conductor of the Music Hall has never asked me to play." Despite his promise to her mother long ago. Or perhaps because of it.

But none of that mattered now. Her father had asked her to come home. The only question that remained was, Why had he asked?

Chapter Two

Three months later they arrived in Boston. Early. A week early, to be exact.

In the end, Deandra and Henry had been unwilling to go to Monaco without Sophie. And Margaret, hoping her Boston relatives would welcome her home, was anxious to send off a note to announce her return. As a result, all four of them stood on the walkway in front of Swan's Grace—a tall town house made of red brick and limestone.

The sun had set and gas lanterns burned golden along the length of Commonwealth Avenue in Boston's prestigious Back Bay. Henry peered up from the street through the darkness. "It doesn't look like they waited up for us."

Sophie glanced at him with a mischievous smile. She couldn't believe how excited she was to be home. "That's because no one knows we're here. I'm going to surprise Father," she explained, before her smile quirked wryly at the thought of the very dark house. "At the time it seemed like a good idea."

Deandra rolled her eyes. "We'll surprise him, all right," she said, using her Lyons Mignon parasol to bat some unfortunate lantern boy who accidentally brushed against her skirt on his way down the street. "Once he gets a look at us, we will be heading to the nearest hotel. I've said it before, and I'll say it again. Your father will not want a man

15

and two women he doesn't even know staying at his house."

"My father is not like that," Sophie insisted. "Besides, what most people don't know is that Swan's Grace is not my father's house."

"Really?" Deandra mused. "To whom does it belong?"

Sophie laughed with delight. "Me."

The landscape was covered with winter snow and ice, but that didn't put Sophie off. She reveled in the barren rosebushes she had planted with her mother as a child, which peeked out from beneath the winter pack. She marveled at the matching swans carved from granite that were mounted on either side of the steps that led to the front door.

Swan's Grace. Dignified and refined. And for half a second, time spun backward and Sophie expected her mother to step out onto the terrace, her arms held wide.

Sophie drew a deep, poignant breath. Her mother had been dead five years. But Genevieve Wentworth was still here in so many ways—in her daughter's music, in the flowers and garden trellises. She was in everything that made up this house, the one material possession in Sophie's life besides her cello that meant something to her.

In the years since she had left Boston, having Swan's Grace had somehow always made her feel safe. If she lost everything, she would always have her home. How many times had she wrapped the thought of every sturdy brick and hardwood door around her like a fortress against the cold?

Lifting the hem of her brilliant blue velvet traveling ensemble, Sophie mounted the steps. At the door she knocked once, then twice. Anticipation mixed with trepidation at the thought of seeing her father. Would he hug her, kiss her, or be distant and reserved? How would her stepmother, Patrice, act? Would she smile and welcome her friends?

But no one answered the door.

After a moment Sophie tried the knob, only to find it was locked.

"That's odd," she remarked.

Deandra made herself comfortable on the back of one of the swans, pulling out a cigarette and attaching it to an overlong holder. The flare of the match hissed in the cold.

Margaret paced, waving aside smoke every time it drifted her way.

Henry tried the door handle himself, even went to the windows and gave each a tug. "The house is locked tight," he announced, taking the cigarette holder from Deandra. "Clearly no one's home."

"How could that be?" Sophie murmured. "Even if the family is out, the servants would be here."

The Back Bay consisted of a long, narrow, orderly grid of streets, with Commonwealth Avenue running down its center as a sort of manicured, statue-lined pièce de résistance. Swan's Grace stood on the corner of Commonwealth Avenue and Berkeley Street, with a walkway, neatly cleared, that veered off through the expansive side yard which ran along the house. And that walkway hadn't cleared itself. Someone had to be there.

"Maybe your father and his new family have moved."

Sophie studied the darkened windows, ice framing the panes like lace. There had been an awful lot of talk the last time she was in town about Patrice being desperate for a new house on The Fens, a posh part of town where the infamous though hugely wealthy Isabella Gardner had built her stunningly opulent palace. Was it possible that they had moved and her father hadn't told her?

Sophie's heart surged with the all too familiar feeling of being left alone. Then she scoffed into the nighttime air. Her father had asked her to return. She was early. No doubt if she had arrived as planned he would have been at the harbor to greet her.

"They must be on holiday," she mused. "Which could explain why the servants aren't here." But then who had cleared the path?

"What are we going to do if we can't get in?" Margaret asked.

Henry smiled, exhaling a breath of smoke and handing the holder back to Deandra. "Not to worry, ladies," he said with a flourish of cracking knuckles. "Stand back."

"You can't break the window!"

"Pshaw. I would never be so crass." He pulled out a small, flat metal file and applied it to the door lock with the expertise of a backstreet hoodlum. In seconds there was a click, but also a suspicious crack, before the door swung open.

Sophie groaned, but Henry gave her little notice. With a grand sweep of his hand, he gestured for the women to enter. "Come on, hurry. It's freezing out here."

Inside, all was quiet. Their footsteps echoed on the black-and-white marble floor, the sound carrying up into the high-ceilinged foyer.

The house was elegant, if understated, with a wide sweep of stairs, fluted archways, and a crystal chandelier.

Walking farther inside, Sophie turned up the gaslights. But still no one appeared.

"This makes no sense," Sophie whispered.

She made her way through the first floor, pulling off her kid gloves one by one, then her cape and waist-length traveling jacket, tossing them aside as she went. It felt good to be home. Everything looked the same, only somehow newer, she realized suddenly. She wrote the changes off to time having passed, not to mention the dark.

But it was the room off the front study that finally stopped her, a sitting room of sorts, and her brow knitted.

Her mind tumbled back to her mother and their plans to make this very space into a music room. But since Sophie was last there, her father had turned it into a library with a desk and bookshelves. Fine hunting prints took up every inch not covered with books.

Her homecoming was not going as she had hoped—the house was not warm and welcoming, her father wasn't there to offer her a joyous smile, and her stepsisters weren't circling around with happy cheers of excitement. Sophie's pleasure started to fade. But stubbornly she held on. A library could be undone.

Her thoughts were interrupted by a sudden commotion of booted steps on marble tiles and Margaret's gasp from the foyer.

"I'd assume you were Conrad Wentworth," she heard Henry state in his favorite sarcastic lilt. "But you're a little young to have a full-grown daughter. Which begs the question, who are you?"

"A better question is, who are you?"

A man's voice, deep and low.

Sophie's head tilted and her mind raced. There was something familiar about the sound, and a shiver of awareness raced through her body. Her palms began to tingle at the thought that only one man had ever filled her with such feelings.

With her heart in her throat, she headed back to the foyer. And saw him.

Grayson Hawthorne.

Her pulse slowed and her breath grew shallow. It was always that way when she saw him. The astonishment that any man could be so striking, sensual in a hard-chiseled way.

With his challenging glare pinning Henry to the spot, he stood in the flickering gaslight. He was a tall, commanding man with dark hair, longer than she remembered, swept back from his forehead. His jaw was strong, his shoulders sculpted beneath his four-button cutaway jacket that revealed fine woolen, hard-creased trousers molded to his thighs in a way that made her heartbeat quicken.

Tilting her head, Sophie remembered how as a child she had followed him around, she always in trouble, while he had always been patient in a shaking-head, rolling-eyes sort of way. Indulgent of that odd duck Sophie Wentworth.

A fond smile pulled at her lips in memory of the child she had been. Had she really been so obvious and devoted?

"If you don't explain yourself," Grayson stated in hard, cold syllables, his gaze never wavering from little Henry, "I am going to send for the police."

"What is all this talk about the police?" Sophie asked, her smile growing wider as she strolled into the foyer in a swish of velvet.

Grayson turned at the sound, and stopped.

Their eyes met and held, and she knew he was as surprised to see her as she was to see him. For a moment the entourage faded from her mind. There was only Grayson. For one startling second time was lost and they were young again. He was her hero, she his shadow. Her heart filled with a surge of warmth and remembered devotion, and she nearly ran across the room to him.

But then he contained his astonishment behind a fathomless mask. Suddenly his eyes regarded her with a bold, speculative gleam that she found unsettling. Time righted itself, and it was clear Grayson was no longer a boy, rather a man.

At her father's birthday party she had learned that Grayson was no longer patient or indulgent. He was ruthlessly contained, controlled. In the years she had been gone, he had gained an uncompromising authority and a predatory grace, the lines of his body hard and well defined.

She crushed her schoolgirl urge to dash over and hug him tight. She was a woman now, not a child. Long past the age where she followed Grayson around or twined her fingers impulsively with his.

A flash of regret raced through her that things had changed. But she was mature now, and independent, as successful as he was—that is, if a person was willing to turn a blind eye to those pesky little money problems she had. *Soon* she'd be as successful as he was, she amended with a nod and a smile.

"Did you hear that, Sophie?" Henry barked, incensed. "This brute has threatened to summon the police."

Margaret wrung her hands. "You can't call for the authorities for being in one's own house, surely."

Deandra scoffed, crushing her cigarette in an antique bowl. "I can see it now. 'Prodigal Daughter Tossed Out of Home.' On the front page of every newspaper in town. It would be all over this rustic backwater by morning." Her green eyes narrowed in thought and she tapped her fingernail against the table. "No question everyone would talk." Her finger stilled and she glanced at Sophie. "If you play your cards right, you just might get arrested. We couldn't pay for publicity like that."

Grayson's expression turned glacial, locking on Deandra as if he didn't recognize *what* she was, much less who.

Sophie covered her burst of laughter with a cough. "Deandra, you are so bad."

"Isn't that what you pay me for?"

Sophie watched as Grayson slowly looked from person to person, finally fixing on her. Her heart gave a lurch and she felt an unaccustomed rush of heat as his dark eyes drifted over her in a way that had nothing to do with the past. Or propriety.

His eyes narrowed. "Sophie?"

"Ding, ding, ding," she chimed, covering her fluttering heart with a laugh. "You win the prize."

One dark brow tilted sardonically, and for a second she would have sworn he almost smiled.

"You're here," he stated, his intense gaze never wavering. "And you're early."

"Ding, ding, right again. You are a veritable feast of correct answers tonight."

His brows flattened to hard lines.

"Alas," she continued as she sauntered forward, her dainty heels clicking against the marble, "we caught an earlier ship out of France. A bucket of bolts held together with baling wire and twine, as far as I could see. But it got us here so I could surprise Father." She stopped abruptly as a thought occurred to her. "How did you know that I was coming home?"

For a second this tall, commanding man seemed confused, or perhaps surprised by what she had said; then it was gone. "Your father told me."

"Ah, well, that explains it. And since you know so much, why isn't my father here?" But the question trailed off, replaced by another. "Why are *you* here?"

His confusion resurfaced; then something dangerous flashed in his eyes. "Don't you know?"

They stared at each other, and she felt curiously disconcerted by the way he looked at her. Strangely possessive.

"No, I don't know, Grayson. If I did I wouldn't have asked."

His gaze burned into her, the arrogance, the sense of possession, making her feel as though he had run his open palm over her skin. Her body tingled, and she was all too aware of this man.

She had liked it better when they were both young, she following him around like a shadow. Their families the best of friends.

A ghost of a smile surfaced as she remembered—her father with Grayson's father, smoking cigars in the study.

Grayson's mother with her mother, sipping tea at Hawthorne House.

Oddly, she had never been enamored of his brothers, Matthew and Lucas. She had liked them well enough, but it was Grayson who drew her, always had. But as adults, the ease they had shared as children no longer existed. The air between them now was charged, heated, just as it had been the night of her father's party.

"I live here," he stated.

She blinked. "What?"

"I said, I live here."

"You live here?" In her home?

Her heart began to pound in a way that had nothing to do with strange possessiveness or burning gazes. But she refused to give in to the rush of uncertainty. "Fallen on hard times, have you?" she quipped, forcing the words from her mouth. "Sorry to hear it. But it's a big house. The more the merrier, I always say."

She had to find her father.

Gathering her long skirts, she started to turn away. But he caught her arm. His long, chiseled fingers curled with surprising gentleness just below her capped sleeve, and she couldn't seem to look at anything else but his golden skin pressed against her own.

For one startled moment she saw his hand, though it was a smaller, younger hand that she saw in her mind. All of a sudden she was a child, awkward, her hair wild and untamed, smudges on her cheeks as he brushed grit from her knee. Her dear, sweet Grayson. Her knight. The only person who had always been there for her—except once, when she had needed him the most.

Her head jerked up and she looked at him, so tall, so strong, not an ounce of weakness about him. "How could you have wanted her?" she whispered.

"What?"

Her breath hissed in with a painful gasp as she remembered where she was, in Swan's Grace, five years later. No one knew about her nocturnal visit to see Grayson years ago. And she intended to keep it that way.

Her laughter was hollow in her own ears, and she tried to pull away.

But he held her there and with the crook of his finger, he nudged her chin. "I'm not sure why there is this confusion, but I am not a boarder, Sophie. I own Swan's Grace now. I thought you knew."

Every ounce of her forced humor evaporated at the words, and she tugged her arm free. "That's absurd."

"I was led to believe Conrad talked to you about this." His eyes darkened even more, that dangerous flash resurfacing, as if there was something else he wasn't saying. "I bought the house from your father three months ago."

Her world spun and she couldn't seem to breathe. She hated the surety she heard in his voice.

But then she got a hold of herself. "That is ridiculous. It is not his house to sell."

"I'm afraid it was."

"It's mine!" A thread of panic flared in her voice.

"But it was in his name. The contract—"

"No!" she blurted out, cutting him off. "It was in his name, yes, but only because of an idiotic document I signed when I turned eighteen, giving him control of my affairs." At the time it had seemed a small price to pay for her freedom. A small price to pay to be allowed to leave Boston and attend Leipzig Music Conservatory in Germany. But her father never would have sold her house, she was sure.

Calm down, she ordered herself silently.

"Document or no, my father hasn't made a single attempt to involve himself in my life in years." As she said the words, she knew they were true, and the calm she fought for began to surface. "Clearly this is a misunderstanding. We will get it straightened out with my father as soon as I find him."

She laughed, suddenly relieved as she regained her composure. Without thinking, she reached across to pat his arm. Instantly his gaze shifted to her fingers against his dark coat, and she would have sworn she felt a tremor race through his body—as if this imposing man felt some sort of vulnerability at her touch. Suddenly she wondered what it would feel like to tangle her fingers with his. To hold tight. To feel Grayson wrap his arms around her as he had when they were young.

With a self-conscious little chirp, she yanked her hand back. "Rest assured, if indeed some mistake has been made and money has changed hands, I will see to it that my father returns every penny."

His elegant panther's body grew still as he lifted his head and considered her with cool, appraising eyes. He seemed to look into her, searching. He had always been too good at reading her thoughts, as if he could see into her soul. It was all she could do not to close her eyes.

"The money is not my concern."

"Well, good. Then there won't be any problems. In the meantime, we are exhausted. Come along, everyone." The sooner she got away from him the better. Tremors and emotion, seeing into souls? Good God, before long she would be eight years old again, idyllic and romantic, believing in knights in shining armor.

But the world wasn't idyllic or romantic. And there certainly was no such thing as a knight in any kind of armor.

The travelers started toward the stairs.

"Sophie," he stated, the word a quiet command.

At the bottom of the steps she turned back. His chiseled features appeared even more grim.

"Yes?" she asked.

"You can't stay here."

His words rumbled through the foyer and her heart leaped. They had no place else to go, and she had no money to pay for lodging. "Why can't we?"

The question stopped him. He stood for a moment and stared at her, this bold, commanding man, his handsome face shifting into hard, frustrated planes as he seemed to carry on some battle within himself.

"For now, let's just say that it isn't proper for an unmarried woman to sleep in the home of a bachelor," he replied evenly.

With that, a slow smile pulled across Sophie's lips, her equilibrium finally, truly restored. She stepped back and ran the tips of her fingers provocatively down the sleeve of his suit coat, ignoring the heat that flared in his eyes. "So it is true. You really have turned into a fine Victorian prude."

Surprise flared, though only briefly, before the muscles in his jaw tightened. Tension crackled in the air, and standing so close to him she could smell the deep, heated scent of sandalwood.

"Alas," she continued, stepping away as quickly as she could without looking like she was fleeing, "I'm not terribly concerned about my reputation. But if you're concerned about yours, the Hotel Vendome isn't too far down the road. No doubt you could secure a suitable room over there."

Grayson slammed the brass knocker against the massive front door of the palatial limestone and marble mansion on The Fens. The street was quiet, gaslights his only company. It was late, much too late for a call. But Grayson wasn't about to wait until morning to confront Conrad Wentworth.

Impatiently he banged the knocker again, pacing across

the gray-slate terrace until he heard fumbling inside. At length, the door pulled open a crack.

Raymond, the Wentworth family butler, peered through the opening, his face creased with sleep, his trousers and waistcoat hastily thrown on, a candle and holder held up, casting a faint circle of light onto the front stoop.

"Mr. Hawthorne," the man stated, alarmed.

"I'm here to see your employer."

Raymond stammered, stepping back, the door opening further. "But Mr. Wentworth has retired for the night."

"Then tell him to *un*retire."

The butler clearly didn't know what to make of the situation, but when Grayson stepped into the house, he didn't stop him.

Boot heels ringing on marble tiles, Grayson strode past two jewel-encrusted lions that perched in the foyer. Unlike most Bostonians, Conrad Wentworth wasn't opposed to displaying his wealth.

Wealth? Hell. If Conrad had bought fewer jewels for his house and his wife they might not be in this situation.

Grayson was only glad he had learned about Conrad's desire to sell Swan's Grace before it had gone to someone else. Though that certainly didn't help them now.

"But, sir—"

"Get him, Raymond."

The butler was saved from making a decision when a light came on at the top of the stairs.

"What is going on down there?"

Grayson turned to find Conrad Wentworth pulling on a silk robe over his nightshirt.

"Good God, Grayson. What is going on?"

"I want to know why the hell you signed a legal document selling your daughter's property without her consent."

Conrad halted on the stairs for a moment, then continued on. When he came to the foyer, his slippered feet hit the tiles with a shuffle, and when he spoke, his voice was a study in calm as he smoothed his sleep-ruffled gray hair. "I signed that document because I had every right to."

Grayson pinned him with a glare. "You told me she was in agreement." He reined in his frustration as he stared at the older man. "And if you didn't tell her about the house, I can only surmise that you didn't tell her about the betrothal."

The house went quiet.

Conrad shifted his weight uncomfortably. With a wave of his hand he sent the butler away, then he strode into a study off the foyer. The room was dark, but a gaslight quickly brightened the fine wood interior. He directed Grayson to one of the two wing-backed chairs that faced a beautifully carved mahogany mantel. But Grayson wasn't interested in sitting.

Conrad cast a quick, nervous glance at him. "No, I haven't told her about the betrothal. But you are wrong about my authority. I am Sophie's father, and I have every right to guide her life."

"When she was younger, but not as an adult."

"Sophie is not just any adult. She has become a famous adult, and she was a child prodigy before that—the kind of woman all sorts of people try to take advantage of. I control a trust that was set up for her when her mother died, which includes Swan's Grace, and it gives me the right to make decisions regarding her affairs."

"If you felt so certain about this trust, why haven't you directed her before now?"

Conrad grimaced. "I've had other things on my mind."

"That is clear." Grayson seethed. "But she's your daughter."

"Sophie is not the only daughter I have!"

"Ah, yes. Your new family. How could I forget."

Conrad flushed red, his stance growing defensive. "I was giving Sophie a chance to fulfill her dreams as a musician. She has succeeded. That magazine article is proof of that. But now it is time she returned home to make a suitable life for herself. She's a woman, for mercy's sake. She can't be a musician forever. More than that, she certainly can't continue to travel around the world with that ill-assorted group of hangers-on the article mentioned. And I plan to tell her about the arrangements I've made just as soon as she arrives."

"Arrived," Grayson clarified impatiently. "Sophie is already here."

"What? She's not supposed to be here for another week!"

"Sophie is in Boston, at the Commonwealth Avenue house, expecting you." His jaw tightened. "Hell, Conrad, you didn't even bother to tell her you had moved."

The older man looked chagrined. "I had planned to explain that, too, when I picked her up at the harbor and brought her here to The Fens." The lines of his face softened. "I had planned to drive her around the Public Gardens, perhaps get out and walk over to see the skaters on the lagoon. I was going to tell her everything."

"And you think that would have been enough? A quick explanation during a stroll through the park? *After* the papers were signed?"

The softness evaporated and Conrad matched Grayson's anger. "She is twenty-three years old, and it's time she learned that there is more to life than music. She needs guidance. And as her father, it is my responsibility to see to her welfare. I'm seeing to it now, and if I have to use that trust to get it done, so be it. She will move in here where she belongs until she is married."

Grayson raked his hand through his hair. "God, what a mess." He looked at the older man with barely held patience. "Surely you understand that this is not the way to get your daughter to settle down. Sophie will only fight you." His gaze narrowed to slits of obsidian. "Which means she will also fight me."

"Let her fight. Whether she wants to admit it or not, I'm doing what is best for her." He gave a sharp tug to tighten the belted sash at his waist. "I will explain the situation to my daughter. I will go over there first thing in the morning."

"Tell her about the house," Grayson said, his temper under tight control. "But I don't want you making things worse by telling her about the betrothal." His eyes narrowed, his voice taking on a cold, hard edge. "I will tell her about our marriage myself. If she finds out that on top of everything else you betrothed her without her consent, she will be like a runaway horse with a bit between its teeth. She would reject the match simply to defy you."

"I am her father. She will not defy me!"

"Then you've forgotten what Sophie is like."

Conrad grumbled. "I haven't forgotten. She's as headstrong as they come. Always has been."

"My point exactly. Now I will have to untangle this mess."

Chapter Three

"I thought the betrothal was finalized."

It was the following morning, and Bradford Hawthorne, patriarch of the venerable Hawthorne family, spoke from the doorway of his study.

Grayson stood at the mullioned window of Hawthorne House, tense and silent, his thoughts concealed as his father's angry voice sliced through the room.

He had woken up at the Hotel Vendome, his mood dangerous as he remembered Conrad Wentworth. Then he remembered the man's daughter, and his mood changed, though it hadn't gotten much better.

Sophie.

A constant in his life from the day she was born, she had followed him around, constantly talking, always asking questions. A whirlwind of trouble he had pulled out of more scraps than he cared to count.

But there had also been a day when she had tried to save him.

At the memory he felt the easing of that hardness in his heart. It was always the same when he thought of Sophie.

Three months ago the match had seemed perfect. Two old Boston families coming together. A shared past that had meaning.

But last night she had been different from the way he

remembered her. She had changed. Or was he fooling himself?

In truth, at Conrad's birthday gala she had smiled with a confidence and self-possession that not many women had. On the surface she had been the picture of propriety, wearing a stunning though demure gown, her hair decorous, her jewels subtle. But her eyes had flashed something not proper at all. Like a fire carefully banked.

In truth, there had always been that glimpse of boldness in Sophie. As a child she had always had a hint of independence. As an adult it appeared that hint had become a fullfledged streak that not many men could tame.

His brow furrowed against the thought that it was those things that had intrigued him. Intrigued him enough that after leaving The Fens last night, he had nearly gone back to Swan's Grace, despite propriety, to sleep in his own bed—with her in it. Just the thought of her made his blood surge hot and low. He wanted to pull her close, cup her round bottom, and press her body to his while he looked into those brown eyes flecked with green and watch them darken with awareness.

Cursing silently, he reined in his thoughts.

He hadn't returned. He wouldn't put it past Sophie Wentworth to send word to every paper in town that he had stayed there. Hell, she'd probably write the article herself—as if she needed an ounce more attention than she had already received from being featured in *The Century*.

Clearly the woman didn't subscribe to the dictate that a woman's name should appear in print only twice in a lifetime, first when she married, then again when she died. And the last thing he needed was a scandal.

Grayson shook his head. There had been too many scandals of late in the Hawthorne family. His younger brother Matthew had been ensnared in one that had rocked proper Bostonians to the core, and had had every New Englander riveted to the daily newspapers as the events unfolded. Matthew was married now, to an intriguing woman who had changed his life. The Hawthornes loved Finnea. Even Bradford had grudgingly conceded that she was good for his middle son. But it hadn't always been that way.

Then there was Lucas, the youngest. He hadn't caused a scandal. But as the sole owner of Nightingale's Gate gentleman's club, he lived one. Grayson was not about to add fuel to the family fire.

He knew his father was counting on him to marry Sophie. The coming together of the two old, distinguished families would be a renewal. It was one of the few times Grayson's intentions had coincided with his father's constant schemes and plans to better the Hawthorne name. Or at least they had coincided until last night. Now he wasn't so sure.

"Damn it, I want to know what you've been doing for the last three months," Bradford Hawthorne demanded, pulling Grayson out of his reverie. "I thought the contracts had been signed. But now you stand there and tell me things are up in the air. I demand to know what is going on?"

Grayson shot his father a warning glance. "My affairs are none of your concern."

"That's the problem," Bradford shot back. "All you have had for the last decade are affairs. It's time you settled down and got married. Damn it, Matthew is married and he's a year younger than you."

"Lucas doesn't have a wife," he offered.

Bradford snorted. "The devil take it. Who'd have him?"

"From what I hear, any number of women would have Lucas," he said with a shrug.

"I'm talking about a proper woman, not some lady of the night who'd like to get her claws into a Hawthorne."

Grayson started to disagree, but decided not to waste his breath. He had been arguing about life, marriage, and his youngest brother for too many years to count. He hadn't found an argument yet that could scratch his father's angry convictions.

The only person who had ever been able to make inroads with their father was Matthew. It was no secret that the second son had been Bradford's favorite child. Matthew had been able to talk to their father in ways Grayson never had. But all that changed after Matthew's face had been scarred in an accident.

Grayson dropped his arms to his sides, telling himself he didn't care about his father and his inability to please the man. But he did care about Matthew and Lucas.

For as long as he could remember, it had been the three of them. Brothers, friends, confidants. Protectors of their fragile mother, who drifted through the house like a whisper. Though if stories were to be believed, when she was young, Emmaline Hawthorne née Abbot had been wild and daring.

But something had happened that took the laughter from her eyes.

Grayson turned back to the Public Gardens. When he had arrived that morning, he had asked for his mother. But her lady's maid had explained that she was not feeling well, and was not receiving visitors.

"You are the oldest," Bradford continued harshly. "You need to provide me an heir to continue the line."

"Matthew has provided you with a child."

"He has provided me with a girl!" Bradford drew a sharp, deep breath, his nostrils flaring. After a moment he visibly eased. "Sweet as she is, Mary will not retain the Hawthorne name once she marries. I need a boy. Only a boy can ensure that the Hawthorne name doesn't die out. You need to provide me with that boy."

Grayson's temper flared, but he held it in ruthless check.

He would not argue with his father. Instead he started to leave.

But Bradford stopped him. "I know how you are. You'll walk out that door and do whatever you please. But I'm serious about this. You get those contracts finalized with Conrad. I want a wedding."

"I don't doubt you do," he stated coolly. "I *will* marry, but only when I'm ready."

Bradford grumbled. "You had better be ready soon. I'm not getting any younger. And if I left it up to you or Lucas, the Hawthorne name would undoubtedly die out—at least die out on the legitimate side. I need a grandson. You owe me a grandson. Damn it, you owe me!"

The men stared at each other, steely dark eyes clashing with harsh, angry blue, until Grayson forced an ease into his voice that he didn't feel. "I owe you? How is that? At sixteen you turned me out of the house."

The words were out of his mouth before he could stop them. They hung in the room, startling and painful.

Bradford shifted his weight uncomfortably and looked away, his face set in stubborn lines. "You should thank me for that. It taught you that life isn't easy. It made you a fighter, it made you succeed."

"Ah, yes, the sink-or-swim method."

Bradford looked back. "You do owe me."

Only long years of practice kept Grayson's emotions in check. "Really, Father? Tell me why."

"Because a son always owes his father."

A late-winter sun was well into the sky when Grayson slammed out the front door. He had locked horns with his father for as long as he could remember. Even when he tried to please the man, he only managed to send them both into a rage of temper. And he had never understood why. He also never understood why his father had forced him to leave Hawthorne House at sixteen. The excuse that he had needed to learn to succeed rang hollow. As a teen, he had worked harder than anyone he knew, had better marks, had more plans. But none of that had mattered.

Stunned and dazed, he had been forced to strike out on his own, finding a rat-infested garret across the river in Cambridge, close to Harvard, where he had already made plans to attend. In the beginning he'd had to fight to survive, the only thing separating him from having to steal for food being baskets filled with meat and cheese, bread and milk. And always a cake—from Sophie.

For months after leaving Hawthorne House, all he'd had were those baskets secretly delivered by servants. And the talking machine. Sophie's words and her gifts of food to sustain him. His eyes narrowed against the memory of the young boy he had been those first weeks. Scared. Cranking the handle of the talking machine over and over again in that drafty, thin-walled garret. The words surrounding him, blocking out the angry shouts and fights between grown men in the hallway.

Eventually he had worked his way through Harvard College, culminating with his graduation from Harvard Law. But as long as he lived he would never forget that it was Sophie who had helped him when he needed it the most.

Instead of hailing a hired hack, Grayson cut across the Public Gardens, a large expanse of land made of curving pathways, footbridges, and plants and trees imported from all over the world.

When he came to the footbridge that would take him toward downtown and the courthouse, where he had planned to go, he veered off to the right and headed for Commonwealth Avenue. And Sophie.

Sophie.

A slow, deep breath filled his lungs. Despite himself, he wanted to see her. Needed to see her.

He cursed the need, but somehow couldn't bring himself to change his direction. His thoughts hardened at the weakness, but then he told himself he simply needed to replace the memory of the bold, provocative woman he had seen last night.

He wanted proof that he hadn't made the single biggest mistake of his life based on the foolish memory of a young girl and a long-ago kindness. Did he yearn only for someone who no longer existed? In the years since she had left Boston, had he in some way always been waiting for her return? And when she didn't, had he simply seen to it that she did?

After he slipped out through the gate and wrought-iron fencing that surrounded the park, he had to stop for traffic before he could cross Arlington Street. The boulevard was packed, and the walkway was filled with warmly dressed pedestrians. When a gap came in the flow of carriages, he stepped off the granite-block curb onto the unevenly cobbled thoroughfare to start across. But he stopped in his tracks as a hired hack sped by. He would have sworn the woman inside was his mother.

"Come on, stop holding everyone up," a washerwoman barked at him.

But Grayson didn't move. The swarm of people who had been waiting to cross parted like a sea and hurried around him as he stared at the retreating carriage. But then he shook his head. That couldn't have been his mother. Emmaline Hawthorne didn't take public conveyances. Beyond that, he had been told she was still in bed.

He continued on, and by the time he came to Swan's Grace, taking the front steps two at a time, he forgot about the woman in the hansom cab.

All thoughts were replaced by music.

Grayson stood for a moment, taking in the sound. His response was swift and intense as the notes soared. He had never heard the piece before, but the deep, yearning sound of the cello pulled at him. The melody was emotional and moving, and he had a fleeting understanding of why Sophie had become famous.

He went to the door and halted. It was his house, his office, but with Sophie inside he felt an aggravating need to knock and did so. No one answered. After another knock he simply turned the knob, and realized the lock had been broken. It became clear how Sophie and her entourage had gotten in the house last night. A smile pulled at his lips and he shook his head. Hell, she really was a maddening little baggage.

Inside, the music was louder, filling the house with a series of short, rapid notes. He headed for the sound, bypassing the office where his desk stood, his footsteps muffled and unheard beneath the music, and found Sophie playing in the library. Despite the cold air, the windows had been thrown open, the curtains flung wide. The furniture had been moved back with careless disregard, while his books lined the walls like an audience.

He had just completed the room the week before her arrival. It was austere and dark, filled with his law volumes and a desk for his receptionist, who, he remembered, had the day off. One less issue to deal with.

But he gave that fact little thought as he took in Sophie. She sat in the middle of it all, winter sunshine and a slight breeze filling the room as she played, her brow creased in concentration. Her hair was pulled up loosely, her skin creamy with a hint of red from exertion. But it was the cello that demanded his attention, pulled between her legs, and he felt a visceral surge between his own at the sight.

She was stunning to watch, beautiful and captivating, her eyes closed, lost to the music.

The two women she had brought along with her sat scattered around the room, one lounging in his fine leather, wing-backed chair, the other sitting up straight, writing as fast as her hand could go. But it was the sight of Henry that made his temper flare, certain that this man must feel the same insistent pull at the way Sophie held the instrument.

Conrad was right about one thing. This ragtag group of hangers-on had to go.

Once again he had the sharp, clear thought that this wasn't what he wanted—not for his wife. But then Sophie looked up and saw him. He saw her surprise. Saw that flicker of joy, however brief, before her bow pulled an uneven note and the music died a harsh, discordant death.

Looking at her now, he felt that same inexplicable shift inside him. She filled something in him that was hard to deny.

"Don't stop on my account," he said, heat warming his blood, his eyes never leaving hers.

The tall woman craned her neck to see him, but she didn't bother to unhook her knees from the arm of the chair. The dowdy one dropped her pad, then fumbled around on the floor trying to gather the papers. Henry looked on with amusement. But Sophie never moved.

"What was that you were playing?" Grayson asked, taking in the way her full lips were parted, showing a hint of pearl-white teeth and pink tongue. He felt an urge to dip his head and taste her.

The words shook her out of whatever place she had been, and she snapped her mouth shut. "It is a piece adapted for me from *La Traviata*."

"The opera? I thought people sang operas."

Her lips pulled into a brittle smile as if he had offended her. "It is not uncommon to have popular operatic pieces arranged for instrumental interpretation. Musicians do it all the time. No doubt even Pablo Casals has done it before."

He wasn't sure where that had come from, but he sensed that the subject was a sensitive one. "No doubt. Regardless, your interpretation was lovely, and I'm impressed by how much effort it takes to play."

The prim one groaned. The sultry one *tsk*ed. Sophie jerked her head around to the little man.

"Henry, you told me I had gained perfect ease!"

The man looked abashed. "*Ma petite,* what was I to do? We have been here only a day after traveling for many. You need time to relax."

"I meant it as a compliment," Grayson stated, bringing four sets of angry eyes around to stare at him.

The light caught Sophie, and he saw for the first time that she looked tired and worried, as if she hadn't slept. He felt an unwanted flare of concern.

She sighed, seeming to rein in her frustration, then nodded her head. "Thank you, but the listener should never feel the musician is having to work hard. The listener can understand that the piece is difficult, but the musician should have mastered it so that the music seems like an extension of herself," she explained.

She set the cello aside, placing the bow on a small, mahogany end table, a long, faint line of white rosin marking the surface like chalk. "You should have been aware of nothing more than the sound and the emotions that the sound makes you feel. Do you understand?"

Before he could answer, she looked back at him. "And furthermore, do you understand that you should have knocked?" she asked, raising a delicate brow in challenge.

He swallowed back a chuckle, amazed to feel his mood lighten. She was beautiful even if she was a little baggage.

He leaned up against the doorjamb and crossed his arms on his chest. "One, I did knock, and two, that was hardly necessary as this is, after all, my house."

Sophie picked up a cup of tea that Margaret had poured. "So you keep saying. Before long I expect you to throw something and stomp your feet like a three-year-old child."

The others laughed. Grayson only looked at her, choosing not to take her bait as she curled her legs up into the chair, glancing at him over the rim of her cup, looking like a provocative little nymph.

"I went to see your father last night," he offered instead.

"What for?" she quipped. "To tattle?"

He cocked a brow.

Sophie eyed him with a mischievous quirk of her lips, seeming to warm to her subject. "Though, in truth, you never were the tattling type. So maybe that hasn't changed, but you do seem different. Hmmm, you look the same." She considered him for a moment. "It's your hair, I think. It's longer than I can imagine you wearing it." Her gaze suddenly danced. "Have you become a derelict, Grayson Hawthorne?"

Grayson's jaw went hard, his good intentions not to become agitated flying out the window when the little man laughed out loud. "A derelict?" he demanded with a scowl.

"Well, it is nearly noon and you aren't at work." She picked up a sugar cube from a dish and popped it into her mouth. "It must be," she said over the sweet, "that you've lost your business and your house, so you've moved in here to save money. Father must actually be out of town for the week and he is simply letting you stay here, and you are too proud to admit that you have become so indebted."

"Ooh," Henry mused. "Fodder for a great story."

"An article," Margaret supplied.

Deandra studied her cuticles. " 'Good Lawyer Goes Bad.' I think that would read well in the evening paper."

"Our Dea is a genius at getting attention," Henry explained.

"Yes," Grayson replied dryly. "I learned that last night."

Sophie tilted her head, her eyes sparkling with amusement. "You should hire her. With Dea at your side, no doubt you'd have a slew of publicity and more clients than you could imagine. You'd be surprised at all the people who come out of the woodwork after you've appeared in the papers." She sliced Deandra a look. "Though I can't promise the caliber of clients she can deliver."

"Business is business," the tall woman replied with a shrug.

Setting her tea aside, Sophie jumped up with a laugh. "Very true. Now tell us, is that why you are here, Grayson, dear? Has your life run amok and you have no place else to go?"

He stood away from the doorjamb, his eyes narrowing, whatever traces of ease and humor he had gained disappearing with the swiftness of a judge's gavel hammering home. "I am here to get *my* files out of *my* office in *my* house at *my* leisure."

She glanced at the others. "If I were a gambling woman I would bet that just about now his jaw is starting to tic."

"Not *starting* to tic, Sophie."

If he thought his tone of voice would intimidate her, he was sadly mistaken. She started out of the room in a breezy swish of long skirts, but just when she would have passed him, she stopped and leaned close.

"You really make this too easy," she whispered. "Baiting you is like taking candy from a baby."

She smiled provocatively and stepped away. But just when she would have slipped by, he flattened his palm against the wall, blocking her path.

Her head tilted back and she looked at him, her gold and green-flecked eyes filled with something he couldn't name. For one unbidden moment she was the young girl who had innocently followed him around. The girl he had known forever. Not provocative. Not forward. Just Sophie.

But then her eyes flashed with something he couldn't name, and she changed—like a stage actress slipping into a new role, he thought fleetingly. Her lips parted. Her gaze drifted down to his mouth, and she was no longer the young girl. He felt an instant stab of desire for the woman she had become. Without thinking, he reached out with his free hand and ran the backs of his fingers ever so slowly down her cheek. He could feel her quick intake of breath—as if he had thrown her off balance.

He curled one long strand of hair around his finger, and he could feel her tremble. In that second he didn't know if he wanted to strangle her for the way she was acting, or kiss her until she went soft in his arms.

But he was saved from making a decision—much less a mistake, given the murmuring audience behind them—when Conrad Wentworth strode into the house.

With Sophie standing so close, Grayson watched as the disconcerted lines of her face went soft and adoring. "Papa," she whispered, as if time had circled back and she were still a child.

Grayson stepped away and she flew into Conrad's arms. "Oh, Father!"

The older man hugged her tight, then set her at arm's length, his smile gentle and loving. "Let me have a look at you. Haven't you grown into the prettiest girl around." He glanced at Grayson. "Isn't that so?"

He conceded the point with a nod. "I agree."

Sophie's cheeks reddened.

"What's this?" Henry asked, shooting Deandra a questioning look. "Do we have a blush?"

Sophie pressed her hands to her cheeks, then laughed out loud and stood back. "Boston women can blush over a compliment as well as any Southern belle."

Conrad cleared his throat. "Why didn't you let me know you were arriving early?"

"It was supposed to be a surprise—a proper surprise that I was home."

"Speaking of proper, Sophie, you need to pack your

bags. You really can't stay here." He eyed her entourage. "And I'm sure your . . . um, friends will be more than happy at the Hotel Vendome."

"Heavens," Henry said dramatically, "the place is getting an absolute profusion of business. What with our brutish Mr. Hawthorne staying there. And now us. Perhaps we should invest."

Sophie ignored him. "Father, what is going on?"

Conrad, however, had to drag his disbelieving glare away from the dapperly dressed little man. "I had planned to explain when I picked you up, but you got home early and didn't give me a chance."

"Explain what? And where are you and Patrice and the girls living if not here?"

"Well, I built a new home on The Fens. A beautiful place, actually. I know you'll love it." He smiled uncomfortably. "Didn't I tell you?"

"No, Father, you didn't, and what does that have to do with Swan's Grace? Mr. Hawthorne said you sold it to him."

Sophie stared at her father, her golden brown eyes darkening with vulnerability, and Grayson realized that she was silently, desperately willing the man to deny her words. She wanted the words to be untrue in a way that ran deep.

Conrad hesitated, glancing around the room before turning back to his daughter. "Well, you see, princess, I did."

She went still. Too still.

Grayson saw a world of hurt and betrayal flash through the golden depths of her eyes, and for reasons he didn't understand, he hated the look, hated that only minutes before she had been laughing and teasing and thrilled to be home.

He needed to tell her about the house and the betrothal, get it out in the open. But right then wasn't the time to do it. Instead he found himself stepping in. "As the ubiquitous Henry has just noted, I am staying at the Hotel Vendome, and I'm fine there while we straighten this out."

"Straighten this out?" Conrad demanded.

"Yes, Conrad." Grayson locked his gaze on the older man. "We will straighten this out."

"But what about the party?"

Sophie looked back and forth between her father and Grayson. "Party? What are you talking about?"

Conrad smiled grandly, seeming to forget the uneasiness of seconds before as excitement laced his words. "Your stepmother and I are holding a huge party at The Fens to announce your—"

"Your homecoming," Grayson interjected, cutting Conrad off.

Conrad's mouth hung open, then his eyes narrowed in anger, his face turning a mottled red. But in the end, he was smart enough not to defy the younger, more powerful man.

"Call it what you like, but all I can say," Conrad finally managed, "is that this had better be *straightened out* soon." He gave a meaningful look to Grayson. "The party is next Saturday."

Things would be straightened out, Grayson thought. But not here. Not with that suddenly haunted look in Sophie's eyes.

Chapter Four

Emmaline Hawthorne, wife to Bradford, mother to Grayson, Matthew, and Lucas, extended her white-gloved hand and gave the driver fifty cents plus a nickel tip. She sat in the carriage for a moment, her primly straightened spine flush against the cracked leather seat. That morning she had taken great care with her attire, slipping on a peach silk gown and her favorite winter-white cape with fur trim.

It had been years since she had been out by herself, and it took a moment before she realized the driver wasn't going to help her alight.

The man's rudeness didn't bother her, however. It actually made her smile that she was about the city, rubbing elbows with every sort of person.

She was less thrilled a few minutes later as she was jostled and bumped on her way to the small building in the South End of Boston. But even that couldn't dampen her spirits. It had taken every ounce of courage she possessed to make these arrangements, telling her maid she was sick so she would be left alone. Bradford would be furious if he found out what she was doing.

But her husband's anger paled in comparison to the sudden, disturbing feelings that had hit her a month before. Life was passing her by. It was as if she woke up one morning and wondered what she was doing. Her husband didn't need her, and he never had after she had brought him the substantial dowry that had allowed him to rebuild the Hawthorne family fortune. Her darling sons didn't need her any longer either. Being much like their father, her three boys had always been independent. Bradford had seen to that. God forbid he find one of them curled up in her arms as a child.

But that was the past, and on that morning when she had woken up and wondered what she was doing with her life, she remembered the years of her girlhood. Years of love and gaiety. She doubted there was a soul in Boston who would believe she used to ride hell-for-leather down the country roads outside of town. She couldn't remember the last time anyone had seen her laughing out loud, or her long hair free.

Certainly not her husband. His interest in her body had waned after the birth of their youngest child. She still remembered the night she had gone to him and he had turned her away, telling her that a proper woman didn't want to make love, only saw it as a duty.

But she *was* proper. She had led committees and attended church and sewn altar cloths. She had raised awareness of the poor and had instituted a charitable foundation to see to the preservation of Boston's historic landmarks. She had been called the epitome of what all proper Boston Brahmins wanted their wives and daughters to be.

Then why did she wake up in the wee hours of the morning with a sick feeling of emptiness in her heart? With desire running deep.

She spent the first two weeks of her new awareness feeling guilty that she wasn't grateful enough for all that she had. When that sentiment failed to make headway in her mind, she then spent the second two weeks deciding what to do about it. It hadn't taken long to know what she wanted to do. Resume her sculpting.

She was fifty. But the mirror still showed smooth and

only gently lined skin. Her hands were still slender. Her body was still curved. She was still strong enough to work the clay.

Emmaline hurried the last steps to the barnlike building that had been an artists' haven for decades. When she was a young woman her father had allowed her to study sculpture. Her dear, kind father who had wanted her dreams to take flight. He hadn't wanted her to be restrained by the reins society had placed around women.

Sometimes it was hard to believe that Bradford, the man who had swept into her life, so full of energy and excitement, could have taken her dreams and ripped them apart. All too soon in their life together the illusions of love had worn away.

Pushing through the heavy front door, Emmaline was hit with the rich smell of clay. The cavernous room was filled with people, a few using potter's wheels, their feet pumping the pedals in a smooth, mesmerizing motion. Others worked on varying stages of sculpting clay, some of it still in large blocks, barely touched, some already being tackled, their masters leaning over them in trancelike pursuit.

Everyone was trying to take the thoughts in their heads and translate them into the malleable earth they molded with their hands.

Emmaline remembered the feeling well, even after decades away from working the clay.

"Do you want something?"

Emmaline whirled around, her long skirts sweeping the dust-covered ground. She came face-to-face with a woman with long gray hair secured in a braid down her back. No demure bun or simple chignon, as any woman over the age of eighteen was expected to wear.

"Yes, I'm here to see Mr. Springfield."

The woman eyed her rudely. "His matron types don't

usually come here. Send him a message, and if he wants to see you he'll meet you at one of those fancy teahouses women like you frequent."

Stunned by the woman's instant and intense animosity, Emmaline was speechless for a moment and she nearly left. But then she remembered those long, sleepless hours.

"Mr. Springfield is expecting me."

"Here?" the woman scoffed.

"Yes, here." Courage she hadn't felt in years surged through her. "I am sure he is in his studio upstairs. I'll just go up there now."

The woman was clearly taken aback by Emmaline's knowledge of this place. But Emmaline didn't wait for her permission. She headed for the stairs.

As soon as she placed her hand on the banister, a door flung open.

"Emmaline!"

She craned her neck and found Andre Springfield at the top of the stairs. "Andre."

"I didn't believe you would really come."

"Well, believe it. I'm here."

The short, round man barreled down the stairs, grabbed her hand, and all but dragged her up to his study on the second floor. As soon as he slammed the door shut, he stood Emmaline in a shaft of light, took her hands, and held them out dramatically.

"Let me look at you!"

He danced her around in circles, and Emmaline couldn't help but laugh. In a matter of minutes she felt the years drop away. It was as if she had never left. He had less hair and she knew she no longer looked eighteen. But none of that mattered.

"Sit, sit! You must tell me all about what you've been doing these last many years." He directed her to a chair, then dashed back to the door, flung it open, and hollered out, "Collette, bring us some tea!"

He was still a whirlwind of energy, and Emmaline smiled to think that not everything had changed.

"Now tell me everything."

"Heavens, we would be here all day."

"Grand! I can't imagine anything I would like more than to spend time with you."

Emmaline lowered her head and glanced at her gloved hands. Andre reached out and nudged her chin. "What is this? Emmaline Abbot blushing?"

"Emmaline Hawthorne now."

"Yes, yes. How could I not know? Your husband is written about in every paper. He is either taking some poor politician to task or signing some new deal to make thousands more dollars. He is everywhere one turns. But I don't want to hear about him. It will ruin my day."

He said the words with a wicked grin, and Emmaline couldn't help her answering chuckle—couldn't seem to manage a bit of offense. Somehow Andre Springfield had always been that way. He could say the most improper things and get away with it.

He glanced at the door. "Where is our tea?" he bellowed.

Just then the door opened, but it wasn't Collette who entered. A tall man with broad shoulders stood in the doorway. He had a full head of hair, graying at the temples. His skin was lightly tanned, as if he spent time in the sun. His eyes were dark and clear. He looked directly at Emmaline and after a long moment he smiled.

Emmaline couldn't move, her breath caught in her chest. Her mind spun and her heart leaped.

"Hello, Em. It's been a long time."

Chapter Five

The slamming door brought her head up from the ledger with a start, the pencil lead in her hand snapping on the page.

Sophie sat back in the desk chair, papers with numbers scrawled all over them spread out before her. She could see a long line of harsh sunlight trying to slice through the closed curtains of the bedroom.

Normally she would have been asleep at this hour. Her entourage still was. But worry over finances had kept her up most of the night. The thought of losing Swan's Grace left her reeling. But she had more immediate concerns just then. No matter how she worked the figures, she didn't have enough to get four adults through to May if she had to pay for their lodging—in Boston or Europe.

Of course, she had known that all along, but at two in the morning she had woken up with a flash of hope that if she redid the numbers, cutting back here, saving there, she'd have enough to get them through. The truth was as harsh as the morning sunlight.

To make matters worse, her father had made it clear that Deandra, Henry, and Margaret were not welcome at his new house, and Sophie wasn't about to leave her friends to fend for themselves. Which left staying at Swan's Grace as the only viable alternative until she could get her father to straighten things out. And he would, surely. Swan's Grace was hers.

In the meantime she had to find a way to maintain residence in her childhood home. Though how hard could it be? she reasoned. Grayson was an old friend. Besides, how much time did a lawyer spend at his residence? Didn't he have cases to try, judges to meet, clients to advise—all of which undoubtedly took place in courthouses and downtown offices?

She kicked herself for goading him yesterday. Not the best way to start ingratiating herself. But being around him made her uneasy, unbalanced, as if at any second he could tip her over.

Today, she promised herself, she would do better. She would be as sweet as pulled taffy, and he'd have little choice but to let them stay.

For a second she thought of the rumors Margaret had heard of his impending marriage. What if he had a wife waiting in the wings to move in before May? But she wrote that worry off. Grayson Hawthorne was not one to do anything quickly, much less marry that way. No doubt he'd make an official announcement, then have a long and very proper engagement. By then she'd have Swan's Grace back and the money to pay her bills.

As the sun burned brighter, Sophie felt a growing sense of relief. Things would work out. During the day Grayson wouldn't be around enough to care if they stayed at Swan's Grace. And at night he could easily stay at the Hotel Vendome. He had told her father himself that it wasn't a problem.

The sound of efficient footsteps clomping across the downstairs floor seemed to vibrate up through the walls. She grimaced at the thought that it might be Grayson, disproving the theory that he didn't spend much time there. But she dismissed the idea. Grayson Hawthorne did not clomp.

She glanced at the huge four-poster bed that had been

her father's—though now Grayson was using it. His belongings filled the room. Fine suits, high-polished boots. A cashmere robe.

In the early morning hours, she had pulled it on, wrapping it around her. His scent clung to the material, clean and musky. She had the fleeting image of his arms wrapped around her, and a shiver drifted down her spine.

He was a man now, not a boy, fulfilling all the promise he had shown years ago.

She groaned at the thought of him. Truly he unsettled her. And staying in a room full of his belongings hadn't been one of her smarter decisions. It made her remember him—made her question her determination to be independent. And that made her mad.

The fact of the matter was, she didn't know how to be anything else. Her mother had taught her to be free, had never made the slightest mention of how society expected a woman to do a man's bidding. She didn't know the first thing about running a household or preparing a meal.

And children.

She pressed her eyes closed at the unexpected thought of holding a baby, Grayson's baby, in her arms. Snuggling close. Someone to love her.

She shook the thought away. She cringed to think of what a mess she would make of a child. Beyond which, she hadn't worked five long years only to toss her success away at the first feel of a cashmere robe around her shoulders. The garment was soft and sweet. Grayson, the man, was anything but.

The clomps from belowstairs broke into her reverie. With little help for it, Sophie secured the tie at her waist, searched the floor for a pair of feather-trimmed slippers, then went in search of whoever was making all the racket.

Just when her foot hit the bottom step, she came face-to-face with a severe-looking woman who looked to be a hundred if she was a day. She wore a no-nonsense hat over steel gray hair, and a starched gown that made Margaret's prudish attire look provocative.

"You look a bit prim to be a thief," Sophie stated without preamble, rolling the long cashmere sleeves up a few turns. "Would you care to explain what you are doing here?"

"I'll not be explaining anything to the likes of you," the woman said with a sniff, her tone censorious as she looked Sophie up and down. "I'll not abide a lady of the night waltzing about a respectable man's home. Get away with you, girl, and believe you me, I'll be having a word with young Mr. Hawthorne."

Young Mr. Hawthorne, as if he were a boy still in knickers. Who could this dour lady be?

Sophie would have laughed her delight had she not been so surprised.

But she was saved from having to do anything when Grayson pushed open the front door. He wore a fine wool overcoat and clapped his gloved hands together to warm them. A rush of cold air came in with him.

He glanced down at the lock as he passed across the threshold, and when he looked up he noticed the two women. Sophie saw his eyes darken when he noticed her. His gaze traveled over her, seeing his robe, the motion like a caress. Then he smiled, surprisingly bright and rich considering he had left her yesterday in a dour mood.

"Make a note to have this door fixed, Miss Pruitt," he said, shutting out the cold before continuing toward them.

He was beautiful, and Sophie's heart kicked. His hair was still damp from his bath despite the weather, and he walked with an ease that few men possessed. It was all she could do not to smile back.

She really had to make an effort not to be pulled in when

he decided to turn on the charm. She couldn't afford to let down her guard for so much as a moment. They had become adversaries. He had Swan's Grace. She wanted it back.

Grayson stopped and looked from woman to woman. "I see you have met."

They looked at each other with asperity.

Grayson chuckled. "I wondered what would happen when the two of you came face-to-face. Let's make it official. Miss Altima Pruitt, may I introduce Miss Sophie Wentworth."

"What is going on here?" Sophie demanded.

Miss Pruitt pulled her sturdy shoulders back. "I'll not be working here if you plan to entertain"—she searched for a word—"*guests* right beneath my nose," she finally managed.

"Rest assured, Miss Pruitt, I would never dream of abusing your sensibilities." He came forward and put his strong arm around the woman's sturdy shoulders. "Miss Wentworth is Conrad Wentworth's daughter, and she is staying here, with chaperons"—he actually scowled at this—"while I stay at the Hotel Vendome. Now why don't you go make us some of that delicious coffee of yours."

Altima sent a sharp, accusing glare at Sophie and her attire, then pulled off her hat with swift efficiency, setting it carefully on the hat rack, before heading for the kitchen.

Sophie watched her go, then turned to Grayson. "Aren't we cordial this morning?"

Instantly she cringed at the flip tone. She had promised herself she would be nice!

"I'll do whatever it takes to keep Miss Pruitt happy." He smiled at her, an inviting smile full of warmth and mischief. "The woman types like the wind, takes dictation like a gazelle, and keeps my life organized with the quiet, unobtrusive efficiency of a queen bee in a honeycomb."

"Enough with your snappy wildlife analogies." He really did bring out the worst in her. "Who is this paragon?"

"My receptionist—though to be more specific, she is a woman I adore," he said with a grand sweep of his hand to his heart. "In short, she's the best receptionist I have ever had. And I've had a few."

"You have a receptionist? Here?" she squeaked.

"Of course. She runs my office."

"You mean your office downtown?" she prompted hopefully.

"No. I advise my clients from Swan's Grace. And I do have clients, Sophie. People who keep me solvent so I can pay those things called bills and not become the derelict you accused me of being."

He stepped close and boldly ran his fingers down the edge of the cashmere lapels, his voice deepening. "Despite what you want to think, I don't need your father's money."

His fingers stopped just before they came to her breasts. She could hardly think, much less utter a coherent word, as heat seared through her, centering low in a way she didn't understand. Could he tell that she had virtually nothing on underneath? Could he feel the way her heart began to pound?

His hands lingered, his dark-eyed gaze burning into her, and for a second she thought he was going to kiss her. But just when she would have leaned close, despite everything, he dropped his hands away. A wry smile tugged at his lips as he took in her attire. "And speaking of clients, one should be arriving any minute. Charming as you look, I'd rather they not see you in my robe."

Heat surged through her cheeks, mixing with dismay. She hardly understood what he made her feel. Desire? Panic?

With a jerk, she looked out the window at the carriages rolling by as if all were right with the world. She was so close to having the pieces of her life finally fall into place—different from how she had imagined it would be when she was a child, but still something she had created for herself. Her whole life she had dreamed of being famous, dreamed of being something more than awkward Sophie Wentworth. How many times had she envisioned herself holding court in Swan's Grace, performing in the Music Hall? Playing Bach.

She had given up Bach, replacing it with showy pieces. She had given up the dream of playing in the Music Hall, replacing it with Europe. But she couldn't replace her dream of living in the only true home she had ever known.

Grayson Hawthorne and his purchase of Swan's Grace had thrown what remained of her dreams into chaos.

But should it really matter? She had a glamorous life. People around the world adored her, would never believe she had experienced an awkward day in her life.

Her gaze shifted and ran over the black-and-white marble floor in the foyer, the stately, fluted columns, the grand sweep of stairs she had descended again and again as a child, a long linen towel attached to her shoulders trailing behind her, making her a queen.

His touch drew her attention and made her breath catch. He cupped her chin and forced her to look at him.

"What is it?" he whispered, his dark gaze serious. "What is it that I keep seeing in your eyes?"

For one blinding second she had the foolish urge to blurt out her dreams, to pour out the worries she had shouldered on her own for so long. But too many years of having only herself to depend on kept the words firmly in check. Because the truth was, she was no longer a child, no longer anyone Grayson Hawthorne would care for if he learned who she had become. Independent and provocative. Pushing the envelope. Anything but proper. And she knew she couldn't give up her dream of Swan's Grace.

She bit back her desire to tell him her worries. She

raised her chin and found her practiced diva smile. "I never would have guessed you'd become such a romantic in your old age. Seeing things in eyes. Really, Grayson, next you'll be waxing on about lips like roses and kisses like wine."

His gaze drifted low. "Your lips are like roses." Then, as if he could do nothing else, he leaned down and pressed his lips to hers. Barely a touch, only a teasing brush, but enough that her insides went soft with yearning.

After a moment he pulled back. "And your kiss *is* like wine."

He ran the tips of his fingers along the collarbone beneath her gown, barely, softly, making her body come to life with a slow sensual burn.

With no warning at all came an image of her as his wife, lying beneath him, tangled in sheets, his hands slipping beneath the cashmere robe.

Whom had he chosen? she wondered with a sudden rush of heat to her cheeks. Whom had he picked to be his wife? For the first time in five years, she felt a flash of regret for the path she had taken. She wished she had understood the rules to a game that had never made sense.

But she had always been different, and to try to change now would be like hammering a square peg into a round hole. She had already lost herself once, five years ago. She couldn't afford to lose sight of who she was again.

Grayson started to say something, but was cut off when the doorbell rang.

"I'll get it," Miss Pruitt announced from the back, followed quickly by the clomp of her sensible shoes.

It was all happening too fast, and Sophie felt rooted to the spot. Grayson seemed to understand.

He tucked a strand of hair behind her ear. "Everything is going to work out, Sophie," he said gently. "We'll talk later. But for now, go."

He turned her around and gave her a little push. Mechanically she took the stairs, turning back at the top to see a smartly suited man enter the house, the austere double doors closing behind them as the men walked into the study.

Grayson was there to stay. Entrenched. He had no intention of going anywhere.

And *his* kiss had been like wine, sending her senses reeling. Making her want more.

She really had to speak to her father, to somehow undo whatever it was he had done. She couldn't afford for Grayson to remain in her life.

For three days running, Sophie sent word to her father every morning. But each note was returned with another stating he couldn't see her. At first she was hurt, then she became angry. But by the fourth day, she was fighting off full-fledged panic. Why had her father asked her to return if not to be with the family?

To top it off, Grayson had showed up at Swan's Grace to work first thing each morning with a regularity and punctuality she could set a clock by. The infamous Miss Pruitt arrived as well, appearing at eight, staying until five, riding roughshod over Sophie and her entourage as though they were a gaggle of wayward geese.

And each of those days, Sophie avoided Grayson like the plague, certain that the minute he found her alone, the *talk* he wanted to have would be to tell her once and for all that she had to move out. Each time he had asked for her she managed to be out, unavailable, or indisposed. Henry told her that after the last time he had delivered her message Grayson had actually growled.

Henry had been delighted. She less so. The man's patience was running dry.

Only once, at the end of a long day, had she actually

seen him. She was sitting in the drawing room, working through a new cello arrangement of *La Bohème* on paper, unaware that he was across the foyer in his office. Miss Pruitt had marched out of the library, knocked on the closed double doors, then entered. Sophie glanced over and saw Grayson sitting behind his desk. He was intent on a client who was talking, the man's back to her. The receptionist set freshly typed papers in front of her employer. Without warning Grayson had glanced up and seen her. Their eyes met, locking with unreadable undercurrents, and all the while the client never stopped talking.

Leaning back in his chair, Grayson had studied her over steepled fingers as if he could understand something if he looked at her long enough. She saw the heat in his eyes. The possessiveness.

With a start, she had pushed up from the divan and gone in search of Deandra, hating the way her knees felt weak and her heart leaped in her chest. The incident had left her oddly unsettled.

And still her father wouldn't see her.

Finally, last night, less than two days before the party her father had mentioned, Sophie simply obtained her father's new address and went to his house unannounced. Upon arrival, for one brief second she had forgotten why she was there.

The Fens was beautiful in an ostentatious sort of way, but it was the party decorations that had moved her. If her father was to be believed, the decorations were for her homecoming party. Didn't that mean he cared?

But whatever delight she had felt quickly evaporated. Other than finally getting to see her precious half sisters, the visit was a disaster. Conrad adamantly refused to get Swan's Grace back, saying the deal was done. No amount of arguing swayed him.

He was angry and dismissive until finally she whispered, "Why? Why are you doing this to me?"

Her father sighed, looking suddenly older than his years. "I am doing this because it's for the best."

"Best for whom?" she blurted out, trying to understand.

His anger returned full force. "Best for this family! Now you will do as I say, and move in here to The Fens. And send those . . . those hangers-on back where they came from."

Angry, Sophie had defied him. She had left The Fens and returned to Swan's Grace, more determined than ever to regain her home.

"What are you doing in here?" Miss Pruitt cried out, breaking into Sophie's thoughts.

The woman's sensible hat was still perched on her head as she entered the library, her reticule clutched in her hands as if she was afraid one of them would steal it.

"Ah," Henry drawled from his favorite cushioned seat in the corner of the book-lined room. "It's our dear Miss Khan. Can we call you Genghis for short?"

Deandra laughed appreciatively, looking up from studying her manicured nails, the layers of her long, shimmering gown rustling as she unhooked her knees from her chair. "Henry, you can be so clever."

Even Margaret had to cover her smile.

Miss Pruitt's lips pursed like a shriveled prune, and her eyes narrowed. But they flew open with dismay when a sudden breeze came through the open windows and played havoc with the papers on her desk.

"Look what you've done!" she cried, dashing to the window to slam the glass panes shut.

"Were those important?" Henry asked, picking up a sheet and starting to read. " 'Mr. James Lampman, formerly of 212 Mount Vernon Street, more recently of 155 Huntington Avenue, wishes to sue for damages after one H. Paul Redman ruined his reputation and his business—' "

The woman snatched the page away so quickly that the paper nearly tore in two. "That is private," she barked. "Now get out of here! Out! Out! Out! This is my office!"

She tried to shoo them from the room, but Margaret stood her ground.

"You can't run us out. Our Sophie needs to play."

Music was as much a part of Sophie's day as breathing. If she didn't have her cello in her hands, music ran through her head. She worked out passages no matter what she was doing, without thought, out of habit.

"She'll practice somewhere else," Miss Pruitt stated. "That is, if you call that noise I've been hearing music." She looked directly at Sophie, who hadn't moved. "I hardly call *The Love Nest* worth a grown person's time."

The statement surprised Sophie, then made her laugh in turn. Miss Pruitt was a smart one. With a smile, Sophie stood from her chair, then handed Henry her instrument. "Tell that to all the men who pay to see me play, Miss Pruitt."

The older woman's look grew knowing. "I know what men pay to see you do."

The room went quiet. Sophie and Miss Pruitt stared at each other. Henry, Margaret, and Deandra stared at them.

A tense moment passed until Sophie, at last, laughed.

"Come along, children. When the woman is right, the woman is right. More than one man who has seen me perform doesn't know the difference between Beethoven and Boston baked beans."

Deandra and Henry exchanged a questioning look before they followed Sophie from the room.

Despite her laugh, Sophie hadn't been as immune to Altima Pruitt's words as she wanted her entourage to think. Long years as a serious cellist couldn't be suppressed completely, making her think of Bach.

If she had tried, really tried, could she have done it?

Could she have played Bach's cello suites and moved a crowd?

Needing to be alone, Sophie went into the study—rather, Grayson's office—clicking the door shut behind her. Grayson was in court that morning, and he wasn't expected until well after noon.

She sat in the desk chair, so much like the seat her father had had when she was growing up. But this was a new chair, changed. Like so many things about her life.

Part of her wanted to board the next ship bound for France and never return. But it hardly mattered. She didn't have the money for passage. She had to sit tight until she received advance-booking money for her June concert in Paris.

Frustrated, she pushed up from the chair and went to the side window. Earlier that morning she had pulled on a simple sky blue day dress with long, fitted sleeves. But despite the sun she felt the need to wrap her arms around herself and briskly rub her arms.

"You look cold."

She whirled around to find Grayson standing in the doorway wearing a dark suit and waistcoat, his white shirt and collar starched, his light wool trousers molding to his strong thighs. Would the impact of his presence ever lessen? Would she ever get used to his hard-chiseled perfection? His height, the darkness of his eyes? The casual ease that was little more than a patina over a barely contained power? Would she ever grow used to the effect he had on her?

She would have fled through the door had he not blocked the way. Besides, she would not be a coward.

As casually as she could, she went to his desk and sat in his chair, hooking her ankle beneath one knee and swinging her slimly booted foot in a desperate effort to appear calm while her heart hammered in her chest. "Nope. Not cold at all. And weren't you supposed to be gone for hours?"

Grayson strolled into the room and sat in the chair opposite her, as though she were the lawyer, he the client. He leaned back and crossed his legs with ease, then looked at her.

"The court session was postponed. Besides, we need to talk."

The time had come. This was it. He was going to tell her to pack her bags and head for a hotel. Her mind raced with what she could say. Where would they go? How would they survive until May?

Nervous, she picked up a fountain pen to keep her hand from shaking. "Of course we need to talk. But first, did you see the flowers?" Anything to avoid the inevitable.

He sat for a moment, then glanced back at the foyer. "It's impossible not to see them. What are they for?"

The pen stopped midcircle. "For me," she explained, then resumed her designs. "There are flowers and candy. Trinkets and baubles. Not to mention invitations by the dozens."

"What's the occasion?"

A smile tilted her lips as she glanced at him. "My homecoming. Word has gotten out that the prodigal daughter has returned."

He stood from the chair and reached for the pen. Their fingers touched, and she felt it intensely—his long and strong, hers smaller, with short, rounded nails so she could press the strings of the cello.

He took the pen from her hand and set it aside. "I'd hardly call you a prodigal."

She sat back, her teeth catching the corner of her lower lip, cradling the fingers he had touched. "What would you call me?"

He came around and stood between her and the desk,

leaning back against the edge. She felt her pulse skitter, and without being obvious, she pressed farther away. But he only looked at her for a long time, really looked, and her discomfort grew.

A strange tenderness softened his obsidian eyes. "I'd call you complicated."

She made a scoffing sound, too loudly. "I'm a simple girl, nothing more."

Pushing up, she tried to move away. But when she stood, the chair didn't slide back, and she found herself so close to Grayson that if she shifted so much as an inch they would touch.

His dark eyes glowed like embers. "You are many things, Sophie, but simple is not one of them."

She started to protest, but he cut her off as he brushed the tips of his fingers down her arm. Just barely.

He was too close, she felt too much. Crossing her arms on her chest, she tried to pull free. But he held her there.

"I make you nervous," he said quietly. "Tell me why."

"You make me nervous?" Despite the truth of his words, pride got the better of her and she pulled her shoulders back. "I don't think so."

He chuckled, and his lips tilted in a way that made her want to reach out and trace the fullness.

"All right, if you won't tell me why I make you nervous, then tell me who all these gifts are from. Childhood friends? Your father's acquaintances?"

"They're from admirers."

Instantly the glowing embers of his eyes sparked with fire. Any tenderness was gone, only irritation remained. *Good.*

"Admirers? You have admirers? Already?"

"Yes," she stated, using the word like armor. "It would appear I have scads of them." And she did, amazingly enough. Men who as boys wouldn't give her the time of day. "Do you want to know who has paid calls?"

"No, I do not." His voice was tight. "You have no business being courted."

"Oh, really," she mused, planting her hands on her hips. "Why ever not?"

He stared at her, that same, strange war she had seen in his eyes that first night raging within him. With a sudden shudder she dropped her hands to her sides and wondered if he already knew about her performances. Was that why he touched her as he did? Boldly, much too forward.

She could tell he was on the verge of saying something very serious, and her palms began to tingle. What would it be? A reprimand? A lecture?

"Sophie, you've been here nearly a week and it's long past time we talked."

He was as solemn as she had ever seen him, that dark possessiveness resurging.

Her breath grew short, though she couldn't say why. Her chest felt much too tight, and suddenly she didn't like the look in his eyes. With all her heart she wished she hadn't started down this path of teasing about admirers.

He took her hand and his voice gentled. "We've known each other for a very long time." He smiled, his full, wonderful lips tilting with fond amusement. "In fact, other than my brothers and parents, I've known no one longer. So I would like to be frank."

Her heart began to pound. "You could try to be Frank, but I'll have a hard time thinking of you as anyone but Grayson." She searched for a smile, tried to laugh.

"No more jokes, Sophie. We need to discuss the reason why your father asked you to come home."

Sound swirled in her mind, a low buzzing, like the rush of wind whispering through willows. Despite the rough start, her father wanted her back to be a part of his new family; it could be nothing else.

"I think you know that I have always cared for you," he continued. "And I would like to think you care—"

"Good heavens! Look at the time." She whirled away from his grasp and hurried to the door with a laugh she didn't feel. "I'm late, absolutely, positively, unforgivably late. I know you understand, since you are about nothing if not schedules and timetables. We'll talk later. Really."

"Sophie!"

But she didn't stop. She dashed out of his office, aware the whole time of his dark, probing gaze on her back.

Chapter Six

Grayson stood in the window of his office, staring out at the snow-lined street without seeing. He didn't know what to make of Sophie and her abrupt departure.

With a sigh, he ran his hands through his hair. He was frustrated and growing increasingly ambivalent about the bride he had chosen. But he also couldn't deny his increasing hunger for the taste of her mouth. The quick brush of her lips had only made him want more. As always, just thinking about her made his body stir.

On the morning he had found her wearing his robe, he could tell she had little on underneath. For one stark moment he had imagined parting the cashmere, cupping the bare fullness of her breasts, running his thumbs over the rose-tipped peaks. And his receptionist was only yards away in the kitchen.

Grayson bit back an oath. His intended was barely home and already she was twisting his thoughts and beliefs into unrecognizable musings.

Conrad had been pressing him to tell Sophie of the betrothal. He and Patrice, not to mention his father, wanted to announce the joining of the two families at the party Saturday night—in truth, the sole reason for the event. Though Sophie didn't know that.

Grayson had returned from court early, determined to

tell her. And he would have, but she hadn't given him a chance.

Impatience flashed through his mind at the thought. This was the woman he had chosen to marry. He had written up and signed a flawless legal document to do just that. She was the woman who would bear and raise his children. Hell, based on what he had seen so far, Sophie needed some raising of her own. The irony wasn't lost on him.

The woman was trouble, and trouble he didn't need.

But still, he couldn't get her out of his mind.

He heard the slam of the front door, then he saw Sophie race out onto the landing. Wearing heavy woolen gloves, she pulled on a coat and buttoned it awkwardly, popped open a parasol against the winter sun, then hurried down the flagstone path.

He didn't believe for a second that she had someplace to go. Though what he wasn't as certain about was whether she had known what he had been trying to say.

He watched as she crossed the street, then strode down the granite walkway that was bordered by a waist-high, black wrought-iron fence, topped with spikes that were more decorative than deterrent. Despite himself, Grayson started to smile. She was outrageous and maddening, but beautiful beyond words.

Her hair was uncovered, a generous hat of bells and bows held in her free hand. Wild golden curls were pulled up and away from her face, but escaping its confines. His fingers itched to pull free the simple ribbon that held the riotous mass in place. He longed to touch her hair, her lips. He thought of her eyes, large and brown, shot with shards of gold and green. Vivid and wild. Yet again, his body surged at the thought.

Suddenly she stopped. Grayson watched, his thoughts churning to a halt, as she slowly sank down to the walkway in front of a place in the wrought iron that had been broken but not yet repaired. With his shoulders stiffening, he saw her curl her gloved fingers around the bent lengths of fencing and peer into the bushes just beyond. Something was wrong.

Sophie pushed up from the ground, then looked frantically from side to side. He started to go to her, but his jaw fell open in amazement when she dropped her hat and parasol on the walkway, gathered up her skirts, and squeezed through the jagged opening in the fence, then got stuck.

Grayson stood half stunned, half furious. Sophie wriggled around, only making things worse, until suddenly twisted lengths of wrought iron poked through the voluminous folds of her coat.

Seconds later, Grayson banged out the front door.

Commonwealth Avenue was busy, the sound of wheels on cobbles and cinders ringing in the air as carriages and wagons vied for the right-of-way. He crossed the narrow lane, the frozen expanse of the grassy mall, then the opposite lane, giving little thought to the cold.

He drew closer as she struggled to free herself. Even from a distance he could hear her muttering curse words that would have made a drunken sailor blush. But she managed only to entangle herself more thoroughly. Grayson was pounding forward when another man whistled his appreciation. For the first time Grayson noticed that with her skirts impaled on the fence, her underclothes were exposed.

"Havin' a problem?" the man called out to Sophie, approaching from a wagon he had pulled over to the side of the street.

Anger sliced through Grayson. "You're going to have a problem if you don't step away this instant."

The man whirled around to see who had spoken, his body tensed for a fight. He was stocky, with the uneven face of a man who was used to using his fists. But one look at Grayson clearly made him think better of it, and he backed off. Whether it was Grayson's look of authority or his broad shoulders and six-foot-four-inch frame that had deterred the man, Grayson didn't care.

"Good Lord. The man was only trying to help," Sophie said, craning her neck to see him.

"He was gawking."

"And no wonder," she stated dryly, renewing her efforts to pull away. "How often do you think he sees a woman with her skirts skewered on a fence?"

Grayson's features hardened. "How foolish of me. I should have left you to his whim."

"Enough," she interjected. "Will you please help me out of here?"

Grayson stared at her for one long, exasperated moment before he took the last few steps that separated them. Then he started to untangle her skirts.

"Come on, Grayson."

"I'm doing the best I can without ripping your clothes off," he ground out.

"Forget my clothes. If you don't hurry I'm going to tear them off myself."

With a muffled curse he yanked at her skirts, pulling them off the twisted metal with a loud rip.

Once she was free she ended up inside the yard in a profusion of ice-covered bushes, the fence between them. Without so much as a word of thanks, she dropped to her knees.

"What in the world are you doing, Sophie?"

"Quick, I need your help."

Grayson couldn't imagine what kind of trouble Sophie had managed to find, though he had no doubt that trouble was exactly what she had. But when he leaped the fence with a curse and squatted down to see what it was, he stilled at the sight that met his eyes.

A dog lay beneath the bush, bloody and beaten.

"Get away from there," he demanded, jerking back, pulling Sophie with him.

But she shook free, her face set in firm lines. "We have to help her."

"The dog is going to die, Sophie. All we have to do is get away from here and call the authorities."

She glanced over her shoulder to look at him, and he was surprised to see tears.

"No," she stated with a steely obstinacy.

Grayson cursed as he looked back at the dog, its eyes clouded with pain, regarding Sophie warily. But the animal was weak—from hunger, he was certain, as much as loss of blood. Soon the dog's eyes drooped closed, its head bobbing before finally sinking down onto the ground. Carefully, Sophie tried to pick up the animal.

"Sophie," he warned sharply, coming forward.

She glanced at him with a look of determination mixed with a sudden flash of desolation that he recognized.

"I will not leave her here to die," she stated, her voice strained but determined. "If she dies she will not die alone."

Their gazes locked, hers stubborn as the muscle in his jaw leaped. "Damn it, I'll carry the blasted dog."

Her expression grew as wary as the dog's had been earlier. But she held her tongue while Grayson picked up the animal, its once golden fur matted with dirt and blood and gritty ice that smeared his Savile Row suit. When Grayson stood, the dog cradled against his torso, Sophie looked at him with a solemnness that made his heart constrict. Silently she nodded her head, as if somehow words would betray her.

For reasons Grayson didn't understand, he felt a flash of certainty that her concern for this dog went much deeper than he could fathom. The sudden darkness in her golden brown eyes spoke of a great deal more than frivolous days playing the cello—of more than the outrageous trouble-maker he had been convinced she was only minutes earlier. But what could she have seen in her life to make her eyes become as troubled as they were now?

"We'll take her home." Sophie pushed up from the ground, mindless of the stains and rips that marred her clothes.

Forgetting her hat and parasol, Sophie cut across the yard. They stepped through a gate onto Commonwealth Avenue, and before Grayson could stop her, she walked out into traffic, forcing drivers to jerk their reins to keep from running her down.

She ignored the angry men who leaped up from their wagon seats, shouting heated curses. "Hurry, Grayson," she called from the road.

He stepped out onto the length of Commonwealth Avenue. Abruptly the angry din of voices broke off at the sight of the bloody dog that lay limp in his arms.

Grayson walked through the sudden, eerie quiet, no sound, no thought, only the feel of the dog's unconscious shudders of pain against his chest. He was certain that as long as he lived he would never forget the sound of that silence and the feel of life ebbing away in his arms.

Sophie threw open the front door of Swan's Grace, then raced past a startled Henry, who stood in a smoking jacket sipping coffee from a china cup. She led Grayson down the back stairs to the basement laundry room.

"Put her here," Sophie instructed.

No sooner had Grayson set the dog down than Henry appeared in the doorway and grimaced.

"Get some towels, Henry," she stated.

"Me?" he squeaked, his cup rattling.

But he was saved from doing anything when the efficient woman called Margaret bustled into the room. Grayson was all but pushed aside when Sophie and Margaret hovered over the battered dog, working as if they had done this before.

By then the animal was barely breathing. Grayson's eyes narrowed against unexpected emotion, emotion that seemed to have tangled in his mind the minute he picked up the dog. He didn't want to care. The dog would die. He had learned that as a boy, had learned that favorite dogs died and fathers refused to let sons care. But if Sophie realized it, she didn't let on.

"I'll build a fire to warm the room," Margaret said.

The woman stepped away, grabbing a towel to wipe her hands. Grayson hadn't moved since they entered.

"I'll do it," he said suddenly.

Sophie and Margaret looked at him as if he had spoken in tongues.

"I'll build the fire," he repeated, his voice low and commanding.

Sophie stared at him with a furrowed brow, as if trying to understand him. But before he could give it another thought, she pointed toward a neat stack of firewood.

"The kindling is over there," she said, then returned her attention to the animal.

He watched her for a moment, her tender hands, her capable but gentle ministrations as she tended the dog's wounds. Without warning a memory surfaced from years before. He was young, no more than four or five years old, knocked into the street by a gang of laughing older boys. He was hurt and bleeding, his wrist throbbing, and tears streamed down his cheeks. Then his father, standing over him like a giant, his face angry as he told him to buck up, to stop crying like a weakling.

Grayson had picked himself up, but when he headed for

his mother, his father had cut him off. "Only a baby needs coddling from his mother."

In the end he had washed his cuts in the upstairs lavatory alone, tears streaking his grimy face, his meal sent up by his father as if he had done something wrong. His cuts and scrapes had healed. And he had never cried again.

Grayson didn't understand the strange pounding of his heart, or why he suddenly remembered the incident—why memories were wrapping around him. A father's duty was to teach his son to be a man, to be strong and powerful. Grayson had become both.

Suddenly he wondered why he was still there. He didn't need this; he didn't want this. Outrageous behavior, traveling the world with an entourage of hangers-on, up to her elbows in dirt and muck from an unknown dog that was sure to die. Once and for all he saw so clearly that this was not what he wanted in a wife.

He wanted an ordered world, important work, a warm, calm home to return to at night. He wanted the life he had spent over fifteen years building.

But the pounding didn't stop and he turned away sharply, tossing wood into the fire with more force than was necessary.

When there was nothing more they could do, Margaret and Sophie leaned back against the wall. Margaret left, and when Sophie told him she didn't need anything else, he stared at her for a long time as he told himself to leave. Forced himself to leave.

With measured steps he returned to the hotel, forcing his mind to a careful blank. He concentrated on the small bed, the cramped space. He had to use the small basin of water in his room when the shared bath down the hall was full.

He grimaced before his lips flattened to a straight line. Memories swelled of the earlier days in the garret, when he had faced the shock of dingy hallways and shared baths with rusty streams of trickling water, and unscrupulous men who would have as easily stolen his razor as used it to slit his throat. He'd been thankful that at sixteen, he hadn't needed a razor all that often.

He searched for a laugh, but found nothing close to humor.

When he went to the small hotel wardrobe to change, Grayson realized that he was down to his last pair of trousers and an older shirt.

Frustration snaked through him, though for so much more than lack of clothes. Too many memories. His life suddenly felt out of control.

The situation needed to be remedied, and soon. But what did he want? What did he really want to do about Sophie and the betrothal? He had no answers.

He had always been a man of quick decision. Once made, he moved forward. But since Sophie had arrived, one minute he couldn't wait to marry her, the next he wanted her out of his life.

When he once again left the Vendome, he was intent on going to his men's club. He refused to think—of Sophie, of the dog, of the past.

But when he should have hailed a hansom cab to take him downtown, he turned instead toward Swan's Grace. Like a moth drawn to a flame.

He found Sophie still tending the dog, and instead of continuing on to his club, Grayson went to his office in Swan's Grace to work. But his concentration was fractured. Every few minutes he found himself standing in the basement doorway.

Sophie sat in a shaft of sunlight that streamed in from a small, high window. He watched, unable to look away, as she touched the dog, barely, softly. Her fingers drifted across a patch of fur on its brow that was unmarked by vio-

lence. She gave no thought to hurting herself, no thought
to hurting the fingers she depended on to play the cello
with such beauty.

So quietly that Grayson couldn't hear, she whispered to
the animal. But he understood. Somehow he knew. She
truly believed she could heal this dog. This stray. This battered soul that was beyond repair.

He came farther into the room. Sophie glanced back at
him, her eyes filled with silent question. He met her gaze
with determination as he pulled out a ladder-back chair
and sat down beside her. For one brief, fleeting moment,
she smiled, the gesture tired but appreciative. Then she
turned back to the dog.

Grayson didn't leave her again.

It was late in the day when Sophie's stepmother came
down the stairs.

"Sophie, are you here?"

Sophie turned and Grayson rose.

Patrice Wentworth was undeniably a beautiful woman,
much younger than her husband, not much older than Sophie herself. She stood in the doorway, dressed in a deep
blue taffeta gown that matched her eyes, and a rich blue-
and-brown-paisley shawl. Her hair was the color of midnight, her skin as white and pure as a bowl of cream.
Grayson had only been around her once before she married Conrad Wentworth. But since that marriage she had
become a jewel of Boston society, attending all of the
city's finest events.

Patrice grimaced as she sidestepped a pile of used towels,
her beaded reticule swinging on her wrist. "Good heavens,
what are you doing down here?"

No greetings, no hugs.

"Hello, Patrice," Sophie responded, a dark, painful look

flaring in her eyes. But then it was gone and only a smile remained.

"Did you bring the girls with you?" she asked.

Patrice's footsteps rang daintily on the stone floor as she approached, clutching her shawl as if it were a shield against the dimness of the basement. "No, I didn't bring the girls— Oh, Mr. Hawthorne, I didn't realize you were here."

"Hello, Mrs. Wentworth," he offered with a formal nod of his head.

The woman smoothed her hair, and her decorously painted lips parted on a beautiful smile. "I haven't seen you in ages."

"Not since you called at Hawthorne House for my mother," he replied, his tone cold and clipped. Patrice Wentworth wasn't his favorite person.

"Ah, yes. Your mother." She seemed to lose interest. "How is she?"

"She is well. Though recently she was a bit under the weather."

"You can't mean it." Her brow rose in surprise. "I could have sworn I saw Emmaline just Monday." She smiled and sighed. "She looked beautiful in a gown of peach silk with a simple inlay of Flanders lace, and a wonderful cape of winter-white wool with fur trim."

His brow furrowed with confusion. "You saw my mother on Monday?"

Patrice placed her gloved hand against her midriff, pulling herself up. "Oh, yes. She looked stunning. She couldn't possibly have been ill."

"You must be mistaken. She was at home."

He could feel Sophie's questioning gaze on him. But he couldn't keep the hard pounding in his mind contained.

"Well," Patrice considered, "I thought it was her." She shook her head and laughed. "Though perhaps not."

She turned her attention to Sophie. "The girls couldn't come, as they are much too busy with all the things young ladies do." She stopped abruptly. "Though I always forget that you were too busy with your music to become involved in the . . . simpler aspects of a young lady's life."

Sophie tensed, he saw it.

"You were always playing, playing, playing." She eyed Sophie. "Of course, my girls don't have a bit of talent when it comes to musical instruments. And you have so much. I sometimes wonder who is luckier. You with your talent or my girls with their brimming engagement calendars." She *tsk*ed. "I suspect that you consider the trade-off well worth it. Especially now that we've all seen the article that ran in the magazine."

"You saw it?"

"Why, yes."

"Did Father see it, too?"

"Well, of course he has seen it." Then nothing else.

Grayson watched as red flared in Sophie's cheeks.

"What did he think?" she asked, as if she couldn't help wanting to know.

Patrice smiled in a way that was clear she knew of her stepdaughter's frustration. "You'll have to ask him that yourself, dear. I would never be so presumptuous as to speak on his behalf."

"Of course not," she responded, the words tight.

"Enough about the article. I've come to make sure you will be at the party. I understand that you had words with your father last night." She shook her head daintily. "Not that I'm surprised. You always were strong willed. But the party is set and there is no turning back. And what would people think if our guests of honor weren't there?"

"*Guests* of honor?" Sophie asked, confused.

Grayson caught Patrice in a hard glare.

"Guest, guests. The more the merrier, I always say."

Patrice glanced over at Grayson and raised a brow defiantly. "You are going to be there, too, Mr. Hawthorne?"

"Yes," he answered tightly.

But Patrice hardly seemed to notice as she gasped, her delicate features blanching at the sight on the table. "Good God! What is wrong with that dog?"

Sophie looked at the animal. "She is hurt."

Patrice's smiles were gone. "Why am I not surprised that you would be down in the basement tending a bloody animal?" Her eyes flashed annoyance.

They stared at each other, neither speaking, until Patrice turned away and hastened from the room, a finely wrought handkerchief held to her mouth.

As soon as the door slammed at the top of the stairs, Sophie seemed to deflate.

"Nice to see you, too, Patrice," she said to the empty stairway.

Grayson stared at the closed door before turning back to Sophie. Her nose was red, her chignon long having fallen about her neck, but all he knew in that moment was that he wanted her. To hold her, to taste her. To brush his fingers along her body to make her want him as much as he wanted her.

He wanted her with an intensity that left him aching like a schoolboy. An intensity that filled him now as he looked at her.

"Sophie," Grayson said, reining in his body with iron-clad control, "you need to get some rest. You've been at this for hours."

"No," she whispered, touching that one unbattered spot on the dog's brow.

Grayson grasped her shoulders, gently turning her to face him. With the palm of one large hand he smoothed back her hair from her face. "Let the dog go, Sophie."

She met his gaze, her eyes growing obstinate. "No! She needs me. I am going to save her."

Then she pulled away.

Her words circled in his mind. *I am going to save her.* Grayson didn't believe the dog would last until morning.

But sometime later, with Sophie nearly asleep in her chair, the dog opened its eyes.

Grayson grew still. Sophie didn't notice. For one long, solitary moment, he sat in the room, unable to move, just staring at the dog, his heart beating hard. Then, more gently than he had done anything in his life, he reached out. With visible effort, the dog tentatively sniffed his fingers and licked his hand.

A tremor raced down Grayson's spine, and the memory of Sophie's baskets of food shot through his mind, her childlike attempts to save him much like her attempts to save this dog.

His hand was unsteady when he placed his fingers to that spot on the dog's brow that Sophie had touched so often. "Do you think she can save me, too?" he whispered into the quiet room.

A low noise sounded deep in Grayson's throat as he leaned back, dragging his hand over his face. He would never let anyone know of the fear and emptiness he had felt when his father sent him away. It hadn't been ambition that made him succeed, rather the desperate desire never to be hungry and cold again. Or afraid. He would never let anyone know that to this day there were nights when he awoke in a cold sweat, the remembered feel of rats brushing against his feet making his skin burn. And the loneliness. It had been a desperate ache that competed with his hunger.

He had moved beyond that. Today he had food at his fingertips, money in the bank. He had cut off emotion. He had succeeded.

But now, for reasons he didn't understand, the past had been dredged up and he had done nothing but remember, turning back the clock to that time when he thought he wouldn't survive.

After a moment, he drew in a deep, steadying breath, then touched Sophie's cheek, uneasy with all that he felt. When she jerked fully awake and looked at him in confusion, he didn't speak, only motioned to the dog.

Sophie gasped as she pushed the hair out of her face. The dog whimpered and tried to wag its tail—barely a movement, but enough.

With that, Sophie's tears spilled over. She threw her arms around Grayson and kissed him full on the mouth. "Oh, Grayson! We saved her," she whispered before carefully burrowing her face in the dog's neck.

Abruptly he pushed up from his seat. Sophie called out to him, but he didn't stop. Taking the stairs, he didn't think about where he was. He only wanted away.

He went straight up to the bedroom that he had made his own. But the unexpected sight of Sophie's belongings mixed with his stopped him cold. As if they already lived together. His best Hessian boots were still where he had left them before she arrived. Her sheer night wrapper was flung with careless disregard over the back of the chair, papers scattered in a jumble across his desk.

The bed was unmade, drawers half closed, her undergarments tossed in with his. The mess sent a flash of heat through him. Anger, he told himself, denying that the intimacy of it all affected him in any other way.

He knew he should return to the hotel or his club. Maybe even Lucas's gentleman's establishment for a stiff shot of brandy. But he knew he wouldn't. Shutting the door, he yanked off his shirt and strode to the deep closet that held his clothes. This time he wasn't surprised when he found her gowns lined up next to his suits, soft velvets and satiny silks next to crisp, pressed wool.

He'd had many women over the years. But he never stayed overnight. When he got up in the morning, he preferred to be alone. He had never woken to the intimacy of a woman next to him. The casualness of her clothes tangled with his. He was from a house full of men—their mother off-limits in most meaningful ways.

Forcefully Grayson emptied his mind, choosing a new shirt, then tossing it on the bed before he went into the private bath and turned the sink knob. Within minutes steaming hot water gushed into the basin. With a minimum of ceremony, he mixed up a lather, pulled out his finest razor, ran it across the strop attached to the wall, then started to shave. The motion cleared his mind, brought an ease to him. An order. The way things should be.

The coil of tension began to unknot.

After no more than two swaths across his face, he bowed his head, planted his palms against the sink, and leaned against the porcelain basin, the razor still in his hand.

What was she doing to him?

How was it that his perfectly ordered world suddenly seemed upside down?

But when he looked up, it wasn't his own reflection he saw in the mirror, rather Sophie's, as she stared at him from the doorway.

"I was worried," she whispered, her voice oddly hoarse. "You left so abruptly."

"No need to be."

He gave little thought to his bare chest, and forced himself to look away from her when he knew he wanted to hold her tight, bury his face in her hair. Make her promise she would never leave him again.

Biting back a curse, he resumed shaving, but stopped again when Sophie came up beside him.

"There is something so incredibly intimate about seeing a man shave."

His hand tensed. "I'd say there aren't many unmarried women, at least of a certain kind, who have seen a man shave."

His tone was meant to intimidate.

Sophie only laughed, then reached out and ran her finger through the white lather, leaving a streak on his cheek. "I'm not that *certain kind*, Grayson." She grew serious. "I haven't been in a very long time."

He pivoted on his heel to face her. "You mean to tell me you have been with men in this type of intimacy?"

She shrugged but wouldn't turn to him. "Well, not exactly. Actually I haven't seen anyone shave but you."

His brow furrowed.

"When you were young. Remember?"

Suddenly he did. He saw it so clearly. Sophie unexpectedly standing in the doorway of his room in Hawthorne House, she only eight, he pretending he needed to shave with any regularity. She had worn a dress with too many ruffles, and her knees had been scraped, no doubt from having tried to play stickball with the boys down the lane. Sophie had always wanted to do everything any other kid did. But the other kids hadn't wanted her around.

Had they understood she was different from them? Smarter? Wiser? Or had her mother's ruffled dresses and superior attitude put them off?

"You weren't quite such a prude back then, as I recall," Sophie interjected. "Not so proper."

"I was sixteen."

"You were fun."

His thoughts hardened, but at the same time his pulse began to throb. He glanced at her mouth. Her lips parted and his blood surged when her gaze drifted low. Taking a towel, he wiped the shaving cream from his face, and though he told himself to turn away, he could do little more than toss the linen aside, then reach for her. He touched her mouth, just barely, his fingertips over the fullness.

Her lips moved with half-uttered silent words.

"Was I?" he asked in a whisper.

Confusion creased her brow.

"Was I fun? Ever?" He waited for her answer, needing to hear it.

Her expression softened. "Yes," she whispered. "But you were more than fun. You were strong and kind."

His fingers slid into her hair, cupping her head. He pulled her to him as if he had no will of his own, and pressed her close. He wanted to curse, wanted to scoff in response to her answer. It was weakness that made him care. He knew it. But the words meant too much.

"Sophie," he said softly against her hair.

Her fingers flattened against his chest. He tipped her head and looked into her eyes. There was so much he wanted to say, but didn't know how. Words, half-formed in his head, disappeared like smoke before he could grasp them. He only knew that, for better or for worse, he couldn't let her go.

The decision was made. He would marry her.

He kissed her then, slowly, languorously, until she moaned. And that was his undoing. Running his hand down her back, he could feel the tremor that raced through her body. He deepened the kiss, his tongue seeking entrance. When she opened to him, her arms came up and wrapped around his neck. She held on to him as if she, too, didn't know how to let go. The thought filled him with satisfaction. After all these years she wasn't indifferent to him.

He grazed her tongue with his teeth, and he felt her breath. Like oranges in winter. Delicious and sweet, but rarely tasted.

His hands ran up her sides, then he brought one palm up to cup her breast. With that touch, everything changed.

"No," she gasped, flinging herself back, her eyes flashing wildly.

But just as quickly, she calmed herself, as though she had turned a page in a book and become a new character.

"Now, Grayson," she all but purred, though there was a tremor in her voice, "you're the proper one here. I don't think I need to spell out why I shouldn't be standing in a bathroom with you half-naked. I simply wanted to thank you for helping me with the dog. It was kind, and I couldn't have done it without you."

She didn't wait for a response. She left as unexpectedly as she had appeared, leaving him alone to stare at the empty doorway. Who was Sophie Wentworth?

He turned away and found his reflection in the mirror. Who was *he*?

Once, life had been different. Once, he would have tried to save that dog. But life had changed, and he had changed along with it. She had credited him with attributes that he didn't deserve. He hadn't saved anything.

He would have left the dog to die—and never would have known that souls wounded beyond repair could be saved.

Chapter Seven

Smoothing the voluminous folds of her taffeta skirts, Sophie felt the thrill of anticipation wrap around her as she stood in her father's palatial home. The house brimmed with two hundred of Boston's elite, all of whom were there to see her.

A grand party in her honor.

She searched the faces for Grayson, then scowled when she realized what she was doing. She hoped he didn't come. He had completely unnerved her in the bathroom of Swan's Grace. The kiss. The intimacy.

It had been with great effort that she had managed finally to pull up the sophisticated, unemotional wall she had built around herself. She couldn't let it drop again.

She had taken great care with her appearance. Her gown was stunning, though demure, the collar high, the sleeves long, with proper white gloves covering her hands. It had been ages since she had cared what people thought about her. But tonight she cared. Deeply. Tonight she wanted to make her father proud.

Making her way through the Italian-marbled foyer, she took in the house. Crystal chandeliers glistened. Candles burned in hand-carved bronze candelabra, imported from France. The treasure of a king, Patrice had explained. Nothing but the finest for her father.

Sophie had often thought her father should have been a

king. What he lacked in bloodlines he made up for in an extravagant display of wealth. He had made so much money in shipping, her mother had told her as a child, that even the most blue-blooded, puritan-minded Bostonians couldn't turn their noses up at the man.

Sophie continued on, but her attempts to cross the room proved to be no easy task, given that everyone wanted to say hello, inquire after her journey home, or comment on the article in *The Century* magazine.

And the men. Every man there, eligible or not, clamored after her. Men who as boys hadn't given her the time of day. They all wanted a dance, or a minute of her time.

The night was proving to be a wonderful success. She was home, and from all appearances, Boston adored her.

Halfway across the foyer she saw the man her stepmother had pointed out earlier. Niles Prescott, with his gray hair combed back and the lines of his face making him look dashing rather than old, was the longtime conductor for Boston's Music Hall. He had been a close friend of her mother's. Too close, she knew some had whispered. He was also the man who had given the debut concert he had promised her to someone else.

Sophie blinked hard when she remembered the crushing announcement of who would perform the solo at the Grand Debut. The Music Hall's auditorium had been filled with students and their parents. Niles Prescott stood at the podium. Sophie had waited impatiently to hear her name called, to rise from her seat, to walk to the stage with the audience thundering their applause. It was the moment she had lived her whole life for.

Sophie felt heat sting her cheeks when she remembered how she *had* stood, the name announced taking seconds too long to register. Then the sight of her greatest competitor walking to the podium. The triumphant smile. The embarrassment, the devastation.

Later, the conductor had said very little to her. But it was enough. *I didn't think you could play Bach.*

A lie.

Sophie knew it had nothing to do with Bach. She thought of her mother and the man. The promises he had made, promises he no longer had to keep once her mother was gone.

But even knowing that, for the first time in her life, Sophie had begun to doubt herself. *Was* it a lie? she had suddenly begun to wonder, insidious thoughts that became indistinguishable from the truth.

Always before she had simply played, Bach being her most cherished composer. After she lost the long-counted-on debut, she started second-guessing what she did and how she did it.

She had fled to Germany's Leipzig Music Conservatory, where she enrolled in the four-year program. She analyzed and studied, practiced and played, until she had taken every class and learned everything any of the professors could teach her. Then finally she gave a debut recital, but in Amsterdam, not Boston. And it had been a disaster.

She had been nervous and self-conscious. The audience's reception had been cold, and she had cringed at the reviews the next morning describing an uninspiring performance by yet another child prodigy. But all of that changed when she created her new show. Flash and dazzle. Jewels and gowns.

It might not be Bach, but for the first time everyone had loved her.

Earlier in the evening, Patrice had mentioned that Niles wanted to see her. Sophie couldn't imagine what he wanted, and she had no interest in finding out. She wasn't sure what she would do if she came face-to-face with him after so many years.

Somehow she slipped through a knot of guests to

escape, and practically ran into Bradford and Emmaline Hawthorne.

"Little Sophie," Bradford said grandly, kissing her hand like a Renaissance courtier.

He was a tall, distinguished man with broad shoulders. He had the ability to be charming, but she remembered too well when he had so callously sent Grayson out on his own. She had hated the man back then, and still couldn't quite bring herself to forgive him.

"Now really, Bradford," Emmaline Hawthorne said, extending her hands to Sophie, "she is no longer a little girl." She pulled her into a loving embrace before setting her at arm's length. "She has grown up to be a beautiful young woman."

Emmaline was soft and dreamy, her age lending her a grace and dignity that youth would never allow. Sophie's own mother had been more practical than beautiful, and Sophie had always marveled at Emmaline's ethereal loveliness.

The older woman's smile softened. "I know your mother would be proud of you. I wish so terribly that she were here to see your success."

Sophie felt a poignant lump swell in her throat, the sudden wish that her mother were with her now hitting her so hard she nearly stumbled. "Thank you, Mrs. Hawthorne," she managed. "That means a great deal to me."

They were interrupted when someone called out her name.

"Sophie!" a woman exclaimed, striding up to them in a cloud of shimmering skirts and sparkling jewelry. "Don't you look smashing," she cried, then extravagantly kissed the air beside either cheek.

It took a second for Sophie to realize that the woman was Megan Robertson. Megan was shorter than her, and rounder in a voluptuous sort of way, with dark brown hair done up in a mass of twists and curls, and large brown eyes. As an adult she was lovely in a Rubenesque sort of way. But when she was eighteen she had been called darling—and had been awarded Sophie's solo in the Grand Debut.

"Hello, Megan," Sophie replied evenly, hating the flash of insecurity that surged inside her as if five years hadn't passed. She was successful now, she had to remind herself.

Megan quickly greeted the Hawthornes, who then excused themselves, leaving the two women alone. Megan whirled back to Sophie.

"You must come with me! Everyone is talking of nothing but you, and I am going to show you off."

Megan hooked her arm through Sophie's as though they were still schoolgirls and began leading her from room to room of the Wentworth house. Sophie didn't know what to make of this girl who had always competed with her, always promising that one day she would be the best. After all these years, was she trying to be kind?

Sophie all but scoffed out loud at the surge of gladness that this once most popular girl would befriend her now. They were adults, not children.

"You remember James Willis," Megan said, waving to a man, then pulling her along to his side.

"James, love. You remember our Sophie, don't you?"

"Of course." The man was dressed in expensive but slightly rumpled evening wear, and the pomade he used wasn't completely successful in taming the cowlick on the top of his head. "It has been a long time."

Sophie felt a devilish smile pull at her lips. "Yes, it's been a very long time. I haven't seen you since you put a frog down my dress."

James blushed a bright shade of red, and Megan laughed gaily. She swatted James's coat sleeve with her fan. "You didn't."

"As I recall," Sophie replied, "you helped him, Megan."

"Oh, yes." She laughed and pulled Sophie on. "How could I forget the way you squirmed around and carried on like you'd been shot? You always were such an actress." She raised her hand. "Thomas! Thomas Redding. Look who I have here."

Sophie felt her teeth start to grind. So much for any hope Megan would be kind.

Thomas Redding was a tall, thin man. As a boy he had spent his time reading books, his round spectacles as much a part of him as his nose. Since then, Sophie knew he had become a highly respected councilman.

He bowed formally and took her hand. "Miss Wentworth, it is a pleasure to see you again. And might I add that the photographs in the magazine did not do you justice."

Megan all but jerked her away, leaving Thomas kissing air instead of knuckles. "He has become so grandiose. Of course he's right, though. You are simply gorgeous. Who would have guessed that little Sophie Wentworth would have turned into such a beauty?" She scanned the room. "Oh, look, there's Grayson Hawthorne. Surely you remember him."

Sophie stopped abruptly as her heart stilled. He stood in the receiving room, his dark hair shining beneath the crystal chandelier, his white formal tie crisp, his black evening jacket accentuating broad shoulders. Even though he was surrounded by people, he stood apart from the crowd. He exuded power, a strength that drew people at the same time it made them cautious.

As always, he was stunningly handsome, but he was also the last person she wanted to see after the kiss they had shared. Just remembering sent a shiver through her body, making her want more.

Still, after all these years, he captivated her as no one else ever had. During her concert tour over the last many months, she had been courted by European princes and

English diplomats, but only Grayson held her attention. Just her luck to be attracted to a man who was as much fun as a cold splash of water on a cloudy winter day. She shuddered to think about a life together, Grayson in bed by eight, no doubt with a hot-water bottle at his feet and a warming cap on his head.

Wouldn't he?

She thought of his kiss, felt the betraying heat flaring low, and suddenly she wasn't so sure.

But then Patrice was at his side, her hand resting boldly on his arm as she told him something. Sophie felt her stomach clench as her stepmother smiled and stepped even closer. The pair spoke for a moment, but then Grayson looked up as if he sensed her presence, and their eyes met across the room.

He looked at her for what seemed like ages before he disengaged his arm from Patrice. After a second her stepmother seemed to realize where he was going, and her blue eyes hardened before she turned away sharply.

"Grayson!" Megan called out.

Instantly Sophie headed in the opposite direction, but the seemingly delicate Megan had a grip of steel.

"Look who I have here," she cooed. "When was the last time you saw our little Sophie?"

Grayson didn't bother to look at Megan. His dark eyes bore into Sophie's, at once sensual and unnerving as he ran his gaze over her. "Just yesterday."

The words made her feel touched, like a brush of fingers against her spine.

Megan's chin went up. "Yesterday? You've already seen Sophie since her return?" She shook her head, then she laughed. "Though I shouldn't be surprised. What did she do? Lurk outside your house waiting for you, like she always did?"

It took a moment for the words to register, but when

they did Sophie felt childish embarrassment burn hot and fast through her cheeks. Slowly Grayson turned his exacting gaze on the shorter woman.

"As it happened, *I* was waiting for Miss Wentworth when she returned," he said, his voice taking on a sharp edge.

Megan looked between Grayson and Sophie. "Really," she replied, all the more intrigued.

Sophie cringed and groaned silently. The last thing she needed was for Megan to think there was something going on between them. Her nemesis would no doubt latch on to that and find a way to embarrass her.

But before anything else could be said, a group of men circled around.

"Miss Wentworth!"

"Sophie!"

"You're a vision!"

"A dream!"

Sophie felt the welcome balm of familiar words, and her pique drifted away. She forgot about Megan. She started to smile, then smiled even more when she saw Grayson's jaw muscles starting to tic. He looked at each man as if wondering which of their bones it would be easiest to snap.

But when he noticed her smile, he raised a brow, then leaned back against a Doric column as if to say, *Two can play at this game.*

She nearly scoffed at the thought. Grayson Hawthorne might play for a second or two, but in three he'd be ready to throttle someone. Namely, her.

"Gentlemen, gentlemen," she said, slipping into the familiar role like slipping on a velvet cape. "Is that you, Dickie Webster? And Devon Bly. Goodness, it's Wade Richmond. Such handsome men you've grown up to be."

They tugged on their lapels importantly and smoothed their hair like preening peacocks. Grayson crossed his arms on his chest and looked grimly amused.

Megan, however, didn't look amused at all.

"Of course you all remember one another," the woman said, her smile tight. "How could any of us forget Sophie? Especially after that memorable day when we all heard her voice on the gramophone. A silly child's toy, really, playing a silly child's game. But it was fun."

Dick Webster and Devon Bly laughed appreciatively. Grayson stood away from the column, suddenly tense as his gaze met Sophie's. Megan looked between them all yet again, her eyes glittering like jewels beneath the chandelier.

"You remember that day, don't you, Sophie, dear?" she asked, her voice creamy with barely hidden delight.

Sophie's heart pounded. Remember? How could she forget? A child's prank, but one that had mortified a young girl who had never quite learned how to navigate the precarious waters of childhood and making friends. Music she had always understood. Music had made sense. But childish games and practical jokes left her stunned and hurting.

She knew it shouldn't affect her. As an adult she should look back and laugh. But all she remembered was Megan tricking her into talking into the brass speaking tube, uttering words that had been so important to her. Then Megan had taken that machine and played it aloud for a group of laughing peers—and Grayson. Sophie especially cared that Grayson had heard.

But the worst part was that he had done nothing. Only watched. Only stared. His young eyes had narrowed in the harsh gaslight that had painted all his friends in gold, as if he were furious.

Why had he stood there? Why hadn't he said anything?

Sophie shook the questions away, the glittering crystal lights coming into focus. She stared at Grayson, and cursed herself for a fool that such a childish prank still had the power to hurt her.

She tore her gaze away from Grayson, fighting back the red that wanted to resurface in her cheeks. "I can't say that I do remember, Megan." She laughed an especially practiced laugh, the sound like silken honey.

"Really?" Megan responded, her brow raised. "If only I could find that talking machine I could play it again to remind you. I'm sure it would make you laugh at how silly we all were back then. I wonder what happened to it? I don't think I saw it again after that day."

Sophie hoped like Hades it was never seen again.

Patrice chose that moment to join them with the conductor in tow. He was still a tall, elegant man. She thought of her mother, and it was all she could do not to squeeze her eyes closed.

Her stepmother. Niles. Megan, and even Grayson. Suddenly she felt like the ugly duckling she had always been, awkward, and underneath paddling frantically just to keep afloat.

"Sophie," Patrice chimed. "You remember Mr. Niles Prescott, don't you?" She smiled up at the man. "I am told he is quite renowned in the music world."

"Miss Wentworth," the man said formally, bowing low, as if he hardly knew her.

How many times had he come to Swan's Grace for tea? How many times had he regaled her mother with wonderful stories of his years in Europe as a musician? His years conducting Bach? Sophie had hung on every word, enamored of the exciting life he had led.

If her mother hadn't spent so much time with the man, would her father not have become so enamored of Patrice?

When he straightened and met her gaze, his light eyes bored into her. "It is a pleasure to see you again. I read the article in *The Century* and was as intrigued as the rest of the world."

"Thank you, Mr. Prescott. I see you've done well for

yourself." She couldn't quite keep the bitterness from her voice. "I hope to attend a performance at the Music Hall before I return to Europe in May."

She felt more than saw Grayson's sudden tension. The sensation confused her, since no doubt he would be thrilled to death at the thought of her moving out of Swan's Grace.

But her thoughts were interrupted when the conductor said, "Actually, I had hoped you might honor us with a performance of your own. It is time that Boston's very own, much-talented daughter played an official concert in our city."

Her heart leaped, beating in that low, all-encompassing way, filling her, surrounding her. To play in Boston. To stand onstage in the Music Hall, the lights trained on her. How often had she dreamed of just that?

But that wouldn't happen. It was too late. She wouldn't play for the denizens of Boston because, as Deandra had not so subtly pointed out, she would curl their hair. She had returned to forge a relationship with her father, not ruin it for good.

"I'm afraid that is impossible," she said.

The man stiffened, Patrice gasped her outrage. Grayson looked on with considering appraisal.

Anxious to get away, Sophie grasped at the first exit she could take. "Oh, look," she said. "I believe dinner is being served."

Patrice instantly glanced around. Indeed, a footman was announcing the meal. Without a word, she gathered her skirts and quickly made her way to the dining room.

The conductor regained his composure. "Perhaps I can change your mind." He extended his arm. "Will you allow me to escort you in to dinner?"

But Grayson stepped forward, taking her arm possessively. "I'll be escorting Miss Wentworth this evening."

Niles stammered until Megan stepped forward. "Niles,

darling, will you be good enough to escort me into the dining room?" she asked. "My husband is nowhere to be seen."

The conductor shrugged and nodded his head, then proceeded to dinner with Megan at his side.

As soon as they were well away, Sophie pulled her arm free. "Thank you for that," she said sincerely. "The last thing I need is to be hounded by Niles Prescott all night."

She started for the dining room, but was stopped when Grayson gently took her arm once again.

"I was serious when I told Prescott that I am escorting you this evening."

"Whatever for?"

"To keep the long line of suitors at bay."

Sophie laughed, growing relieved, curling her hand through the crook of his arm without thinking. "There has been a long line this evening, hasn't there?"

Grayson scowled. "Hasn't anyone taught you the fine art of being modest?"

"Of course." Her eyes sparked with amusement. "But it seems an unnecessary waste of time. At least around you."

With a noise that sounded suspiciously like a growl, he pulled her close. Her eyes widened, then drifted to his lips.

"Are you going to kiss me again, right here in front of Boston's most proper society?" She was amazed at how steady the words sounded, even in her own ears.

"No," he said, his voice gruff. "Not here." His hands ran up her arms—strong, capable hands, his thumbs coming up to graze her mouth like a promise. "But soon."

Despite herself, a shiver of anticipation raced through her at the words. And when he took her elbow, she let him, understanding in that moment as he led her in to dinner that regardless of her best intentions, the long-fought-for wall she had built around her emotions had slipped lower by a notch.

*   *   *

The massive room was filled with twenty round tables, ten guests at each. Nearly as many footmen streamed in, bringing silver dishes piled high with extravagant fare.

Both Sophie and Grayson were seated at the head table with her father and Patrice. Emmaline and Bradford were there as well. The two older men sat in deep conversation, though it was clear that Emmaline was straining to make conversation with Patrice. At least in some arenas, Sophie thought with childish satisfaction, Patrice hadn't been able to take Genevieve Wentworth's place.

She would rather have been seated at a table with Deandra, Henry, and Margaret. But her entourage had not been invited, and no amount of begging had changed that fact. She almost hadn't gone. But they had insisted, saying they hadn't come all this way to have her turn her nose up at the very thing she wanted—her father showing that he cared.

Conrad sat between Sophie and Patrice, with Grayson to Sophie's left. She was all too aware of his nearness, the brush of his forearm against hers when he reached for his knife, his long fingers picking up his tall crystal glass. With renewed effort, she attempted to fill in the crack in her wall. It was safer that way, safer not to care. Caring only ended up hurting.

But she would not let him see that she was off center. Leaning close and teasing, she said, "You're impossible to get away from these days."

She expected a laugh, or better yet, a scowl. She didn't get either. Instead he looked at her intently, one bold finger reaching up to crook beneath her chin despite the crowds around them. "Do you really want to get away from me, Sophie?"

Disconcerted by the way he made her feel—one minute

like a recalcitrant child, the next like a desirable woman—she wrenched back. "Yes, I do."

This time he smiled. "Liar."

With that he turned his attention to the woman on his left.

Sophie concentrated on the hand-carved candelabra that lit the room, the high-polished silverware reflecting in the light. The cups were filigreed and the plates accented in gold, jeweled, much like the women in the room.

Dinner was served in nine courses. She hardly noticed the meal, too busy was she trying to avoid Grayson. But she nearly knocked the contents of her wineglass across the snowy white tablecloth when he turned to her and offered her a taste of the decadently rich chocolate soufflé with a drip of sugared brandy poured down the middle.

"No, thank you," she managed, turning away abruptly to the sound of his all-too-knowing chuckle.

At the end, huge folding doors were slid back to reveal a stunning ballroom with crystal chandeliers and sheer white draperies pulled back from French doors opened to the black-velvet night. And then music erupted. A stunning Dvořák waltz from a twelve-piece orchestra, inviting the guests to join in.

The crowd gasped in awe at the fairy-tale scene. Patrice looked on with exhilaration at what was clearly a social triumph.

Conrad smiled to the crowd, then said, "I believe I'd like to dance with my girl."

My girl.

The words her father had always said to her as a child. The words that sang in her heart. The words that preceded a glorious dance. He did care. He hadn't forgotten.

With her heart in her eyes, she stood from the table. But she froze half in, half out of her chair when Patrice stood as well, her father taking her stepmother's hand and leading her to the high-polished parquet floor for the dance.

Sophie couldn't seem to move.

Silence fell across the table, tension shimmering through the small circle like waves of heat on the summer-scorched cobbles of Boylston Street.

But before other heads could turn and take in her dismay, Grayson stood up and had her on the dance floor, pulled so close to his chest that she could feel his strength.

She wanted to melt away, melt into the floor.

"I'm sorry things have changed so much since you left," Grayson said, his voice filled with genuine regret. The words wrapped around her much like the music. "Your father hasn't handled your homecoming well."

She hated that he understood her pain, must have seen it in her eyes, and pride forced its way into her voice. "Good heavens, Grayson, I never thought for a moment that my father was going to dance with me. I was on my way to the ladies' retiring room. I'd be there now if you hadn't swept me onto the dance floor."

His look made it clear he didn't believe a word she said.

"Don't flatter yourself," she scoffed. "I didn't need your help."

She calmed herself, then shrugged her shoulders with practiced indifference. "But if your overactive, manly pride needs to think so, who am I to contradict you?"

"Manly?" he asked.

His voice lowered, a vibration of sound that sent a shimmer of feeling through her body.

"Do you think I'm *manly*, Sophie?"

She wasn't sure if he was serious or not, but she didn't like the way he pulled her closer, the way his hand spread across her back with such assurance and strength. Her skin felt tingly and too sensitive as he studied her.

"Don't look at me like that, Grayson Hawthorne," she warned.

"What look is that?" His mischievous smile grew heated.

"That . . . *manly* look."

"You mean this?" He set her back a bit, his dark-eyed gaze traveling down to where their bodies nearly touched.

"You're impossible." Frantically she tried shoring up her wall. She refused to feel anything, and she tried to step away.

Grayson chuckled. "I'm not ready to let you go, sweetheart. We haven't finished our dance—or our discussion. As I recall, you were just telling me how manly I am."

The words surprised her. She almost laughed at the thought that he was toying with her. Grayson Hawthorne playing the cad was an event to remember. But she didn't laugh. Instead she decided on a new tack sure to have this proper man escorting her back to the table so fast they'd leave scuff marks on the parquet floor.

Slowly she ran the tip of her tongue along her upper lip. "Is that what you would like me to do? Tell you how manly you are?"

She moved closer and his eyes darkened.

"Would you like me to show you right here?" she challenged, her voice soft and sultry. "On the dance floor?"

His eyes never wavered from hers, and she was certain he was considering her offer. But he surprised her with his words.

"Is this how it will always be between us? Each pushing the other, playing chicken to see who will back down first?"

"Sounds like my kind of game. Why don't we try it? I'd be interested to see who would actually win."

He touched her cheek, his finger tracing the line of her jaw as he forced her to look at him. "I'm not interested in battles, Sophie. What do you say we start over?"

She was quiet for a moment; then she pulled back, the dance floor becoming crowded around them. "That's the difference between you and me. As far as I'm concerned, it's the battles that make life interesting."

"There is more to life than battles."

"Like what?"

"A home and family."

She glanced at her father dancing with Patrice. "Perhaps."

"And children."

Her eyes shot back to Grayson. "So it's true! You are looking for a wife."

He hesitated. "What if I said I am?"

"I'd laugh."

She felt him stiffen and she smiled.

"I hardly think my marital pursuits are cause for amusement."

"True. And based on the considerable amount of gossip I've been hearing, there are an ample number of mamas anxious to bring their daughters to your attention. Tell me that you aren't seriously considering Monica Redmond."

"Who said anything about Miss Redmond?"

"No one. But I saw you talking to her earlier, and even I've heard that she's looking for a husband. Furthermore, I have been led to believe that you are considered something of a catch"—she glanced at him with a coy smile—"even if you are destitute and forced to live in my house."

He bared his teeth. "I hardly call paying large sums of money to reside at the Hotel Vendome reason to say that I am living at *your* house."

"You might not be sleeping under my roof, but you spend nearly the rest of your day at Swan's Grace."

"My office is there," he stated.

"True, but it seems a silly place to work. And the few papers I've seen on your desk hardly seem worthwhile."

His eyes narrowed and his features went hard. "You've gone through my belongings?"

"Of course I have," she stated, unable to keep her lips

from quirking. "What did you think, that it was above me to search through your drawers, given the chance? Though I was hoping to find something of some interest. Like some hapless soul's divorcement papers, or better yet, a tantalizingly juicy lawsuit. Maybe even an arrest warrant of sorts. Surely even your clients get tossed in jail."

He stood like stone, his face a disbelieving mask.

Sophie chuckled, relieved to be the one causing discomfort. *Finally.* "You're upset."

"I hardly think *upset* covers what I feel."

She bit her lip to keep from laughing, then looked at him through lowered lashes. "If it will make you feel better, I'll let you come over and search through my drawers."

She drew the last word out, letting it roll off her tongue provocatively. She expected him to sputter, and if she were lucky he might even turn red.

But he offered little more than a flicker of dumbfounded surprise before his face washed clean of expression.

A clever man, she mused. He was smooth and able to play the game better than she had thought, she realized when his hand drifted low, slipping to that place on her gown under which those very crudely called "drawers" circled her waist.

In the next minute he danced her through the open doorway and out onto the flagstone terrace, cold, clear moonlight filling the blackened sky.

"I think you actually *are* trying to get into my drawers, Mr. Hawthorne," she said with mock primness. "But if you think it will be that easy, you've been dealing with the wrong kind of women these last many years."

"Or you've been dealing with the wrong kind of men."

She laughed appreciatively despite herself.

But then his chiseled face grew serious. No more heated smiles or sensual grazes over skin. It was the face she remembered, the face of the young boy she had known a life-time, dark and stormy.

"Did you really not remember the talking machine?" he asked without warning.

The words surprised her, and her head tilted in confusion at the sudden change in subject. "The talking machine?" she replied, her heart beginning to pound.

"Yes, Megan Robertson's gramophone."

Her heart skipped and she felt vulnerable, just as she promised herself she would never be again.

"Do you really not remember what you said about me on that machine?"

She stared at him, then couldn't help asking, "Do you remember?"

"You said you loved me." He said the words with force, almost as a challenge.

She looked away, her mind drifting back as it had so many times this night. "I believe my exact words were that I loved you. Forever. I loved you with all my heart. And one day I would be your wife."

She turned back to him and saw something she couldn't name in his eyes. Regret, need?

She felt them both, and hated them each in turn. Because forever was a long time, and sometimes things happened that got in the way.

Chapter Eight

"This has gone on long enough. Sophie has to be told."

Patrice's smooth brow furrowed with agitation as she paced across her husband's study, her dark coil of hair shining in the muted light. It was late, the party was over, and the guests had gone home. But Patrice still looked dazzling and vibrant in her shimmering gown.

"Now, darling," Conrad said, looking every one of his nearly fifty-two years, "I've talked to Grayson several times. But I can't push him. We have to let him do this in his own time. And he will do it. I'm certain. Besides, there is time enough to tell her. She has barely been here a week. Even I see now that I expected things to move too fast."

"They can't move fast enough, as far as I'm concerned. In the time she has been here, she has managed to gain the attention of every eligible male in Boston. I can't tell you the line of men who begged me for an introduction to-night. Of course I didn't comply," she said with a sniff. "I only brought Niles Prescott to her attention."

Conrad tensed at the mention of the man, and thought of his first wife. He hadn't wanted to invite him at all. Why dredge up old wounds? But Patrice had been adamant.

"And do you know what that daughter of yours had the audacity to do?"

He sighed.

"She turned down an invitation to play at the Music

Hall! Good Lord, she travels all over the world performing, but she won't play in her own hometown." Her cool eyes turned heated. "These are the people who supported her and nurtured her along the way. Not that pack of impoverished, overbred peasant stock who call themselves European royalty."

"Actually, it was her mother who nurtured Sophie's talent, not Boston, and not Europe, for that matter—at least not until recently. If I'm not mistaken, her first concert in Europe wasn't a success. I'm not sure what made the difference."

Patrice gave her husband an impatient look, then resumed her pacing. "Regardless, she is successful now, and Niles said if Sophie performed, the show would be the premier event of the year. There would be parties leading up to the concert. Parties and dinners. It would be a social coup."

"For whom?" he asked with surprising acumen.

"For me!"

She stopped abruptly, her gaze meeting her husband's; then she ran a jeweled hand down the bodice of her expensive gown and drew a deep breath. "Regardless of what you think about who did or did not support her, Sophie owes Boston, dear."

Turning his gaze away, Conrad thought of his only child by his first wife.

He had loved Genevieve as a husband should. But before she died, her days had been absorbed in Sophie and her music, with little time for a husband or having a larger family.

Not long after Genevieve's death he had married again. There was a significant age difference between Conrad and his new bride, but she was a stunning woman who captivated him, making him feel younger than his years. They had three lovely daughters who were sweet and . . . simple in the best kind of way. *Thank God for that.*

Sophie was anything but simple.

As a child she had lived for music. As an adult she still lived for music. But as he had told Grayson, it was time she settled down. As her father, it was his responsibility to see that she did—no matter what he had to do to achieve that goal.

"I think it's best she turned Niles down," he said. "I don't think she should play the cello any longer, at least not in public. She is a grown woman now. It's time she turned her attention to a husband and children."

Patrice whirled around. "Fine!" she exclaimed, her blue eyes like fire. "But if that's the case, then we need to stop beating around the bush and tell her about the betrothal. It's time, Conrad, long past time."

A knock sounded on the door. When Conrad turned the knob, he found his best friend's son.

"Grayson, I thought you would have been long gone by now," Conrad said in surprise.

Grayson raised a questioning brow and glanced at Patrice as he entered, then looked back at Conrad. "I was asked to meet you here."

Confusion swept through Conrad before a sharp dread began to fill him, and he turned his gaze on his wife. "What is this about, Patrice?" he asked, his tone exacting.

"I told you, husband, this has gone on long enough."

Grayson's eyes narrowed dangerously, and he brought his arms up and crossed them on his broad chest.

Grayson Hawthorne had grown to be a man of great wealth and power. He had a reputation for scrupulous fairness, but also for unmatched ruthlessness when someone crossed him. A person could see the power of him in the way he moved, the way he spoke, even in the fine, chiseled lines of his dark countenance.

Conrad tugged at his rumpled dinner jacket, feeling a flicker of concern caused by the younger man's hard stare.

"What has gone on long enough?" Grayson inquired, his voice deceptively soft.

As soon as he asked the question, Grayson saw Conrad's unease. He also saw the flare of pleasure in Patrice's eyes. Grayson knew right away that she was up to no good.

Annoyance flickered through him as he came farther into the room and shut the door.

Conrad glanced nervously at his wife before turning back to Grayson. "Patrice and I were just discussing your betrothal."

A fire burned on the hearth, reflecting on fine oil paintings and bronze sculpture. After doing some digging into Conrad's financial status, Grayson had learned that Conrad's finances were not as healthy as they once were.

"What are you waiting for, son? The longer we wait the harder it will be to tell her. You're not having second thoughts about this, are you?" Conrad asked, his voice growing guarded.

Grayson no longer doubted his intent to marry the man's daughter. Regardless of the fact that she was headstrong and had made it clear she had little interest in being a proper lady, he couldn't give her up.

He stood in Conrad's study, surrounded by bookcases filled with volumes of gold-embossed, finely tooled leather. When he was young he had read every single book in his father's library. He had finished the last one the week before he was sent out on his own.

It had been those stories, frequently, that had helped him through the long nights in Cambridge, with men shouting and cursing each other in the dank hallways, fighting in the streets. Grayson had gone over the tales of Odysseus and Julius Caesar in his head, their journeys and successes, to forget the sounds.

Within a few short months, however, he hadn't needed the stories. He had learned to fend for himself. Like Odysseus. Like Caesar. He had learned to use his fists, fighting off bigger men, some wild, unrecognizable emotion surging inside him that gave him more strength than his sixteen-year-old body normally would have had.

By the time he turned seventeen, everyone close by knew to steer clear of him. It had taken years after he had finished Harvard Law to smooth over those jagged edges. Long years of ruthless control to lose the wildness. Because of that, everyone had left him alone. Everyone except Sophie.

Her baskets eventually gave way to letters and small trinkets. A shirt or sweater. Always arriving when he needed it most. Those gifts had been a mainstay in his life, along with scraping to get by and obsessive studying.

But one day, the year she turned eighteen, the gifts and letters had ceased. He had learned shortly afterward that she had left Boston. Foolishly, he had been disappointed that she had left without a word to him. Disappointed and oddly alone. For so long Sophie had been such a part of his life. Then suddenly she was gone.

Whenever he felt that he desired her at the deepest level, he turned away from the thought. He wanted her, yes, but he didn't need her. He merely wanted to make Sophie Wentworth his own. Or so he told himself.

"I'm not having second thoughts," he said to Conrad. "But we've got to give her the chance to get to know me again. We've been over this."

"Damn it man, she's known you her whole life."

"True, but until last Sunday she had seen me only once in five years, and that was at the birthday gala Patrice had for you."

Women had wanted Grayson for as long as he could

remember. He had never given it much thought until recently—until Sophie.

He was no fool. He wanted a willing bride in his bed. And because of that, he realized, he would have to take the time to court her. Amazingly, he found himself looking forward to the idea.

Besides which, Grayson reasoned, with the arrogance of a man used to getting what he wanted, he was certain he could win Sophie over. He just needed time.

"She's not as much trouble as she seems," Conrad said.

Grayson stared at the man with disbelief.

"Okay," Conrad conceded. "So she's a little troublesome."

"A little?"

"Damn it, Sophie needs someone to keep her out of trouble," Conrad blurted out.

Grayson's mind absorbed the man's tone more than the words. "Is there something you're not telling me?"

Conrad grew uncomfortable and studied a small daguerreotype on his desk of Sophie holding her cello. She was young in the picture, her mixture of pride and defiance clear even in the murky brown-and-white tint.

"No," he finally said. "But you remember Sophie and her escapades." The older man ran a hand through his thinning hair, seeming tired and resigned. "She makes everything into a drama. Always has."

Grayson was quickly being reminded of how true this was. Nothing was easy with Sophie.

"So you can see why I want her married to someone with a level head on his shoulders, someone I can trust to keep my daughter out of harm's way." Conrad shrugged. "The sooner the better."

"I think we should tell her tonight," Patrice interjected, her look challenging.

Grayson barely afforded the woman a glance before he

returned his attention to her husband. "No, Conrad. Not yet."

The statement shimmered through the room, hanging in the air as the quiet command it was, each man eyeing the other. "As I've already said, let her get to know me again. There is time enough before she needs to learn about the betrothal. Then I will be the one to tell her." Grayson's gaze pinned the other man to the spot. "Are we clear on this?"

The words were barely out of his mouth when another knock sounded on the door. Both men turned not to the entrance, but to Patrice, who raised her chin defiantly.

"Come in," she called out.

Conrad leaped for the door, his gaze skewering his wife. "Don't you dare say a—"

But the door opened before he could get there.

"Father," Sophie said, entering into the room with a fond smile. "Thank you so much for the party."

She meant every word. While the event hadn't turned out exactly as she had hoped, she was grateful that he had tried. And in the end there had been more ups than downs, leaving her with a shimmer of excitement running through her veins.

Conrad flushed red. "I'm glad you enjoyed yourself, dear. But in truth, I can't take credit. It was your stepmother's doing."

Sophie felt a childish flicker of bitterness sweep over her at the thought of the woman, but she covered it quickly and turned. "Thank you, Patrice."

The resentment fled entirely then, and was replaced by nothing more complicated than end-of-the-night excitement. "It's been years since I have seen so many people I knew from my youth." She laughed gaily, sweeping through the room as though she were still dancing.

But then she stopped abruptly when she noticed Grayson, though even he couldn't dampen her spirits. "What are you doing here?"

"I have business to discuss with your father. Perhaps you could excuse us for a moment."

She tilted her head, suddenly aware of an odd tension that shimmered through the room. "But I had a note asking me to come to the study."

"Yes, but it was a mistake."

With eyes that had intimidated some of the most powerful men in Boston, Grayson shot Patrice a quelling look.

Sophie didn't understand what was going on, but frankly she was still too content to care. She was exhausted, and the excitement of the night was starting to wear off. She longed to slip between cool, downy sheets and drift into a dreamless sleep.

"Fine," she said with an indifferent shrug. "I'll ask Jeters to drive me back to Swan's Grace." She twirled around suddenly and laughed. "I want to get to bed so I will be refreshed by midday." She headed for the door and pulled it wide as if she were dancing with it, her low-heeled dancing slippers clicking on the hardwood floor just beyond the Oriental carpet. "Donald Ellis is taking me out to Brookline for a picnic tomorrow afternoon. And after that, Allan Beekman has asked me to dinner at Locke-Ober's."

"You will do no such thing!" Patrice snapped.

The words sizzled through the room, stopping Sophie abruptly, the doorknob still held in her hand.

"Patrice," Grayson warned ominously.

"What is going on here?" Sophie asked. "The three of you have been acting strange since I walked through the door."

"You will not go anywhere with any man, do you understand me?" her stepmother asked.

"Why not? What harm is there in a picnic with a man I have known since he was in short pants, or dinner with an old family friend?"

"It is time someone told you that engaged women do not go on picnics with men who aren't their intended. And you are engaged," Patrice added.

Sophie froze. Conrad groaned.

Tension, like fire, shimmered through the room. Sophie felt it, white and hot against her skin.

Emotion flared, but she forced it aside and laughed. "That is ridiculous. I haven't been home long enough to meet anyone new, much less become engaged. Who in the world has been spreading such rumors?" She looked at Grayson, her eyes chastising. "Have you been trying to get me into trouble again?"

He didn't reply. He stood like a tight coil ready to unleash, his handsome features dark and murderous.

At length he ran a large hand through his midnight black hair. "I think you know I don't spread rumors, Sophie."

"Then who said such a thing? And who could I possibly be engaged to?"

"To Grayson," Patrice stated triumphantly, though she wasn't looking at Sophie. Her eyes were locked on the man in question.

Sophie went still, and she felt every fiber of her being pulling in on her as she stared at her stepmother in shock.

She forced another laugh, this one hollow and aching even in her own ears, as she looked at Grayson. "Enough with the jests."

"This is no jest, Sophie," he said after a moment, deep, troubled regret etched on his face. "We are betrothed."

All traces of laughter vanished. "You've got to be out of your mind. We've hardly exchanged a civil word since I got here, and certainly not a word about marriage."

She jerked around to face her father.

"It's true," Conrad said without having to be asked. "I made the arrangements before you returned to Boston."

The words were like a blow. Her eyes bored into her father. "That's why you asked me to come back, isn't it? So you could marry me off, not so I could be with—"

She bit the words back, swallowing them with effort.

There had been times in her life when she understood that the next sentence uttered would change her life forever. She realized this was one of those moments, realized somewhere in her mind that she already knew the answer to her unfinished question.

Her father still didn't have a place for her in his world.

She felt her heart tear, ripped apart by indifferent hands as if it were no more consequential than a child's craft made of thick colored paper.

Beyond that, her father had taken it upon himself to change her life. Irrevocably and without her consent. Yet again he had betrayed her.

Her knees felt like putty when she realized that her life had changed some time ago and she simply hadn't known it. She had danced through the days seeing what she thought was the truth, when all the while it was a lie. She hadn't been free. She hadn't been loved.

How long had it been since her father had changed her world without telling her? A month? A year?

Deep down, had she actually sensed that her life had shifted the minute she got the letter from her father? Was it possible that she'd had some clue early on? Had she understood that some other reason besides love prompted him to ask her to return?

She shook the thoughts away. She didn't want to hear what Grayson was saying, wouldn't accept it. If she acted as if the words hadn't been spoken, she could make them go away.

"I'm really tired," she said, feeling disjointed and dizzy.

"And Donald is picking me up at noon. I've got to get some rest."

Patrice gasped. "Haven't you heard a word that has been said here tonight? You aren't going on any picnic."

"I hope it snows. There is nothing more divine than a beautiful winter carriage ride to the country when the landscape is crisp with new-fallen snow."

She started back for the door, her mind an odd blank.

"Stop this," Patrice demanded.

"Perhaps I'll take my cello along, with a basket of fruit and cheese."

"What has gotten into you?" her father blurted out.

"Maybe even some warmed wine would be nice. People drink wine like water in France. Did you know that?"

"Sophie."

Grayson's voice filled the room, filling the void in her mind like no one else could. Reminding her. Making it impossible to keep the words at bay, as she wanted so badly to do.

With the haze and fog cruelly swept away, she whirled to face him. "What?" she demanded. "What do you want from me?"

He started to reach out to her, to wrap his fingers around her arms and pull her close, as he had done so many times since she had arrived. That possessive gesture. Now she knew why. He felt that he owned her.

She yanked her arm away and watched as his expression grew grim.

"We are engaged, Sophie, and I cannot allow you to go on a picnic with Donald Ellis, or dinner with anyone else."

She felt steel fill her soul, and she welcomed the hardness.

"Then *un*engage us. Good God, I've never known two more ill-matched people in all my life."

"I disagree," he replied.

She whirled back to Conrad, her heart pounding so hard

she was sure everyone could hear. "Then you undo this, Father."

Conrad's lips pursed, then he said, "I can't. God, what a mess this has become."

"Why?" Her voice started to rise. "Tell me why you can't undo an unforgivable wrong?"

Conrad looked as if he wanted to shrink away. But Patrice was not so bothered.

"Your father can't undo the betrothal because money has changed hands."

Sophie's shoulders stiffened, a pain sweeping through her that was hard to imagine, but her eyes never wavered from her father. "If you've given him some sort of dowry, ask for it back."

Conrad's face blushed red. "Actually, it was Grayson who settled an amount on us. And I've already spent the money, Sophie, love."

The endearment seemed to spur Patrice on. "While you've been enjoying yourself in Europe, we've had bills to pay."

"Bills to pay?" Confusion filled her. "Father has more money than Croesus. Everyone knows that. Or if you don't have enough money to pay your bills, why build this house? Good God, the halls are all but jewel encrusted, and there are enough servants to run a large hotel."

Then she stopped, her heart wrenching in her chest. "You have bills *because* of this house," she whispered, as brutal understanding came clear. "You sold me and my home without my knowledge or consent to pay for this . . . this monstrosity."

"I hardly call this a monstrosity," Patrice bit out.

"Then what would you call it? What would you call a garish mausoleum that you bought and paid for with my money, my house—my soul?"

"Good Lord, Sophie," Patrice scoffed. "Stop being so dramatic."

"Dramatic?" Sophie asked, pulling the word out with scathing sarcasm. "Oh, that's right. Sophie is always dramatic. Anyone else would be considered upset or furious—indignant over a wrong that has been done. But I'm always dramatic. Well, let me tell you how dramatic I am." She turned to Grayson. "I'm not about to be sold off to the highest bidder. And if I have to, I'll pay the money back myself." She would, even if it took her the rest of her life to pay off the debt. "What is the amount? I'll even pay interest. You can make a decent return on your investment," she finished coldly.

"I don't want your money. I want you as my wife."

"But I don't want you!" Not as a husband, not as someone who would demand he control her life. She couldn't take that; she couldn't be molded into something she had never learned how to be, unable to guide her own destiny, dependent on others to make her dreams come true. Didn't Grayson understand that, Grayson who had known her for so long and so well? Didn't her lifelong friend understand that she couldn't be caged? No matter how much he drew her.

And the truth was, he didn't really know her anymore. He only thought he did. He had no idea who she had become.

Grayson didn't respond; he only looked at her with grim determination.

"I'll fight it," she stated. She stopped pacing and took in the three people in the room. "I am not a commodity to be traded."

"You can fight it, but you won't win," Grayson said with quiet solemnity. "I drew up the contract myself. Only I can let you out of it."

"Then do it!"

He looked at her for an eternity, emotions that she

couldn't fathom drifting across the sculpted planes of his face—at war with himself, as if he wanted to let go of her but couldn't. "No, Sophie. I can't do that."

"You can't or you won't?"

"It hardly matters. The result is the same. But I will give you time to get used to the idea. Promise me you won't do anything rash in the meantime."

"The only promise I'll make is that I will never marry you. I don't care if you have a contract. I don't care if you have bought and paid for me."

With that she turned as calmly as she could, fighting back the tears that burned in her eyes, and started through the doorway. But at the last minute she stopped and turned back to Grayson.

"One last thing. Niles Prescott asked me to perform at the Music Hall."

"And you said no."

"I've changed my mind. Tell him yes."

Patrice clasped her hands together, her mood instantly changing. "This is wonderful news. It will be a grand event! Everyone who is anyone will want to attend."

Sophie looked at her stepmother, her bitterness no longer contained. "Everyone who is anyone? Do you really think there is more for you to conquer, Patrice? Do you have to have every man loving you? Wasn't my father enough of a prize? Wasn't it enough for you to come into Swan's Grace to nurse my mother, and instead take her place?"

"Sophie!" Conrad gasped.

Patrice's eyes narrowed.

"There was nothing untoward going on between Patrice and me while your mother was still alive."

No, nothing untoward in a physical sense. But only because Patrice was too smart for that.

"Apologize to your stepmother this instant," Conrad demanded.

"I don't think that is necessary. She'll get her concert, and the cream of society will attend. That should mollify her," she said, her eyes locked with Patrice's. "In fact," she added, her chin rising, her mind racing with what gown she would wear—the low-cut red velvet, or the ruby satin with more lace than bodice, "I suspect that indeed it will be a grand event, one Boston won't soon forget."

Then she looked at Grayson. "And since you are so good at drawing up contracts, draw one up for this. I want a specific date and terms of payment. I'd hate for Niles Prescott to have second thoughts at some point down the road, and try to back out. My time is valuable," she offered, and smiled her best diva smile. "I bet you didn't realize I go for a hundred dollars an hour."

Then she quit the room, leaving her father, stepmother, and Grayson in a crystalline moment of completely stunned silence.

Chapter Nine

The clay was soft in her hands, smooth and cool, yielding to her touch.

Emmaline sat on her high stool in a simple cotton gown, her gray hair in one long braid coiled at the back of her head. The smell of clay filled the room. Clay and glazes. Firing and heat.

Breathing in, she sat up straight and arched her back. It was early, the day after the Wentworths' party at The Fens, an event that had been oddly strained. She had sensed that the only person there who had enjoyed herself at all was Sophie.

Dear, sweet Sophie.

Emmaline knew that Bradford wanted Sophie and Grayson to marry. He said a good marriage always distracted from scandals. And even she had to concede that Matthew and Lucas had certainly caused their share of those. Now her husband was depending on Grayson to make Boston forget what his brothers had done.

Yes, a marriage could do just that. But that wasn't what she cared about. She believed Sophie could make her son happy. Grayson had spent too many years being serious and responsible, with a breathtakingly tight rein on his control. Sophie had spent too many years being independent and wild. Together, Emmaline believed, they would find the perfect balance. No couple could be too much of only one trait.

But what if her son did to Sophie what Bradford had done to her, trying to force her into a mold that never fit?

She shook the thought away. Grayson was demanding, but more of himself than of those around him. He was good and kind, and he would make Sophie the perfect husband. Plus, Sophie was strong and confident. How else could she have become so successful on her own?

As a result, when Bradford had told her of the impending marriage, she hadn't mentioned the rumors she had heard years ago in the women's circles she moved in regarding her dear friend Genevieve and that awful Niles Prescott.

It had been so long ago that Emmaline couldn't imagine that anyone remembered the gossip and innuendo. But Bradford might not see it that way.

Emmaline stretched the muscles that weren't used to sitting on a backless chair so high off the ground for such extended hours. While working, she had forgotten about everything but the clay before her.

Not that her suspended state of mind had helped the work, she thought as she studied the misshapen lump before her. She had made more mistakes than progress, but still, it felt good to be laboring with her hands after all these years.

She grimaced when she thought of the story she had made up so she would be left in her room undisturbed— yet again. She had mumbled something about a sick headache. She wanted to make up an excuse so she could go out. But her husband always insisted she be seen about town with a companion. In truth, a chaperon.

The thought made her bristle. Surely her son wouldn't turn out as harsh and demanding as his father.

But the sick headache had worked well enough. Not that

it would take much to keep people away, especially her husband. Bradford Hawthorne hadn't come to her room, much less her bed, since shortly after Lucas was born. And that was nearly thirty years ago.

For a long time she had given little thought to her husband's absence. She had been too busy with three young boys to raise, servants to oversee, menus to plan, and good works to contribute to society. And when she finally had begun to wonder, she hadn't had the energy at the end of the long days to worry about it. She had been sure that as soon as the boys grew more independent, and the Hawthornes' place in financial circles had been well and truly reestablished, she and Bradford would come back together with all the passion he had directed her way during their courting.

She had been wrong.

Embarrassment stained her cheeks as she remembered the times she had tried to attract him. The provocative nightwear. The intimate dinners. But at the end of each night, she was dutifully kissed on the forehead and sent off to bed like a child.

She bit her lip and looked out the grimy window as she remembered the night she had swallowed her pride and boldly gone to her husband's bed, her heart in her throat. The sudden sight of him standing at the window in his shirtsleeves, so handsome, so strong. But when he had turned to her she saw the hardness in his eyes that she somehow always managed to forget. And his words.

"What is it, Mrs. Hawthorne?"

Even in the intimacy of the bedroom he was formal.

Her courage had started to desert her, but she had come too far.

"I thought . . . well, perhaps . . . we might, or rather you might want . . ."

Her words trailed off as his gaze boldly ran the length of

her. For a moment she was encouraged, but then his eyes met hers.

"I will pretend I don't understand your meaning, Mrs. Hawthorne. I would hate to learn that my wife thinks of the baser aspects of life as anything other than a duty to conceive children. You have given me three sons. Your duty is done."

He had turned back to the window then. Emmaline had stood frozen, mortified, desolate, and desperate to shout at this man who so callously turned his back on her. Her duty was done, but that didn't mean she didn't have desires. Or was she different? Was she truly wanton and improper? Did other wives truly want nothing to do with their husbands after they had children?

But she asked no questions. Made no demands. She only turned slowly, mechanically around and slipped back through the doorway to her room.

The following morning her belongings had been moved to the opposite end of Hawthorne House.

"Emmaline, love! I'm so glad you are here and working! Your sculpture is . . . interesting!"

Emmaline jerked in surprise on the stool and nearly fell off. But Andre Springfield caught her.

"Gathering wool, were you?" he asked, his smile as bright as the day.

"Guilty as charged," she said, thoughts of Bradford fading away. "And you are being much too kind in your assessment of my work. It is interesting only if you find a misshapen block of clay intriguing."

He threw back his lion's mane of hair and laughed, startling the other sculptors in the cavernous room.

"Come," he said, pulling her away, "have tea with me. Colette has it ready."

"Andre, I can't."

"Of course you can."

He didn't wait for her response. He dragged her out of the room and onto a glassed-in back terrace, the gardens dormant just beyond. It would be beautiful in spring.

He held a chair for her, then took one for himself. He poured for each of them into old, chipped cups of fine china. From a coat pocket he produced a bottle.

"May I sweeten your cup?" he asked, the bottle poised to pour.

Her surprise at the decadence brought a smile to her lips. She remembered long days in the summer when she was struggling to be an artist. Wine and cheese. Long conversations in cafés on street corners. But those days were gone. "No, Andre, but thank you."

He laughed. "All the more for me then," he said as he poured a generous portion of what looked like brandy into his cup.

He didn't bother to stir. He reached into another pocket and produced a pipe and a packet of tobacco. With the ease of someone used to smoking, he made quick order of the implements, then sat back with a sigh as he lit a match. But just as he brought the flame to the pipe's bowl, he hesitated, looking at her through the orange flare.

"You don't mind if I smoke, do you, Emmaline?"

"Of course not," she all but stammered.

"Good," he said, then sucked on the stem as he brought the flame to the tobacco.

"God, life is fine," he offered on an exhale of smoke. "I might not have much money, but I have a satisfying life." He busied himself straightening the china and matches, then looked at her. "Can you say the same thing, sweet Emmaline?"

Flustered, she sat back in the chair, grimacing when her spine hit a bent slat of the metal chair.

Andre nodded knowingly. "I see you can't."

"I hardly think that grimacing after nearly maiming

myself on a piece of metal constitutes an answer. I was thinking."

"Thinking about how unfortunately correct I am."

"I have a lovely life. My boys are wonderful. My home is beautiful. My life is full." *But not satisfying.*

The unspoken words hung in the air.

"And what about your marriage? Is that full, too?"

Her inclination was to cry out the truth, to finally share the secret disappointment she carried with her. She and Andre had always been able to discuss all the things men and women didn't talk about. Love. Life. Hopes and dreams. She realized now how much she had missed his friendship.

But long years of training since her marriage never to show one's feelings, much less talk about them, kept the words securely back in her throat. She could hardly speak at all over the lump.

"My marriage is quite full, thank you," she said primly, the effect somehow lost as she sat with a man not her husband who sipped brandy in the middle of the day.

"Then why are you here?" He leaned forward, his tea sloshing carelessly as he planted his elbows on the rickety table. "I thought the minute you saw Richard Smythe, I'd never see you again."

She looked away.

"He still affects you. Is that why you are really here?"

Her head snapped back and she met his eyes. "I am here to sculpt. Nothing more. I have no interest in ever seeing Richard again."

"Perhaps you should tell him that."

"I'm married, Andre. I shouldn't have to tell him anything. But I will if I need to."

"I think you do. And now is your chance."

Her breath caught when Andre sat back and looked toward the doorway.

She whirled around and found Richard standing there, much as he had only a week before when he suddenly had appeared, leaning against the doorjamb. Amused. Arrogant. Breathtakingly handsome. Making her want to reach out to him.

"Em, I knew you'd be back."

Outrage mixed with her pounding heart, and she tried to push up from the table. But the chair was heavy, and her long skirt caught on the crooked arm.

"Let me help you," Richard said, suddenly at her side, his voice a breath against her ear.

She slapped at his hands and managed to break free.

"Don't tell me you are going to run away again." His smile was wide and full, revealing straight, white teeth. "I tried to talk to you last time, but you slipped out the front door and into traffic before I could catch you."

"You have no business trying to catch me." The words were strained; even she could hear that.

"True, but I never had any business catching you. Not now. Not back then."

She felt his words like heat to her skin.

"And we both know that there was a day when I did."

"Stop!" She slapped her hands over her ears. "Stop this instant," she said more quietly. "My coming here is not about you!"

He reached out and gently took her hands away, but he didn't let them go. "If that's true, then what is it about? You had to have known I would be here."

She turned on him then, his arrogant assumptions unleashing her long-held anger. "I'd have to know? Why? How? All I know is that years ago you disappeared without a word of good-bye or explanation."

She pulled free with a yank and she could feel her hairpin give way. The long braid loosened, and tendrils escaped to curl about her face. She was fifty years old, standing in a pottery house with wild hair, feeling like a wayward schoolgirl. "Don't stand there and tell me what I know or don't know. I am here to sculpt. Nothing more."

And she was. She wanted something for herself. She wanted more in her life that said something about her. Something more than being the Ladies Society's most diligent member, or her sons' mother. Or Bradford's wife. She pressed her eyes closed. A wife in name only.

"I am here to sculpt," she repeated, all traces of weakness gone from her voice. "And if I have to go someplace else to do it, so be it."

"But you won't go someplace else," Richard said, a smile in his voice, as if she hadn't said a word against him. "You'll come back. And I'll be waiting."

Chapter Ten

How dare they?

Long hours after the gala, Sophie paced the east drawing room of Swan's Grace, reeling with shock. How could her father and Grayson have made decisions about her future without so much as a word to her in regard to what she wanted? Good God, would she spend the rest of her life at the mercy of men?

But on the heels of that thought came another. Grayson had chosen her.

A swift joy pierced through her anger before she ruthlessly stamped it out. She had already seen that Grayson wanted her, but that desire was strictly physical. And physical attraction wasn't enough.

If just once he had mentioned love, no doubt she would have been putty in his hands, with every one of those five long years of struggle dropped aside as swiftly and as easily as his cashmere robe. Because if he loved her, didn't that mean he could accept her for who she really was?

But he hadn't mentioned the word, not even some approximation. She knew him well, and undoubtedly the truth was that he saw her as an asset. A marriage between two fine, old families. He was treating her like a possession, just as her father had. Used by one, bartered away by another as if she were no more than a business transaction.

Betrayal snaked through her.

She had learned long ago that Conrad Wentworth lived by standards, traditions, propriety, and social order—sometimes more vehemently than blue-blooded Boston Brahmins. But that, she had learned as life began to teach her lessons beyond reading and music, frequently was the case with men and women who weren't born into the world they inhabited. Those people took on ways with fervent dedication that insiders took for granted. Her father espoused those beliefs, never wavering.

Except for once, when a month after her mother died he had married her nurse.

But time had passed, and as long as Conrad Wentworth had money, Boston could forgive him anything. Even Patrice.

Though as long as Sophie lived, she would never forgive the woman who had come into her home and insinuated herself into their lives, dissolving the adhesive that held them together. Her father had seemed oblivious to Patrice's manipulations, coming into their home to help his wife, and ultimately taking the woman's place.

Bitter anger welled up inside her. Sophie knew her father's calling card into the most prestigious drawing rooms of the old town had been her mother's centuries-old name and his fat bank accounts. He had already lost her mother. If he lost his coins as well, Sophie suspected Bostonians wouldn't be so forgiving.

Because of that, her father was using her to replace the silver and gold he had lost. And he had the power to do it since she had signed a document that put him in charge of her assets and her life.

Even she understood now that she had given him the power to do whatever he wanted with Swan's Grace. She had also given him the power to sign agreements on her behalf. But never in a million years would she have believed he would use that power to sell her home and sell her into marriage. The notion was archaic.

In hindsight, she could hardly credit being so foolish as to agree to such an arrangement. It seemed idiotic now. But at eighteen, after losing her mother and the promised debut concert—losing her direction in life—she hadn't cared. And when her father told her Patrice would be her new mother, she would have done anything to get out of Boston. Signing that document had been her ticket out.

Forcing her mind clear of thought, she sat on the divan and attempted to play. She needed to play, needed to feel the music fill the emptiness in her soul.

It was early in the morning, the sun barely a hint on the horizon. She started a few measures of an adapted piece from *The Marriage of Figaro*, a favorite of audiences. But today it held no interest for her.

Next she tried *The Love Nest*. Still nothing. No feeling. Until finally she moved through the opening bars of a simple piece called *The Waltz of Swans*, which a composer and admirer had written for her. With that, she managed to forget. The long C, the soothing A. The G that made her heart soar. Time was lost, her escape found.

"I thought you said you were going to practice."

Her mind halted, her escape lost. Last night tumbled in on her, and her hand froze midstroke.

Sophie glanced at the doorway as Henry entered the room. The dog she had found lay curled up on the divan, improving every day.

Word had been put out that the animal had been found, but as yet, no one had claimed her. Sophie hated to think that she was thankful no one had shown up. The last thing she needed was to become attached to this dog. She would be leaving just as soon as advance money arrived.

But what about the house? Could she give it up now? Could she toss aside the one thing she had relied on in order to escape the manipulations of men? Could she live without the knowledge that it was there for her?

"I *am* practicing," she said with force.

To prove her point, she began again, music filling the room.

Henry held a cup of coffee in his hand. He wore a black satin smoking jacket with fine gray flannel trousers and a paisley cravat at his neck. "No, you're playing."

"Playing, practicing, what's the difference?"

"You know better than I what the difference is. Practicing is working on technique, mastering sections of a piece. Running through scales," he added pointedly.

Sophie made an indistinct sound in her throat, then immediately started the prelude of another audience favorite called *Love Circus*. Her breathing grew even with the heartfelt opening passage played all on the G and C strings, the intensity and passion filling her. "I hate scales," she said on an intake of breath as she kept the cadence.

"Of course you do, no one likes scales, but everyone has to practice them."

She continued on with *Circus* as though he hadn't said a word, her mind distant, savoring the andantino, the wonderful lilt and swing. She relished the syncopated rhythms. "I practice *my* technique by finding new gowns and combining them with stunning pieces of jewelry. We both know that is what my audience wants to see."

She bit her lip, concentrating, as she prepared for the ritardando in the last measure, her finger sliding up to a high B-flat and G before hitting a perfect F-sharp like the trill of a bird's song.

Finished, she whipped the bow away with a flourish, feeling pleased, triumphant. The piece of music was perfect for her show. Beautiful but accessible. The trick seemed to be to find works that an audience could hum after a performance, works that stayed with them. Hence the reason for performing a great many opera pieces that had been adapted for the cello. It had entailed learning a whole new way of playing.

Most of the difficult concert pieces she had grown up on were appreciated for their complexity and sophistication, frequently nothing a person could hum. Except for the Bach cello suites. They were difficult, yes, sophisticated and complicated, true. But a truly talented cellist could enthrall any sort of audience with the pieces—if one had the ability to create magic.

Once she had believed she could create magic with her cello. Once she had believed she was born to play Bach. Now she created magic with jewelry and gowns instead.

"I think I'd like to wear a tiara for my next appearance."

"A tiara!" Henry demanded.

The burst of sound brought the dog's head up from where she slept on the brocade divan.

"Shhh, sweetie, it's okay. Uncle Henry was just being loud."

The dog thumped her tail against the cushions, then sank back down and tucked herself in more comfortably.

"Yes, a tiara, with diamonds."

"Are we planning wardrobes?" Deandra asked as she walked into the room, her own cup of coffee held in her hand, her ostrich-plumed mules matching the ostrich plume around the neckline of her peignoir.

"Good morning," Sophie said.

Deandra finished a sip, then returned the cup to its saucer with a clink, her ostrich-plumed sleeve slipping back down to her wrist. "Good morning, loves."

"Sophie wants a tiara," Henry stated.

"I think that is a fabulous idea," Dea said after another sip.

Margaret walked in, dressed in a severely cut woolen

gown buttoned to her neck. She held a tray of tea items in her hands. "Everyone's up early. Should I start breakfast?"

Deandra shook her head. "You'd think there'd be servants around here. If we are going to be here until May, why don't I look into hiring some?"

"Oh, no." Sophie said the words too fast, drawing everyone's attention. She forced a smile, thinking of her limited funds, reminding her, among other things, that buying a tiara was completely out of the question.

Her smile felt brittle on her lips. "I think it's better we wait until I have this house situation straightened out before we start hiring servants. In the meantime, we can all pitch in and take care of things."

"Us, take care of a house? Sophie, are you feeling all right?" Henry asked.

"I'm feeling fine." Determined, she returned the bow to the strings, sawing up, then back.

"Of course she is fine," Margaret said from the doorway, her mood remarkably lightened since receiving a note from a cousin inviting her to the family country house for a weekend. "And she's right. The last thing we need around here is more people. Good heavens, between all of us, Mr. Hawthorne, and that receptionist of his, not to mention his clients, the house is bursting at the seams." Her eyes widened as she came in and set down the tray. "Speaking of houses bursting at the seams, how did the party go last night?"

The bow sawed unevenly, turning a C into a muddied, screeching jangle of sound.

"That good?" Henry asked, slipping into the wing-backed chair just before Deandra could get there.

"Out of my seat."

"Sit on the divan," Henry said with a snicker.

Deandra pulled herself up to her imperious height. "The dog is there."

"Birds of a feather should flock together. . . ."

A brief silence sizzled through the room before Dea's eyes narrowed and she started for Henry. But Sophie jumped in, waving her rosined bow between the two like a surrender flag. "Children, children."

Henry chuckled and hunkered back down against the buttery leather, his coffee cup held close to his chest like a shield.

"Henry, I hardly call that the gentlemanly thing to do," Sophie admonished.

The little man sliced her a crooked grin. "Since when were you concerned about propriety?"

"Since we got here," Margaret interjected. "Didn't you notice that she spent hours deciding on the perfect gown for last night?"

"Did she really?" Henry mused.

"She *has* been a bit different lately," Deandra commented.

"*She* is sitting right here," Sophie demanded. "And *she* is no different now than ever before."

"Oh, really?"

"Yes, really!"

With that she leaped into another popular piece adapted from an opera, the notes deep and brooding, her playing fast and furious.

"I take it last night didn't go so well," Margaret remarked.

In answer, Sophie dug into the strings, finding an angry F-sharp, the note leaping out from the others.

"Oh, dear," Henry said with a sigh, then stood up from the chair, walked over to the divan, and sat, seemingly unaware of what he did.

"Tell us what happened," Deandra said, lowering herself into the wing-backed chair.

Within seconds, Margaret, Henry, and Deandra were circled around Sophie, leaning close.

"There's nothing to tell."

A knock sounded on the door. They ignored it.

"Of course there is something to tell. You only play the overture to *Don Giovanni* when you're upset."

Another knock sounded, followed by the ring of the bell. They didn't even glance that way.

"A lot you know," Sophie replied, her tone disgruntled. "I was planning to add the piece to my repertoire."

"And I'm the queen of England," Henry scoffed.

Deandra shot him a sharp look. "Then we should get *you* the tiara."

"Funny, Dea."

"I thought so."

"Enough!" Sophie broke in. "After all this time, you'd think you two could get along."

"Ah, but we do get along." Henry leaped up and set his coffee aside, along with Deandra's. Then he swept the taller woman up from the seat and threw his arms around her. His head came to her bosom. "I adore you, Deandra," he cried, his voice muffled by generous cleavage.

Deandra laughed, and even Margaret couldn't hold back a reluctant smile. Sophie shook her head and felt a surge of love for this group of people she had gathered around her, just as the sound of the door handle being turned clicked in the foyer.

"Am I interrupting?"

Sophie, Deandra, and Margaret turned to find Grayson standing in the doorway of the east drawing room. Henry didn't hear the approach.

Grayson held his hat in his gloved hands; his heavy top-coat was buttoned to the top, only a hint of woolen scarf showing at his neck. His powerful build filled the doorway. Sophie hated him for looking so good, so calm, as if he had done nothing more to her than invite her over for tea. At the very least he could have the decency to look chagrined.

"Yes, you are interrupting," she stated.

But Grayson wasn't listening. He stared at Henry, who was slurping and moaning and carrying on with great enthusiasm at Deandra's breast. Deandra chuckled and raised her delicate brow.

"What is going on here?" Grayson demanded.

Henry finally heard, and popped his head out from between Deandra's ample breasts, and at the sight of Grayson he smiled licentiously. "I was just enjoying myself. You're just in time to have a try."

Grayson's expression went cold, Deandra sputtered her laughter, and Margaret looked confused.

"A try at what?" Margaret asked.

Sophie boldly met Grayson's eyes, then turned to her assistant. "Henry was just being bad, Maggie, love."

Henry let go of Deandra and came forward and bent over in front of Grayson. "*Very* bad. Perhaps you'd like to spank me."

This time there was no mistake about meaning.

"Henry!" Margaret exclaimed, her face blanching before turning a bright shade of red. "What will Mr. Hawthorne think?"

"We hardly need to concern ourselves with what he thinks," Sophie stated, setting the cello aside, "as our *esteemed* guest is not above improper or, dare I say, underhanded actions himself." She smiled bitingly. "Do you think I adequately described what you've done, Mr. Hawthorne?"

Grayson got that look about him, hard and cold, his jaw tight.

"What has he done?" Henry wanted to know, straightening like a jackknife.

Grayson didn't respond, his eyes locked with Sophie's.

"He's gone and gotten himself engaged," she supplied.

"To whom?" Margaret asked.

"To *moi*."

Deandra, Margaret, and Henry turned to her like precision soldiers. "What?" they cried incredulously.

"Tell them, darling," Sophie said to her newly betrothed, drawing out the endearment.

Still, Grayson didn't utter a word, but the look on his face said clearly enough that he wasn't happy.

"All right, if you insist, I'll tell them." She looked at her friends. "As it turns out, he bought me at the same time he bought the house. Signed, sealed, and delivered and he didn't even have to get my permission. I'd say that's a savvy businessman."

"Oh, my goodness!" Margaret moaned. "How can you sit there and be so cavalier about this?"

"What would you expect?" she asked, looking at Grayson rather than Margaret. "Tears and hysteria?"

"Actually, yes," Deandra supplied.

She wasn't about to share with them how true that was, how she had woken that morning sick and dizzy and wanting nothing more than to scream her outrage. How could she explain that the boy she had adored had become a man that was the very antithesis of what she wanted in life? He had grown up to be a man who made the rules, while she had grown up wanting only to break them. And she *had* broken them. Too many times to turn back from.

As much as she wished her mother hadn't died and life hadn't changed in such a way that she'd needed to flee Boston, she couldn't deny that experiencing life on her own had been a revelation. Could anyone who hadn't experienced the heady intoxication of freedom understand its attraction—its addiction? Independence had given her freedom. How could she go back? Even for Grayson Hawthorne.

She wouldn't let Grayson or her friends see her distress. All she could do was find a way to undo all her father had done.

"This is awful," Henry cried. "You can't get married."

"Rest assured, I'm not."

The words sliced through the air, followed by silence.

"How do you plan to get out of it?"

Grayson's voiced shimmered through the room, down her spine, in a way that muddled her thoughts.

Sophie shook her head, then flicked the cello bow aside. "I'm going to take you to court."

Margaret sat down, hard.

Deandra started to pace. "Hmmm. Actually we could work this to our advantage." She held her hands up in the air as if framing a headline. " 'Desperate Groom Snags Reluctant Bride.' No, too boring. How about 'Desperate Measures of a Desperate Groom'?"

Henry twisted his lips and considered. "It sounds good to me."

"It sounds like libel to me," Grayson said, his voice clipped.

"And you say you're a lawyer," Deandra scoffed. "Tell me what's not true about either of those statements?"

Grayson stared at her in a way meant to quell her tongue as he slowly unbuttoned his coat, then set his winter things aside.

Deandra only continued. "Sophie clearly *is* reluctant, and you certainly look desperate to me."

Grayson's dark eyes narrowed.

"I agree," Margaret supplied.

"Very desperate," Henry added. "We all could testify."

"And both you and I know, Mr. Hawthorne," Deandra explained, "that libel occurs only when a person knowingly and with malicious intent expresses defamatory statements. As far as I can determine, we see our statements as nothing but God's own truth."

Margaret beamed. "Impressive, Dea."

Henry clapped. *"Brava, mademoiselle!"*

Sophie bit her lip to keep from smiling with the surge of love she felt for her friends. "Headlines won't be necessary, dear ones. As I see it, a quick trip to any judge in the land will have me out of this contract in no time. This is the 1890s, after all. Which means I will be unengaged *and* I will get my home back. So if I were you, Grayson dear, I'd trot on over to the nearest office building and find myself a new address from which to transact business."

"But that's the thing, Sophie," he said, his voice deep and low in a way that made her insides tremble, "you aren't me."

She raised her chin and chided herself for trembling like a schoolgirl. "Well, well, aren't we clever this morning?"

"Clever enough to know you will never win. In the meantime we need to talk." Grayson glowered at the entourage before turning back to Sophie. "Alone."

"I can't think of a thing that needs discussing, unless you've had a fit of conscience and have come to say it was all a huge mistake." She hesitated, hating the surge of hope that laced her tone. "Is that why you're here?"

"No."

"Then we have nothing to discuss."

"Actually, we do. I have the contracts for your concert," he stated.

"Concert! What concert?" Deandra demanded.

Sophie felt a betraying tinge of red singe her cheeks. But she would not regret her impetuous discussion. "Did I forget to mention that I'm going to perform at the Music Hall?"

"Good God!"

"You're not!"

Deandra crossed her arms and studied her. "Aren't we full of surprises this morning? First a betrothal, then a concert here in Boston. At the Music Hall, no less."

"Now might I have a word alone with you?" Grayson asked, his polite tone strained.

"No," she repeated, setting her cello aside, then she started out of the drawing room. "Just leave the documents on the desk and I'll get to them later. Come along, dear ones."

The group started out, Sophie herding them along like a gaggle of geese. But just as she came to the door, Grayson stopped her. Henry and the others turned back as well.

"Leave!" Grayson barked at them.

"Don't you dare!" Sophie shot back.

Henry and the women glanced between Sophie and Grayson before they grimaced and headed for the kitchen.

"Traitors," she called after them.

"No," Grayson said, his voice ominous, "they're just smart."

"Now who is being dramatic?"

He raised a dark brow. "I take it drama is a sensitive subject for you."

She scoffed. "Hardly. I was just tired last night." She ducked beneath his arm and left the room.

Unfortunately, Grayson followed, though she felt the moment when he stopped abruptly. They had entered the library, his horrid paintings of hunting dogs and shot pheasants stacked up against the dark walnut wainscoting like an oversize deck of playing cards. Streaked on the wallpaper were several swaths of colored paint.

"What the blazes have you done?" he demanded.

"What does it look like?"

"It looks like you've opened a play school and used the walls when you found yourself short of finger-painting paper."

Sophie smiled. "Wasn't that witty. Actually, I am re-decorating." With paint instead of new wallpaper, because paint was in the basement and there was no money for anything else. And she couldn't stand the dark room and dismal paintings a second longer.

"I just had that wallpaper put up."

"Good God, you paid for that?"

"Quite a lot."

"Then you were had." She turned around and took in the walls. "I think I might go with red."

"You can't paint the room red!"

She tapped her finger against her cheek and studied her surroundings before looking back at him. "A bit much, you think?"

His jaw went well beyond the tension stage. He looked furious. It was all she could do not to rub her hands together in glee, and a thought occurred to her. Perhaps she wouldn't need a court case *or* a concert to run him off.

"Maybe I should go with a cheerful yellow, or a nice, calming blue." She tilted her head as if in serious contemplation. "What do you think? Yellow or blue?"

For half a heartbeat, Grayson actually seemed to consider the question, before he shook his head and his face grew murderous.

But Sophie headed him off. "I think a calming blue. Then we both could benefit from the redecoration. I could play in a beautiful setting, and you could just sit here to ease that straining jaw of yours. That can't be good for your health."

"*You* aren't good for my health," he snapped.

"Exactly. More reason for you to call off this silly betrothal and give me back my house."

"Not on your life. And you can forget your plans for redecorating."

"Good Lord, why are you so upset?" she asked. "Based on our earlier discussion, one of two things is going to happen. Either I'm going to get my house back, or I'm going to have to marry you. Whichever scenario plays out,

I'm going to live here, and I need a music room." She smiled devilishly at him. "Are you a gambling man, Mr. Hawthorne? Do you want to put a wager on which way the chips will fall?"

"A gambling man would place his money on the lawyer who knows the law."

Her smile evaporated.

"You are going to rue the day that you got yourself engaged to me, Grayson Hawthorne, a gambling *woman* would bet on that."

His eyes narrowed. "Be careful what you do, Sophie."

"I'm scared. Can you feel me tremble?"

For one long second the words hung unanswered. Sophie saw the change in him, fire flashing bright in his eyes. He leaned back against the receptionist's desk. Slowly he reached out and took her arm before she had time to step away, then pulled her between his strong thighs. Demanding and intimate at the same time.

His voice went low, his grip surprisingly gentle but heated over her skin. "I'd like to pull you beneath me and make you tremble with the desire I see in your eyes."

The change in him was so quick and so intense that he left her off center. Her breath caught when his hand trailed down her arm, then slipped beneath her long sleeve at her wrist, a simple brush of his fingers over delicate skin.

"In your dreams," she managed.

She saw the calm that came over him, like a warrior getting ready to go into battle, and she grew nervous. Things went better for her when he was agitated. And when she wasn't between his thighs.

"You are in my dreams. Every night."

He said the words in a low voice that brushed over her senses, his fingers drifting higher up her arm to the curve of her shoulder and neck. She could feel his heat, drawing her like a fire in the cold. He smelled like sun-dried grasses swaying in the breeze. And male. Dark, sensual male.

"And when we marry, I *will* make you tremble."

She jerked away and slapped her hands over her ears. "Stop! I am not going to marry you. Not now, not ever. Don't you understand that?"

Very gently he pulled her hands away and held them in front of him. "Is it because the contract was signed without anyone consulting you? Is that what has you so upset and determined to thwart me?"

His fingers circled her wrists, and she was sure he could feel her fluttering pulse. "For starters," she managed.

"That was your father's doing, not mine. I was led to believe you were agreeable."

He was so near, his hard body playing havoc with her thoughts. "And you think that absolves you?"

"Why doesn't it?"

"Because you didn't tell me of the ruse you were trying to pull off once I got here."

"This is no ruse." His thumbs grazed the sensitive skin on her wrists.

"So you keep saying," she said, stringing the words together with effort. "But you should have told me the minute you realized I didn't know about the betrothal."

"I told you about the house." He grew quiet and turned her hands over, staring at her fingers. "At the time I didn't know how much more you could take."

She sucked in her breath, felt that same ache in her heart for a childhood that had been filled with hope and promise.

"Sweet Sophie."

His kind tone was almost more than she could bear, and she lowered her gaze.

"Let's start over," he added.

She felt hope surge inside her, and her head shot up.

"That's wonderful," she said with a gasp. "We can start over and do things right this time."

"Fine."

He lifted her hand, and just when she thought he would kiss the back, he turned it over and pressed his lips to her palm. The sensation shot through her, straight to her knees.

"Will you do me the honor of becoming my wife?"

Her eyes pressed closed, and her lungs filled almost painfully. His wife. A childhood dream come true. She planned to say no, told herself to do just that. "Do you love me?" she asked instead.

The words caught him off guard, she could see it. His spine straightened and his dark eyes grew unfathomable. "Love is hardly a prerequisite for marriage," he answered, like a lawyer advising a client. "You will have my respect and the protection of my name. As my wife, I will hold you in the highest regard."

Sharp, piercing disappointment shot through her. Foolishly. She had known what he would say.

"We will be perfect together," he added, though the meager words seemed to cost him.

But they weren't perfect together. He knew nothing about her anymore. "No," she said, then pulled her hand away. "You don't know the first thing about the woman I have become."

She heard the quaver in her voice, couldn't seem to stop it. But she was acutely aware that her head barely came to his strong shoulders, putting her at eye level with his broad chest. She didn't dare look down to his tapered waist, didn't dare let him distract her in any way.

"Then tell me. Tell me who you've become," he insisted.

For half a heartbeat, the truth tangled on her tongue. But in the end she couldn't tell him about the outrageous gowns and provocative concerts. About her mother. And Niles. She couldn't bring herself to tell Grayson about the night she went to his garret and found him with someone else. She couldn't utter the words. Instead she said, "I am someone who can't be caged."

He made a sharp noise in the back of his throat. "That is just an excuse."

"Call it what you like, but I won't marry you, Grayson."

His eyes went even harder, though there was something else there. Something darker, something elusive—the same look she had seen when his father threw him out on his own.

"What is it about me that you find so objectionable?" he demanded.

She hadn't expected that, and the answer was nothing. He was perfect, perfect except for the fact that he was domineering, possessive. And he would expect her to be perfect, too. But she wasn't about to say that.

"You aren't accepting."

He stiffened. "Accepting?" Then he shook his head. "What are you talking about?"

"I come from a long, distinguished line of judgmental people, and I recognize one of the inner circle when I see them. Some people embrace others' differences. You, on the other hand, reject those who are different. You hate women like Deandra, you shudder at a man like Henry. And you have little time for a lady like Margaret."

She stopped as just then a thought occurred to her, and she studied him. "You don't realize there is another way to be."

"You know nothing about me," he said tightly.

"Don't I? Don't you look at people with sweeping generalizations, making pronouncements based on what you want to believe—that either people are like you . . . or they're wrong?"

She realized with a start that she wanted him to deny her accusation, to tell her that he had the ability to look beyond a person's failings. But he only stared at her with harsh, unforgiving eyes.

Yet again, disappointment seared her.

"Oh, Grayson, you want a proper wife. And in addition to not understanding who I've become, you've forgotten who I used to be," she said with a rueful smile. "Somehow, whether it was caused by that article in the magazine or by the night you saw me at my father's birthday gala, you've begun to picture me as someone I'm not."

"That's ridiculous."

"Is it? What do you remember from our childhood?"

He didn't answer.

"Do you remember how I followed you everywhere? As much as I hate to admit it, Megan wasn't exaggerating about that. Or do you remember how crazy I made you when I constantly turned up without warning?"

"You didn't make me crazy."

"No? How about when I followed you into the Beacon Hill carriage house?"

A light flashed in his eyes.

"If you need reminding, I fell out of the loft after I leaned too far over the edge to see what you were doing. Do you remember that?"

"Perhaps," he answered, his tone clipped.

She knew he remembered every detail.

"You were using the stable's watering spigot to bathe."

"And you were mortified speechless!"

"I was *momentarily* speechless, and only because you were naked as the day you were born." A daring smile pulled at her lips. "You were beautiful."

His gaze shot warnings.

"Naked, and so large. I asked if I could touch you. Do you remember that? Would you like me to describe some more?"

"I think I remember quite enough."

Her smile fled. "Good, and remember well. We both know that I'm not like you. I was never polite or proper. And I can't live with someone who will always think I'm wrong."

They stared at each other, dark eyes clashing with golden brown. But there was nothing more to say. She saw in his expression that he finally understood the truth of her words. It was over. Finished.

Sophie dropped her gaze, then stepped past him. And this time he didn't try to stop her.

Relief filled her, though she felt a stab of regret as well. Part of her was still the little girl who spoke into that talking machine, the little girl who dragged a three-quarter-size cello around everywhere she went, making it hard not to be noticed by the young boy she always followed.

But when she got to the bottom of the stairs his voice rang out.

"Sophie."

Unable to do anything else, she turned back. She stared at him as his face transformed. The darkness fled, the anger dissipated, leaving only a confident smile which made her breath catch.

"I don't give up that easily," he said with a warrior's deceptive softness. "You've known me long enough to understand that." He walked up to her and gently framed her face with his strong hands. "You're a woman now, not a child. We *are* perfect together. It's just going to take me a little longer to make you see that."

She could hardly absorb the words as his gaze drifted to her lips and she was sure he was going to kiss her. Her mouth went dry, and she felt the tingle of her skin where he touched her. But he didn't kiss her. He only leaned close until she could feel his breath against her ear.

"You will be my wife," he whispered. "I promise you that."

Her heart leaped, and she cursed the fact.

Then, very abruptly, he set her at arm's length. "In the meantime I have work to do. Perhaps later you will join me for a cup of tea." Then he stepped away all too calmly, striding through the doorway to his office.

Unsettled, she blinked as she regained her composure. "Don't count on it!" she called after him with a frustrated growl.

He had the audacity to chuckle.

Chapter Eleven

As promised, Grayson set out to win her with a possessive assurance that both intrigued her and made her uneasy. He wooed her as if he had all the time in the world, assured that in the end he would have her.

In turn, Sophie set out to let him know that he wouldn't.

But regardless of her determination, he seemed even more intent, simply shrugging his shoulders and smiling during those times she played raucous music whenever a client appeared. He didn't so much as blink when she indeed painted the library a tawdry shade of red. Did little more than cringe when the all-too-efficient Miss Pruitt packed up her desk and quit in no uncertain terms. And when she and her friends had a drunken champagne-and-caviar party, Grayson had merely taken a fluted glass, toasted the group, then left for the hotel after the simple request that they not burn the house down.

It seemed that the more outrageous her actions, the more convinced he was that he was winning.

Sophie assured herself that he wasn't.

On the fifth day of Grayson's pursuit, it had been a quiet morning when Sophie sat down to play. It was cold outside, and a fire burned brightly on the hearth, warming the room. She had dressed in a rich pink ostrich-feather-and-velvet lounging ensemble with matching ostrich-feather mules, more suited for a bordello than a drawing room.

Just when she started warming up for a new piece that had been adapted from the popular opera *The Fairy Queen*, which she wanted to add to her repertoire, Deandra walked into the room.

"I've decided to make a few changes to the show," Sophie stated, halting the bow in midstroke.

"Really?"

Sophie leaned back. "I see an even bigger event, with more flash and greater sparkle." She ran her tongue along the edge of her teeth, then smiled impishly. "Even some men."

"Some men?" Margaret asked, entering behind Deandra.

"Just one or two. One to hold my chair, another to hand me my cello. Big, handsome men. We'll dress them in fine woolen trousers—just a little too tight—and fine silk shirts. I see it as an extravaganza, the likes of which Boston has never seen before."

"The likes of which the Ringling Brothers Circus has never seen," Margaret lamented, shaking her head.

"As long as you're going for big," Deandra said, "why don't we shoot you out of a cannon, then those men of yours could catch you and present you to the audience like a gift."

Sophie laughed. Margaret groaned.

Deandra tapped her cheek with the end of a pencil in consideration. "You know, we actually could—"

"I will not be shot out of a cannon. Even I have my limits. I just want to make sure that there is no mistake about what kind of a show I perform."

"Like there will be one iota of doubt the minute you drop the cape from your shoulders?" Deandra eyed her. "What is this about? You are already daring enough that you should offer smelling salts at intermission instead of champagne. Why do you need an extravaganza?"

Sophie sniffed and studied her nails. "Because I want Grayson Hawthorne to have an apoplectic fit when he witnesses his bride-to-be in action."

"I thought you were going to take him to court."

"I will if I have to. But it occurred to me last night that a court case could drag on for years. And the fact is, Grayson just thinks he wants to marry me. Just like Bostonians think they want me to perform for them. They want me now because my photograph has been in magazines and they hear I'm famous."

Deandra nodded slowly in dawning understanding. "But once they see you perform, carried out by a bunch of brawny men . . ."

She would gain her freedom.

But at what cost?

She shook the thought away. She would not marry, nor would she lose Swan's Grace. She would fight for her independence and her home. She would do battle for the two things her soul depended on. She would fight for the life her mother had given her.

And if by the time the concert arrived Grayson Hawthorne hadn't already thrown up his hands in defeat over her tactics to run him off, he would start running the minute he saw her play. The very proper man would back out of the betrothal so fast heads would spin. Then she would let *him* out of the contract, just as soon as he returned Swan's Grace.

"Just tell me what you want me to do," Deandra said. "In fact, we might get some ideas in New York. I heard Lily Langtree is singing at Carnegie Hall at the end of February. Henry suggested we take the train down and see her show."

A trip? On a train? A trip that would cost money? Sophie's stomach fluttered.

"I can't," Margaret said.

Thank God, Sophie thought, her sigh of relief seeping out of her like air from a child's balloon.

Margaret and Deandra eyed her curiously.

"Don't mind me, I was just yawning." Then she did just that, stretching extravagantly. "Why can't you go, Maggie?"

Margaret's brown eyes filled with barely contained excitement. "Because that's the week my cousin Lucinda invited me to the country. Apparently most of the family will be there. You don't mind if I go, do you?"

Sophie's thoughts shifted completely, away from money problems and to Margaret. "Mind?" She squeezed Margaret's hand. "I'm thrilled for you. I know how much this invitation means to you."

Eventually Deandra left the room, as did Margaret. Once she was alone, Sophie's mind was filled with mixed emotions, the past and the present—with what her life had been and what it would be when this was all over. It would be the same, she told herself, the same life that she had loved. Traveling, concerts. And once she regained Swan's Grace, she would spend the off season at her home with her friends around her. Money would no longer be a problem. They could come and go as they pleased. Life would be exciting and full. It would be, she told herself firmly when doubt flared.

Perhaps she would become like Isabella Gardner, with her risqué art and extravagant parties. Once Boston got over the shock of the wealthy woman, they had embraced her with open arms.

Encouraged by her plan, she noticed her hands had started moving of their own volition, her fingers and bow finding notes that she hadn't played in years. Startled by the unexpected direction, she forced herself back to the familiar strands of *The Waltz of Swans*.

But before she realized it, she sought out a G, then tumbled down to a D with a smooth, rolling bow gesture back and forth across the top three strings. The prelude of Bach's First Cello Suite in G Major.

Could she have done it?

Could she have ultimately triumphed had she been given the debut recital at the Music Hall?

Had she taken the easy way out when she started to play the provocative popular pieces instead?

Had Niles Prescott been right about her all those years ago when he didn't give her the show?

She brought her hand away as if she had been burned, the bow knocking against the table from her haste. The truth was, she had played the opening bars of Bach, and it had sounded perfect. Even she recognized the brilliant color, the perfect tone.

She listened for a moment, confirming that the house was silent. Deandra and Margaret had returned upstairs. No one would hear.

Taking a deep breath, she ran through the first bar again. Her hand began to tremble, tears burned in her eyes. Years tumbled back, and she could practically feel her mother's presence in the room.

"Do you understand, Mother?" she whispered. "Do you understand what I am doing and why? You were my tie to Boston, and you're not here anymore. But I need Swan's Grace, I need to know it's here and it's mine."

Outside, the dormant rosebushes stood strong against the cold wind, while the long, bare branches of a willow swayed like a dancer.

But the room remained still, offering no response.

She leaned back in the chair, the hardwood trim biting into her back. Her mother was gone, there would be no answers.

Jerking forward, she returned the bow to the strings and concentrated on *The Waltz of Swans*. One bar, two. The notes easy and lyrical. But it wouldn't flow. The notes coming from the cello tangled with the notes in her head. G-D-B . . . A-B-D-B-D. Notes from the Bach that demanded her attention.

Sharply she lowered the bow, and she would have left the room altogether if the music hadn't wrapped around her. Like a promise? Or a curse?

With her hand still trembling, she glanced one last furtive time toward the stairs, then gave in to the pull and started to play. G-D-B . . . A-B-D-B-D. The same section, again and again, until she leaped off and continued on, playing with her eyes closed. Dreaming. Hoping. Feeling each note like a mother wishing for a child.

She didn't think; she played as she had when she was young. She lost herself to the sound, the sweet, resonant vibration of the chords against her body as she worked the suite as if she had played it only yesterday. She played so intently that she didn't hear the front door open, didn't hear the booted steps coming through the doorway. She didn't hear anything until she stopped as she came to the end.

"God, that was incredible."

Her head popped up, the bow slicing crazily down the strings as she jumped in surprise. "Grayson."

"Hello." A beautiful smile pulled at his full lips.

She stared at him, trying to focus, her heart pounding as much from the music as from his unexpected arrival. The promise of the Bach and Grayson's handsome form standing there was almost too much to take.

"What was that you were playing?" he asked.

"Nothing," she stated, laying the bow carefully across the table.

"It didn't sound like nothing. I've never heard it before."

She waved her hand dismissively. "It's just the opening notes of a Bach cello suite."

"Really?" he asked, surprised. "I didn't know Bach wrote suites for the cello."

"There are six of them, though not many people are aware they exist. In fact, for years the person who found them thought they were little more than bowing exercises. How wrong they were."

"Do you play them in your concerts?"

"Good heavens, no," she said too quickly. *Calm down,* she told herself.

"Why not?"

Calm was elusive, and her palms grew sweaty. "Because they're a bore."

She hated the way he considered her, looking at her as if he could see into her soul.

"Then what do you play?" he asked.

"A bit of this, a bit of that. All pieces my audiences adore. Why are you here?"

Grayson could tell she was trying to change the subject. But he let her. He had no idea why the stunning music she had been playing when he walked into the house would bring a stain to her cheeks when she was asked about it.

He had heard the sound as he walked up the road after having spent the morning in court. He had approached from Berkeley Street and had seen her through the side window as he drew near. He had easily spotted her hair, like a golden flame. Standing before her now, he saw her beauty like a lick of fire. With her hair neither blond nor brown, and her startlingly vivid eyes, it was easy to see traces of her Norman descendants—warriors who fought brutally for what they wanted.

Did she have more of them in her than their coloring? Was that what made her a challenge?

Or did she fill a need in him?

For years he had fought off the desire for something he couldn't name, fought off an emptiness. He had found ways to cease his circling thoughts, to forget—in long hours of work, in the soft flesh of women. But that was only temporary. Always he woke, knowing that the woman next to him wasn't what he wanted. They never filled the void inside him; the sex served only as a way to fill his mind momentarily with a blank slate, as if nothing had been etched there long ago.

There were other means to forget. Music. Sweeping crescendos and dazzling denouements. But mostly there was work. Business deals and court cases had consumed his thoughts and energies. He had risen to the top of his field, worked obsessively. But once there, what did he have?

He had worked a lifetime to gain his father's respect. But regardless of his accomplishments, he couldn't say he had achieved his goal. He hated the familiar feeling of futility. And as always, he didn't know why he continued to care. Why did the need circle around inside him? It made him weak. And weakness was unacceptable.

"Hello. Are we sleeping?"

He blinked and found Sophie standing before him, fluttering delicately ringed fingers in front of his eyes.

"I was thinking."

"You do too much of that."

He watched as she sauntered across the room, her shimmering gown trailing behind her like a waterfall of gossamer gold, the stain gone from her cheeks, her equilibrium regained. One minute she was sultry and flip, the next she was vulnerable.

That was something he didn't understand about her. He had heard of musicians who were artistically brilliant, but their talent was twined with a monstrous self-centeredness.

Someone who didn't look deep enough might think that of Sophie. But Grayson had seen the caring, the giving.

When they were young. Recently with the dog. With her ragtag group of friends whom she looked after like a mother hen.

"You still haven't told me why you are here," she said, her heels clicking on the floor as she walked across the room to the tray of tea items.

"I amended the Music Hall contract I brought you before, adding the additional terms you asked for. You drive a hard bargain. But they agreed to everything."

She whirled around to face him. "How could they?"

He studied her, wondering what he saw. Regret? "I thought that is what you wanted."

"Well, yes. But . . ."

She stared at the sheets of paper he held in his hands, her porcelain cheeks so pale that he could see a faint hint of freckles across the bridge of her nose.

"Is something wrong?" he asked.

With a start she glanced up at him. "No, no. Nothing's wrong. I just thought . . . I mean, I didn't think they would agree so readily."

"But they have. Are you thinking about backing out?"

He watched her chin rise.

"Never. Where do I sign?" she demanded.

After a second of studying her, he pulled a pen and a bottle of ink from a small writing desk. Setting the papers flat on the surface, he handed her the pen.

Sophie stared at it, her eyes closing for one brief second, before she strode forward with determination. Taking the pen, she brushed against him, barely a touch, but he felt it to his core as she passed to stand in front of the contract. Then she stopped. She didn't move, and Grayson could see the column of her neck, the delicate wisps of hair curling over smooth skin. She smelled like sweet soap and springwater, not heavy perfume.

"Do you realize how much I want to kiss you right now?"

Her thoughts broke apart at his words, but she didn't turn around. "I'm a cellist, not a mind reader."

His answering chuckle filled the room. "Do you have a glib response for everything?"

"I try," she said dryly. "You'd be amazed at how glib and entertaining I can be."

He hesitated, felt all joking fade from his mind. "I'm beginning to think it has nothing to do with entertainment. I think you use it as a defense."

This time there was no glib response, and she went very still. "Ah," she mused, her tone forced, "a disciple of Dr. Freud, I see."

"Who?"

She shook her head, and he could tell that she breathed in deeply.

"Forget it," she said. "You wouldn't have heard of him yet."

"You're filled with lots of names and titles I haven't heard of."

She started away, but he wouldn't let her go. Not this time. He caught her arm, his fingers sliding gently across her skin. "You aren't going to keep me at a distance."

His hand skimmed up to her shoulder, then his other hand, until his palms cradled her face.

"I won't let you push me away, Sophie." His thumbs ran gently over her cheeks.

She didn't respond, but she looked at his mouth, the way it was full and sensual, strong. She felt a shiver race through her, a slow, throbbing heat building up inside her. He did that to her, made her yearn.

"In the years you were away," he said, his voice deep and low, "you've built a wall around yourself."

His palms drifted down her neck to her shoulders, strong and confident, making her want to lean in to him—making her want the very kiss he said he wanted to give her.

"You are an odd mix of bravado and shyness"—he took one long curl and wrapped it around his finger—"conceit and self-deprecation. I understand that." His eyes met hers. "But what I don't understand is why." His finger slipped from her hair and he leaned down, his lips so close that they were nearly touching hers. "I intend to find out."

It took a moment for his words to penetrate her mind, but suddenly they did and she jerked back, her heart racing. "Leave me alone, Grayson. I don't want you prying into my life. And I certainly don't want your kiss."

She ended on a lie, and they both knew it. They stared at each other until he merely smiled with that irritating self-confidence, and nodded his head. "Fine, for now," he said, his voice a sensual brush of sound. "I'll give you time. I've said that all along."

With that he turned her around to face the papers, but she could hardly think. Her pulse raced and she was much too aware of his large hands on her shoulders—of his promise to dig into her life. Would he learn about her mother and Niles Prescott and why she had left Boston? Would he learn about her past?

"Sophie?"

She only stood.

"You're going to be wonderful. If you play like you did when I walked in, Boston will love you. How could they not?"

Her heart raced.

"Sign the contract, Sophie. I have work to do."

She tried to focus on the pages, feeling backed into a corner. Despite all her plans and bravado, how could she go through with it? How could she let Boston see her show?

When she only stood there, he lowered the pen, stepping beside her, and studied her with an all-too-curious look. "What are you afraid of?"

In a flash she grabbed the pen. "I'm not afraid. Of anything!" She had stopped being afraid a long time ago. Then she brought the pen to paper and signed angrily. "There, are you happy?"

"This isn't for me, Sophie. It's for you. The question is, are you happy?"

"As a clam."

Grayson considered her, trying to understand what he saw in her eyes. Was he right when he thought that she was trying to keep him and others at arm's length?

But then he noticed a slip of paper resting beneath her cup of tea. The name Percy Walters caught his attention.

"What is that?" he demanded.

Sophie looked down, then pulled the soggy note away and read. Glancing between him and the slip of paper, it was obvious that whatever was written there made her happy.

"Oh, yes, I forgot. This came yesterday around noon. Maybe one." She shrugged. "Something about some Percy Walters's court date on the twentieth being moved up from one o'clock to eleven in the morning."

She handed him the message, the sheet limp.

Grayson felt fire start to burn in his mind. "Do you know what day it is?"

She clucked her tongue as she glanced around the room as if looking for a calendar, her equilibrium yet again regained at the thought that there was hope yet that she could run him off.

"It is the twentieth," he bit out.

"Really," she said, relieved that he was no longer talking about digging into her past. She glanced at the clock on the mantel. "Oh, look at that. Five till eleven. You'd best hurry or you'll be late."

He counted to ten.

"You know," she offered, "I'm not much for giving advice, but none of this would have happened if you had a real office with a real receptionist."

"I have a real office, and I had a real receptionist. You ran her off."

"I can think of a few things to call Miss Altima Pruitt, but *receptionist* isn't one of them. Good riddance, as far as I'm concerned. But fortunately for you, as long as you're here, I don't mind taking a message or two."

"That's what I'm afraid of."

She smiled like a cat who got the cream—like a cat who just might win the war yet. "If you hurry, it's possible you could make it in time."

An hour later, with Miss Pruitt little more than a bad memory, Grayson at court, and everyone else gone, there was no one to answer the shout of hello Sophie heard in the foyer.

With heels clicking on marble and her feather boa swirling as she walked, Sophie came into the entryway to find a middle-aged man wringing his hands. His eyes went wide at the sight of her—or maybe it was her attire. It was hard to say.

"I'm here to see Mr. Hawthorne," he stammered, then glanced at the empty office. "I had a twelve o'clock appointment."

"Did you really?" she asked, her tone a lament. "As it happens, there has been a pesky little change in plans. Your Mr. Hawthorne had to dash off to court."

"Do you expect him back?"

Sophie grimaced. "Unfortunately, yes."

"Then I'll wait."

"It could be hours."

"Fine."

"Suit yourself." She waved toward the drawing room, then she started for the stairs.

"Do you think I might have some tea while I wait?"

"Tea? You want me to make you some tea?"

"If it's not a bother."

"Hmmm," she murmured, shrugging her shoulders at the newness of the idea.

When she was growing up, her mother had insisted her time be spent playing and practicing. Sophie had never learned to run a household—though she was learning rapidly, since she couldn't afford servants. But she had yet to progress to the kitchen. That was Margaret's domain. "Why not? I'm sure we can drum up a cup. Come along."

Startled, the man followed her to the kitchen.

Despite having spent a minimum of time in the kitchen over the years, Sophie procured the kettle and cups with ease, searched out the canister of tea leaves, and had the stove going as though she did it every day. Once she had the brew steeping on the counter, she found her favorite tiny cakes in the cupboard and set them out on a Wedgwood plate.

She poured two cups out. "Sugar?" she asked.

"No, thank you." The man sipped. "Perfect." He sighed, leaning against the counter. "I can't tell you the kind of week I have had."

Sophie *hmmm*ed noncommittally as she plopped a sugar cube into her cup, then rummaged through a velvet-lined box for a spoon.

"I had so hoped to have my . . . err . . . difficulties resolved today," he continued. "Or at least have a plan of action put in place."

"I certainly understand about needing a plan of action," she mused over a sip of tea, then dropped another cube in the cup. "Anyway, Grayson is bound to return, and no doubt he will solve your difficulties."

"Do you think?"

Sophie finally looked at the man. For the first time she noticed his furrowed brow and the dark circles under his eyes. She couldn't stand to see someone in need. "Of course." She smiled at him, stirring, the silver clinking against china. "Things always have a way of working out, even when you don't think they will." She had come to depend on that sentiment over the last few days.

"Even with a divorcement?" he blurted out, his face turning bright red.

"Ah, a divorcement." She *tsk*ed and set the spoon aside. "I'm sorry, Mr. . . ."

"Cardwell. Willard Cardwell."

The man began to ease, and the next thing she knew he was telling her every aspect of his predicament. She cringed at the personal details, couldn't imagine anyone wanting to talk so openly about their life. She was a strong believer in one's private life remaining private.

But Mr. Willard Cardwell didn't appear to live by the same standards, and she quickly learned that he and the missus had been married five years, had four children, and his wife was suddenly fraught with sick headaches. By the end of his tale, Sophie was so caught up in the story that she didn't think about the fact that the conversation was entirely inappropriate.

"Good God, Mr. Cardwell. Who wouldn't have headaches after having a child once a year, four years running. The woman needs a rest!"

He sputtered and puffed up. "But I'm a man, after all, and I have—" He cut himself off abruptly, his face flaring red.

"You're a man and you have needs. Tell me something that's news."

"Then you see, I have little choice but to get a divorcement!"

"Who told you that?"

"Mr. Hawthorne."

"Grayson Hawthorne told you that?" she demanded, incensed.

"Actually, not in so many words. He told me I needed a mistress. But I can't afford such a woman! I can only afford a wife, and mine no longer has any interest in me."

"Pshaw. What does Grayson know?"

"He's a lawyer! The finest in town."

"Let me tell you something, Mr. Cardwell. Grayson Hawthorne might be knowledgeable as a lawyer, but he doesn't know the first thing about women. If I were you, I'd not waste my good money on a lawyer or a mistress." Then she leaned close and told him just what she thought he should do.

The man was shocked by her suggestion. Sophie shook her head and sighed. Men really were too much.

"If you have a problem with that," she added, "at least buy your wife a fabulous necklace. Your mistake is that you're not thinking with your heart. Woo her, Mr. Cardwell. Make her feel like she is more than a brood mare. Make her feel cared for."

"But jewelry is expensive."

"So is Grayson Hawthorne. I've seen what he charges." She had, when she had gone through his desk, which was sparse and well-ordered, just like the man. Only a small locked cabinet remained beyond her reach. Henry had offered his services, but even she had limits. Though often she had wondered what he kept inside.

"True, Mr. Hawthorne is expensive." He considered, his tea long finished. "Perhaps I should give it a try."

"If I were you, I'd take her to dinner on occasion, as well. Bring her flowers. Candy."

He looked at her, the furrows in his brow easing. "And maybe the . . . the . . . your suggestion. Thank you, Miss—"

"Wentworth. But call me Sophie."

"Sophie, I appreciate your candor."

She patted his hand. "I'm always glad to help."

She walked him to the foyer. But just as she pulled open the front door, Grayson hurtled up the granite steps, his hair falling forward, making him look like a tardy schoolboy.

"Willard, I apologize for being late." He glowered at Sophie and raked his hand through his hair, his other holding his black leather satchel. "There was a little mix-up with my schedule."

"No problem, Grayson. In fact, I just received the best advice I've gotten in ages from Miss Wentworth here. If all goes as planned, I won't be in need of your services, after all." He tipped his hat and strode to his waiting carriage.

Slowly Grayson turned a baleful eye on Sophie. "What did you say to him?"

"Something you should have said when he first came to you."

"What was that?"

He enunciated each syllable through gritted teeth, making Sophie smile wickedly.

"I suggested he use contraceptive devices."

That took the wind out of his puffed up sails. He stood for several seconds, his expression incredulous. "Contraceptive devices?" The words seemed to tangle in his mind.

"You've heard of them, haven't you?" she asked ever so innocently, fluffing her fluttering sleeves, "those things men slide down over their—"

"Christ! You didn't," he demanded, his normally implacable features pulled into a mask of disbelief.

"I did." She tossed the end of the feather boa over her shoulder. "I never would have guessed at how good I am at giving advice. If you'd like, when I have a bit of free time, I could give you some pointers."

His eyes blazed, and he looked as if at any moment he

would strangle her—with great delight. "You are ruining my law practice."

"Now, really, it's unbecoming to blame others for your shortcomings."

Frustration flashed across his face. "I have no doubt you've set out to run off my clients intentionally."

"Would I do that?" she asked with a thick, honeyed drawl.

"In a heartbeat. Unfortunately, I don't have time to deal with that now. I have a hearing in another hour. If anyone arrives, do not so much as look at them. If I find out that you have been *advising* another client of mine I'll—"

"You'll what? Take me to court? Sue me?" she challenged.

His jaw worked furiously, but he didn't respond.

"I didn't think so." Then she smiled at him, baldly, before she turned on her dainty heel and disappeared down the hall.

This time he didn't chuckle.

Chapter Twelve

The tables started to turn in earnest a week later, though not in her favor.

On Thursday, Henry and Deandra departed for New York to see Lily Langtree. Deandra had insisted they see the show for inspiration and ideas. Besides, she added, they had friends there that they wanted to stay with.

Standing there, Sophie hadn't had any idea how to tell them that what little money she had was dwindling faster than she had anticipated.

But in the end, since they had yet to learn the money was dwindling at all, she had scraped enough together to buy two train tickets. Thank goodness, Margaret was going to Lexington to visit her cousin. Three tickets would have put her in dire straits. As it was, she'd had to borrow from the meager allotment of coins she had set aside for emergencies.

A low thread of panic started to rise. She'd never had to juggle money before. She had always had the luxury of buying what she wanted, whenever she wanted. Even when she had borrowed against future earnings for the jewels, she'd hardly batted an eye. In her mind she considered it an investment in the future. And the investment had paid off. She was booked solid for the upcoming season. Soon she would have money.

Only she realized now that it wasn't coming in fast enough.

Sophie took a deep breath in hopes of calming herself, absently rubbing her hand over the dog's sweet head.

When Henry and Deandra had pressed her about the importance of going to New York to see the Langtree show, Sophie had started to confide in them about the situation. But the words stuck in her throat.

She wrinkled her nose as she realized she wasn't sure they would stay if she couldn't continue to pay their way. And right that second she couldn't afford to lose the only semblance of family she had.

She snorted out loud at how pathetic it was that she had to buy her family. But even knowing that, she couldn't bring herself to tell them. As a result, she was on her own until the following Monday.

It had snowed overnight, hopefully the last of the season, the cinders and sludge covered up with a fresh dusting of white. It promised to be a glorious morning.

She flipped the end of her feather boa over her shoulder, pulled out her cello, tuned it, then started to play. The dog stood up and stretched, then circled around until she plopped back on the soft cushion as music filled the house.

Sophie played whatever she wanted, fast and slow, cheerful and moody. The session went well, but it was hard to concentrate on the show. Soon she was bored, and her friends had only just left. Even the thought of Grayson arriving held some appeal. Too much appeal, if truth be known.

A knock gained her attention. Excited despite herself, she dashed to the front door and swept it open. Her mind froze at the sight of Niles Prescott standing on the slate tiles, his wool coat a flashy burgundy, his scarf a mix of blue and gold, his bowler perched on his gray hair at a jaunty angle.

He stood on the threshold with a smile on his face, as if five years hadn't passed and he had arrived for tea.

What had her mother ever seen in the man that she would bring him into their home?

"I think we both know she is not here," she snapped, and started to slam the door.

He flattened his gloved palm against it with an indulgent chuckle. "Now, now, Sophie. Is that any way to treat a family friend?"

"Let's not pretend we're friends, Mr. Prescott."

"*Tsk, tsk,* you're still upset about the Grand Debut."

His audacity made her blood boil. "Upset?" She fought to remain casual. "You ingratiate yourself into my family, take advantage of my mother's largesse, promise me the solo, then . . ."

Words failed her.

"I what? Gave the concert to someone else?"

"Yes," she blurted. "For starters!"

He shrugged indifferently. "I'm giving you a concert now."

"And you think that makes up for everything?"

"Doesn't it?" He brushed lint from his sleeve, then glanced up at her with amused gray eyes.

She felt the flare of her nostrils as she took a deep, searing breath. "Get out."

"Now, Sophie."

"I said get out. We have nothing to discuss."

"Ah, but I'm not here to see you, my dear. I'm here to see Mr. Hawthorne about a little thing called a contract that you so wisely asked for."

But stupidly agreed to. Her world spun.

"Grayson isn't here. Now good day."

Before he could protest, she slammed the door, then purposefully ignored his muffled demands and pounding fists.

She walked from room to room, waiting for him to leave, and for the first time she wished she had gotten the lock fixed. She stopped and shuddered at the sight of the library. Painting the wallpaper red really had been a childish act, but it had gotten rid of Altima Pruitt.

The dog followed every step she took. When the pounding on the door finally ceased, she leaned down and hugged the dog tight. "You really are a sweet thing. Come on, Sweetie. Let's get something to eat."

They went to the kitchen, only to find that the cupboards were bare. She shouldn't be surprised, however. When Margaret had offered to take care of stocking the shelves before she left, Sophie had known her food allotment had already been spent on train tickets. So she had produced one of her famous smiles and told Margaret there was no need. But now she realized she had to eat something.

Sophie thought of a place her mother used to go on Beacon Hill. Sloan Market. How Sophie had loved shopping there, always leaving the store with candy and sometimes even a slice of cheese from the butcher. Plus, all her mother had to do was sign for the food and a bill was sent later.

Within minutes, Sophie was bundled up and headed for the store. When she came to the courthouse on her way, she felt a start of awareness that Grayson was inside. She wondered what he was doing, could imagine him standing tall, wooing juries with his respectable looks and fine voice.

She started to smile, then realized what she was doing. Muttering about foolish musings, she hurried by, then slipped inside the warm, inviting confines of Sloan's.

Grayson shook his client's hand in the courthouse rotunda before they both headed out. Buttoning his coat, he headed for the Back Bay, but four steps beyond the large plate-glass window of Sloan Market he stopped dead in his tracks. His head cocked in confusion; then he took four steps back, certain his eyes were deceiving him. But when he peered through the gold lettering on the clear glass there was no question that the person standing at the counter, a long line of impatient customers behind her, was his betrothed.

Sophie was sure her cheeks were as bright as the shade she had painted the library walls.

"I'm sorry, Miss . . ."

"Wentworth," she said, her smile forced. "From Swan's Grace."

"Wherever," the young clerk said with a huff, snapping the thick black ledger book closed. "But you can't just sign your name, then walk away with groceries. What do you think this is?"

"I told you that I was referring to an account," she said as quietly as she could through clenched teeth, the line of people behind her on the verge of revolt, "with a bill being sent at a later date."

"And I keep telling you I don't have any Wentworth at Swan's Grace in my book. Now either hand over the money or put the goods back."

"Yeah, hurry up, lady," a man behind her stated. "We don't have all day."

Mortification stung Sophie's cheeks and she stared at the items on the counter. "How much does it come to?" she finally asked.

"A dollar fifty."

A dollar fifty! Who would have guessed groceries could be so expensive? She ran her eyes over the tin of her favorite cakes—why go to all the trouble of making them yourself when you could buy them?—her favorite sardines. It wasn't as though she were trying to buy caviar.

Praying that she had more money in her reticule than

she thought, she pulled out her coin purse. She flicked her finger through the change. A meager thirty-five cents.

With a wooden smile, she reached out and took away a jar of peach preserves. "There, now how much?"

Someone in the line groaned. The clerk blew out his breath in an exasperated puff. "A dollar twenty-nine."

With a self-conscious shrug, she took the tin of sardines and set them aside. "Now what is the total?"

A woman stamped her foot. "If you quit buying fancy gowns with feathers, and hats with birds, you might be able to afford groceries."

"Heck, just put back those expensive cakes and you could pay for a thing or two," another woman barked.

Sophie turned with a jump, and started to say something to the hecklers. But her mouth froze, the words hanging unspoken on her tongue when she saw Grayson. He stood just beyond the line, a look of confusion on his face.

"Is there a problem here?" he asked, stepping forward.

"No, no problem," she said quickly, whirling back to face the clerk. *Of all the rotten luck.* She leaned close. "Please just pack up thirty-five cents' worth of things, and hurry," she whispered frantically.

Grayson worked his way to the counter.

"Hey, mister, there's a line here."

Grayson turned to the woman and gave her a smile that would have melted the hardest of hearts. Sophie remembered that expression so well, a smile he had used many times when they were young to get her out of the worst of predicaments.

He directed the full brunt of his charm on the woman. "I know there is a line, madam, and I wouldn't dream of cutting in. But if you don't mind, I'll take care of this . . . situation so we all can get on with our days."

Situation.

Sophie's cheeks flared even redder. But then she saw the

woman who had only seconds ago heckled her all but swoon right there on the Sloan Market floor. That was when she got mad.

Sophie jerked around. "On second thought, I don't need any groceries."

Snapping her change purse shut with a click, she stuffed it in her reticule and started to leave.

"Fine," the clerk said with a sneer, "and don't bother coming back."

But she didn't get any farther than a half step toward the front door when Grayson blocked her path and restored her purchases to the center of the counter.

With those strong hands that had caressed her, he pulled a five-dollar gold piece from his pocket and faced the smirking clerk. Grayson's smile was gone as he set the coin down with an ominous click against the high-polished wood.

The clerk's eyes widened, and his knowing grin evaporated into the coal-heated air.

"Here is your money," Grayson enunciated. "It's a wonder anyone shops here when they are attended to in such a rude manner. Perhaps I should have a word with Mr. Sloan."

The clerk sputtered and awkwardly rang open the cash register, fumbling to make change.

"You'll have a word with no one," Sophie snapped, taking the recently returned items and setting them aside. "I will pay my own way."

Grayson's eyes bored into her, dark and exasperated. "Why are you being so stubborn about this?"

They stared at each other, a battle of wills taking place in the store.

"I am no longer a child, Grayson," she said, almost in a whisper. "I don't need you to save me."

His expression grew troubled, his body suddenly tense. "But what if I need you to save me?"

Her breath caught, and confusion clouded her mind.

"Mercy sakes alive, we don't got all day."

With a start, Sophie and Grayson focused on the line of people. Then, before anyone could say another word, Grayson tossed her items in a box and secured it on his hip, his strong hand at her back as he guided her to the door.

"Hey, what about the change?" the clerk called after him.

"Keep it."

They came out into the brisk air, Grayson walking so fast it looked as if he were marching.

"Stop, please!" Sophie demanded, whisking away from him.

But he kept going, hitching the box under his arm. His mind churned, stunned that he had uttered those words out loud at all. In a store. In front of Sophie.

After a few seconds, he heard Sophie start after him. Seconds later she came up beside him, though neither of them stopped walking.

"What did you mean, save you?"

He gave a wry look that he didn't feel. "I was joking."

"I don't think you were."

He shrugged, never missing a step.

"Grayson, talk to me."

"Ah, now you want to talk, when it's about me rather than you."

She crooked a smile and looked like a little imp. "I've never claimed to be fair."

"You got me on that one."

"So you aren't going to tell me what you meant," she said.

"Ding, ding, ding, you win the prize."

He repeated her words from the night she arrived, making her laugh, the sound echoing against the new-fallen snow.

"Well, then," she began grudgingly, "I guess I have no choice but to move on to new topics and thank you for taking care of the grocery bill." Her smile melted away like snow beneath a spring sun.

"You're welcome."

"I could have paid."

He glanced over at her with a raised brow.

"I could have," she insisted.

He stepped off the curb to accommodate two women who were walking their way. He tipped his hat and nodded his head, and the ladies smiled and cooed at him.

Sophie groaned and rolled her eyes.

This time he laughed and seemed to relax. "Jealous?" he asked with a smile once he was back on the walkway.

"Not on your life."

"You used to be jealous when I was with other women."

She shot him a look. "I was eight."

He smiled appreciatively. "True."

"And a moron."

"You? Never."

She kept on going. "I was, and we both know it. But I've changed a lot since then."

"We've all changed, Sophie."

"You more than most, I'd say."

"Don't tell me we are back to that again."

She glanced over and studied him as they turned left, and she noticed his smile was no longer so smug.

"I'm not so different, Sophie."

But he was. They both knew it, too. After being kicked out of his home, he'd had something to prove. That he was successful. That he was perfect. She wondered if he understood that about himself.

She stopped at a hill that by afternoon's end would be covered with children coming out to play. She glanced between the snowy slope and Grayson. "Prove that you haven't changed."

His head whipped around. "I don't need to prove any-thing," he said, his tone that of a lawyer in court.

Sophie smiled. "I'll save you, Grayson. I'll save you from a life of little more than drawing up contracts, acting proper, and doing the acceptable thing. And I'll do that by putting a little excitement in your life."

His jaw went tight.

"Slide down that hill."

"Which will prove little more than that I'm a fool."

"It will prove you know how to have fun."

"Even if I wanted to, which I don't, there is nothing to transport me."

" 'Transport me'?" she repeated, giving him an in-credulous look. Then she shook her head and scanned the landscape, catching sight of a red-slatted sled. "You're in luck. Surely a sled is *transport* enough."

There it went, the tic in his jaw beating like the hall clock. She wasn't sure if the proof made her happy or sad.

But she was given no chance to think it through when Grayson dropped the box of goods on a bench with a clunk, and stormed over to snatch up the guide rope.

She stood stunned and watched his retreating back as he marched up the snowy hill, his ever so proper coattails flapping, snow no doubt filling his fine leather shoes, the brightly colored sled following along in his wake. She cringed for a second, then laughed up to the skies and raced after him.

At the top she panted from exertion. He stood very still, without looking at her, staring at the city that stretched out below. The sight of him took her breath away. The past dis-appeared. The future wasn't a thought. There were only the two of them on this hill, the beauty of him, as always, sur-prising her.

"Why did things have to change?" she whispered.

He turned to face her, his eyes solemn. "Do you really wish things had stayed the same?"

"I wish my mother were still here."

He sighed and reached out to hook his arm around her shoulders, pulling her against him. Amazingly she didn't feel the need to flee. She savored the warmth of him, the scent of male, warm despite the cold.

"True, but you've gained so much as an adult," he said. "Do you want to give all that back?"

"For my mother? In a heartbeat."

They stood in silence, an ease wrapping around her much like his arm. "I wouldn't go back," Grayson said so quietly she almost didn't hear. "I wouldn't be young again to save my life."

It had been horrible for him. Even she, so much younger than he was, had understood that. But just like her, he couldn't change the past. They could only move forward and make what they could of the future.

She savored the wonderful moment one last second, then she pushed away.

"Come on, Hawthorne, hop on that sled."

He straightened, coming back to himself. After a second he glanced at the red slats and grimaced, as if he wondered how he had gotten there. "Maybe another time."

He started away.

"Chicken."

His eyes narrowed and he turned to face her.

"Baaak, baaak," she taunted.

"I am not a child to be dared into action."

She folded her arms into wings and strutted in a circle.

"I am not a chicken."

"Of course not," she replied, pulling her knees up high beneath the long skirts of her gown and jutting her chin.

With a curse, he pointed the sled down the hill. "If I

break my neck, it is nothing worse than I deserve," he grumbled, then lowered himself to the wood.

But he was a big man, no longer a boy, and his knees popped up like tents.

Sophie's eyes went wide before she couldn't help herself. She burst out laughing until tears rolled down her cheeks.

Glowering, he leaped up. "This is ridiculous."

"Baaak."

"Then you get on it with me."

That shut her up.

"I hardly think I have anything to prove when it comes to having fun."

A smile pulled on his lips. "Baaack," he mimicked, the sound drawn out in a taunt.

"Damn you, Grayson Hawthorne." After which she marched over and plopped down.

Seconds later Grayson mounted behind her. The feel of his arms around her was like a shock. But the shock gave way to unbridled joy as they set off down the hill.

The late-winter sun had turned the new snow to crusty ice, and they slid with growing speed, her boa blowing out behind them like a feathered flag. Wind caught in her hat, tugging it from her head. For half a second they each tried to snag it, but it flipped on the breeze and tumbled away.

Sophie laughed, relishing the moment of unencumbered freedom. Then suddenly they hit a bump and left the ground, before hitting with a crash, the sled tumbling out of control.

Landing on her back with a thud, Sophie stared up at the brilliant blue sky, too surprised to move. Puffs of white clouds drifted by, and she thought she could lie there forever. The peace, the sense of life not pressing in on her. The lack of worry.

Only seconds later Grayson leaned over her, blocking out the clouds and sun.

"Sophie," he stated, his eyes dark with concern, his brow knitted. But the effect was lost with the snow that frosted both his hair and his expensive cashmere coat. He looked more like a snowman than a proper Victorian solicitor.

"Sophie, are you all right?" he demanded, his voice growing hoarse with worry.

With that she laughed. She couldn't help it.

Grayson froze, then slowly leaned back on his haunches.

"I'm fine, but I'm not sure you are."

"This isn't funny. You could have been killed."

She raised herself up on her elbows and smiled. "But I wasn't. Though if looks could kill . . ."

His scowl deepened, then he started to push up. But he stopped when she caught him in the side of the head with a snowball. She nearly laughed again at the look on his face. Startled, amazed. Then slowly his expression shifted, his eyes narrowing.

Sophie silently cursed herself, knowing she should have quit while she was ahead. Slowly he started toward her.

"Grayson," she warned, scooting back.

But he caught her ankle, his fingers surprisingly gentle, but still like manacles against her thick wool stockings.

"Now, Grayson, really." She forced a smile.

"Now, Grayson, what?" he asked, his voice a rumble of sound as he slowly pulled her to him.

"You are acting irresponsibly."

"Isn't that what you wanted?"

Yes. "It hardly matters what I want. I'm simply thinking of your reputation," she reasoned. "We are in a public place, after all."

"You weren't too concerned about reputations and public places when you forced me to ride down this hill."

"Forced? I doubt I could force you to do anything you didn't want to do."

He shrugged, a crook of his lips beginning to show. "True." His smile widened. "You badgered me into doing it."

"I do not badger."

But the words trailed off when she found herself so close to him they nearly touched.

He had let go of her ankle, and he reached up to brush his gloved fingers down her cheek. "I've missed you," he said.

Self-conscious, she snorted. "You weren't missing me last week when I was advising your client."

He chuckled, his fingers still brushing against her cheek. Her heart beat hard and she told herself to flee, but she couldn't. She stared at him, her mind racing.

"That was last week," he said, before his face darkened. "You have a way of making me forget." He hesitated. "But I've never forgotten the baskets you sent me when I lived in Cambridge."

She felt the red that flushed her cheeks. He hadn't forgotten. "God, I was so silly. Sending those things like you needed me to help you with food."

"I did."

The words made her heart snag in her chest.

"You saved me from needing to steal during those first months when I didn't have any money."

"I can't imagine you without money."

"Imagine it. You should have seen the place I lived in."

"Oh, but I did see where you lived!"

This time it was Grayson who went still. "What are you talking about?"

Instantly she cursed herself for mentioning her nocturnal trip to Cambridge all those years ago. She did her best not to think about the night she had slipped inside that dismal garret and found him. The beauty of him, the naked, hard planes of his body held in the hands of someone else.

Shocked and devastated, she had backed out silently. To make matters worse, the next morning it had been announced that the Grand Debut solo had gone to Megan Robertson.

Sophie had fled for Europe on the first ship out of Boston Harbor, the document signed giving her father control of her affairs.

"It was nothing," she said, brushing snow away from her skirts to keep her hands busy. "I just happened to be in the neighborhood once."

"Good God, when?" He leaned away.

"Before I left for Europe," she said casually. Though she didn't feel casual at all. If only he had been alone, life would have been so different.

"I always wondered why you didn't say good-bye."

His words surprised her, since she hadn't gone there intending to say good-bye. At the time she hadn't known how wrong things were about to go.

But suddenly he was smiling broadly, making him look for all the world like an errant schoolboy. She realized he was inordinately pleased.

"I knew I couldn't have been so wrong about you," he said.

His joy was contagious. And the nighttime visit was suddenly in the past. She felt his joy, felt that old bond, as if they were connected. And before she knew what she was doing, she pelted him with another handful of snow.

This time he wasn't surprised. He grabbed up some himself, and when she tried to scramble away, he pinned her in the snow, then stared at her. His smile faded, that deep intensity filling his features.

She could only stare back. Then he tossed the snow aside and lowered himself until they lay face-to-face.

"I'm going to kiss you, Sophie."

Tell him no. Get away. Run as fast as you can.

Her fingers curled in his snowy lapels as he leaned close.

The kiss was sweet and gentle, and her heart soared. His lips tasted hers, brushing back and forth. He pulled back and met her gaze.

"Sophie."

The implacably hard, ruthless man had faded away, making it more difficult than ever to resist him. Making her feel safe. He looked at her, his dark eyes suddenly aching, desperate. In that moment he looked vulnerable as she never would have imagined this man could be. His strength drew her and repelled her in turn. She couldn't afford a strong man who would try to dominate her life. But this vulnerability of the soul drew her in a way that made pushing away seem impossible.

Her heart tightened with something she couldn't name. Panic? Perhaps. But it felt like something more. As though she wanted to give in. Despite everything.

With a start she turned her head away, pressing her cheek against the snow. But he cradled her chin and pulled her back. She could see the passion in his eyes.

He didn't say a word, he only dipped his head again, and this time the kiss was a demand. He lowered himself with a groan, his arms wrapping her close. And she was lost.

He caught her lower lip between his teeth, gently, barely. Then he slanted his lips over hers. She hated the shiver of feeling that raced down her spine, much less did she understand it. She only knew that she wanted his touch, seemed to need it in some elemental way.

He groaned when her hands slipped up around his neck, and she felt the minute he started wanting her more. She relished the knowledge, though she knew she shouldn't.

Opening his coat, he pulled her inside. She could feel

his heat and the strength of him. His hands ran up her sides, his thumbs grazing her breasts beneath the bodice of her gown. The simple touch sent sensation jolting through her. But the jolt mixed with fear, and she stiffened.

Grayson sensed the change and he pulled back to look at her. She saw his eyes, his achingly dear face, mixed with that unfamiliar desperation she had never seen before—as though he needed her more than she understood, in ways she had never guessed.

"What is it?" she asked, reaching up and touching his cheek.

The darkness in his eyes flared, sharp, fierce. Yearning. But then he turned his head and kissed her palm, pulling one finger slowly into his mouth.

Darkness and fear were pushed to the murky edges of her consciousness as he pressed his lips to the tender spot beneath her ear. Everything was swept away then. Only Grayson was left, and the intensity he brought to life in her body. Tumbling in the snow on a winter day, in a town to which she had sworn she would never return.

He started to pull away. But she only held him close. "Don't leave me," she whispered.

He stared at her. "I won't."

He pulled her tightly into his arms, neither of them aware of the cold snow or the world around them as he rolled over, taking her with him until she was on top of him.

"Hey, mister, what are you doing with my sled?"

It took a second for the words to penetrate her senses. When they did, she craned her neck to find a little boy leaning over them, his eyes accusing.

Grayson froze, then pulled them both up from the snow with an athlete's swiftness.

The child's eyes went wide over the sheer size of Grayson and the clearly expensive clothes covered in snow.

"I was just borrowing your sled, young man. I appreciate the loan."

The boy stepped back as he glanced between Sophie and Grayson. "Sure, sure." Then he grabbed the rope and ran across the snow, the sled jerking back and forth as he went.

After a moment, Grayson turned back with a wry smile. "He won't be back for a while."

Sophie had to orient herself, trying to grasp what had happened before the child showed up. "If ever," she managed.

She headed for the street.

Grayson caught her arms and brought her into his embrace. His laughter trailed off to a satisfied smile. "You please me, Sophie Wentworth."

With one strong hand, he tilted her head and kissed her deeply before he set her back, then retrieved the box and headed for Swan's Grace.

Her knees felt weak, and as she watched him go, she wasn't sure if she wanted to chase after him or nail him in the back with another snowball for his arrogance. Please him, indeed.

Chapter Thirteen

"Have you set a date yet?"

"Good morning to you, too," Grayson said as he entered his father's study in Hawthorne House the following day, a late-winter storm brewing outside.

His boot heels rang against the hardwood floor before hitting carpet, the sound instantly muffled by thick-piled wool. It was Friday, nearly noon, and Grayson had spent the morning in court. He came by now after receiving word from his father to join him for lunch.

Bradford grumbled. "I don't need sarcasm. I get enough of that from Lucas."

"Have you talked to him then?" Grayson asked, surprised, as he folded his long frame into one of the wing-backed chairs in front of his father's desk.

Bradford finished up with a document in front of him, then looked up. "He just left."

Grayson sat forward. "Lucas was here?"

"He came by looking for you."

Bradford slammed his fist against the desktop, making pens and a letter opener jump. "He had the audacity to stand there and tell me he was having an outstanding year. Hell, with each day that passes, more and more people learn that my son owns a gentleman's club."

"I doubt everyone knows."

"Anyone who matters."

Grayson studied his father. Without warning he thought of Sophie telling him that he expected people to be like him or they were wrong. Was there another way to be in life? Was he turning out to be like his father, a man whom he could barely tolerate?

He had worked hard to live up to what was expected of him, then worked harder to fit back in to the world of his family until it became habit. Was there a place between wildness and strict propriety?

He cursed silently.

"Mother must have been thrilled to see Lucas," he said, forcibly changing the course of his thoughts.

"I didn't tell her he was here."

Grayson stared at his father incredulously, an incredulity born of frustration. "She'll be furious."

"Your mother does what I say," he replied angrily, tossing the pen into its holder, "and I won't allow her to see him until he straightens out his ways."

"Then she is likely never to see her youngest son again." His fingers curled around the chair arm as he fought the urge to pummel his own father. That wildness within him flared, wildness that had begun to rise back to the surface since Sophie arrived.

"Damn it, what did I do to deserve such a derelict of a son? An owner of a saloon, for God's sake."

"A gentleman's club, I believe it's called."

The older man focused on Grayson. " 'A rose by any other name is but a rose.' "

"Ah, I see you even make changes to Shakespeare. Does anyone please you?"

"What has gotten into you?" his father snapped.

Grayson wanted to know as well. Recently he found himself questioning aspects of life, things that had always been clear. Society. His place in it. What he wanted in a wife. Sophie made him second-guess himself.

His shoulders tensed. He felt restless, disturbed. And it was all because of Sophie. But he was long past the thought of setting the betrothal aside. Because he couldn't.

He could tell himself that she was a challenge; he could tell himself that they shared a past and their families knew each other. But the truth was that she filled him, filled the gaping loneliness that had never eased.

Up until now, he had moved through life with a minimum of disturbance, gliding through the events of each day with mastered cool control. In hindsight, he could hardly believe he had rolled around in the snow in a public place, much less with the woman he was to marry. And the fact of the matter was that his bride-to-be had rolled around with him, her fingers curling into his lapels, pulling him close. His body responded to the memory.

This time his curse was audible.

"What?" Bradford demanded.

"Nothing."

His father muttered. "The last thing I need is yet another ill-mannered son. That was the one thing you always had going for you, you were respectful."

Grayson's jaw went tight.

"The fact of the matter is," Bradford continued, "with Matthew gone, the future of the Hawthorne name is left up to you. Which brings me back to the original question. Have you set a date for the wedding?"

"Not yet."

Bradford's gray eyebrows peaked first, then he exploded. "Damn you! What is taking so long? Word has gotten out, no doubt from that blasted Patrice, that there will be a marriage. Before long, all of Boston will know you are supposed to marry Sophie. Beyond which, her father is my oldest friend and an important man in society. Everyone is expecting an announcement.

"After that messy debacle with Matthew," he continued, "not to mention the continual disgrace of Lucas, if this marriage isn't announced soon, everyone will assume Conrad backed out. And who could blame him?" He shook his head bitterly, then looked at Grayson, his gaze scathing. "Do your duty. Get this wedding over and done with. I won't stand for another scandal tainting the Hawthorne name. And a broken betrothal will give people just what they need to start talking. Again."

Bitter, futile anger swept through Grayson. "I will let you know when a date is set," he stated coolly.

Bradford stared at his son, then grumbled. Muttering, he glanced toward the door. "Luncheon should be ready."

If his mother hadn't promised to join them, Grayson would have left. But he saw so little of her. As a result, Grayson and his father strode into the dining room. But Emmaline was nowhere to be seen.

"Where's Mother?" Grayson asked as a footman handed him a large hand-painted china plate from the sideboard, which was covered with an assortment of luncheon fare.

Bradford served himself a heaping portion of mashed potatoes, roast, and gravy, then sat down and took a sip of mint tea from a tall crystal goblet. "She'll be here." He shot him a hard glance. "She wouldn't miss lunch with her precious eldest son."

Just then Emmaline walked into the dining room in a cloud of gossamer silk, her soft gray-white hair pulled up with pearls. Bradford hadn't waited before beginning his meal, and barely acknowledged his wife when she entered.

Grayson kissed her cheek and noticed instantly that something was different about her.

"Hello, dear," she chimed, her voice more like a school-girl's than that of the graceful matron he had known his whole life.

He studied her, wondering at the difference. For a brief moment he thought of the day he had been certain he had seen her in a hansom cab. But he disregarded the thought as soon as it entered his mind.

Bradford continued to eat, obscured behind one of the many newspapers that were delivered to him daily.

"You look beautiful, Mother," Grayson said, holding her chair.

"Oh, why, thank you," she said with a shy though pleased smile. But she bypassed the chair.

In a move that amazed Grayson, she walked directly to her husband, then hesitated only a moment before she took a deep breath and rested her delicate hand on the man's shoulders.

Bradford snapped his head up, the ironed sheets of newspaper crumpling when he lowered his meaty hands. "What are you doing, Mother?" he demanded.

Emmaline flinched, but she persevered. "It looks to be a dreary day. Winter can be so long in Boston."

Craning his substantial neck, Bradford peered up at her. "Are you feeling ill?"

"No, no, husband," Emmaline said with a nervous trill of laughter. "I was simply thinking that on a day such as this . . . perhaps we could have a picnic." Her features softened and she met his eyes. "In the sunroom. Like we used to."

"Like we used to? Good God, woman. When in blazes have we ever gone on a picnic?"

Her fingers tensed on the dark wool fabric covering his shoulders as she glanced furtively at Grayson, red staining her cheeks. "Before we were married, Bradford. Back when you were courting me."

Grumbling, he turned back to his paper. "Bah, we were young and full of nonsense."

"But I still feel young," she said, the words seeming like a whisper of thought.

"What?" he demanded.

"I said I still feel young," she repeated, her hands falling away, her smile forced.

"Well, you aren't, Mrs. Hawthorne," Bradford stated, "and you'd do well to remember that fact."

Grayson felt acutely uncomfortable to have witnessed such a scene.

Finally, when the interminable meal was over, Bradford headed for his study, Emmaline headed for the stairs, and Grayson headed for the door. But all three were deterred when the front bell rang.

Seconds later the butler stepped into the dining room.

"Mrs. Hawthorne," he announced in imperious tones. "A letter for you."

He extended a silver tray with a crisp white envelope on top with handsomely embossed initials in the seal. *R. S.*

His mother stared at the crisp white stationery as though it were lethal. But when Grayson started to take the missive for her, she leaped forward and snatched it away.

She fell back into her chair, fluttering nervously. "I'm sure it's nothing."

No one else said a word, and Bradford didn't appear to notice that his wife was suddenly acting strangely. He simply bade Grayson a tight good-day, then headed for the door.

As soon as his father was gone, his mother abruptly pushed up from her seat.

"I'm not feeling well. I need to lie down. You'll have to excuse me."

Then she strode from the parlor without looking back.

Emmaline hurried down Charles Street. She was half incensed, half trembling like a butterfly as she thought of the note.

Em,

> *Either you come to me, or I'll come to you. I'll be*
> *waiting at the Old Corner Book Store.*

> *Richard*

How dare he?

Regardless of her outrage, her heart sputtered at the thought of meeting him at the place where they had met before—so many years ago.

She had seen him several times at the sculpting house. Each time she had been polite, but distant, not allowing him to get close. But she had felt the attraction, the pull, heated and intense, as if she were no more than seventeen.

This morning, she had sought out her husband, hoping to find some way to fight off the feelings she felt returning for this other man. But Bradford had provided no reprieve.

Emmaline hailed a cab and sat impatiently as the carriage fought its way through the dense downtown traffic. She remembered the days as a girl when she had managed to sneak away from her lessons and go to the place where Emerson and Longfellow used to meet. The Old Corner Book Store had been a meeting ground for a considerable circle of authors. The place had also filled her with a need to do something more than sip tea and crochet altar cloths for the rest of her life.

For the first time, she had been exposed to ideas and thoughts so unlike any she had heard from her governess or other young ladies in the polite drawing rooms of Boston Brahmins, or the schoolrooms of the Boston well-to-do. It was at the bookstore that she had first gotten the idea to sculpt—to shape her vision, not with words as the writers did, but with her hands. To create. She had loved those long days of conversation, loved the sense of self she had found for the first time.

But that peace and satisfaction was short-lived, as she had been betrothed to Bradford Hawthorne already.

The two-seater snared in traffic, and they came to a complete halt. Shouts and curses rang out as each carriage and driver jockeyed for the right of way. Impatient, Emmaline grabbed the speaking tube and informed the driver that she was getting out.

Before he could say no, she hopped down onto the cobbled street, handed him some change from her reticule, then picked her way through the horses and carriages. She didn't stop until she arrived at the barn-roofed store at the corner of Washington and School streets. With her heart in her throat, she walked in through the door.

It took a moment for her eyes to adjust, but when they did it appeared that no one was there. She walked further inside, the smell of musty old books filling her with memories of another time. Closing her eyes, she felt the bittersweet memories of the past. How had things turned out so differently?

"Em?"

She blinked and saw him. So tall. Still so handsome, his graying hair only adding to his good looks.

"I'm glad you came."

Her spine stiffened and she held her beaded reticule close. "You didn't give me much choice."

Richard chuckled and tilted his head, conceding the point. "No, I didn't, did I?"

His frankness took the bite out of her anger, and she nearly smiled. *Dear, arrogant Richard.* He was still the same.

When they were young he had stepped into her life and all but demanded her attention. She had been engaged at the time, and she had ignored him for weeks. But he had persevered, coming to Andre's pottery house, talking to her while she worked, regardless of the fact that she hadn't responded. He had regaled her with stories of his life. Of his parents, whom he loved dearly. Of his siblings. And as the days mounted, she found she looked forward to his arrivals.

A month into his pursuit, things changed. His story that day had ceased midstream, then he had said, so simply, so purely, "I fell in love with you the first day I saw you."

Just that, on the heels of one of the many elaborate parties celebrating her betrothal, where Bradford had clearly been more interested in the other guests than in her. She had turned to look at Richard that day—and started down a path that had nearly destroyed her life.

The smells of clay and firing ovens seeped into her mind. And it was a moment before she remembered thirty-two years had passed.

Richard took her gloved hand, but she pulled it decidedly away.

"You're upset with me?" he said, his tone admonishing.

"Of course I'm upset. You had no right to put me in that kind of position. That note could have fallen into the wrong hands."

"You never did like ultimatums." He ran his finger along her sleeve. "And you always were beautiful when you were angry."

"Don't think you are going to charm your way out of this one. If my husband had read that note, there would be hell to pay."

Richard scowled. "Don't ruin a perfectly lovely day with talk of your husband. I try my best to forget that he exists."

"If you think for a second that I'm going to forget that fact, you are sadly mistaken."

"*Tsk,* such a waste. But enough about that. I have a surprise for you."

"I'm not interested in a surprise."

"Are you sure? Are you absolutely certain that you don't want to see the first-edition Jamesian sonnets I found?"

Her eyes widened.

"I thought that might pique your interest."

She closed her expression. "I am not interested in sonnets."

"The volume includes 'The Raven's Love Song.' "

The title was like a knife to her chest. "Why?" she asked after long seconds had passed. "Why are you doing this to me? I'm no longer a silly young girl with dreams of fancy in her head."

His face grew serious. "I am doing this because I have never forgotten you."

This time it was Emmaline's turn to scoff. "Tell some other gullible woman your stories. I'm no longer that naive."

"Oh, Em." He reached for her hand, and when she pulled away, he bowed his head and conceded. "I'm sorry if I hurt you."

"Sorry!"

The clerk had appeared from a back room and now sat on a tall stool behind a counter. The young man's head popped up at her outburst.

"Sorry?" she said in a hiss.

Richard took her elbow, and before she could think, he guided her out of the store and onto School Street.

"What are you doing?" she demanded when he steered her along, hardly noticing the cold.

"We need to talk, and we can't with so many people around."

"We have nothing to discuss. Furthermore, I have no intention of being alone with you."

He stopped and turned to face her, his features suddenly serious. He looked at her for an eternity, just looked, before he dropped his gaze and studied the hand that he held, stroking the gloved surface with his thumb. "I never forgot you. I tried. God, how I tried. You have to believe me." His thumb ceased its motion and he glanced at her. "I truly am sorry that I hurt you. But I had to go," he whispered. "I really did. And now that I've seen you again, I can't believe I ever left."

Her throat tightened.

"Just talk to me. I ask nothing else. We'll go to a café, or a park bench, or somewhere out of the way where people you know won't see you. But please, Emmaline, don't run away from me again."

She closed her eyes, feeling dizzy from the sound of kind words washing over her. How long had it been since someone had spoken to her as if they cared? How long had it been since someone sought her out? Her husband wanted no part of her.

Was this destined to happen, that Richard would return? Would everything have been different if Bradford had been kind to her this morning?

She didn't know; she only found herself walking by the man's side, the straining winter sun wrapping around them, tinting them in a muted gold, making her feel years younger. And she couldn't deny the bubble of excitement that sprang up inside her.

It was horrible and wrong. She knew that. And she told herself she would catch a hansom cab at the next block and return home. But block after block she allowed herself to be guided along, Richard's hand on her elbow, the touch proper, but not.

He was bold, his fingers on her sleeved arm as intimate as a passionate kiss.

"Tell me about your life," he said, steering her around a puddle in the street.

"There is nothing to tell."

"Of course there is. Tell me about your concerns." He looked down at her. "About your dreams."

And oddly she did. They walked for more blocks than she cared to count. With each step they moved farther away from downtown, farther away from the life she had been born to lead.

"You've certainly done your share of charity work, and clearly you love your sons," he said when her words trailed off. "But what have you done for yourself?"

The question startled her. She hadn't thought about doing anything for herself. Not in years, until she returned to her sculpting.

He must have sensed her confusion. "Tell me, Em, what do you like? What do you want just for you?"

She couldn't answer. Not because she didn't want to, but because she realized she didn't know how. She knew what her husband wanted, and her sons. She knew what her friends and the community wanted. She had spent a lifetime seeing to those needs. But in all that time no one had asked what she wanted, what she cared about. For the first time in years she felt pursued and desired, cherished and interesting. She put from her mind what she was doing, slipping away and meeting this man.

"You want to sculpt again," he said. "Why else would you have contacted Andre Springfield?" He glanced down at her. "Unless you contacted him because you really had hoped to see me."

She shot him a scowl. "I wanted to sculpt."

"Then why don't you go more often?"

"It is so hard to get away."

"You deserve that. You deserve to think about yourself for a change. And if it's hard to get away, why don't you have a tutor come into your home? Women of good families do it all the time."

A bud of excitement swelled inside her at the thought. Would Bradford allow it?

"I could come to your house and teach you."

She whirled to face him. "Good God, no!"

Richard chuckled, then feigned an innocent look. "Now, Emmaline, I wouldn't cause a single problem."

"Just as you didn't cause a single problem this morning by sending me that note."

He didn't even have the good grace to look abashed. He only chuckled more, his wide smile and white teeth flashing in the sunlight.

"All right, so perhaps it's not a good idea that I come to your house. But go to Andre's more often. Forget about me. Do this for yourself, for Emmaline Abbot."

"Hawthorne," she corrected sharply.

"Ah, but you were once Emmaline Abbot, a beautiful girl who loved as no other."

"Emmaline Abbot, the girl you left without so much as a word."

"You always were a stickler for details."

He propelled her along the walkway, stopping to buy her a hot cocoa and then a brown wrapper filled with candy.

"Do you remember the time we took the trolley out to Brookline?" he asked.

"No," she said too sharply.

"I think you do."

"Well, maybe a little." A reluctant smile surfaced.

"You danced around without your slippers, as I recall."

She felt the surge of color in her cheeks. "I was a foolish girl."

He turned her to face him, surprising her. "You were a beautiful young woman." His hands slid up her arms, his thumbs brushing her collarbones. "You still are beautiful," he added, his voice growing gruff. "Very beautiful." His gaze drifted to her lips.

Her breath caught and her eyes drifted low. How easy it would be to lean close, to feel a man's lips on hers. How many years had it been since she had been kissed? And was this desire that she felt really about Richard, or was it simply due to a lack of love?

"I thought of you often," he whispered, his hand drifting up to her face, cupping her cheek. "I wondered what you were doing with your life, if you were happy or sad." His thumbs brushed her skin. "I don't want to lose you again."

He leaned forward, and she knew that he was going to kiss her. Would it still feel the same? Would he still make her yearn?

Her heart pounded, but at the same time her mind cried out a frantic warning.

"Do you want me, too?" he asked.

With a cry, she jerked away. "No!"

He very gently took her hand. "Yes, I think you do. But not yet." He raised her hand and kissed her palm.

She pulled away as if she had been burned.

"I've waited this long, Emmaline, but I won't wait much longer."

She turned away sharply and lifted the hem of her gown. Then she rushed down the granite walk and never looked back.

The carriage stopped at the busy juncture of Atlantic Avenue and India Street. Earlier, just as Grayson had motioned to a hired hack, he had caught sight of a woman slipping out of Hawthorne House. A mix of foreboding and anger had sliced through him, and he had followed.

But following wasn't so easily done. He had lost the carriage in traffic soon after leaving Beacon Street. Grayson had told the driver to continue on, up and down the curving streets, with no success. But just when he would have given up, he was certain he saw her. With a man.

Stepping down from the carriage, Grayson tossed the driver a coin, then started walking. He crossed the street, weaving through drays and horses, craning his neck when a carriage blocked his view, gilt lettering announcing a delivery service.

Frustrated, he barely waited for the wagon to pass before he continued across the cobbles, and found that his mother was gone. Only the man remained.

Before Grayson reached the other side, he was blocked again, this time by a vendor pushing his cart. And when his path was free, the man was nowhere to be seen.

Blood rushed through Grayson's temples as he started to run. He darted from person to person, trying to see their faces, finally grabbing a man from behind.

"Hey, what are ya doing?" the tall stranger demanded.

Grayson realized in an instant that he had the wrong man, and he let go as if burned.

Out of breath, Grayson stood in the middle of the shipping district, an ominously dark sky brewing overhead, pedestrians parting as they walked around him, giving no notice to the fact that he stood there with eyes wild and wide open.

Both the man and his mother had disappeared like smoke in the wind, just as it started to rain.

Chapter Fourteen

Grayson arrived at Swan's Grace, his thoughts in turmoil. After leaving India Street, he had returned to Hawthorne House. At first there had been a flutter of confusion when he asked to see his mother.

"She's busy, Mr. Hawthorne," said a maid at the same time as another offered, "She's in bed, Mr. Hawthorne."

The women grew flustered. "We mean . . . we mean . . . your mother is busy going to bed."

His mood had darkened even more.

During the ride from the docks, he had convinced himself that he only thought he had seen his mother. He hadn't seen the woman's face. It could have been anyone. But with the flustered confusion, he had grimly concluded that it had been Emmaline Hawthorne.

His forbidding thoughts had been interrupted when a few minutes later she descended the stairs in "at home" attire, her lady's maid seeming to breathe a sigh of relief when she appeared. Without preamble, he had asked her if she had been to the harbor. She laughed, perhaps too loudly, then dismissed his claim that he had seen her, explaining that she had been home all day.

Was that the truth? Why would she lie? And if she hadn't been home all day, why would his mother, a woman beyond reproach, meet a man not her husband on a bad side of town?

Grayson slammed the front door of Swan's Grace shut, his boot heels ringing on the foyer floor. At the sound, Sophie's dog appeared around the corner, stretching as if she had been asleep. "Sophie," he called out.

He needed to see her, like a palliative to his racing thoughts. He didn't like thinking about his feelings for Sophie. The desire, intense and raging, was like nothing he had ever experienced before, as if he couldn't survive without her. This woman was driving him nearly as insane as his mother was.

"Sophie," he demanded, his voice echoing against the marble and high ceilings.

But no one came. The house appeared to be empty except for the dog. He swore softly.

He had work to do, and he told himself to go to his office, but he couldn't still his mind. Grayson strode from room to room, Sophie's pet hobbling along at his side, limping awkwardly. Grayson searched but found nobody. Sophie clearly wasn't at home.

He had an important social engagement he needed to attend that evening, and his closet at the hotel was empty, the clothes that had accumulated in a pile beside the wardrobe finally taken to a washerwoman to be cleaned. But he had plenty of clothes upstairs.

As he headed back to the foyer, the dog continued to follow along. Grayson stopped and looked down. The dog looked back. They were a sight. He knew it. Two pathetic, mismatched souls.

"Go on," he said, motioning toward the kitchen.

The dog merely cocked her head, then followed after him as he continued on.

Grayson started up the stairs, but was stopped by a struggling sound. Glancing back, he saw the dog trying to make it up the stairs. Trying. Wishing. Needing to be saved.

An ache swelled inside Grayson and he grumbled. But

when the dog stopped, stood there panting, and looked up at him with those big brown eyes, Grayson could only hang his head and curse again, then he marched down the steps.

"You are as maddening as Sophie," he said more harshly than he felt. Then he scooped up the mutt and started back up the stairs, muttering the whole way.

Not three steps up, however, the knocker announced someone's arrival. He marched back down, set the dog carefully on the floor, then pulled the front door open at the very moment the knocker sounded again.

"Well, well, well," a man said, "have you given up the law and become a butler?"

A reluctant smile curved Grayson's lips. "Lucas," he said, reaching out to shake his youngest brother's hand.

Lucas smiled, avoided his hand, and pulled him into a firm, nearly bone-crushing embrace.

"How have you been?" Grayson asked, standing back to look at Lucas. "More to the point, where have you been? I haven't seen you in ages."

"Here and there." Lucas shrugged.

"Come in."

"I can't stay. I'm in a hurry."

Lucas Hawthorne was a tall man, as tall as Grayson, with the same dark hair and broad build. The biggest difference was in their eyes. Lucas's were startlingly blue, just like their father's.

Grayson was striking, but Lucas looked like the rake he was, handsome, with a devilish smile pulling at his lips.

He owned the infamous Nightingale's Gate, Boston's very own exclusive gentleman's club. Dancing, drinking, gambling, all in the finest surroundings. To gain entrance to the elegant confines, a man had to have money, and lots of it. Grayson knew that men wanted to gain admittance in droves.

The youngest Hawthorne was gaining a reputation as much for Nightingale's Gate as for the fact that he was the errant son of the blue-blooded Hawthorne clan. Rarely did a family that dripped such respectability have a son who owned an infamous establishment. Or if they did have such a relative, they kept the unfortunate fact concealed.

And that was just what Bradford Hawthorne had tried to do, only to be thwarted by his youngest offspring, who took great pleasure in letting all the world know about the life he led. Bradford hated him for that as much as anything. But everyone knew the sentiment was returned, in spades.

Grayson knew all this, as well. He had tried to bring the two men together, had tried to get them to talk. But each was as stubborn and tight-lipped about what had caused the rift as the other.

Lucas pulled out a beautifully wrought engraved invitation on thick vellum. The most proper of Boston matriarchs couldn't have done better. "This is for you."

Grayson read it quickly. "A masquerade," he stated, shaking his head, "at Nightingale's Gate." His countenance grew stern. "Is this wise?"

"Come on, big brother," Lucas cajoled, amused when he should have been chastened. "You'll be surprised to find how many people you know attend my annual event."

"Sounds like the perfect opportunity for the Boston police to fill their jail cells."

Lucas only laughed, then glanced down. "Who's this?" he asked, clearly surprised at the sight of the dog leaning up against Grayson's perfectly creased flannel pant leg.

At the sight of Sophie's pet, Grayson looked as surprised as his brother. "A new addition to the household," he grumbled.

The dog wagged her tail and panted.

Lucas dropped to his haunches and ran his fingers through the scattered tufts of fur. "You look like you've been around the block a time or two, and met up with some mean sorts, my friend."

"The dog was all but dead when Sophie found her," Grayson explained, remembering the feel of those shuddering breaths against his chest, hardly aware that he spoke.

Lucas looked confused as he straightened. "Sophie?"

Grayson refocused his attention. "Yes, Sophie. She's back."

"Little Sophie Wentworth. And Sophie has a dog." Lucas laughed out loud, then studied his brother. "Actually, you look fit to be tied. Don't tell me it's because of a dog."

"If you really must know, it's Sophie who is driving me to distraction. But that's beside the point."

Lucas laughed harder at this. "Sophie always did have the ability to stir things up. God, I haven't seen her in ages. Does she look the same? Hair wild with tangles, and eyes much too big for her face? And those ruffles. Tell me she doesn't still wear so many ruffles that she looks like a sheep."

Grayson's lips quirked fondly. "No, she hardly looks like a sheep. She's grown into a beautiful woman."

"I'd like to see her."

"Unless you're willing to come by for dinner sometime, I don't see the opportunity arising. You certainly won't see her at Nightingale's Gate."

Lucas laughed. "Why not? Bring her to the masquerade tonight. No one will know it's you."

"No one will know it's me because it won't be."

Lucas laughed out loud. "One of these days I'm going to get you there, big brother."

After Lucas left, Grayson stood in the doorway for several minutes until he heard the dog whimpering at his side. Without thinking, he tossed the invitation on the foyer table, then lowered himself to his haunches. "What is it, girl?"

The dog whimpered and burrowed her head against Grayson's thigh. Despite himself, he chuckled and ruffled the dog's fur. "You want some attention, do you? Unfortunately I've got to run. But first I need a suit."

He started for the steps, but this time when the dog started to follow, Grayson held his hand out and said, "Stay." And the dog did.

"You clearly were trained by someone, my friend. But by whom? Do you have a family who is looking for you?"

The dog cocked her head, then sank down onto the tile floor as Grayson headed up the stairs.

Sophie returned, slipping inside the house just before it started to rain. Her cheeks were pink and her hands ached from the cold. She'd have to warm them thoroughly before she could play.

As she pulled off her hat, she was surprised to find Sweetie lying patiently in the foyer. Sweetie, as she had begun to call the dear animal, had improved greatly, but she still had a difficult time.

A second set of notices for the animal had been posted, and not a single person had shown up to lay claim. Though she had promised herself she wouldn't become attached, she knew she had. Each night Sweetie slept in her room, and each morning the dog followed her downstairs to hear her practice. Like a shadow. Like a constant. Like someone who really loved her, for herself, regardless of how she looked or how she played.

Sophie closed her eyes and didn't understand the tears that burned, the sense of love and healing, of hope. Never in her life had she had something of her own to love. Her cello didn't count, because an instrument couldn't love her back. And while she loved her entourage, she knew it wasn't the same. They liked her, had come to care for her, perhaps. But the fact was that the minute she couldn't pay their salaries, her *friends* would be gone.

"Have you been waiting for me this whole time?" she asked, setting her hat aside.

Sweetie rolled over to be petted. Sophie laughed and obliged. "Just for a bit, then I really, really have to practice." For days she had played very little. It was as if she could hardly make the bow move over the strings. Every time she launched into *The Waltz of Swans* or even *The Love Nest* her hand wavered, and the next thing she knew she was daydreaming about performing Bach.

Straightening abruptly, she peeled off her coat and tossed it aside, then tugged her gloves from her hands and set them on the foyer table. A thick invitation caught her attention.

The weather was getting worse, and she heard the rain start to pour down from the pewter gray sky. Sophie wished she had gone with her friends to New York after all. Money be damned.

She hated the rain. Always had.

She needed something to do—besides attempt to practice.

With a flicker of excitement, she opened the envelope and found an invitation to a masquerade ball at a place called Nightingale's Gate. Most every day she received invitations to some event or another. But nothing sounded as deliciously decadent as a masquerade ball. Just the thing to brighten her mood.

A discreet knock sounded at the front door. She started to ignore it, though she quickly realized that it could prove to be a much needed interruption. Perhaps one of Grayson's clients. A suitor. Maybe even an old friend. Anyone would do just then.

But when she pulled open the door, Sweetie limping along at her side, she stopped cold. A well-dressed man and a little boy stood at the threshold. For half a second their faces were serious, but in the next, the boy cried out and fell to his knees. The dog whimpered and hobbled forward, straight into the boy's arms.

"Goldie!" the boy cheered, before he sobered and took in the animal. "What happened to you?"

Sophie could hardly think, much less speak. And the quaking inside her started again.

The little boy buried his face in Sweetie's neck, and Sophie could feel his tears and her own.

"Oh, Goldie," he cried, his voice muffled.

"Do you know this dog?" she asked needlessly.

The man stepped forward and extended his hand. "I am Norville Green. This is my son, Danny, and we saw your notice posted about Goldie. Dear God, what happened to her?"

"I'm not sure," she barely managed. "She was hurt when I found her a few houses away from here."

The man shook his head. "We were having a picnic in the park when she ran off chasing a squirrel. When she didn't return we searched for hours. My son has been despondent ever since." He knelt down before Sweetie. "From the looks of her, it's amazing that she survived." He glanced up. "How can we thank you for caring for her?"

The pounding tightened her throat. Silly, she told herself, it was only a dog. Not her dog. She had told herself that again and again.

"No need to thank me. I'm just glad to see that Sweet— I mean, Goldie, has someone to love her and care for her."

Reluctant to let her go, but knowing she could do nothing else, she lowered herself to her knees. Sweetie seemed torn between the little boy and her, going back and forth as best as she could.

Sophie made it easier. She gave the dog a quick, hard hug, then pushed up. "Well, I'm glad you found her. Perhaps you'll come by once in a while."

The door shut behind them, and Sophie leaned back against the hard wood, feeling it press along her spine. She squeezed her eyes tightly shut. Not knowing what else to do, she walked inside Grayson's office and sat in his chair, pressing against the leather, imagining it was him.

She felt caged inside by more than rain. Even the thought of a gala masquerade party didn't ease her mind. She felt alone, giving her too much time to think.

What was she doing?

Did she really want to go back to the life she was leading in Europe?

She gave a hard shake of her head. Europe had been good to her. Loving her. Wanting her in a way that she had never been wanted before.

Though Boston seemed to want her now. The callers. The flowers. The endless invitations. Didn't they?

She cursed the insecurity, cursed the fact that mere weeks in this town could make her feel like time had stopped, then circled back to when she was different from everyone else—hearing music in her head, hearing it once and knowing it by heart, her mother telling her she was special. Everyone else hating her because of it. The desire to play with other children, ordinary children's games, but her mother saying she might hurt her hands.

How many times had she cursed the fact that she was a prodigy, wishing she were like every other child she met? But even she understood that she was different. She might have longed for a doll, but she hadn't had any interest in playing with one. Hopscotch, checkers, jacks? No interest. Chess? Maybe. But music? Notes and measures, rests and interpretations? All of these had fascinated her for as long as she could remember. And because of that, the other children had thought her strange.

She closed her eyes against the memories. But one memory wouldn't be pushed away. Being four years old and Grayson, older than his years, defending her, then bending down on his knee and brushing her tears away, kissing her nose, then ruffling her hair when he sent her on her way. She had fallen in love with him that very moment, then had followed him around every chance she got.

A click in the distance gained her attention. When she glanced out of the office, she caught sight of Grayson. He had opened the front door and stood there looking out into the rain, clothes of some kind held forgotten in his hand.

Without warning she remembered the night she had found him with another woman. Seeing him there, naked. Was he still so hard and strong? she wondered. Would she ever touch him so intimately?

The thoughts shot through her mind before she could stop them as she took in the commanding planes of this handsome man. As usual, he wore a dark suit with a crisp white collar attached to his creaseless white shirt. But today she could just make out a paisley waistcoat, a hint that there was more to him than his austere exterior.

He didn't appear to know she was there. He stared out into the dreary day, much as she had earlier. His expression was different now, disturbed somehow. The arrogance was gone, though he looked every bit as commanding. Even lost in thought he seemed a force to be reckoned with.

Carefully she tried to slip away.

"I know you're there."

"You have eyes in the back of your head, do you?"

"More like those shoes of yours aren't meant for stealth."

She looked down at her Louis mules with two-inch, fashionably curved heels. "So they aren't."

Grayson turned slowly from the door, then leaned back against the casing as he took Sophie in. As always, her beauty hit him hard, her fiery soul burning beneath.

"I have someone coming to fix the lock," he said.

She looked confused.

"You know, the lock Henry broke when breaking into the house."

She only shrugged. "Who's going to break in and steal your belongings?"

He took in the length of her, slowly. "It's not my papers and files that worry me."

He would have sworn she blushed. But if she did, she quickly recovered and sauntered into the foyer.

"I'm bored," she stated. "Why don't you take me out for tea? Or better yet, take me dancing."

He would have smiled, but thoughts of his mother and Lucas concerned him.

"I'm not in the mood for tea," Grayson said, forcing his family from his mind. "And I doubt there is a dance hall in Boston open at this hour, not that I would take you to one if there were," he stated, and even he could hear the sharpness in his tone.

She raised a brow. "*Tsk, tsk.* You're upset. Is my invitation too forward? Should my daddy have called your daddy to see if you could come out to play?"

A smile sprang to his lips, and he set his suit aside and walked toward her. For every step he took, she took another one backward.

"We can play, if you'd like," he offered, one dark brow tilting devilishly. "Though I'm not sure we should ask your daddy."

There was no mistaking the red that surged in her cheeks this time.

"Shouldn't there be clients here?" she demanded.

He stopped and groaned. "Don't tell me you've forgotten to tell me about another appointment."

"I haven't forgotten anything," she answered. "Though I have been taking messages for you all week."

Several steps later, she ended up behind his desk, he in front of it.

"You mean you've started answering the door?" he asked.

She sliced him a dry look. "How could I help it? It got easier to answer the knocking than to ignore it. People can be persistent. In fact, I think you're more sought after now than ever before." She leaned forward and lowered her voice. "I think I'm a draw. And clearly I have a knack for this. Take that nice Mr. Cardwell as an example. You remember him, don't you? I advised him on his divorcement."

"Yes, I remember. Did he come by to say he is suing me for malpractice?"

She scoffed. "No. He patched up his differences with his wife, and his marriage is once again bliss—based on my advice. Proof that people don't really want stodgy, pompous, boring types after all."

"You think they'd rather I be wild and outrageous, like you?"

She shrugged. "I think they'd settle for an occasional smile."

His face darkened, all teasing and lightness gone, the awful, troubled look she had noticed when she first walked into the room resurfacing.

She studied him, then couldn't help the kind smile that pulled at her lips. "But he greatly appreciated your advice, as well. You are the most highly regarded lawyer in Boston."

"He said that?"

Her nose wrinkled. "Well, no, but you looked like you needed some kind words."

He looked at her in disbelief and shook his head.

So much for cheering him up.

"So tell me," she said, her palms flat on the blotter, her eyes sparkling mischievously, "what's the occasion?" She gestured toward his colorful waistcoat. "Do you have a date?"

"I hardly think a date is appropriate, given that I'm betrothed to you." He came around the desk.

"So you keep saying." She gave an unladylike snort.

"Then why are you at Swan's Grace now? You don't appear to have any appointments. And you usually don't show up here this late in the day." Her lips tilted. "Isn't it time for you to do something boring, like take a nap?"

"If you'd like, we could go upstairs and crawl into bed together. Though I'm not sure I want to nap."

Sophie laughed appreciatively. "You really are getting good at this."

"I've resigned myself to long years of practice from now until death us do part. Speaking of which, we have to set the date for our wedding."

"I thought you said you were going to woo me."

"I've tried."

"If that was wooing, I'd hate to see what not wooing is." She waved her hand, dismissing him as if she didn't believe for a second that he would marry her.

"You *will* be my wife, Sophie."

"Really?" she asked, her voice suddenly low and smooth like molasses.

Instantly Grayson was suspicious.

"Do you mean to tell me that you want a wife who wears provocative clothes?" She walked around the desk to stand before him, her head tilting back to look him in the eyes. Then she slipped her hands under his lapels and rested her palms on his waistcoat. "A wife who wears feather boas?" She smiled provocatively, then, with a flick of her wrist, slid the feathers free and wrapped them around his neck.

The motion caught them both by surprise. Suddenly, they were close. Sophie didn't like the change at all—Grayson standing so near, the desk behind her, the tables turned, giving him the advantage.

"Are you flirting with me, Sophie?"

She scoffed, though her voice was shaky. "No, I was just playing."

She tried to step away, needing to put distance between

them, leaving the boa around his neck. But he took hold of one end and pulled it off, then looped it around her gently, pulling her back.

"I don't play games, Sophie. Nor do I break promises. And I promised your father I would marry you."

"I, on the other hand, have no such qualms about breaking promises." She tried stepping aside. "I am a master of crossed fingers and expedient prevarications. Besides, I didn't promise anyone anything."

"But your father did, on your behalf."

"You just can't let that go, can you?" she griped.

The boa held her there as securely as a rope. Her flash of good humor fled, and she felt her frustration from earlier return. "Damn it, why do you want to marry me? Give me one good reason. We used to be good friends," she said after long moments, looking away. "Why ruin that?"

"I'm not interested in being your friend, love." He touched her chin, his fingers a gentle caress as he forced her to meet his gaze. "I want to be your husband."

"I've already told you, Mr. Hawthorne," she said, enunciating each word, "I'm not going to marry. I will not be any man's possession."

His eyes narrowed. "A man doesn't own a woman."

"Perhaps not literally. But look at Patrice."

"She is certainly not a possession," he insisted. "She is a wife. The mistress of a man's home. Mother to his children."

"*His* home. *His* children. A woman is told what she can or can't do." She hesitated, then forged ahead, heedless of dangerous territory. She had gone too far to turn back. "Look at your mother."

She felt the tension snake through his body.

"My parents' relationship is like any other. That is what marriage is."

"But it shouldn't be!"

"Why?" A look came into his eyes. "Tell me why," he demanded, his voice suddenly intense, as if he wanted to believe there could be something different.

But she had no profound explanation, no example of anything other than what he had described. "It's just not fair that a woman is forced to do a man's bidding," she said with a sigh, not knowing what else to say.

Grayson's face grew grim, and she thought for a moment that he was disappointed that she didn't have a better explanation. "If I've learned anything in this world," he said, "it's that life isn't fair. The sooner you understand that, the easier it will be for you."

"Accepting that won't make me any better at marriage. I won't make a good wife, no matter what you think."

"That's nonsense."

"You need someone who will sit at home and act like a proper lady."

"You wouldn't have to sit home, Sophie. And how hard can it be to act proper?"

Her throat tightened. He didn't understand. Not her. Not her life.

"This is a silly conversation," she said at length, forcing a smile as she swallowed back the lump in her throat.

He tucked a wayward strand of hair behind her ear.

"You're just nervous. You will be a wonderful wife, and a wonderful mother. I've seen that with how you deal with the dog." He glanced at the foyer, then his brow furrowed. "Speaking of dogs, where is yours?"

"Gone." She bit her lip to keep it steady. Suddenly the day pressed in on her in a way that seemed unbearable. She hated the burning in her eyes and the tightness in her throat, could hardly explain to herself why she felt so lost. "Her owner showed up a few minutes ago."

He sighed and wrapped her in his arms. "Why didn't you tell me?" he said, his voice so gentle it made her ache.

"It's just a dog." She bit her lower lip. "I had started to call her Sweetie."

"The perfect name for a dog you loved." He brushed his lips against her forehead. "I'm sorry, Sophie. If you want, we'll get a new one."

"I don't want a new dog! And I'm fine, completely fine." She swallowed hard.

He kissed her eyelids, then pulled her head beneath his chin. "You're not fine. You'll never forget Sweetie. And she'll never forget you."

A second passed. "Do you think?" she asked softly.

"You, Sophie Wentworth, are unforgettable." He kissed the top of her head. "There is a party I am attending at a client's house. Come with me. Then tonight we will drink a toast to Sweetie."

"Sorry, I already have plans."

"What plans?"

Her mind raced to come up with something. The last thing she needed to do was go anywhere with Grayson. Then it came to her. "I have an invitation to attend a party of my own." The masquerade.

"No doubt from one of your slew of admirers," he grumbled.

She smiled. "No doubt."

"Cancel," he stated autocratically, then headed for the door. "I'll return for you at eight."

Chapter Fifteen

It was nearly eight that night, and soon Grayson would be arriving at Swan's Grace to escort Sophie to his party. Only Sophie wouldn't be there to greet him.

Masked and costumed for the masquerade ball, she stood at the ornately gated entrance that led to the establishment called Nightingale's Gate.

It felt deliciously decadent, and her mood began to brighten.

The rain had stopped, but the night was still cold and the sky was still ominous. Sophie wrapped her black satin cape around herself more tightly.

Despite the opulent walkway, the town house itself looked respectable and unassuming. Though based on the attendees who had passed by her so far, she surmised that this was not a party meant for proper Boston matrons seeking a bit of innocent costumed fun.

Of course, that gave it all the more appeal.

She could just imagine the scowl on Grayson's face if he found out she had attended. After a long, bad day, it was that thought more than her desire to mingle with this crowd which sealed her fate.

Because of that, any chance of her doing the smart thing and returning to Swan's Grace was banished.

Securing her demimask on her face and easing her knotted grip on the long cape and hood, Sophie gathered her skirts and was swept up in the crush of guests entering the receiving room of Nightingale's Gate.

Once she was inside, her slowly budding delight grew. While the anteroom looked circumspect and respectable, the receiving room was anything but. The paintings alone would make a grown man blush.

And the women. By now they had shed their wraps, revealing gowns that left little to the imagination. With her long, hooded cape that she refused to relinquish, Sophie was by far the most modestly dressed woman in attendance. Wouldn't Henry and Deandra have a laugh over that fact, had they been there.

"Your invitation please."

A deep voice sounded at her side. When she turned, she found a man dressed like a velvet-clad courtier, his gloved hand extended. She hadn't been able to find the invitation anywhere when she looked for it as she was leaving. No telling where she had set it.

Hoping for the best, she glanced at the man's extended hand, then offered her own in greeting and smiled.

The man, however, was not amused. "Your invitation," he reiterated.

Obviously the polite, amusing route wasn't going to work. So she pulled back her shoulders, raised her chin, looked down her nose, and said, "I didn't bring it."

He only smiled blandly, and said, "Then you don't get in." He turned to a couple who entered behind her.

The thought of going home—or worse yet, going to Grayson's proper party—pushed her on. "I was invited," she stated imperiously. She had been, though by whom she had no idea.

For the first time the man seemed uncertain, and he peered at her more closely. But before he could speak, another man stepped forward.

At the sight, Sophie's heart slowed. The man wore a

black cape and black half mask, looking for all the world like Lucifer from the underworld—the devil himself in unrelieved black. But it wasn't his clothes that startled her. It was his eyes, deep blue, peering out at the world from beneath the mask, spoiling his underworld image.

She felt a moment of unbalance, as if she should know this man.

"Is there a problem here?" he asked politely.

His voice melted over her, familiar somehow, but she couldn't imagine how she would know him.

"Madam," he repeated, "is there a problem?"

Sophie mentally shook herself. "My question exactly," she stated crisply.

The courtier-thug shifted his weight from foot to foot. "She doesn't have a . . . I wasn't sure. . . ." Then he stopped.

The newly arrived man glanced at Sophie, a smile pulling at the full lips that were revealed from beneath his mask. "You seem to have taken the words right out of his mouth. No small feat considering Brutus is not a man to deal with lightly. But surely you understand that his . . . concern is derived from the fact that at a party such as this—"

"A party that I was invited to," she interjected, her tone bold and confident. "Though little did I know I would be treated like a common criminal upon arriving."

At this Lucifer threw back his head and laughed out loud. "A woman after my own heart," he said, his blue eyes glittering appreciatively. "Not to worry, Brutus. I'll see to our guest."

Indeed, the devil man escorted Sophie into the grand ballroom. An orchestra played at the front of the room, the music resounding off the walls, washing over her—a seductive Strauss waltz called "Wine, Women, and Song." A good choice considering the event. Men in masks, women with covered faces and dazzling headdresses.

The man handed her a glass of champagne that seemed to appear from nowhere.

"Lovely," she said as she took the shallow crystal, then sipped.

The man eyed her speculatively, his eyes studying her.

"Tell me," he said, "do I know you?"

"No, never met." *Drat.* She glanced at him furtively, wondering if perhaps they had.

"You seem familiar."

"Since I'm wearing a mask," she answered, "how could that be? Given your disguise, I'm sure I wouldn't recognize you if you sat next to me in the Public Gardens tomorrow."

Lucifer placed his hand over his heart and chuckled. "You wound me deeply, madam. Am I so forgettable? I know I would never forget someone as lovely as you."

Sophie smiled, eyeing him over the rim of her glass, welcoming the velvet feel of champagne slipping through her limbs.

"But enough of that," he said. "I agree you shall remain anonymous. At least for now. I have always loved a mystery."

She declined another glass of champagne. One was her limit. Then Lucifer pulled her into a dance. He led her around the hardwood floor as if they moved in a dream. He held her close, too close, and she had the sudden thought of Grayson. Grayson held her like this. Grayson's voice rumbled the same way. Somehow this devilish man reminded her of a man who wouldn't be caught dead in a place like Nightingale's Gate.

Sophie chuckled at the thought.

"What is so funny?" her host asked, whispering against her ear.

"You remind me of a man I know who is the very picture of propriety."

"How so?" he demanded, his voice rumbling in his

chest as he leaned forward to brush his lips boldly across her neck.

She pushed back sharply, but he held her secure. She met his eyes. This man was not like most men she knew. He was like Grayson, not easily controlled with sultry looks and bold words.

She looked at him as he expertly turned her around the floor, her heart pounding harder. "Just like that. The way you . . . kissed me. The way you hold me, the way you talk. It makes you seem so like Gray—" She cut herself off. "It makes you seem like the other man."

She would have sworn the devil man stiffened. But when she looked more closely, a smile still pulled at his lips.

Seconds later the waltz ended and he guided her to the side. She told herself that the hand which led her was not as suddenly forceful as it seemed, and that his laughter had not grown forbiddingly dangerous.

A footman brought her yet another glass of champagne, and this time she took it gratefully. When she turned back, her host was deep in conversation with the courtier from the door. When they broke apart, Brutus hurried from the room.

Sophie started to excuse herself, suddenly thinking better of spending too much time with the likes of Lucifer, but just then a new man with a patch over his eye and an odd, hooked contraption covering his hand approached.

"Might I have this dance?" Captain Hook asked.

But it was the devil who answered. "No," he said curtly, then he pulled her back onto the dance floor, the crystal chandelier glistening overhead.

Grayson needed a woman.

He needed to sink his flesh between the legs of a willing female and purge all thought from his mind. But that was the problem. The only woman he wanted was the very woman who was making him lose his mind.

Sophie.

He stood in the foyer of Swan's Grace and cursed the fact that it was empty. He had arrived early with a locksmith. It was long past time the broken lock was fixed. She had insisted that she would see to it, each time telling him someone was on their way. But still the lock remained broken, allowing anyone who dared to slip inside.

Grayson paced as the man finished his repair, but by the time it was done, the house was still empty. No doubt she wasn't there just to make him crazy.

His jaw cemented. *Damn Sophie and her fathomless eyes.*

Earlier he had considered taking a mistress to ease his need. Someone who understood. No strings, no ties.

His face grew grim. Everything had strings; nothing came without a price. Sophie, he decided, was costing him his sanity. And he hadn't even married her yet.

He bit back a curse. But soon she'd be his wife.

Not soon enough—or too soon?

He no longer knew.

"Mr. Hawthorne."

Grayson turned to find Lucas's right-hand man standing in the doorway. He couldn't have been more surprised to find the burly man standing in the foyer of Swan's Grace. Instantly he grew concerned. "What is it, Brutus?"

"Your brother would like to see you, sir."

"Tonight? Can't it wait?"

Brutus hesitated. "It's ... an emergency. At Nightingale's Gate."

Nightingale's Gate was brightly lit when Grayson strode into the main ballroom wearing the long cape and half mask Brutus had provided at the door.

"Your brother insisted," Brutus had said.

"There you are," Lucas said heartily, clamping his hand on Grayson's shoulder.

"What's wrong?"

"Nothing's wrong," the younger man replied, though his smile was devilish. "I just hated to think you hadn't accepted my invitation."

Grayson eyed his brother closely. He wasn't sure if he should be relieved that nothing was wrong or perturbed at being dragged here for no reason. "I already have plans."

"Do you really?"

"I am escorting Sophie to the Tisdales' ball this evening."

"Ah, yes, Sophie. You mentioned she was back."

"What is this about, Lucas?"

The younger man chuckled. "Nothing, nothing. But tell me, how is your little Sophie doing?" Lucas asked unexpectedly.

Grayson glanced at him in question, suddenly suspicious. "Why do you ask?"

Lucas shrugged. "Just wondering. Earlier, you were a bit . . . out of sorts over her. Are you sure you're not really in love, big brother?"

Grayson couldn't have been more startled if he tried. Sophie had asked the same question. As if she believed the sentiment truly possible. Love? Did he love Sophie? Of course not. She would be his wife. A woman to have his children, make his home.

He tamped down the surge of unexpected emotion he couldn't afford, and drew his features into a sharp blank, then shot Lucas a cold look. "Getting fanciful in your old age, are you? I would think you'd be the last person to think about love—or even believe it was possible. And if you did think love possible, surely you don't think the sentiment worthwhile. Mother's love for our father certainly hasn't served her well."

Lucas was quiet for a moment. "I'm not so sure she ever loved him."

Grayson glanced at Lucas, wondering what he meant,

before turning back to the crowd. "Love certainly is not an issue between Sophie and myself." He said the words with more force than necessary, and Lucas looked at him with a raised brow. But he wasn't about to admit the need he felt for his betrothed, the weakness. He had been raised to be strong. Hawthornes weren't weak.

Finally Lucas shrugged before he turned as well to gaze out across the crowded room. "You know," Lucas said, clasping his hands behind his back, "it seems as though I heard something about her a while back."

The brothers stood side by side.

"You probably heard about the article that ran in *The Century* magazine."

"Perhaps, though I'm not sure that's what it was. But it will come to me. Nothing escapes my attention."

Grayson hated those bits and pieces of proof that Lucas was tied up in things he shouldn't be. But Lucas was a grown man, and didn't listen to brotherly advice.

As to Sophie, no doubt what Lucas had really heard was that she could bring a grown man to his knees, Grayson thought dismally. But he didn't say that. "No telling what you heard."

"Hmmm," Lucas said in contemplation. "But enough of that for now. Join me for a game of cards."

"No, thanks. If there is no emergency, I'll be going."

But when he started to veer in the opposite direction, Lucas caught his arm.

"This way, big brother. There's someone I want you to see."

Grayson looked at Lucas oddly, but when he started to pull away, he noticed a woman at a gaming table. A dazzling woman of startling seduction.

Four men and the one woman circled the dealer. The men acknowledged his approach first. The woman was the last to turn. When Grayson's gaze met hers, each of them froze.

Grayson could tell little about her face, which was covered by a demimask and shadowed beneath her hood. But her body was another matter altogether. With her cape flipped back over her shoulders, her form was fully revealed—and even more alluring than from afar. His heated gaze raked over her.

He thought she gasped at his bold appraisal, but when he looked closer, he could make out little more than the glittering eyes beneath her mask. Golden brown and daring.

White-hot desire stabbed through him, and he cursed when he remembered the invitation had been on the entry hall table while he had gone upstairs to retrieve his clothes. She really was a maddening little baggage.

Once Sophie's heart restarted in her chest, she knew immediately that Grayson recognized her.

Damn.

He stood a few feet away, just looking at her. He was dashing in dark evening attire, a crisp white shirt and collar, a flowing cape, and a black silk mask. She felt acutely aware of herself, of her low-cut dress, the tight bodice—the kind of gown she wore to perform. Her skin tingled with a mix of panic and excitement.

But on the heels of that awareness came something else. What was Grayson Hawthorne doing in a place like this? Did this man who demanded respectability from those around him not actually demand as much from himself?

She could hardly give the thought credence.

But there he stood in a house of ill repute, looking as though he belonged. She thought of the invitation and realized that it must have been sent to him. Not to her.

Suddenly the evening was more interesting than she had anticipated.

Awareness shimmered through her veins with an intensity and boldness that made her heart trip, and she stood.

"Where are you going?" one of the men at her table called out. "We're not finished with the hand."

"I fold," she replied without looking back.

Grayson watched her as she approached, and she felt the intensity of his touch without even being near him. Despite everything, she wanted him to touch her again.

The mask made her bold, since she knew the crowds around her didn't know who she was. It freed her of Sophie the awkward prodigy. Of Sophie the famous concert cellist. Allowing her to step out of herself, the past slipping away.

Their gazes never broke as she drew closer, her heart pounding so wildly that she could hardly hear.

"Hello," she whispered.

"Hello."

One word, simply spoken, but a deep gruffness told her he was not immune.

"What brings you to a place like this?" she asked.

"I was sent for."

"Really?" she asked, surprised. "Why?"

"Because you were here."

Her eyes narrowed. "Who told you?"

"My brother."

"Matthew? Matthew's here?"

"No, Lucas."

He gestured across the room to the devil man, who raised his glass in salute.

"That's Lucas?" she demanded.

But then she smiled and signaled a masked waiter, who supplied her with another crystal glass of champagne. "I should have known. The traitor. Though a dashing traitor. Good God, I haven't seen him in years. How is it possible that only one of you turned out to be a bit of fun?"

Instantly she felt the tension that snaked through him at

the words. He didn't speak for several moments, some kind of battle going on within him. Until she touched his arm.

He looked at her again, his gaze forbidding.

"Let's not fight," she whispered. "A truce. Just for tonight. We can resume the battle again tomorrow."

Annoyance flashed in his dark eyes beneath the mask.

The dance floor was crowded with couples holding close, too close, kissing in the dim, golden light of candles. Grayson turned to look out over the room.

"No one will know who we are," she persisted, hoping she was right, ignoring the feeling that suddenly someone was watching too closely. Instead her mouth opened on a silent gasp when she noticed a man's hand running down a woman's back, cupping her hip before curling between her legs.

Another couple stood in the center of the floor, locked tightly together, no longer pretending to dance. The pulse of the dark melody drummed through the air, somehow primal. Sophie felt it, and she could tell Grayson felt it, too.

He turned back and looked at her, his dark eyes like liquid smoke, searching. The music's beat surrounded her, seeping into her.

"Dance with me, Grayson."

She didn't recognize her voice. She felt like she was dissolving with desire, the distinct, determined lines she had drawn around herself long ago fading in this high-ceilinged room filled with strangers and masks.

His gaze drifted to her lips, then back, forcefully. "We have other obligations," he answered.

"Please," she whispered.

He hesitated and bit out a curse. Then with practiced ease he pulled her onto the dance floor, pulling her close as they stepped into an intimate waltz.

They made a turn around the floor, and she felt it the moment he began to relax, that way he had about him when he seemed to give in to the battle, and the stiffness slipped away.

"You look beautiful tonight," he said, his hand secure against her back, twirling her in perfect cadence to the beat.

Her answering smile tilted on her lips. "Are you trying to soften me up with sweet words?"

"I'm not trying to do anything. I'm simply enjoying seeing you happy—with your defenses down."

She laughed. "My defenses are never down."

"Why?"

She tried to take a step back, but his strong hand curled gently around her waist.

"I was joking."

"I don't think you were." He executed a perfect turn, his strong thigh coming between her own as they moved. "I've said before that I think your joking is all a pretense." He looked down, his hand pressing her closer than propriety allowed. "I also believe you want me."

Her heart seemed to stop, and it was difficult to find her voice. She forced a laugh. "Big words for a man who's been told point-blank I won't marry him."

But he wasn't goaded this time. "It won't work anymore, Sophie."

If possible, he pulled her even closer, until she didn't know where she ended and he began. Blood rushed through her veins, making her weak. She felt cornered, her defenses faltering.

"You can't stand there and deny that you want me," he added. "Not anymore. I see the way you look at me when I enter a room. That means something, Sophie."

"It means I need to have my head examined."

"It means we have a past together. You know things about me that no one else does. And there are things about you that only I know. We belong together, Sophie."

His voice was a caress of sound, and she wanted to believe him. The look in his eyes sent her heart skittering madly. She was mesmerized by his intense, unreadable gaze as he slowly leaned forward until his lips captured hers, despite the crowd.

He kissed her as he drew a breath, seeming to breathe her in, out of herself, until she was lost.

His earlier kisses had filled her body with an aching desire beyond what she understood. But this was different. This filled her dreams. No demands. Just a gentle coaxing. Just enough to make her want to lose herself forever. And for that moment she did. She lost herself to the feeling as he brushed his lips gently over hers, side to side, slowly, making her want more.

She felt the key to her heart click, felt it trying to open just a little more. She realized with a start that she wanted to give in. She wanted to be his wife, wanted a normal life, fame and houses be damned.

She nearly moaned out loud when he broke the contact. It took a moment for her mind to clear, and she realized he was looking at her and they had stopped dancing. His gaze took her in, as if he were trying to understand something. As if he were trying to answer some question that churned in his mind.

But then his face cleared. "Come on, sweetheart. It's time we went. You've had your dance, and the Tisdales are expecting us." He took her hand and started leading her toward the door.

Just like that, he tried to command her life, not asking her what she wanted, caging her. Taking, whether she wanted to give or not.

Defiance surged, inevitably, the lines returning well before tomorrow, clear and unmistakable. She pulled free. "Damn the Tisdales. And damn you, with your inflexible timetables and boorish behavior. I'm not finished dancing," she stated, thankful her voice was steady.

Perhaps it was the champagne, or maybe it was the night, but she returned to the hardwood floor to dance by herself. The music had changed, the beat low and pounding, sensual. Men and women danced, too close. It was decadent, pulsing. And Sophie began to move.

She swayed to the rhythm, her hips moving provocatively. Her heart beat hard, her gaze locked defiantly with Grayson's. The guests began to watch, the men eyeing her appreciatively.

Others set their drinks down to take in the scene. Bartenders stopped tending bar.

"Sophie," Grayson warned from where he stood, his dark eyes flashing beneath the mask, his hands planted on his hips, his cape spreading over his shoulders and elbows to show a hint of the red silk lining underneath.

Gamblers at gaming tables turned to the dance floor; cards froze in dealers' hands.

"If you don't come with me now," he warned, "I'm going to toss you over my shoulder and carry you out like a sack of grain."

Her eyes glittered beneath her full-lidded gaze. "You wouldn't dare." She twirled around, her skirts lifting to reveal jeweled slippers and a glimpse of stockings.

A murmur of appreciative voices swept through the high-ceilinged room. And a gasp. But Sophie barely noticed.

"You realize, don't you," Grayson stated, "that at this very minute, bets are being placed on who is going to win this little skirmish."

She spun slowly, her arms extended, her head tilted back, and she relished the feel of her cape swinging wide. "Who do you think is going to win?"

He acted so fast that she hardly knew what happened. One minute silken material billowed like clouds around her ankles; the next she was swept up in his arms, the sounds of claps and cheers ringing through the decadently lit surroundings as Grayson boldly carried her from the grand hall. But he didn't head for the front foyer.

He took her down a long, deserted hallway, closed doors lining the length, hard marble tiles making every step too loud and echoing. She wasn't sure if she wanted to laugh or curse at his high-handed behavior. Though either option faded from her mind when he lowered her to the floor, but didn't let her go.

Her body pressed against his, his arm holding her secure. She felt consumed by his gaze, hot and trembling. She started to push him away, but with one large hand he captured hers to his chest.

"If you've set out to bewitch me," he said, the words a raw whisper of desire, "you've succeeded. Bewitched and beguiled. Driven me crazy."

Then he kissed her hungrily, his hands sweeping beneath the cape to her shoulders, down her back to her hips, until he pressed her against the hard, unmistakable ridge of his manhood.

"Make no mistake about how much I want you, Sophie."

For a moment she tensed. But then she reminded herself that this was Grayson, not someone else, not some other man from the sea of faceless men who wanted her. She wanted to feel Grayson's touch. At least for tonight. One magical space of time where masks washed the slate clean.

She clung to him, and he kissed her again, his lips trailing back to her ear.

His voice was gruff. "We are meant to be together, Sophie."

"Yes," she answered. *For tonight,* she thought.

She felt his tongue graze her skin, his teeth nipping as he drifted lower. Gently he pressed her back against the wall. She circled her arms around his shoulders, and he pulled her up against him. He cupped her hips, and she felt an intimate throb of heat. She wanted him, felt the desire much as she felt the music deep in her soul.

One touch, one kiss, and she all too easily forgot everything but this man whom she had worshiped since she was a young girl.

Was it possible that the past might not matter?

The thought startled her, then led to another.

Could there be a way to give in to this man and begin a new life?

A surge of hope washed through her that left her weak and yearning as much for what might be as she yearned for his kiss. She hadn't thought a life with Grayson was possible since she fled Boston five years ago. But Grayson was here, at this less than perfect place, his brother the owner. Was he different than she thought? Was it possible that he wouldn't cage her? Was the passion he felt for her enough to overcome the past?

Suddenly he stopped and took her hand.

"Where are we going?" she asked.

"To do what I should have done long ago."

He swept her up and carried her to a private room, kicking the door shut with a resounding bang. Instantly he set her down as his mouth hungrily covered hers. His hands framed her face, his lips slanting over hers.

He kissed her, his hands sweeping beneath the cape to her hair, down her back to her hips, cupping her round bottom, pressing her against his manhood as he groaned.

Sophie gasped, but the sound was lost when he nipped her lower lip, sucking it in.

"God, I want you," he said, his voice hoarse.

The words made her heart still. His lips trailed to her neck, her head falling back. Clinging to him, she felt his lips move lower, his hand coming up to cup her breast, the sensation making her quiver and burn.

Gently he leaned her back against the wall, his knee nudging her legs apart.

He kissed her, his tongue plunging within her mouth in a rhythm as old as time; then he groaned, pulling back.

He pressed his lips against the hood of her cape. "I knew it would be like this between us." His words were more accusation than statement.

Then he ravaged her mouth with an exquisite torture. Hot. Insatiable.

Joy swept through her and she nearly cried. Instead she held on and returned his desire.

The mask made her bold, her hands exploring as she had never dared to explore before. His breath grew ragged. He caressed her in ways that brought her body to life, making her yearn for his touch.

When he swept her up in his arms and carried her to the chaise, she wrapped her arms around his shoulders. He set her down and followed in her wake, coming to rest above her, his weight supported on his elbows.

His hand caressed her side, sliding up until he worked the fastenings of her gown. With expert ease, he slipped each fastening from its mooring, then pushed her chemise aside until she felt the kiss of air against her skin.

She gasped when his strong hand grazed the skin of her breast, brushing delicately before he cupped the swell, his thumb circling over the nipple.

"You are so beautiful," he whispered against her.

His kisses trailed over her forehead and cheeks. Kisses that she had longed for, wanted, couldn't live without.

And in that moment it hit her.

She *couldn't* live without him—despite the fact that she had been mad at him since she found him with another woman. And she *had* been mad at him, she realized with a dizzying sense of understanding. Mad and angry and hurt that he hadn't been there for her when she needed him most.

But suddenly she knew what she wanted from life—the very thing she had fought so hard against. Him.

She had thought she knew what she wanted from the world, but she really hadn't. And now she could only hope that it wasn't too late—not too late to show him that she wanted to laugh with him, to be with him—to show him that she loved him.

She realized then, her breath swept away, that she was still in love with Grayson Hawthorne—and that she wanted him for more than this night alone.

How was it possible? her mind raged. How could she fall for a man who would expect perfection from her?

But that was just it. The hope that had been building burgeoned, full-blown and stunning.

Grayson wasn't like that.

He proved he didn't expect perfection just by being in this room in a house of ill repute. Grayson could be wild— he could be outrageous. And as much as she hated to think about it, wasn't that what he had proven when he had been with a woman not his wife?

The realizations tumbled in on her. She wanted to sing and dance, to shout her joy. Because she could marry this man after all.

Sophie wrapped her arms around Grayson's shoulders, hardly aware of where she was or what she was doing. Her body was alive with love for this man as much as with the sensations he was bringing to life in her body.

But at the sound of the voices coming down the hall, emotion ceased and she froze.

"I'm just sure it was her. With Grayson Hawthorne," she heard a familiar voice mutter.

Grayson stilled.

"I'd believe it of Grayson—his brother owns the place— but Sophie Wentworth?" a man asked.

"Don't be fooled. It was her, and they came this way. I have every intention of finding her."

There was no mistaking the sound of Megan Robertson's voice, overloud and echoing against the tile floor.

"Even if it is her," the man asked, "what does it matter?"

"It matters to me. She waltzes back into town and acts like she owns the place. If people find out she came to Nightingale's Gate, then they won't be so blindly enamored."

Grayson felt Sophie flinch. He wanted to step into the hallway and put a halt to the conversation, but didn't know how without revealing Sophie's presence.

"She certainly has taken Boston by storm," the man mused. "Actually, based on that article, I'd say she has taken the world by storm."

"Doing what?" Megan demanded. "Did it escape your notice that there is not a single mention of what pieces she plays?"

"Hmmm, now that I think about it, you're right."

"Of course I am. The fact of the matter is, I know the music world, and I have never read about a concert without being told what works were performed. There is not one mention of what Sophie Wentworth plays . . . or doesn't play. She's a fraud, I tell you. She always has been. I remember well all the speculation that she would solo at the Grand Debut. But who did Niles award the concert to? Who did he ask to perform?"

Grayson felt the coiled tightness of Sophie's body, as if she wanted to spring out and defend herself, but couldn't—or didn't know how.

"He asked me," Megan finished with a flourish.

"Didn't that happen right after Sophie's mother died? Wasn't that when he invited you to give the concert?"

Megan sniffed. "Yes. And what does that tell you?"

The man was silent, and Grayson felt Sophie press her forehead to his chest, hard.

"Think about it, Peter. Think about how much time Niles Prescott spent with Genevieve Wentworth. They had an affair, I tell you."

"No!" Peter breathed, scandalized.

"Don't be naive. I can't believe you didn't hear the rumors. And the minute she died, he no longer had to pretend Sophie was any good."

"I can't believe it!"

"Well, believe it. And do you want to know why Sophie ran off to Europe? Because of sheer embarrassment. The supposed prodigy had been taken down to the place where she belonged. A distant second peg to me."

The pair had stopped outside the door. Grayson cursed when he realized that in his haste he hadn't secured the lock.

Sophie lay there as if waiting for the inevitable. But with the same expertise with which he had moved them about on the dance floor, Grayson whisked them up from the chaise and behind a thick velvet curtain just as the handle turned.

"I just know she is here somewhere," Megan said, her voice no longer muffled by the walls.

Heels clicked into the room, a closet was thrown open. Footsteps came closer, and Grayson held Sophie tight when Megan came to the window and looked out into the night.

"I am just sure I saw her."

So close.

"Well, she's not in here."

"Hmmm," Megan said speculatively, and Grayson was sure they were caught.

But then she and her friend started away, and their voices faded in the distance. Silence returned, the quiet broken by nothing more than the sound of rain hitting the windows.

Sophie didn't move long after they heard the click of the

door. At length, Grayson glanced down at her, expecting her to be upset. For a second he thought she was, but then she spoke.

"Well, she certainly has a way with words."

He heard the flip tone and knew the walls were once again erected.

"Sophie, don't do this," he said. "I've heard you play," he added gently. "I know you are talented."

Her cheeks flashed red and her brow furrowed. Then she laughed, but the sound was forced and hollow.

"That's the thing, Grayson. You haven't heard me play."

Her gaze grew fierce. But her lips began to tremble. Suddenly, as if a dam had given way, her eyes blurred with tears, and she drew a tiny, shuddering breath before she jerked away from him. She fumbled with the curtain, then her dress, finally pulling her cape closed.

"Sophie, tell me what you're talking about."

But she wasn't listening. She threw open the door, then fled to a back exit and pushed out into the cold, biting rain.

"Sophie!" he called out.

But she didn't stop; she held her skirts and ran out into the alley, no coat, no shawl, protected by nothing more than the thin black cape and the gossamer-sheer silk of her gown.

Chapter Sixteen

Grayson started after her, but a voice stopped him.

"My, my, look who we have here."

He turned sharply, and found Megan sauntering back down the hall.

"I told Peter that if I waited long enough I was bound to find you. He went upstairs, but he'll be back." She peered past him. "I know you're back there, Sophie. You might as well come out. By this time tomorrow all of Boston will know that you were here, dancing like a harlot."

"You are wasting your breath. Sophie isn't here, Megan. As to telling Boston anything, one, you have no proof. And two, how do you mention anyone's presence here without revealing your own?"

Her shoulders went back defiantly. "I'll find a way!"

"You will not." His voice was cold and unrelenting with menace. "You've done enough to Sophie. It's time you left her alone."

She gasped at the words. "Me?" she demanded, a sudden, intense anger flashing through her eyes. Without warning, her proper patina melted away as if it had been little more than a pretense. "She's the one who did everything! She's the one who everyone paid attention to. It didn't matter that she was awkward and gawky. Everyone might have thought she was odd and troublesome, but they also believed she should have had that solo debut instead of me. I deserved that concert," she hissed, as if trying to convince herself. "And now with that wretched article in *The Century* magazine, all anyone can talk about is Sophie this, Sophie that! Proving that they had been right about the solo all along. I will not have it. Do you hear me? I will not have it! And I will not sit by while she gets this new concert." Her chin rose. "Or you."

Grayson went still, and suddenly Megan's face crumpled. "Oh, Grayson—"

"Sophie isn't upstairs." Peter Marshall stopped abruptly, and Megan turned her face away to hide her sudden tears. Peter seemed confused, before he gave Grayson a knowing look. "Hello, Hawthorne. Fancy meeting you here. Have to admit, Megan, I'm surprised you were right. Where's Sophie?"

"She isn't right," Grayson bit out. "Sophie isn't here. And if I hear that either of you have said one word about her, you will answer to me."

Then he raced out the back door and into the rainy night.

He didn't think about anything but finding Sophie. But once outside, there was no sign of her.

After looking left, then right, he chose the direction that led to the Back Bay. Surely she would head home. He caught a hansom cab to follow her, but when he arrived he found Swan's Grace empty.

He tried The Fens, to no avail, and had to make up some excuse as to why he thought she might be there and why he was soaking wet. Next he went to Hawthorne House; thankfully he found only the butler, who informed him that Miss Wentworth had not been there.

He searched the Public Gardens and Boston Commons. He hailed another cab, ignoring the frigid cold and rain that seeped to his bones as he rode up and down each of the orderly grids of streets in the Back Bay, only to come up empty-handed.

The moon was well hidden in the heavy night sky when the hired hack pulled up in front of Swan's Grace once again. Frustration mixed with growing despair as he stepped down onto the walkway. And there he saw her.

She sat on the top step, huddled against one of the granite swans, nothing to shield her from the rain and cold.

"Sophie," he whispered, not wanting to think about the way she made him feel.

Slowly she looked up, and he couldn't deny the relief that flashed through her eyes when she saw him.

He stopped in front of her and they stared at each other, he on the walk, she at eye level on the top step, her clothes soaked through, the loose tendrils of her hair dripping with rain.

But a smile trembled on her lips. "You fixed the lock."

His throat tightened with emotion. "Someone had to."

She chuckled, though oddly, before her face crumpled. Only then did he realize that her body shivered with cold, and her skin was much too white.

He didn't like the blue tinge in her lips. He had seen it once before when he was young and Matthew had gotten caught in a storm much like this. Wet and cold made a deadly combination. Fortunately his father had acted quickly, putting Matthew in a hot bath before his body shut down.

"We've got to get you inside."

He took the steps, but when he helped her stand, she collapsed against him. In seconds he swept her up into his arms, then had to fumble with the keys and the lock.

"Damn!"

"It was easier before you fixed it," she mumbled like a drunkard.

His worry grew. He needed to get her warm, and fast.

"Where is that blasted Deandra or Margaret when you need them?" he demanded as he strode into the marble entry, kicked the door shut, then tossed the keys on the foyer table with a clatter.

"Away for the weekend. Having fun," she murmured.

"Damn," he repeated.

Sophie focused on his face, though barely, a muddled smile lurking. "We're alone. Are you going to have your way with me?"

Grayson's eyes narrowed. "Funny."

"I thought so." She giggled, her head falling against his chest.

"Hell."

"Aren't you a plethora of curse words this evening?" Then suddenly she shook her head, as if clearing her mind. "And put me down." She drew her body up, her eyes opening wide. "I'm fine. I don't need you to carry me."

He studied her, and she looked him directly in the eye.

"I really am fine."

Grayson growled, but in the heat of the house she did seem better.

"I just sat out there for too long, is all," she added.

After a moment's hesitation, he finally set her on her feet.

Sophie took a few steps, her long gown dripping water on the foyer floor. "See, I've never been better."

She started toward the stairs, then stopped. "I hope you don't mind that I don't see you out. I'll just run along and get changed."

But Grayson didn't move, and when she came to the stairs she wavered for a second before she sank down on the bottom step, her head slumping on her arms, long, convulsive shivers racing through her body.

"Hell," he ground out, a swift stab of fear piercing through him.

Sweeping her up in his arms, he took the stairs two at a time as he carried her the remaining distance to his room.

He set her down on a small upholstered bench in the massive bathroom suite, then ran hot water into the porcelain tub at the same time he peeled off the layers of her clothes as if she were a rag doll.

He disregarded the fact that someone else should be undressing her, since there was no one else to do it. He put from his mind the reality of her delicate skin and her generous curves. He thought only about getting her warm.

"Come on, sweetheart. Help me."

Sophie's eyes fluttered open. She seemed to focus, first on him, then on the fact that she was sitting there with next to nothing on. "My clothes," she squeaked.

"This is hardly the time for modesty."

And yet again he wondered about the contradiction of Sophie Wentworth. Only hours before she had danced provocatively at Nightingale's Gate. Now she acted like an innocent as he tried to save her life. Which was she, an innocent or a provocative woman who knew too much about life? He hated to think that it mattered to him.

But there was no time for thought. Quickly he tested the water before lowering her into the tub, nothing left of her clothes but her chemise and pantaloons.

Her eyelids fluttered but didn't quite open when she touched the water. When he had her settled, he ripped off his coat and rolled up his shirtsleeves, then took her hands and started to rub them vigorously.

"Leave me alone," she mumbled, her tongue stumbling over the meager words.

"I will not leave you alone," he told her, taking her foot and starting to work.

He rubbed her extremities and kept the water almost hot, and soon color started to return to her skin. When she groaned and tried to pull away, this time with some strength, while muttering, "You're hurting me," he started to relax.

"Sorry, love, but I have to get you warm."

He leaned back on his haunches and for the first time looked at her. Her hair had come loose and floated on the surface like strands of spun gold. Her chemise and pantaloons clung to her body, so thin and sheer they might as well not have been there. Rose-tipped breasts were outlined, as well as the golden triangle of hair between her legs.

She was stunning.

"He didn't believe I was good enough."

His head jerked up and he found her staring at her hand—first the palm, then the back, water dripping down her fingers like tears.

Confusion filled him. "What?"

She met his eyes and blinked. The look on her face was of devastation and unbearable pain.

And it all came clear to him. The bravado. The excitement over people's praise. Such a contradiction. She pretended not to care, but in truth, she cared so much that it hurt.

With a weak splash, she lowered her hand. "Nothing."

"Come on, let's get you out of there."

He picked her up with ease and set her on her feet. She wavered for a moment, but she steadied herself before he could catch her.

She appeared tired, but her sadness seemed to drip away along with the water, replaced by a growing defiance and anger.

"Why did you run away tonight, Sophie? Because of what Megan said about your mother? Or because Niles Prescott asked Megan to perform instead of you?"

She snorted, seeming to pull herself up. "I didn't run away. I left. It was a dismal party and I saw no reason to stay." She raised her eyebrow in a moment of meaningful clarity. "Good God, did you taste that champagne?"

"You looked like you were having a perfectly grand

time. And that champagne happens to be one of the finest in the world."

"That's right! I was having a grand time in a house of ill repute, dancing decadently. Proof that I'm not proper or perfect! And I never will be, Grayson!"

Her knowing look faded and she turned away sharply. Then, regardless of the fact that he was still in the room, she started tugging at the remainder of her clothes.

The wet chemise clung to her, refusing to give up its hold. She tugged, then jerked, then ripped at the material.

"Here, let me help."

But when he stepped forward, she whirled on him.

"Don't you understand anything? I don't need your help! I don't need anything from you. I don't need anything from anyone! I made it on my own, and I will continue to do so!"

By now tears burned in her eyes, then spilled over down her cheeks, and her hands fell to her sides in defeat. Her teeth had begun to chatter again, but not with life-threatening cold. She just needed to get dry.

Grayson didn't understand what he felt, didn't understand the need in him that had nothing to do with desire. Slowly he reached out to her again, and when she didn't resist, he gently began to free her from the wet muslin.

What stores of strength she had built over the years were spent. He understood that with such sudden clarity that it nearly bowled him over. Crying silently, she watched his fingers as he worked at the fastenings of the chemise. But they were knotted, and finally he tore them loose, until the material lay in a puddle at her feet.

Her breasts were full and well rounded, her waist slim. She was more beautiful than he had ever imagined.

His fingers nearly trembled as he tugged at the tie of her pantaloons. The thin cotton gave up more easily and fell to her feet, revealing beautifully sculpted hips and long legs.

But she didn't move. She stood like stone, the material like shackles around her ankles. And when he lifted her chin, he saw the emptiness in her eyes, a desolation that had nothing to do with standing naked in front of him.

Grabbing a towel, he wrapped it around her, then swept her up. He laid her on the high four-poster bed he had used as his own for a few short months. As if she were a child, he rubbed her dry before wrapping her in his thick cashmere robe.

With a patience that surprised him, he gathered her close, then set her in front of the fire. He poured a crystal glass of brandy, then sat down behind her, pulling her between his knees as he leaned back against an overstuffed chair. After coaxing her to take a sip, he slowly began to work the tangles from the long, curly strands of her hair.

Whether it was hours or minutes, he didn't know. They shared the brandy, sitting in a quiet cloud of golden firelight as he pulled the soft bristle brush through her hair in long, sweeping strokes. She didn't utter a word the entire time, just sat staring at the flames.

"Talk to me, Sophie," he said when her hair was dry and her body warmed.

She tensed and tried to get up, but he wouldn't let her. He turned her around to face him. She was still between his bent knees, though now she was kneeling on her own. He could see the emotion in her eyes. She seemed cornered, desperate. But then the look changed, shifted, and she reached out and touched his lips.

His body leaped, hard and demanding. But with steely control, he gently took her hand away.

"No, Sophie. I'm not going to let you change the subject. Touching me or kissing me isn't going to change anything."

"Of course it will," she said, her voice a practiced whisper of breath.

He recognized it now. "Stop!" he said fiercely. "You can't hide from the past any longer."

Silence sliced through the room.

"Ah, Sophie," he whispered. "Are you ashamed of what people say your mother did with Niles Prescott? Is that what has been holding you back from me all this time? That doesn't have any bearing on you. As to the concert, I'm sorry you didn't get the solo. But you will play the Music Hall now, and you will show them what they missed."

Her face turned to a mask of genuine surprise before it crumpled completely. Tears sprang from her eyes and she tried to jerk away. But still he held her, cupping her face, before he leaned forward and kissed her gently on her forehead and cheeks, on her eyelids so softly. As if his touch could truly heal her.

Chapter Seventeen

He was close.

Too close, or not close enough?

She could feel the heat of him, the strength, and she wanted nothing more than to lean into him, to let him hold her, cherish her. His gaze was dark as he studied her, and she knew he was trying to see into her soul. For one brief second, she almost let him.

Instead she closed her eyes, turning her head.

"I don't have to see your eyes to understand," he whispered, as always knowing. "I believe we are meant to be together."

Her head snapped back, and she felt a blaze of feelings. "Do you really think that?" she demanded, Megan's words having cruelly reminded her that there was no place for her in Boston.

"Yes."

So kind, so gentle.

She wanted to scream her frustration.

"You don't understand anything! It is impossible."

"Why? Tell me why! Because your mother had relations with another man?"

The words took her breath. She felt strangled and trapped, remembering. "Don't blame this on my mother." But did she?

The thought leaped out at her. Determinedly she quelled

it. She loved her mother. Missed her mother. Appreciated all she had done for her.

"Then why?" he demanded.

"Because I saw you with Megan!"

The words sliced through his kindness. "What are you talking about?" he asked, his tone dangerous.

"I saw you with Megan in your garret in Cambridge."

She saw the surprise, then the frustration and regret that filled him.

"The night you said you saw where I lived," he whispered to himself.

"I came because of your note."

"What note?"

"After my mother died you sent a note saying to come to you." Her voice quieted. "When I needed you, your note arrived." She blinked and focused on him. "But when I got there Megan was—"

"The bitch," he stated coldly. "I never sent a note."

The words beat in her head like the pounding of a drum. Her throat tightened. Her world spun.

"What does it matter who sent the note?" she asked. "You made love to her. I saw!"

"I did not make love to her, Sophie."

"You were naked!"

"I was getting out of the bath and she was there."

"And clearly you wanted her. That is hard to deny!"

His lips thinned to a flat line. "I'm a man," he said in cold, hard syllables. "God, she reached out and touched me. I was alone and young."

Sophie turned away sharply, remembering the hardness of Grayson. And his eyes, dark and desperate, strained as feminine hands moved on him, holding him, stroking him. She standing paralyzed, watching, shocked, sick, but unable to look away. And Megan looking up, seeing her. Smiling that triumphant smile.

Sophie had backed out silently, then once outside she had run. "How does being young and alone make it all right?"

"It is all right because I sent her away."

She blinked and her brow furrowed.

"She came to me, yes. But I sent her away, Sophie."

She jerked around to face him. His expression was as serious and gentle as she had ever seen it.

"There have been women in my life. I won't deny that. But do you really think I would make love to someone who had hurt you in so many ways?"

The words strangled her, and her mind reeled with what he had just said. She didn't trust her ears. "What are you saying?"

"You know what I'm saying."

He hadn't made love to Megan. She could hardly absorb the words. Or the portent.

She stared at him, her heart soaring, and for one startling moment she nearly flung her arms around his strong shoulders. But in the next second her heart stilled.

He hadn't made love to Megan.

As if it were a cruel joke, she suddenly understood what that meant. He hadn't betrayed her with someone who had lived her whole life trying to hurt her.

Mistakes and regrets spun in her mind. Her stomach roiled. But it was too late for that.

She jerked away and started to scramble free.

But he caught her bare ankle.

"Quit running! You have been running ever since your mother died."

A strangled sob rose in her throat, and she kicked to get free. But he held secure, pulling her back to him.

She was crying now, tears burning a path down her cheeks for so many reasons. "I hate you," she choked out.

"No, you don't," he whispered, as if the simple words

were terribly important to him. "You're just mad at me. And perhaps at yourself."

Her sob burst out, and she gave in. The walls tumbled down and she flew into his arms, holding him as fiercely as she had ever held anything before.

"I'm sorry. So sorry," she whispered.

They came together like two halves of a whole, no place for thought, only sensation.

Her tears were hot and he kissed them away, his strong hands framing her face. His fingers slid back into her hair, tangling in the strands he had just dried. His tongue traced her lips. "Open for me, love."

She did, savoring the rich, brandy-laced taste of him. Without breaking the kiss, he pulled her into his lap as he came back against the overstuffed chair. Her knees pressed into the thick rug on either side of his thighs. She had nothing on beneath the robe, and she could feel the soft woolen flannel of his pants against her most intimate skin. Sensation shimmered through her, and she gasped when he moved just so.

His hands slipped beneath the heavy cotton, the sash belt loosing its hold as he ran his hands along her sides, coming around to cup her breasts, his thumbs circling her nipples. A moan started low and tried to pry its way free. But she swallowed it back, breathing in deeply as his hands drifted downward over the gentle curve of her belly, until his fingers grazed the tight curls between her legs. This time she couldn't hold back the sound.

Their lovemaking turned frantic then, each surrendering, each forgetting all else. He ran his hands over her body, and she gasped as liquid heat seared her.

They came up on their knees, the robe falling away completely, and she wanted to lose herself in his arms.

She tore at his shirt, but she couldn't work it free. She had the fleeting thought that she had something to prove—

to herself, to him. About the past. Something that she would make him understand once and for all.

But she pushed it away. She could do nothing else but love him. Once. Something to hold dear and remember.

He swept her up, and she circled his neck as he carried her back to the bed. But he surprised her when he laid her down and didn't follow.

"God, Sophie. If I don't leave you now, I won't be able to." He said the words as if they cost him greatly. "But soon we will be married. I will make love to you then. Long and slow and sweet."

Her arms locked around his neck. She didn't respond with words, she pulled him back to her lips.

He groaned at the touch and she could feel him fighting her. But when she flicked her tongue against his lips, he was lost.

He came down beside her with a low, greedy cry. "You make me lose control," he said with a rasping breath of accusation.

She gasped as heat seared her body when the soft material of his evening shirt brushed ever so lightly against her breasts, bringing them to taut peaks.

Outside, the rain beat against the windows like a native drum. She felt the throbbing in her soul, making her body burn as it never had before.

She understood that she was giving in, and she wanted nothing more than this. This man. This way. And she couldn't do anything else but press her hand over his when he brought his fingers to her heart.

Drifting lower, the heel of his hand grazed the side of one breast before he cupped the soft underswell. Her eyes fluttered shut when he brought his lean, black-clad thigh between her own, spreading her legs. He nibbled at her lips, sucking gently, lingeringly, his tongue tracing the outline of her mouth before plunging deep inside.

He played her as skillfully as she played the cello, alternately giving then demanding. When she tried to turn to him, he gently held her still. Balancing himself on one elbow, he looked at her. "Sophie," he murmured, his low, hoarse voice filled with raw desire.

But before she could respond, he ran his hand between her breasts, lingering at the gentle swell of her belly. He traced her knee, pulling it up, then very slowly brought his palm up the inside of her thigh before continuing on to find the soft, hidden folds of her womanhood.

Her breath came quick and shallow when he slid one finger inside her wetness, circling around before he inserted another. She cried out her pleasure, and, unable to help herself, she raised herself to him.

She grew frantic, wanting something she couldn't name. But when she moaned her frustration and moved her hips, he gentled her.

"Not yet," he murmured, stroking her slowly, then deeply, then softly teasing her nether lips.

With infinite care, cradling her shoulders with his arm, he brought her to a fever pitch of wanting and needing, but not knowing how to give in.

"Grayson?" she whispered.

"Yes, love," he said gently, "I'm here."

Her body sought him, soared toward something. But suddenly she tried to get free.

"What's wrong?"

She came up on her knees and boldly pulled at his shirt. "I want you," she cried. "Completely. Not you showing me or teaching me. I want to find whatever it is together."

"Dear God," he whispered, his voice barely a sound.

With a panther's grace, he tossed the shirt aside, allowing her to run her hands up his back, the hard, subtle ripple of muscles widening into broad shoulders. She took his kiss, then demanded more.

She melted into him, wanting to feel him, to feel this body that was meant to be hers. She wanted to know every inch of this man whom she loved.

And when she thought she couldn't take it a second longer, he came over her and settled between her thighs. With his breath coming in sharp bursts, he raised her knees as he caressed her tongue with his own, sucking and nipping. His body moved, pressing against her secret opening, teasing, pulsing until she was wet and ready. Only then did he moan his surrender and thrust inside her.

The movement took her breath, and the world froze around them, each coming back a bit to stare at the other, the truth about her past no longer deniable. She wasn't a virgin.

"Sophie," he breathed, deep, welling emotion etched across his face, burning in his eyes like tears.

But she didn't respond, couldn't. She only pulled him closer. "Love me, Grayson," she whispered, moving against him until he groaned and began to move within her, slowly, steadily, making them forget.

He loved her then, as if trying to become one with her, his strokes long and slow, complete, then faster. Sweet, maddening love until they both shattered.

Afterward she lay in his embrace, their arms and legs entwined. A moment of perfect bliss.

She tried to keep her mind blank. Wanting to savor this cherished space of time, she tried to keep thoughts at bay. But as minutes ticked by, reality circled faster and faster with each word Grayson didn't utter.

Her heartbeat began to hammer, not from passion, but from growing despair. She had known it would come to this, but still it wounded her to the core.

Finally she pulled out of his arms, fighting back hot, burning tears. And as he had that day in the foyer of Swan's Grace, he let her go.

Slowly he swung his feet over and planted them on the carpet. But he didn't stand. He looked at her, his expression unreadable.

The blankness made her want to weep, but it didn't do her any good. Only strength helped. Only bravado. She had learned that long ago.

"Now you understand why we can't marry," she stated, forcing the words to be strong. "Because the truth is, Niles Prescott didn't make love to my mother, he made love to me."

Chapter Eighteen

The silence grew deafening as Grayson's face became etched with something she couldn't name—shock, anger, despair.

She felt too hot despite the chill that clung to the room now that the fire had died. Her head swam and her body began a slow, deep shudder. She had to get away. But he surprised her when he caught her hand, staring at their intertwined fingers before he raised his chin and met her gaze.

"What are you saying?" he asked, tension radiating in each syllable.

"You heard me, Grayson," she said quietly, hating the words.

He shook his head slowly, as if he could deny what she had said. "You had relations with Niles Prescott? A man old enough to be your father?"

She couldn't move, much less speak.

"Sophie, explain yourself." His voice grew rough, strained.

"Yes! All right, yes! I had relations with Niles Prescott."

He took hold of her arms. "Tell me that he raped you, and I'll see that he pays."

Her face flushed red and she closed her eyes, seeing that night from long ago. Rape? Had Niles Prescott raped her? He had told her it was her fault. Wasn't it?

"No, it wasn't rape," she answered woodenly.

His features grew incredulous. "Then why? Because you thought I had made love to Megan? Did you think to get back at me?"

Her head jerked up. "No! Of course not!" But how to make him understand when she hardly understood herself how things had gone so wrong?

"Then why would you lie with him?"

She felt dizzy and weak. She caught a glimpse of herself in the mirror, the passion-swollen lips, the tousled hair, the robe lying in a puddle on the floor. With shaking hands she retrieved the cashmere and pulled it around her.

"Sophie, answer me."

"What do you want me to say? That I was a fool, that I made a mistake? I admit it—does that make you happy? Or do you want me to tell you how one day my mother was laughing and making plans, then the next she was dead from influenza?"

A month before her eighteenth birthday, her mother was suddenly gone, her father stunned with grief and unreachable.

"Or do you want to hear how Patrice showed up at my house to take care of my dying mother, only to end up as my father's new wife little more than a month after she died?"

Grayson's eyes narrowed as he took in her words. "What does that have to do with Niles Prescott?"

Her shoulders slumped as she remembered the days she had tried to see her father, trying to break through his grief, only to be kept away by Patrice. "It has nothing to do with him," she whispered, turning to the window, "and everything."

How could she make Grayson understand that she had felt so alone? How the note she had thought was his had arrived when she needed him most. How frantically she had gone to him, only to find Megan there, her hands boldly caressing him.

After she had fled that garret, she had gone to the music school to lose herself in her cello. Niles Prescott had been there, so kind, her mother's friend, and he had held her while she cried. But Niles's comfort had turned to something else.

Sophie felt bile rise up inside her. The shame. The disbelief. The need to wake up from a bad dream, even all these years later.

How many times had she asked herself why it had happened? But answers remained elusive. Had it happened because she was so inexperienced? Foolish? Desperate to be loved?

But the explanations never mattered. All that mattered was that she had sex with that man. And then the crowning blow—he had given Megan the solo. In a matter of a single month, she lost everything. Her mother, her dream, and any chance that she could marry a respectable man.

A series of wrong turns and mistakes had changed her life completely.

"Nothing and everything?" Grayson demanded. "You think that's explanation enough?"

She met his eyes. "There's nothing I can say that is going to change the reality. You want what every proper Victorian man wants. Expects. A perfect, virginal bride. Can you deny that?"

He stared at her, but didn't utter a word.

With a spurt of breath to hold back tears, she knew what she had to do. With measured steps, she walked to the writing desk and pulled out pen and paper. Her hands shook as she quickly scrawled out the words.

Grayson turned to stare at the window, and he seemed surprised when she returned to stand before him. The anger had fled and he looked like a sixteen-year-old boy, spurned and aching. Confused. She longed to reach out, to pull him close. But he was no longer a boy, he was a man, hard and exacting.

"Sign this, Grayson," she said.

Mechanically, he read. His eyes narrowing, he looked back at her.

"This terminates our betrothal," he stated, as if he didn't know what to believe, how to believe anything in a world that had turned upside down on him.

"It's best this way," she said with a businesslike mien she didn't feel, her heart tearing in two.

He stared without seeing, but just when she realized he was going to rip the scrawled document in shreds, she added, "And I want Swan's Grace back as part of the deal."

He lifted his head and looked at her. "What are you talking about?" he asked dangerously.

"It's mine, Grayson," she said. "My father never should have signed it away."

It was then that the confusion and aching despair fled, replaced by a hardness that took her breath. Fury surged, heated and all-consuming. He looked at her as no one had ever looked at her before. In that second she realized that he had come to hate her. So purely, so quickly. Wasn't that the way intense emotion changed? Never slowly, never over time.

"Damn you," he cursed. "That's all you've cared about this whole time. Swan's Grace."

Savagely he took the pen and paper from her. With furious strokes he wrote something on the bottom of the page. Then he signed his name. When he was finished, he tossed the pen down with a clatter, ink spattering the desk like blue-black tears.

"There, you've gotten what you wanted. Your house back and your freedom."

Her freedom. She couldn't speak over the despair closing her throat. She had been so mired in the battle that she had lost sight of what it was that she had truly set out to win. Freedom, yes. But freedom from the only man she had ever loved, and always had.

The truth hit her like a tidal wave after months, if not years, of keeping it at bay. How could she afford to love a man who couldn't love her in return? Because she knew, and deep down inside he knew as well, that he had spent a lifetime demanding perfection. For his father, for the Hawthorne name, and ultimately for himself—for the man he had grown up to be. More proof was the fact that he had turned Megan away.

His silence and his signature on the paper screamed the truth.

When the room remained quiet, he cursed one last time, then yanked his shirt back on. With angry movements, he dressed with precision, then headed for the door. But when he came to the threshold he stopped and turned back, his dark eyes stark and empty, as if he had lost more than she knew.

"Regardless of what you think, I never had any intention of caging you. I only wanted you to share my life."

Then he was gone, the door banging closed with finality, her broken heart breaking even more.

Grayson slammed into Nightingale's Gate. Brutus came around in a flash, his eyes wild for a confrontation. But at the sight of his employer's brother, he got hold of himself.

It wasn't the first time that Grayson had to concede that his younger sibling was involved in the darker side of life. But it was that very fact that brought him there now.

"I want you to find out everything you can about Sophie," he stated without preamble when he strode into Lucas's plush, second-floor office, Brutus racing along behind him like a lamenting mastiff.

"Sorry, boss. He wouldn't let me announce him."

One side of Lucas's mouth quirked as he glanced between the two men. Then he waved his right-hand man away.

"You really shouldn't do that to him," Lucas admonished with mock severity. "Brutus never knows how to deal with you. You never let him do his job as he sees fit."

"I'm not here to exchange pleasantries."

Lucas chuckled. "I can see that. You want me to dig into your betrothed's past."

Grayson was still too . . . stunned, enraged . . . disappointed, to phrase his request in anything other than the bald truth. "Yes."

"Then I take it the marriage is on hold."

"Hell." Grayson ran his hand through his hair, surprised by the stark truth. "The marriage is off."

He pressed his fingers to his temples. She had made love to another man—a truth that he had blindly wanted to deny, despite the fact that she had tried to tell him in so many different ways. He could only blame himself.

"Don't tell me the ever-proper Grayson Hawthorne found his bride-to-be wanting?"

"Careful, little brother. I'm not in the mood for this."

"No," he said in quiet contemplation, "I don't suppose you are. Tell me specifically what you are looking for."

"Anything you can find. And while you're at it, look into Niles Prescott."

Lucas raised a brow.

"Don't ask," Grayson stated. "Just find out what you can about the man. I want to know where he is from, how he got his job." He looked his brother in the eye. "I want to know everything, down to what he drinks in his morning tea."

"Care to tell me what this is all about?"

"Let's just say that I'm finally listening to what Sophie

has been telling me all along. Something is different about her performances, and I intend to find out what it is before she goes onstage at the end of the month."

"Consider it done. Anything else?"

"That's it."

Every ounce of despair was pushed back, and he welcomed the raw rage that surged up and flickered through his veins. Rage he understood.

Chapter Nineteen

Sophie didn't want to think. With meticulous care, she sketched out plans for the music room, then threw herself into the project with determined energy. But regardless of her attempt to empty her mind, thoughts wouldn't leave her alone.

She had spent nearly five long years reweaving the cloth of her life. Four years of dedicated study at Germany's prestigious music school, then another six months making a life for herself. She had found her entourage, gathering them around her with painstaking care, then creating a show that won fans over by the hundreds. But now with one pull the threads were coming apart.

Grayson knew her secret.

For years she had wanted desperately to undo those few hours that divided her life into before and after as sharply and as swiftly as a cleaver severed a whole into two halves. She was an adult; she knew she had to move beyond a foolish mistake. Over the years she had tried to tell herself it wasn't her fault. But she couldn't forget that she had gone to the music school, late and alone.

And as long as she lived, she would never forget the look on Grayson's face when he realized she wasn't a virgin. The sense of betrayal. The disappointment.

Her guilt mixed with a growing sense of anger. This

newfound anger surprised her after years of little more than guilt and the need to put the past from her mind.

She glanced out the foggy window and saw a man approaching. She leaped up from the chair. She hoped it was Grayson returning to talk things through.

But when she looked closer, she saw it was Niles Prescott who strolled up the front walk of Swan's Grace, his hat at a fashionable angle, just a hint of woolen muffler peeking out from beneath his fine camel coat, his walking stick hanging rakishly from his forearm. For the first time in five years she allowed the stinging bite of fury to surge up.

She didn't bother to wait until he knocked. She went to the foyer and whipped open the door.

At the sight of her he raised a winged brow. "Does this mean you are going to let me inside this time?" he asked with a debonair smile, clearly not aware of the fury that seethed before him.

"Yes," she said tightly. "You couldn't have arrived at a better time."

Seeming pleased with himself, he strolled into the house. When he turned back, he extended an envelope. But his hand stilled at the sound of the slamming door.

"What is that?" she demanded.

"It's the first payment due you for the concert." His smile grew hesitant at the look on her face. "But perhaps I should come back another day."

She snatched the envelope away. "I think not." Instantly she looked inside, her heart pounding. *Money. Please God, let it be enough to get us back to Europe.*

But the amount written out on the bank voucher was only half of what she needed.

She felt sick and angry and furious. At Niles, at herself. At Grayson. In her heart she had known that Grayson needed someone virginal, had known that all along. But suspecting the truth and having it confirmed were two different things.

Her breath hissed out of her.

"I'll just be going," Niles said.

She pinned him with her gaze. "Not yet. It's time we talked."

"I have an appointment."

"It will have to wait. I've been running from this for five years. I'm tired of running. Tell me why."

"Why what?" The man shifted uncomfortably.

"Why didn't you give me the solo?"

Niles's shoulders lifted with righteous indignation. "You weren't good enough."

"Liar."

His eyes widened.

"I was good enough."

His surprise went out like the flame of a candle, and his lips thinned as if he, too, had been waiting for this moment. "You were wild and undisciplined. What kind of a girl shows up in the late hours of the night without a chaperon? A girl who has no morals, and certainly one who doesn't deserve the prestigious solo in the Grand Debut."

"What kind of a man takes advantage of that girl?"

Red flared in his cheeks.

"I might have been wild and undisciplined," she continued, "but I was innocent."

His brows set defensively. "I hear you aren't so innocent now. The American public might not know much about you yet, but I do. I've heard about your concerts. You are outrageous, just as you were as a child. But I have kept that little secret to myself. Soon enough Boston will learn about the kind of concert you give. I'm interested to see what people will think when they witness firsthand what I sensed all along."

The words were like a blow. "You asked me to play just so I could fail?"

He gave a harsh little laugh. "Maybe then Boston will forget how horrible Megan was when she performed." His voice began to rise with each word he spoke. "Maybe then they'll forget that you were supposed to have had the concert. Maybe then they'll understand that you didn't deserve it. You are no better than most girls, thinking they can get their way with pretty smiles and sweet words. Well, I showed you!"

The truth that he had used her, then tossed her aside, hit her square in the chest.

His eyes locked with hers, and he sneered. "And now you will show Boston that you don't know the first thing about good music, especially not Bach."

Grayson left the courthouse and headed for his office in Swan's Grace. He had to make up for lost time. More than one of his longtime clients had expressed concern that he was distracted. Never had he felt so out of control.

But he stopped cold at the sight of a dray wagon at the curb.

HAMMERMILL MOVERS. THE BEST IN THE BUSINESS.

When he pushed through the front door he had to jump out of the way of two burly men carrying bookshelves. *His* bookshelves.

"What the hell?" he muttered.

He stopped the men. "What are you doing with that?"

The front man grunted. "Moving it."

"Why?"

The man shrugged. "Don't know. Have to ask the boss lady that." Then he continued on, carrying the walnut case from the library into his office, where the rest of the bookcases now stood.

Grayson set out to find the *boss lady*.

He found her standing in the doorway to the library. At the sound of his voice she turned to face him. They stared at each other, questions and words hanging unspoken in the air.

He saw the devastation in her eyes, golden brown darkening until the flecks of green were obscured. She hesitated, and for a second he was sure she was going to say something. But at the very last minute she seemed to think better of it and turned away.

"What are you doing?" he demanded.

"I'm removing the furniture from the library."

His hand knotted at his side. "I can see that. The question is why?"

"Because I am turning it into a music room—just as it was always supposed to be," she answered, her tone brisk and businesslike. "I didn't know where you wanted the furniture delivered. So I'm stacking it in your office until you decide. You can either help or get out of the way."

"I will get out of the way permanently," he said tightly, "just as soon as I find new office space. In the meantime I have clients to attend, and I have little choice but to work out of Swan's Grace until that time. I'd appreciate it if for once you'd maintain some semblance of normalcy and allow me at the very least not to lose what remaining clients I have. Advising them in an office crowded with bookshelves set about every which way does not instill confidence."

He went in search of the movers, but the men had already trundled into their wagon and were rolling away. Glowering, Grayson stormed into his office, but he didn't get very far for all the bookshelves.

"Damn you, Sophie!" he bellowed.

But when he looked back and found her standing there, obstinately unmoving, arms crossed on her chest, he muttered a curse, climbed over a stack of law volumes, and made his way to his leather chair. He was going to regain control of his life if it killed him.

The next day he returned and found Margaret, Deandra, and Henry standing in the foyer, having just arrived from their travels, their suitcases in disarray on the floor around them.

"What is going on?" he asked with tight precision.

The three whirled around, and he could see the worry on their faces.

"We're not sure," Deandra answered for them. "We just got back, and Sophie has hardly said a word. No sooner did we walk into the house than she came down the stairs as quietly as you please, then took to the library like a woman obsessed."

"You'd better talk to her, Dea," Henry said.

"No, you talk to her. You're always good with her when she is like this."

"But this is different. She's so . . . single-minded and resolute. Though about what, I have no idea."

"True," Deandra and Margaret murmured.

"I'll talk to her," Grayson stated, striding forward.

But he stopped in his tracks when he entered the room.

Sophie stood on a small ladder in the empty library, a bucket on the floor and a paintbrush in her hand. But it wasn't paint that she smoothed on the bright red walls. After a second he realized it was water. She was soaking the painted wallpaper.

Henry came up beside him, the two men staring at the woman before them.

Sophie didn't turn around.

Finally Henry cleared his throat and called out to her. She turned back, nearly toppling from the ladder, and probably would have had Grayson not lunged forward and caught her, the wet paintbrush landing against his worsted wool jacket with a splat. Held in his arms, their faces so close, she stared at him for one long moment, then pushed at his shoulders.

"Put me down," she stated.

Grayson did as he was told, the climate of the room as cold and frigid as a bleak winter day.

"What happened in the short time we were gone?" Henry wanted to know.

Sophie looked at him, the water-soaked paintbrush still in her hand, before she slowly looked at Grayson and smiled dryly. "We finally came to an agreement about the direction of our futures."

She tossed the brush into the bucket with a splash, pulled on a pair of strange-looking gloves, then peeled up an edge of the wallpaper with a workman's tool. Then she pulled hard, the paper coming away with a yank.

"Look at that; it works."

Muttering a curse, Grayson turned on his heel and slammed into his office.

It was much the same after that. Day after day she tore the library apart bit by bit, peeling off the paper and prying off the newly installed walnut wainscoting. In time, there would be little left besides four stark walls and the hardwood floor. And when she wasn't working on the library, she was practicing the cello.

Despite his fury, every time the music began Grayson found himself sitting back, the tall shelves and books cluttered around him as he listened. Since the first time he had seen her play, she amazed him. But now her talent mesmerized him, making it hard to turn away. How many times had he climbed back over the books to stand in the foyer, needing to see her play?

Most string musicians were neat and disciplined, conveyors of music, almost invisible so the music could stand out. But it was Sophie a person noticed. Her body moved against the instrument, seeming to bend the notes to her will. As if she had something to prove.

It was stunning to watch, drawing him in, wrapping around him, making him wonder if he could possibly live without her.

After a lifetime of understanding that he couldn't afford to be weak, what did it say about him if he needed someone so badly?

A week after Sophie told Grayson about her past, a packet arrived from the courthouse. Inside she found the deed to Swan's Grace. Grayson was as good as his word and had reverted the title to her name. But nothing was included regarding the dissolution of their betrothal.

What did it mean? That he was having second thoughts, or that it simply took longer to dissolve an engagement than to transfer title to a house?

But more than that, which reason did she hope it was?

It was late in the afternoon, Grayson had already left for the day, and she stared at the document as she sat at his desk. She also stared at a pile of bills that needed to be paid.

When she had asked for Swan's Grace back, she hadn't thought about paying the bills. Her life was circling faster and faster in the wrong direction. She could hardly think by the time she went through each invoice for the umpteenth time. And yet again, she knew she didn't have enough to pay them.

"Knock, knock."

Sophie barely heard the words. She stared at the hand-scrawled notices from the gas and coal companies. Not to mention the grocery account which Grayson had established at a market nearby. She cursed herself for not thinking about such monumental details as paying bills.

"Sophie."

As though coming out of a trance, she snapped her

head up and found Deandra standing in front of the desk, squeezed precariously between two bookcases. Henry had shoehorned himself into one of the plush leather chairs.

Sophie searched for a smile. "Hello."

"You look like you saw a ghost," Henry mused.

Deandra considered her, tapping her long fingernails against her cheek. "Something is wrong, Sophie. Tell us."

She forced a laugh. "It's silly, really. It's just that things haven't gone as well here as I had hoped." She shrugged her shoulders with a nonchalance she didn't feel. "But I'll be fine."

"This is ridiculous," Deandra stated. "It is clear this place has caused you nothing but misery. You've gotten out of the betrothal. You've regained the title to the house. You can return to Europe anytime you want. I see no reason why we should stay any longer."

"I couldn't have said it better," Henry chimed in, leaping up, bumping a stack of books that tumbled to the floor, and rubbing his hands together with glee. "Give that Niles Prescott his money back and let's head for Monaco."

"If we start packing now," Deandra said, "we can catch the first ship out on the tide tomorrow morning."

Sophie's temples throbbed, her pulse racing. What could she say? How could she tell them the truth?

"Henry," Deandra continued, "go up and get Margaret. She's good at taking care of travel arrangements." Dea turned to Sophie. "Margaret can find out the rate at the shipping office. To save time, just give her a blank bank voucher to fill out there."

With that, the dam finally burst. "I can't give her a voucher!"

Henry froze half out of the chair. Deandra crossed her arms, her eyes narrowing.

"What do you mean, you can't give Margaret a voucher?" Dea asked in much too calm tones.

Sophie's hands curled into futile fists at her sides. But she had gone too far to turn back now. Raising her chin, she looked at the two people who had been more a part of her life than anyone else had in years. "I can't give Margaret a bank voucher because . . . there is no money in the bank on which to draw."

"Then give her coin," Henry stated, as if it were all so simple.

But Deandra didn't say a word, and it was clear in her eyes that she understood the truth.

"There is no coin left, is there?" Dea stated.

"Not enough. But there will be soon," Sophie added hurriedly. "You know as well as I do of the amounts that are due us."

"Why didn't you say something?" Deandra asked, her tone eerily neutral.

Sophie's shoulders slumped. "I didn't know how."

Deandra shook her head and turned to leave. That was when Sophie saw Grayson.

Her body flinched at the sight of him standing in the doorway, so tall, as always taking her breath away.

Embarrassment flared in her breast. How much more humiliation did she have to endure?

"You have no money?" he asked, his voice low.

With those words, all that she had tried to hold together burst inside her.

"No!" she blurted out, this time defiantly. "I don't have any money, I can't pay these bills, and until I play the concert at the Music Hall I won't have enough to get us back to Europe. I admit it. I've made a mess of things. Is that what you wanted to hear?"

He looked at her hard. "I take no joy in your problems."

He strode into the room, barely affording a glance to the narrow path he had to maneuver. "If you will excuse us," he said to Deandra and Henry. "Sophie and I have some financial matters to discuss."

They left the room, and Sophie had the fleeting thought that they would flee upstairs to pack. But her attention shifted when Grayson walked to his desk and looked through the bills that lay in a heap on top of the ledger.

"What are you doing?" she demanded.

"I am determining how much money is owed."

"Those bills are mine, as is Swan's Grace."

"It won't be for long if you can't pay your bills."

"I will pay them!"

"When?"

"Just as soon as I'm paid."

He glanced at the invoices. "Not soon enough." He took up the ledger and snapped it shut, the bills inside. "I'll take care of this in the morning."

She hated the relief that swam through her veins. "I'll pay you back. Every penny. For those bills. For this house." She scrambled for a pen and paper, scrawling a few words across the sheet. "Here. A contract promising to repay every cent."

He took it slowly, staring at her before dropping his gaze to read. When he looked back he raised a brow. "Don't you think you've had enough of contracts for a while?"

Red singed her cheeks. But he only crumpled the single page and tossed it into the trash bin. "Consider it as payment for a debt I already owed."

She narrowed her eyes and tilted her head in a mixture of confusion and hurt she wanted to deny. "What debt is that?"

"Money for the baskets you sent."

If he had struck her he couldn't have hurt her more. "I didn't send them so that you would owe me."

"It doesn't matter why you sent them, only that you did.

Now I have found a way to repay you. Let's just say the debt is clear."

And then he would be through with her. He didn't have to say the words for his meaning to be understood.

Anger washed over her in scalding waves. "You're saying that just to punish me."

"Punish you for what?"

"For Niles. But I can do that quite well enough on my own," she stated, hating the bitter taste on her tongue. "You can't forgive me because I'm not a virgin. But you said yourself that you aren't a virgin either."

She watched his eyes narrow.

"You might have turned Megan away, Grayson, but have you turned every woman away?"

His expression went hard.

"Have you?" she demanded.

"No," he answered tightly.

"Then why is it okay for you but not for me?"

"Because I'm a man!"

The words shimmered through the room, settling between them.

"And that makes it okay?" she asked softly.

"Yes. No. God, I don't know. It's different for a man."

"Why?"

He raked his hands through his hair. "You ask too many questions, Sophie. You want to change the way people think until it meets what you want. Well, you can't just change the world."

She shook her head as the anger drained out of her, and it was all she could do not to laugh her despair. "I always thought of you as brave. Fighting against your father's unfairness. Championing an awkward little girl who everyone else thought odd. That is what I loved about you most. Your bravery."

His jaw tightened.

"I knew that you had become a proper gentleman, fitting into a society that had always rejected me. I saw that the night I returned for my father's surprise birthday party. Until then I guess I always held a small bit of hope that eventually, if I could succeed, prove that I was talented, you would be able to accept me for who I had become. If you couldn't, who could?" She tilted her head and looked at him. "I think I still held a glimmer of that hope until I saw the look in your eyes when you realized I wasn't a virgin."

"Don't turn this around on me, Sophie. You're the one who wanted out of the betrothal. You're the one who cared only about Swan's Grace. I simply gave you what you wanted."

"No, Grayson. I gave *you* what you wanted. A way out of a betrothal to a woman you no longer wanted without losing your honor. Convenient, huh?"

They stared at each other for long moments before she turned on her heel and quit the room.

Chapter Twenty

Emmaline saw Richard nearly every day.

For a few stolen hours during the afternoon, she felt young again, as if she had recaptured youth, emotion rediscovered. She no longer felt as if her life were over.

Richard was like a drug. Once begun, it was hard to stop. Every day she told herself she wouldn't see him again. But then she'd give in, telling herself she would stop tomorrow.

They met at quiet, out-of-the-way places. Places that were easy to get to, but far enough away that they wouldn't be seen by friends or family. Fishing piers. Distant parks. Forgotten squares.

The weather was beginning to warm, flowers threatening to bloom, trees starting to turn a bright, tender green. But on days that still held a strong bite of cold, Richard wrapped his coat around her shoulders, his hands lingering, warming her in a way that had little to do with the added material.

They talked and laughed. He looked at her. Just looked for long minutes, his heart in his eyes, until one day when he ran his finger along her chin, down to her hand.

"You can leave Bradford," he said, lacing his fingers with hers.

Guilt flared at the thought that she wanted to.

"I have money now. I can support you, Em."

"This is not about money, Richard."

"Then what?"

What was it about? she wondered. Certainly not honor, she thought with a cringe of guilt.

For years she had turned a blind eye to Bradford's dealings with their sons. She especially hated the way he treated Grayson, though she had believed that her husband, even in his harshness, was teaching Grayson about honor. She believed in honor.

She hated lying, and she hated lying to her sons most of all. Yet somehow even that didn't make her stop seeing Richard now.

She hated to think that she had no honor.

However, it didn't seem as simple as that—though no doubt every wrongdoer consoled himself with that phrase. But she was not having relations with Richard, she told herself in the middle of the night when she lay alone in her huge, plush, and empty bed.

She put from her mind the fact that meeting a man not her husband for any reason would ruin her. Despite that, she couldn't deny the deep fluttering of almost forgotten feelings that made her breath catch and her heart beat too hard. A mere accidental brush of Richard's hand against hers made her lips part and her knees grow weak.

And she knew he felt it, too. She could see how much he wanted her. The way he danced around her, a brush, a touch, coming close, then whisking away. Making her want him more.

But she was a married woman.

She reminded herself of that daily. Though it was hard to keep that fact in her mind when her husband turned her away and barely noticed she was there.

And when Richard met her at a quiet teahouse in the South End weeks after he had reappeared in her life, whispering in her ear that he wanted to make love to her, her mind screamed no.

But her heart yearned for his love.

Chapter Twenty-one

Sophie woke the next morning and hurried through her ablutions. Once dressed, she dashed to Deandra's room. But it was empty, the bed neatly made, none of the usual boas or feathered mules tossed about in disarray.

Dread started to pound inside her as she went to Margaret's room and found it quiet and still, the assistant's desk clear of the normal stacks of correspondence and files. Then she went to Henry's, only to find it the same way. Neat as a pin, with not a hint of his flowery cologne or dapper suits. And other than Margaret, none of them were known to leave their beds, much less their rooms, before noon.

Reeling, Sophie came downstairs, steeling herself against the sight of her entourage packed and ready to depart, their luggage stacked on the foyer floor. But the black-and-white marble was as empty as the rooms had been, and there wasn't a person in sight.

With her skirts puffing around her, she sank to the bottom step, distressed over the fact that they hadn't even said good-bye. Though it was foolish to feel so hurt. She had understood all along that her relationship with these people had revolved around money. They would be her friends if she paid their way. That was what an entourage was. She was a fool to have come to feel anything else for these people. But she had. She had grown to love Margaret

277

like a sister, and even Dea had become something of a mother to her.

And Henry. A rueful smile threatened at the thought of the little man. He had become like a brother or a cherished friend, always trying his best to say the right thing and very rarely succeeding.

How pathetic she was to have to buy her friends and to seek approval and self-worth from strangers when she performed.

A sound from the kitchen finally gained her attention. Slowly, hope beginning to grow, she headed for the back of the house. When she pushed through the door she found Margaret working at the stove, Henry reading the newspaper, and Deandra going through a stack of documents.

"You're still here," she said, her breath rushing out.

All three looked at her. "Of course we're still here," Deandra said, sitting back. "Where did you think we'd be?"

"But your rooms are empty."

"No, they are simply cleaned up for a change. We are used to having servants do our every bidding."

Sophie's spine stiffed. "I'm sorry," she offered, her chin rising.

"Don't be sorry. You'll pay for servants again soon enough. I'm going through your contracts now to see what is due you and when."

"In the meantime," Henry said, "I'm going to get a job. These classifieds are filled with them."

"You mean . . ."

The words trailed off, and Margaret strode up to her in her efficient manner. "We are staying. Whether you have money or not. Whether you have a future or not. Who knows where the three of us would have ended up had you not taken us in. Now it's time for us to return the favor."

"But what about your cousin?"

"My cousin doesn't want me, nor does she need me. My place is here with you."

Sophie threw her arms around the primly dressed woman who had become a friend. "I love you."

Henry leaped up. "I want a hug, too!"

And before too long, the three of them held tight, only Deandra holding back, an odd look on her face as she sat at the table—wistful and disdainful at the same moment.

"Come on, Dea," Henry cajoled.

After a second, she flew into the group and held tight with a laugh.

"We're going to make it," Margaret said.

"Never a doubt," Henry added.

They pulled back with smiles on their faces.

"Thank you." Sophie felt an intense joy. Then she headed for the newspaper. "Henry, how about sharing those classifieds with me? I'm going to get a job, too."

"Not on your life," Deandra stated, back to her business-like self. "More than ever you need to practice. You are going to get this Music Hall show over with so we can get payment; then we are going to head back to Europe."

Back to Europe. The only viable option, since her father had no room for her in his life. And the truth was, until she had finished the summer and winter tours, she couldn't afford her childhood home.

After all the battles, she could still lose Swan's Grace anyway.

A wave of disquiet swept through her. She turned away, knowing she couldn't redo the mistakes of the past. She could only make sure she didn't make any more mistakes in the future. And she would do that by playing. By truly playing.

As she was meant to.

The thought reared up, surprising her. She wanted to dazzle Bostonians, yes, but with talent rather than spectacle.

She might have lost everything else about her past, but she would not lose her pride.

She realized with blinding insight that she had wanted it all along, but had held the desire at bay.

Determination whirled through her blood. Determination and fire. She would play Bach. Because despite what Niles Prescott had made her believe, she had talent.

Her heart pounded. She wanted this more than she ever dreamed possible. For months she had tried to deny it. But now the feelings burst forth and wouldn't be held back.

She wanted to show Niles Prescott that he was wrong. She wanted to show her father that he should be proud. She wanted to show Grayson that in many ways she had not failed. And show them she would.

With that decision, Sophie devised a schedule, then clung to routine like a lifeline. She started practice earlier every morning, rehearsing into the late hours of the night. Her world became ordered with the precision of a metronome. Purpose and excitement filled her, as intoxicating as a drug.

She practiced in the library, paintings stacked in the hallway, wallpaper half gone, the room empty except for her chair and a music stand. In moments of frustration when a piece wasn't going well, she poured her energies into stripping more of the wallpaper. But then the solution to a difficult section would come to her, a strip of paper hanging half off the wall like a tongue lolling out of a mouth. She would leap back into her chair to play what she heard in her head, the problem solved, until the next one arose.

At the end of the first week of practicing, her confidence rose as the notes started making sense in her head.

Euphoria and wonder filled her. Purpose became her constant companion.

But as one week turned into two, her euphoria began to

falter. No matter how hard she tried, she couldn't pull the suites together. She might understand how the works needed to be played, but despite her determined effort, she couldn't make the cello soar as she wanted.

After long months of simply letting her music flow free and wild, the bow had become awkward in her hands. The change from spectacle back to respected concert cellist required controlled movements. But those modifications made her bowing inconsistent. Her left hand clenched up, her body went tense. Even simple scales became torture.

And at the end of the second week, what progress she had made was negated completely. She fought to hold on to her conviction that she could succeed. Her excitement faded, and confidence became as elusive as waves rushing back to the sea.

Through it all, Grayson was there every day. Several times Lucas had arrived, and the men had conferred behind closed doors. Grayson had also hired a solicitor who specialized in property to find him a new office.

By the end of the third week, doubt had crept in and firmly took hold, making her wonder how she ever could have thought she could play a single unaccompanied Bach suite, much less five of them.

Fear pushed every ounce of excitement away. And by the time she woke the next morning, she could hardly breathe when she stood from the bed.

She wanted to go to Grayson. To talk to him. Sit with him. Have him tell her everything would be all right. But everything wasn't going to be all right. She couldn't play Bach, and soon Grayson would be gone.

With only a week left before the concert, Sophie dressed hurriedly, barely securing her clothes before heading downstairs.

But she stopped in the foyer when she found Grayson standing in the torn-apart library. He stood in profile, so strong in his dark coat and pants, his face chiseled. Would he ever fail to move her?

He turned slowly and looked at her. When he did she could see a flash of brightness, as if he were happy to see her. The simple gesture made her heart swell. But then the flash was gone.

"Good morning," he greeted her, his tone the kind he used with business associates, professional and straight-forward.

"Good morning," she said with a poignant rush of feeling. Where was intelligent, witty conversation when she needed it? But she couldn't deny how glad she was to see him, even if he was cool and distant. "Would you like to join me for tea?"

For a second his countenance softened, seemed almost wistful as he started to reach out to her. But at the last minute his eyes hardened, as if he suddenly remembered the past. He dropped his hand away.

"I'm due in court. I stopped by for a file."

He turned away and strode to his office, cursing when he banged his knee. Sophie was left standing in the foyer. Hurt and angry, she marched in behind him, reacting to more than his bland dismissal.

"Do you really hate me so much?" she demanded from the doorway.

Grayson looked up from the papers on his desk.

His dark eyes were filled with emotion she hadn't noticed when he arrived.

"Don't," he said, the word part warning, part plea.

"Why not? I understand that you don't want to marry me any longer. I've understood that all along. But why do you have to ignore me, like we were never friends?"

"We are too old to be friends, Sophie. Adults are not friends, at least not men and women. Now if you'll excuse me, I need to read this file before I am due in court."

*   *   *

Her father arrived that afternoon, his long, narrow face lined with concern. Patrice was at his side.

"Good morning, princess," Conrad said kindly. "Your stepmother and I are worried about you."

"What for?" she asked, trying for nonchalance.

"We haven't seen you in weeks, and—"

"And rumors are circulating that your engagement to Grayson is broken!"

"Patrice." Conrad turned to his wife.

"What? What kind of future will our daughters have if she mucks this up?"

Our daughters, as if Sophie weren't one of them. The words seeped into her heart, filling every corner.

"Where are we going to get the kind of money that Grayson paid you for her?"

Sophie flinched, but she pushed the words from her mind. She concentrated on the floor, the black-and-white marble like squares on a chessboard.

Her stepmother took a step closer. "Doesn't she care that we will be ruined if she doesn't marry Grayson Hawthorne?"

"That is enough, Patrice," Conrad stated, his voice simmering through the foyer.

Sophie's head shot up and she looked at her father. She couldn't have been more stunned when he came forward and cupped her arms gently, in a fatherly way.

"I've spent many nights these last weeks thinking of little else besides what has happened here," he said. "As long as I live, I will never forget the look on your face when we told you of the betrothal. I can see how distressed you are still. No father is immune to that." His voice grew strained. "Not even me. That's when I realized that I hadn't been thinking about you when I signed the agreement. I was thinking of myself." His smile was sad. "But know that I truly thought a betrothal with Grayson would be the best thing for you and for him."

"Good Lord, Conrad," Patrice snapped.

"I said, enough!"

Tension shimmered through the air as the man and his wife stared at each other. It was clear that Patrice wanted to snap back at her husband, and normally she would have. But something had changed, perhaps in that moment. And after several silent seconds, Conrad looking at her, his gaze hard, she only turned away.

Conrad pressed his eyes closed fleetingly before refocusing on Sophie.

"I will do whatever I need to do to make this right."

"Oh, Papa," she whispered, her throat aching with sudden, unshed tears. "Everything is going to be fine. The betrothal is broken."

Patrice gasped.

"And Grayson has returned Swan's Grace to me."

"Good God, how will we ever repay him?" Patrice wailed.

"You don't have to," Sophie stated. "I will. I have a career as a cellist, and I will repay Grayson Hawthorne every penny he spent."

"Oh, Sophie," Conrad said. "Always so strong. Whether you know it or not, you've always made me proud. That is why I came here today to tell you that, so you could go into this concert without worry."

Her heart lurched.

"You deserve this performance," he continued. "You deserved it long ago. Now it is yours, and I don't want my foolishness to ruin it in any way. This Saturday you will be the tremendous success I've always known you could be." His face lit with a hopeful smile. "Afterward I will find a way to repay Grayson myself."

"Oh, Papa," she repeated.

The concert. She felt sick at the thought. If she couldn't

play Bach, then she'd have little choice but to give her usual show.

"I love you, Sophie."

But would he after he saw her play?

As soon as the door clicked shut, she faltered. Her mind felt disjointed with alarm. She couldn't talk, she couldn't do anything but work her way through the Bach suites again and again, hoping that at any moment they would pull together, until her world consisted of little more than notes that threatened to strangle her.

She couldn't perform the spectacle. Not now. Not after her father's precious words.

The feeling welled up in her all at once, the pain and the longing almost choking her. How foolish to let her worth become wrapped up in a single performance.

She had to get out, escape the doubt, out into the open. With frantic steps she left the house and walked up and down the Back Bay's grid of streets, counting, each step taken to a rhythm in her head like the tick of a hall clock.

Panicked, Sophie continued to walk, looking neither right nor left. The air was finally warm, and she walked through the streets relishing the dark as the sun went down. She walked until she came to the Hotel Vendome. Bright and cheerful. She looked up at a front window and wondered if Grayson was inside.

What was he doing? Sipping brandy? Preparing for court?

Did she dare walk into the Vendome and knock on his door?

Grayson sat in his sparse hotel room, the small writing desk covered with documents and contracts. He had a great deal of work to do, files to read, contracts to draft. But he had sat there for hours without reading a sentence or writing a word, his mind filled with Sophie. The feel of her hair, the taste of her skin.

He cursed the weakness. He was an ordered man. He understood that. And Sophie had turned his world upside down. But no matter what she had done, he couldn't forget her.

The solicitor he had hired brought property after property to him for his perusal. Each of them would have been fine for a new office. But he hadn't bought any of them.

He needed to be strong as he had always been, controlling his life with a calm certainty. However, he felt anything but calm. He was furious at himself. At Niles Prescott. The fury was eating away at him. But always in his mind there was Sophie.

His countenance darkened even more when a knock sounded.

"What are you doing here?" he demanded as he pulled open the door.

Henry smiled, then simply stepped past him, strolling into the room and looking around as if he were considering buying the place.

"Hello to you, too. I take back the suggestion that we buy stock in this humble abode, as it is much too . . . humble for my tastes." He chuckled, then noticed Grayson's ominous glare. With a shrug he added, "As to why I am here, I can think of many reasons." His smile turned lurid.

"Careful, Chambers, you're treading on thin ice."

The little man shivered and smiled. "You brute, you."

Grayson took a step toward him, but Henry held up his hands. "Don't hit me, at least not before we've talked."

"We have nothing to say."

Henry's smile fled as if it had been little more than a disguise, and he sighed. "But we do. I'm here about Sophie."

Instantly Grayson was alert. "What's wrong?" he demanded.

"You tell me. What happened between you two while we were gone?"

Silence sliced through the room, each man staring at the other.

"That is none of your concern."

"Sophie's too proud to admit it, but she needs you."

"Get out," Grayson stated coldly, his frustration seeping through.

"She does need you, just as you need her. Quit being so stubborn and go to her."

"I said get out!"

Seconds later Grayson stood alone in the room. It was dark outside, the night pressing in around him. He had work to finish. He had a hearing first thing in the morning, and he couldn't afford for anything to go wrong with this case. He needed to sit back down and concentrate.

Instead he slammed out the door.

It was nine o'clock, the horizon dark. At Swan's Grace he didn't bother to knock. He used his key and entered, surprising Deandra, but Henry nodded silently.

"I'll tell her you're here," Dea said, standing from her chair.

"Let him announce himself," Henry responded.

Deandra looked at him as if he had lost his mind. "She'll be furious."

"Will she?"

Grayson didn't wait for the two to stop their arguing. He took the stairs in a few pounding steps, then came to the master suite.

He didn't knock.

He pushed through the door, then stopped in his tracks at the sight of her, her gossamer wrapper sheer against the golden light. She stood in front of the long oval mirror, staring at herself.

What did she see?

"You always take my breath away," he whispered, unable to stop himself.

She gave no start of surprise, and she didn't turn to look at him. "Why?" she asked, so softly he almost didn't hear. "Because you think I'm beautiful?" She reached out and touched the glass. "I was never beautiful before. But now men clamor for my attention and swear I am the loveliest woman they have ever seen."

Closing the door with a click, Grayson strode across the room, but stopped just short of her. "They are right."

Pivoting so fast her hair fluttered around her shoulders, she turned to face him. "What is different about me? Why am I pretty now?"

"You were always pretty."

"To you, but to no one else."

What could he say? When she was young, her hair had been unruly, her eyes an indistinct brown. But now that she'd become an adult, those very same features had come together in a way that was striking. Unruly had become provocative. Indistinct had become golden brown.

He wanted to touch her, much as she had touched her image in the mirror. But he kept his hands at his sides. "Now everyone else sees what I saw all along."

"No, they see someone new." Slowly she turned back to her reflection. "I changed. And it's the results of the change that they love. The wildness. The distance I put between myself and them. That is what they crave."

"As you said yourself, every man wants what he can't have," he stated.

Her smile was bitter, and she met his gaze in the silvered glass. "No. Every man wants what he thinks *no* man can have."

Grayson's eyes narrowed against the words.

"Isn't that the truth?" she demanded softly. "They love her as long as she's beyond their reach, then they hate her if they realize she's not so elusive, not so perfect."

He only looked at her in the mirror, his gaze implacable, and that made her furious. "Isn't that how you feel?"

He took her arm abruptly and whirled her around to face him. "Yes, I love your wildness, but I hate it as well. Yes, I want you, but I resent that desire."

"Why?" she demanded. "Because another man had me first?"

"Because you make me lose control!"

The words shimmered violently through the room. They stared at each other, thoughts lost in the startled moment.

"Oh, Grayson, you can't always be in control. Every once in a while we all need to scream and shout."

His jaw cemented, and he let her go as if she burned him. He turned sharply to leave.

"Don't go," she whispered. "Don't leave me."

He bowed his head.

"Leave me tomorrow. I'll understand. But don't leave me now."

He swore and continued from the room, turning the brass doorknob. But he could feel her there, in his mind, in his soul. In his heart.

With a curse, he slammed the door shut and strode across the carpet in a few short strides. He pulled her to him, his mouth coming down on hers, hard. But she took what he gave, her arms wrapping around him as if she were drowning.

He swept her up in his arms and carried her toward the bed.

Sophie felt her heart in her throat. She needed this man, needed to be close. She knew she should have demanded that he leave the minute he entered the room. He already thought so poorly of her. Instead she all but demanded that he stay—proving that she was the kind of woman she had never wanted to be.

But hadn't she already proved that? Hadn't she already known that she couldn't play the music she needed to play? Wouldn't she confirm everything she was afraid she was once and for all when Boston heard the only kind of repertoire she was capable of performing?

He set her down so that she faced him in front of the bed. "I can't stay away," he whispered, his voice strained and desperate.

Her eyes burned with emotion. She could see the accusation in his eyes, and the bewilderment.

"I don't want you to," she answered.

He pulled her to him then, fiercely. In seconds their clothes were tossed aside, and she couldn't help it when she reached out to touch his chest. So strong, so broad, sweeping down into a narrow waist. But he wouldn't stand still for long.

His hands ran down her arms to her hands, making her tremble. With incredible gentleness, he lifted them to his lips, kissing the backs, then her palms. And when his hands drifted up her belly, over her ribs to cup the fullness of her breasts, she did nothing more than sigh.

Winding her fingers through his hair, she gasped when he pulled one nipple deep into his mouth. His tongue laved the bud into a taut peak before taking the other, sucking and laving, a slow lava beginning to churn low in her body.

He traced her body as if he wanted to know every inch of her. Her jaw, her ribs. But when she pulled him back to the bed, he stopped her.

She looked at him in confusion.

"Not yet," he whispered, his voice raw and sensual. "Raise your leg for me, love."

Shock sliced through her.

"Like this," he said, as he gently ran his strong hand down her hip to her knee, then lifted her leg, bracing her foot against the low bench that ran along the end of the bed.

Instantly she felt the heat of embarrassment burn her skin, but combined with that was the heat of sensual yearning.

"Yes," he breathed. "Let me touch you." His fingers drifted to the nest of curls between her legs.

"Grayson," she cried out, grabbing his shoulders.

"Shhh." He gentled her, seeking the lips of her sex. His eyes were dark, penetrating. "Open for me."

He circled his finger slowly until she relaxed.

"Yes, Sophie," he crooned, stroking.

Her gasp rapidly gave way to a sigh that caught in her throat. Her embarrassment fled entirely when the yearning turned into an intense desire, and that made her ready for his touch.

Then he penetrated her with one strong finger.

Her body tensed, but he didn't stop. He stroked her, his finger sliding gently inside her, slowly but intensely, until she sensed her own wetness.

"God, you make me want you," he said in a breath against her skin, then slipped a second finger inside her, cradling her when she trembled.

He stroked her deeply, covering her mouth with his own to kiss her, their tongues entwining. Her body began to pulse, all vestiges of inhibition tossed aside.

But with infinite tenderness he pulled out of her, and her body cried out in disappointment. He only smiled with such love and gladness, then pulled her down on top of him on the thick mattress.

Their bodies came together intimately, touching, but not yet joined. He cupped her hips as he kissed her, running his hands up her back. She was timid on top, not certain what to do. His strong hands guided her, his tongue thrusting into her mouth.

Her body was alive with wanting and passion, and a wildness that was pure and not practiced. She wanted him, desperately. And needed him to want her, too.

"Love me, Grayson. Please."

With something close to what she would have sworn was a cry, he came over her, his elbows pressing into the mattress to support his upper body. He stared at her for one long second, his body trembling. "I need you, Sophie. I always have." Then he kissed her deeply, as if he couldn't get enough.

He sucked her tongue into his mouth, stroking her, as he pulled up her knees, settling between her thighs. Calling her name, he thrust inside her. She felt the tension in his body as he waited for her body to adjust to him. Then he began to move, slowly at first, a maelstrom of emotion building until they were both panting and yearning. He cupped her hips, pulling her up to meet his bold, fevered thrusts.

She clutched his shoulders, his face buried in her neck, panting, thrusting, until she felt her body convulse with her release. He cried out her name, and when he did she could feel an explosive shudder rack the hard length of his body.

He collapsed on top of her. She bore his weight, the heaviness comforting, until he rolled to his side, bringing her with him. She could feel the beat of his heart, strong and rapid. They lay that way, wrapped together, silence all around them. She wanted to stay that way forever.

But then he spoke.

"I don't understand you. You are an odd mix of bravado and vulnerability, confidence and shyness. Boldness and inexperience. You act worldly, but when I stroke you, slip my fingers inside you, you shudder, then come like you have never experienced an orgasm before."

Embarrassed, she turned her head away. But he gently grasped her chin and turned her back. She looked into his eyes and thought she had never seen such desolation.

"Whoever you really are," he whispered, "I do need you. You are my weakness, Sophie. And I can't let you go."

With his words, her heart stilled, because she understood that this strong, aching man believed he couldn't afford any weaknesses.

The question was, Why?

Chapter Twenty-two

Saturday, the day of Sophie's concert, the note arrived. Emmaline stared at the missive.

Please see me. Quincy House hotel. Room 3A.

No name. But she understood.

Sinking lower in a hot, deep, fragrant bath, Emmaline thought of Richard. Her world seemed as soft and muted as the images in the steam-covered mirrors. The note had drifted from her fingers to the small Oriental rug on the floor.

She ran her hands slowly through the water. Just holding the note had made her heart leap. Seeing his bold writing, knowing that he had held the page, made her body tingle and yearn.

Exhaling sharply, she pushed out of the water, her decision made.

An hour later, after dressing carefully, Emmaline came down the stairs, knowing she would go to him.

Good God, what was she doing? Sneaking out of the house like an unmanageable schoolgirl. Again. But she had found the outings impossible to resist. She anticipated a simple brush of hands in the park. Longed for a gentle smile. A promised story. Each of which happened. But never a kiss.

Though not for much longer. Richard had said before he wouldn't wait, but he had, barely, his lips coming so close to hers that she could feel his heat.

Was it really so wrong, considering her relationship with Bradford?

The question circled more and more through her head when Richard was near.

It was a beautiful day, the late-morning sun filling the house. Luncheon was already planned and she wouldn't be needed until this evening, for the concert that all of Boston was talking about.

Grayson had sent word that he would bring by the tickets for the event later that day.

Her brow furrowed at the thought that something was wrong between Grayson and Sophie. Neither was happy, though Emmaline had no idea why.

When she had inquired about the cause earlier in the week, Grayson had stiffly kissed her forehead, telling her not to worry.

As if she were a sweet young thing who needn't bother her little head.

She wanted to reprimand him. She was his mother. She was older, wiser. But somehow her son had lost sight of that fact.

Why did children have to grow up into adults who thought they knew more than their parents?

Lost in thought, her hair pulled up loosely, secured beneath a beautiful spring hat, she wasn't paying attention when she reached for the knob on the front door.

"You're going out?"

Emmaline froze, her hand extended, her reticule swinging on her wrist. "Bradford, I didn't see you there."

"I noticed."

He stood in the doorway of his study, the pocket doors slid back on either side. A book lay forgotten in his hand as he studied her. He was so handsome, standing in this home they had built together. Her heart raced, and she could feel guilt stinging her cheeks.

"Where are you going?" Bradford asked.

Emmaline stared wordlessly before she quickly dropped her gaze. Searching for calm, she smoothed her gown. "Out. Just for a bit." Her hand stilled, and she quickly looked up. "Unless you have a better idea. I don't have to go, not really. I could stay here, with you."

Bradford's gray brows came together. "A better idea? What are you talking about, Mother?"

She strode forward, her steps determined, her long day skirt rustling gently in the high-ceilinged foyer. When she stopped in front of him, she didn't think. She took his hand and pressed it between her own. "I don't know. Let's go for a ride through the park. Just you and me."

"The other day it was a picnic; now it's a ride in the park. What has gotten into you, Emmaline? You've been acting very peculiar recently."

Her hands dropped to her side, sudden, futile anger flashing through her. "I hardly call wanting to spend time with my husband peculiar," she stated with more force than she had used in some thirty-odd years.

Bradford's countenance grew ominous. "Mrs. Hawthorne, remember who you are speaking to."

"Remember? How could I forget! How could I forget for one second that I am the unwanted wife of a man who is too cold to understand that he is loved!"

Not waiting for a reply, she raced for the door. But his voice stopped her. No contrition. No softness.

"I asked you before, Emmaline, where are you going?"

She whirled to face him, recognized the implacable look. "I'm going out, Mr. Hawthorne. Whether you like it or not."

Then she walked out the door with the dignity of a queen, knowing what she was going to do.

Not thirty minutes later, Grayson strode into Hawthorne House. The concert was only hours away, and he still had no idea what to expect.

He had yet to hear from Lucas regarding Niles Prescott or the details of Sophie's earlier performances. And time was running out. He fervently hoped that Sophie's implications about being wild and outrageous were only to make him crazy.

He couldn't make sense of her, and his preconceived ideas about the people in his life were falling apart with each day that passed. An innocent virgin? A respected conductor who would have sexual relations with a girl young enough to be his daughter? And his mother. Slipping from her safe and respectable home, slipping away from her husband, for what Grayson was increasingly sure were assignations with another man.

Fury raced through his veins like ice water. When he got his hands on Niles Prescott he would make him pay. And he would find out what his mother was up to.

His ordered world had been turned upside down until he could make little sense of anything. He hated the lack of control. He had survived by making sense of the incomprehensible. He had made it through being turned out of his home at sixteen by gaining control of his new world.

How was it possible that all these years later the order he had gained could fall apart so completely?

Grayson's day was filled, giving him little time to think. He barely had time to drop off the tickets to the Music Hall for his parents. But when he entered Hawthorne House, his father stood in his study, staring out the window.

"Father?"

Bradford wheeled around to stare at him, and Grayson knew right away that something was wrong.

"What is it?"

"Have you seen your mother?" Bradford asked, his voice odd, somehow disjointed.

"No, but I just got here." He glanced toward the stairs. "I assume she's in her room."

"Then you've assumed incorrectly. Your mother is not at home. Do you know where she might be?"

Grayson stared at his father, remembering the times he had been certain he had seen his mother out. In a hired hack. On the docks.

"I have no idea," he said, protectiveness surging inside him. But he would find her. "She's probably in the garden, or perhaps she ran to an unexpected meeting."

Grayson reached into his coat pocket and pulled out the tickets, hardly aware that he did. "These are for the concert."

Bradford took them absentmindedly.

"You'll be next to Conrad and Patrice in the first row. You should get there early."

"Are you expecting a crowd?"

Grayson's brow furrowed. "Every ticket has sold. Standing room only. The auditorium will be packed."

All of Boston would be there to see who knew what kind of show.

But he'd worry about that later. First he needed to find his mother. Before his father did.

Emmaline walked into the Quincy House hotel, pulling her veil close as she bypassed the front desk and went immediately to the narrow set of stairs. The Quincy was a four-story brick building in downtown Boston that catered to bachelors who lived there year-round. A woman slipping in alone would not go unnoticed, though she was thankful it was not the kind of place where she would be questioned either.

Her palms were moist as she came to the third floor. After looking left, then right, she went to the right, not stopping until she came to room 3A. But when she raised her hand to knock, she hesitated, her mouth going dry with uncertainty.

She stared at the door, scarred from wear, but well polished by a caring staff. She could hardly fathom that she was there.

But her path was clear.

She told herself to flee and never look back. But she couldn't leave.

Her knock was sharp and hurried. When the door swung open, Richard stood there, his smiles and laughter gone. He looked at her as if he couldn't believe she had actually arrived, and his heart glowed in his eyes.

"Emmaline," he said, his voice nearly a whisper.

And she understood then that this man truly loved her.

Grayson sat at his desk at Swan's Grace. The place was a shambles—the library torn apart and unfinished. Furniture scattered. Paintings forgotten in the hall.

Disarray reigned. His life felt much the same way.

If Sophie was there, she didn't let on. The house was quiet as a tomb. His finger circled slowly on the rim of a crystal glass. He stared at it without seeing.

He had searched downtown and at the docks. But he had found no trace of his mother.

A knock gained his attention. When he looked up, he found Lucas striding into the room, eyeing the mess with amusement.

"I believe I found what you're looking for," the younger man said, squeezing through the narrow rows Grayson had constructed.

Grayson stood, for a brief moment confused. How did Lucas know about their mother?

"A man I deal with in Vienna just got word to me."

Grayson realized in an instant that Lucas was talking about Sophie.

"Apparently my contact spoke with a man named Herr Wilhelm who saw Sophie play here in Boston when she was young, and in Vienna just before she returned here."

"Tell me she gives a performance that will dazzle Boston."

"Oh, she will dazzle them, all right, but not in the way you would like."

Grayson ran his hand through his dark hair. "Hell."

Lucas glanced at the folder, then back. "I also found information on Niles Prescott."

Grayson's eyes narrowed.

"The night before the announcement was made as to who would win the annual debut recital, Prescott changed the name of the recipient."

"And he changed it from Sophie to Megan Robertson," Grayson surmised.

"Yes. Apparently it wasn't the first time he did that either, changing the name of the winning student at the last minute. But only when it involved a girl."

Both men's faces shifted into ruthless planes.

"What do you want me to do?" Lucas asked.

Grayson met his eye. "Nothing. Leave Niles Prescott to me."

"Fine. Though first, you'd best look at this," Lucas said, extending a discreet folder. "It contains all you need to know about Sophie's concerts."

But Grayson had barely got it in his hands when another knock battered the front door. Knowing no one else would get it, Grayson set the folder down on his desk, then strode out and answered it.

"Mr. Hawthorne," a man cried, out of breath, as if he had run a long way.

"Hastings?" Grayson said in surprise at the sight of the family butler.

"Your mother's lady's maid found this on the floor," Hastings said, his brow furrowed with concern as he extended a single sheet of folded stationery. "I thought it would be best if I brought it to you."

Grayson eyed him, understanding that Hastings had made a choice between him and his father. His eyes narrowed as he flipped open the note. He read once, twice, then twice.

"What is it?" Lucas asked from behind him.

Hastings's eyes went wide.

"Master Hawthorne!" Hastings blurted, panicked. "I didn't see you there."

"That's an understatement. What's all this about?"

"Nothing, little brother," Grayson said carefully. He would handle this himself.

And before another question could be asked, he strode out the front door, anger pushing him on.

His hands brushed against her arms, his palms drifting along her skin, barely, just a hint, stopping at the puffed spring sleeve. She felt a sweet, tender shudder of yearning, a heady feeling, making her want more.

"Em," he whispered, his breath warm against her ear. "You are incredible."

Whether she was or not, he made her feel as if she were beautiful and young, with life and possibilities stretching out before her.

His hands slipped up her neck, briefly cupping her cheeks before continuing on to her hair. With a few gentle tugs to the pins, the long coil tumbled like a waterfall down her back and shoulders. She felt it against her skin, the strands brushing over her as gently as his fingers did.

She wanted to feel more. Needed to feel more—as if she were finally living.

Perhaps sensing her thoughts, Richard pushed the capped sleeves from her shoulders, running his fingertips along the soft ridge, slipping beneath the material at her arms.

Her head fell back and he kissed her neck, a gentle sucking that made her body tingle and yearn.

He wore shirtsleeves, his coat and tie gone, and when he stepped away, setting her at arm's length, she felt an urge to touch the golden vee of skin at his neck.

But before she could summon her courage, he turned her around until her spine was to his chest. Then he pointed.

"Look," he said.

When she did she saw herself, her reflection in a mirror in the corner. The sight surprised her.

"You are so beautiful."

"I'm old."

"No," he whispered.

She watched, mesmerized, as he bent his head to brush his lips against her hair, his strong hands on her shoulders. In the mirror, she saw someone she hadn't seen in years, a woman with eyes shining, hair flowing, and a smile that erased years from her face. But more than that, she saw a woman who looked happy, so happy she could cry.

His hands drifted down her arms, then across to her abdomen. Very slowly, he pulled her back against him.

"Do you understand how much I want you?"

His voice was deep and low, and she could feel that he wanted her. Her mind tightened with something she didn't recognize. Panic, perhaps, but it was more than that.

She turned in his arms as understanding came clear. "I want you, too." Despite everything, or perhaps because of it.

He didn't respond, merely looked at her. Her heart raced, and she knew she should pull back—for so many reasons. Propriety, decency. The fact that she was married. Instead, when he pulled her close, she went to him.

His kissed her then, his mouth meeting hers, his tongue seeking entrance. She opened to him, then shuddered with intensity when his tongue touched hers.

Sensation she hadn't experienced in decades came back to her, filling her until she felt weak with desire—and gratitude. She wanted to cry for the touch, to weep at the pleasure that she had thought was lost to her.

Right or wrong, she would always remember this day and this kiss, perhaps remember it more than the kisses she had received from him years before. Because now it was like a gift, something she had thought she'd never have again.

His hand ran up her back, molding her to him. Despite his age he still had the hard, well-defined physique of an athlete.

The need to flee was gone, pushed aside by the sensation of his fingers burning a path across her skin. And when he replaced his fingers with his lips, she could only sigh.

He looked at her again, hesitating, as if giving her one last chance to pull away. But she didn't move; she met his probing gaze before he closed the distance between them, then touched his lips to hers once again.

The kiss was tender but demanding, and she had the fleeting thought that she wanted something more from this than simply the embrace. She wanted to feel loved and cherished.

She had turned to this man once before when she had needed to feel loved. She had wanted someone in the world to see her, to make her feel as if she weren't overlooked, as if she were cared for.

And she realized then that she was seeking the same thing from him again.

Understanding that, how could she go through with it?

The thought startled her.

Earlier she had thought she was older and wiser. Was she?

But more than that, could she live with herself knowing she had lost her decency? Not once, but twice.

The thought seared her, taking her breath much as his touch had taken it earlier. She had no answers, no answers other than one.

She deserved to be loved, but not by a man who wasn't her husband.

With that she pushed away.

Richard's eyes were clouded with passion. "What's the matter?"

"I can't do this!"

It took a moment for him to gain control as he pulled a deep breath. "Em, I love you. Surely you know that."

"All I know is that this is wrong, at least for me."

"Your husband ignores you! How could it be wrong to be with someone who loves you?"

She stared at him. "If you really loved me, you never would have asked me to act without honor. Honor isn't only for men, Richard. Women have it, too."

"Emmaline," he whispered, stricken.

But she no longer heard. She frantically pulled herself together, this time knowing that she would never see this man again. She deserved something more in life, and she would find it.

But when she pulled open the door, her mind froze. Her world spun as she realized her insight had come too late.

Grayson stood at the door.

Chapter Twenty-three

Grayson stood on the threshold of room 3A, trying to make sense of the scene before him.

His mother was with another man.

Thoughts collided, and he hardly understood the feelings that snaked through him. He felt as if he had been punched in the stomach.

During the careening carriage ride to Quincy House, he had willed the few scrawled words to be a misunderstanding. Emmaline Hawthorne would not be sneaking out for an illicit rendezvous in a cheap men's boarding hotel. The idea was ludicrous.

Clearly there was some other explanation.

But standing in the dim hallway, his mother looking at him with guilty distress, her hat gone, her hair unraveling, a man behind her standing next to the bed, Grayson couldn't deny it any longer.

Weeks earlier, it *had* been his mother out with a man. It had been his mother looking so young and alive that friends and acquaintances had remarked on the change.

And his ache turned to anger. Anger he welcomed, anger he understood.

His gaze moved from the woman who had given birth to him to the man across the room. A man who had touched his mother.

Grayson saw him up close for the first time, and for a

startling moment his mind went still. Confusion wrapped around him. Somehow this man seemed familiar, looked so like a Hawthorne.

But the spell was broken when Emmaline grabbed his arm. "Grayson," she said, trying to find the words to explain. "It's not what you think."

"Like hell it isn't."

His reaction was primal, but he did nothing to control it. He set her aside, then came into the room like a man possessed, hooking his hands into the other man's collar. Grayson didn't register the look of surprise or regret on the man's face as he slammed him into the wall. Pictures rattled, and the man lost his breath in a rush. But Grayson didn't care.

With little thought for right or wrong, he wrapped his fingers around the strong neck, fury and rage pushing him on, fury born in a tiny garret in Cambridge.

"Grayson!"

Emmaline flew at him, attaching herself to his arm, yanking with all her might. But he barely noticed her. Long pent-up rage let loose, swirling around, making him crazed. But that didn't stop him.

His grasp tightened, and the man's face went red, his veins bulging.

"Grayson, you're hurting him!"

"I'm trying," he bit out.

Emmaline stilled, and a quiet settled in the room. "Then you'll have to hurt me, too, since I'm as much to blame for this as Richard."

Richard.

The words sank in. The intimacy of a name.

With a roar Grayson let go, his breath coming in short, staccato bursts. Slowly he looked from his mother to the man. "Stay away from her," he stated, "or next time you won't be so lucky."

Richard gasped, slumped against the wall, his hands clutching his neck. Grayson didn't give him a second look as he took his mother's arm in a firm grip and led her from the room, then out to the waiting carriage. Like an angry parent guiding a truant child, Grayson helped his mother inside. No sooner had she found her seat than she tugged her arm away.

"I am not a three-year-old, Grayson Hawthorne."

His eyes narrowed. "I know. You're my mother."

She looked away. "For what it's worth, nothing happened. At least nothing that matters."

"I find you alone in a hotel room with a man not my father and you say it doesn't matter?" he snapped.

She looked at him long and hard before she sighed. "Oh, Grayson. Life is not always black-and-white. Sometimes there are shades of gray that you have never been able to understand."

"And an affair is one of those shades of gray?"

She closed her eyes, and she suddenly looked older than her years. Grayson felt a spurt of concern.

The carriage rolled through the streets, drawing closer to the world they both knew, and he had the fleeting thought that it had all been a bad dream. Staring at his mother, he took in the familiar face and clear, comforting eyes, and he thought it wasn't possible that she could have illicit relations.

But then they hit a bump, jarring his thoughts, reminding him firmly of reality.

"No," she answered. "An affair isn't anything but wrong. But life isn't that simple. The paths that lead us where we end up are never that clearly marked."

Grayson stared straight ahead.

"If you feel the need to tell your father, I will understand."

They pulled up to Hawthorne House, and before he

could help her, she hopped down to the walkway. She stopped him when he tried to follow.

"Your father is at his club on Saturday afternoons. No doubt you'll find him there."

Then she walked to the front door and never looked back.

When the driver asked where to head, Grayson told him to drive. He didn't know where he was going, didn't care. He needed time to think. But he would not go to his father.

They drove through the streets until they ended up at Swan's Grace. Wasn't that always the way with him? Somehow every path led him back to Sophie.

But as soon as he walked in the front door, Margaret was there, waving her arms as if to shoo him away.

"I cannot have this! Sophie has a concert tonight. She needs peace and quiet, not this revolving door with people coming and going as they please."

"What are you talking about?"

"First you, then your brother, then that butler, now your father."

"My father?" he asked ominously.

"Yes! He's in your office. This is unacceptable. Sophie needs to prepare for tonight!"

Surprise sliced through Grayson when he found his father standing behind his desk.

"Did you plan on telling me, or were you going to hide the truth?"

It took a second before Grayson realized that his perfectly proper father had been drinking.

"What are you referring to?" he asked carefully.

"You know damn well what I'm talking about. Your mother and Richard Smythe!"

Grayson's eyes narrowed as he slowly came forward.

"Don't think I don't know where your mother has been. And don't think I don't know you were there. I'm no fool.

Though she'd like to make me one. Just as she did all those years before. And now this!" he bellowed, waving a sheet of paper unsteadily in his hand.

Grayson took in the folder of information Lucas had brought earlier, details about Sophie's concerts, lying open on the desk. Judging from his father's countenance it was worse than he had surmised.

Steadily he strode forward, forcing his voice to a calm void that he didn't feel. "I didn't realize you were in the habit of going through other people's papers."

"I do when they are staring me in the face. Who wouldn't? Damn you! Why didn't you tell me what kind of woman you are marrying?"

Grayson didn't bother to tell his father that the betrothal was off. "Let me see the file."

But Bradford wasn't listening. His attention shifted and he glanced toward the doorway.

"Ah, the woman in question," he said with an eerie calm. "Tell him, Sophie. Tell him how you play that instrument of yours."

Grayson turned to face her. The first thing he noticed were her eyes, brown and wide, shot with green, that darkness he had seen so many times before pervading her whole body. She looked wild, provocative. And defiant.

She glanced from Bradford to the folder he held, staring at the sheet. "My guess is your papers there tell it all." Then finally she turned to Grayson. "Did you send out inquiries on me?"

"Hell, yes, he did!" Bradford bellowed. "Inquiries that produced the fact that you are scandalous and—"

"Father!"

The word crashed through the office. The men stared at each other until Grayson returned his attention to Sophie. "I want to hear it from you."

She raised her chin mutinously, or perhaps as if she were finally throwing in the towel on any vestiges of hope.

"What?" she demanded. "You want to know that my gowns are extremely low cut, so I can make every man in the audience lust after me?"

His thoughts solidified, going hard, unyielding.

"Do you want to know about the pieces I play? Provocative works that have little to do with skill and everything to do with making my followers yearn. For me. All men, of course. That's why they clamor after me backstage. Send me gifts. Flowers, candy. Invite me to their beds."

Thoughts flooded through him in a rush.

"Or do you want me to tell you about how I pull the cello between my legs, slowly, like a lover?"

Bradford made a strangled sound, but Grayson's gaze never wavered. And Sophie didn't back down.

"Do you want to hear more?" she demanded.

"I get the picture."

"Are you sure? Don't you want to ask me if I enjoy it?"

"Do you?"

Her eyes flared, then darkened. "Every second."

He should have known. He should have realized. He had seen the way she played when she didn't know he was there. He had felt passion and desire while he watched her all but caress the cello as she ran the bow across the strings.

"You can't do anything right," Bradford bellowed. "Not even find a decent wife."

Something inside Grayson snapped. Long years of doing his best, trying to please this man, exploded inside him.

Wheeling around, he confronted his father. "What do you want from me? Once and for all, tell me!"

"I want you to have been my son!"

He barely heard Sophie's intake of breath.

"Don't look so surprised," Bradford said in a hiss. "You

rove more and more each day that you don't have a drop
f my blood running through your veins."

Bradford's words snaked through the room, his eyes
narrow slits. Grayson stood like stone, trying to take in the
words, trying to understand what his mind refused to grasp.

"You're a lowly bastard, and you show it with every deci-
ion you make. And no doubt you already know. Did you go
o that hotel and have a nice little reunion with your father?"

Suddenly, with a certainty that nearly doubled him over,
e understood so much.

He was illegitimate. A bastard.

And then he remembered the man. Tall and broad. Just
ke him. But he was just like Bradford Hawthorne as well.
hen he thought of the eyes. Dark, like his. So unlike the
lue of the Hawthorne family.

He was illegitimate. And with the words came the real-
zation that someplace deep inside he had sensed it all
long.

"You're worthless," Bradford raged, pounding his fist
gainst the wall. "I raised you as my son—as my heir," he
ellowed. "And what do I get in return? Nothing! Well, let
e tell you, you're as worthless as that no-good Richard
mythe who lured your mother into his bed all those years
go. She was mine, damn you! *You* should have been mine!"

How hadn't he put it together sooner? The strained rela-
onship between his parents. Bradford's disdain for him
tanding in stark disparity to his adoration of Matthew.
Understanding suddenly came as to why he stood apart
om the world, why he tried so hard to be perfect.

Because he wasn't perfect at all.

"And now you sit by while the woman who will soon
ear the Hawthorne name prepares to scandalize Boston
ith a concert that isn't fit for a burlesque show, much less
e prestigious environs of the Music Hall. She's no better
an you!"

Grayson had stood mutely through the diatribe, but at this he reacted. "You will not say another word about Sophie," he bit out, only the shred of some invisible band holding him back.

"I will say what I please, and bastard or no, you still bear the Hawthorne name, and you'd better put a stop to this concert or you will rue the day that you were born."

Bradford turned on his heel and practically ran Sophie down as he stormed past her.

Dear God, how hadn't she guessed?

Slowly Sophie turned to Grayson. She didn't know what she expected, but not the harshness she saw in his eyes. Or was it tears?

Her heart broke for him, for this man who had become strong and formidable in an attempt to hide what he saw as weakness, to hide his love for a man who didn't return the sentiment. And now he knew why.

"You didn't know," she whispered, praying that he would somehow cross the room to her.

He didn't move. He stared at her, his feelings inscrutable behind a dark, implacable mask. Her heart missed a beat when she noticed the tautness of his jaw and the twitch of muscle just below his temple. He might hate her for not being a virgin, but she couldn't turn away from him.

"Bradford Hawthorne is wrong," she stated. "You are a wonderful man, a fine man."

But still he remained like stone, his expression as flat and smooth as a hard, impenetrable wall, just as she had seen him a thousand times before. This time, however, she saw that the dark fury in his eyes was not fury at all, but devastation. Suddenly she saw it so clearly.

In that moment all the heated words that had flown between them died away. Like her, he cared so much, too much, but he didn't want others to know that he did. He id his vulnerability behind a wall he had built around imself, much like hers, holding at bay anyone who came ear his heart.

How had she not recognized the very traits she had earned to wrap around herself to survive?

He had said once that he wanted her to save him. She ealized now, with heartbreaking certainty, that he wanted er to save him from himself. Grayson wanted the love of a nan who wasn't his father, and thought that if he were erfect enough he could finally win his approval. He beeved he needed to be perfect, and he needed her to be perect, too.

Without uttering a word, Grayson started out of the oom. But she stepped in his way. He hardly seemed to xert any effort as he set her aside and continued on toward ie front door.

"Regardless of what Bradford Hawthorne thinks, you re perfect, Grayson. You're perfect just as you are."

He stopped but didn't look back.

The reprieve encouraged her, and she hurried on with onesty, complete and unvarnished.

"I love you, Grayson, as I have loved little else in my fe. I have loved you since I was four years old and you deended me for the first time." She willed him to turn back, ut he didn't move. "I just never thought you could truly ove me in return." She forced a laugh into the brittle air. After all that happened when my mother died, I didn't beeve such a perfect man could love a woman who was anying but. Then I became what I believed I was. Wild and ithout virtue, luring men with provocative ways."

His sigh echoed against the walls. "We're a pair, you d I. Me, trying to be perfect. You, doing everything you n to prove that you aren't. You were right all along. We aren't meant to be together. In the end we would only destroy each other."

Then he strode out the door, leaving Sophie to stand alone, fighting to breathe.

Chapter Twenty-four

Grayson returned to his room at the Hotel Vendome. He refused to think about what had just happened. He no longer recognized the life he had lived or the world he had so painstakingly built.

Everything he depended on had slipped away into something he no longer understood. Sophie. His mother. The man he had always believed to be his father.

Instead he learned that he was the illegitimate son of a man who would seduce a woman. A man without honor. A man whose blood flowed through his veins.

A knock sounded on the door, but he ignored it. He stared out the grimy window at the streets below without seeing.

The knock came again, this time harder.

Still he ignored it.

"Grayson, open this door."

He closed his eyes against the sound of his mother's voice, pressing his forehead to the cool glass pane.

"Grayson, please."

He pushed away from the window and strode across the room. Opening the door, he found his mother standing in the hallway.

"I don't think this is a good time for us to talk," he stated coldly.

She strode past him into the room without being asked;

then she turned back, her soft gray-blue eyes glittering. "
think it is."

"I'm not interested in discussing your meetings with
another man."

Her lips thinned. "Neither am I. That is for my husband
and me to discuss, not my son. What I will do is make cer
tain you don't find yourself in the same trap. I see you
forcing Sophie into the same position I was forced into
years ago."

His eyes narrowed. "I think you should leave."

"I will not. I will not stand by any longer, as I have done
my whole life, and do nothing. Don't force Sophie into
mold. She can make you proud as a wife; she can make
you happy, if you just give her a chance."

"Too late. Sophie and I are no longer betrothed. The
contracts have been voided."

"Because of the way she performs?" she demanded.

"How did you know about that?"

"Your father told me."

He turned sharply away and strode to the window. "He
is not my father."

Emmaline went very still.

"Yes, I know that Bradford Hawthorne isn't my father."

"He told you?"

"In no uncertain terms."

She sighed, and though Grayson wasn't looking at her
he could feel something essential seep out of her with that
shaky breath.

"Oh, Grayson."

Then silence. Bone-deep silence.

"I'm sorry," she whispered, then drew a deep breath
"But my past doesn't change the fact that I love you. Very
much. I wouldn't give you up for the world. And I didn't"

"No, she didn't."

They both turned toward the sound of the voice and found Richard Smythe standing in the doorway.

Emmaline gasped. Grayson felt fury race through his body, and something else. He stared at the man who was his flesh and blood. It was like looking into a mirror. He even recognized the arrogant tilt of the man's chin.

Grayson wasn't sure if he was sickened or intrigued. *This* was his father—a man who had seduced his mother, then left her.

"Leave," Grayson said, his tone filled with barely contained fury.

"Hear me out," the man said arrogantly, sounding just like him, before adding, "Please."

Grayson's hand curled into a fist at his side, but when he didn't reply, Richard proceeded. "I loved your mother very much. I love her still. But I didn't know she was with child when I left." He drew in his breath slowly. "I can't tell you the shock I felt when I saw you hours ago. Dear God, I had a son."

Grayson cursed, and Emmaline began to weep.

It was then that Richard turned to Emmaline. "But I also realized while I stood there that even if I had known you were with child, I no doubt would have left anyway. Perhaps sooner."

Grayson felt shock reverberate through the room, followed by a bitter sting from the words. He hated that he felt anything.

"You were right when you spoke of honor," Richard continued. "And it has taken me over thirty years to realize that I have lived my life without it. I love you, Emmaline. I want to spend my life with you, honorably, not in tawdry hotels, not through stolen meetings. And I want to come to know my son."

"But I don't want to know you."

Grayson's words shimmered through the room, and he

felt his mother's questioning gaze. He didn't want to know this man. He realized that other than a start of curiosity, he felt nothing for him. He only wanted him gone.

As if his mother understood, she turned back to Richard. "If you are serious about doing anything for me," she said, "then you will leave again. There is no place for you in our lives."

"But Em—"

"No." She said the word with force. "I have to find a future on my own. And you missed your chance to have a son."

"Then you're going back to Bradford?"

"I don't know what the future holds. I only know that I have to figure it out on my own. I've sent a note to my son Lucas. I plan to move to Nightingale's Gate."

"You're what?" Grayson asked, stunned.

"It's time I found a life for myself. I can't continue to live under Bradford Hawthorne's despotic thumb." She returned her attention to Richard. "It's time you leave."

"Don't decide yet. Take some time and think about it."

"She told you to get out."

The men eyed each other, one wistful, the other hard and cold.

But eventually, reluctantly, Richard walked from the room.

Grayson watched the door shut, staring at it for a long while, trying to understand what he felt.

"I did send the note to Lucas."

His mother's voice broke into his thoughts. Her voice was strong, a strength that Grayson had rarely, if ever, heard in her.

"I'll make decisions about my future from Nightingale's Gate. But know that Richard Smythe is my past. I realized that fact in the hotel room before you arrived. Though there is one thing I already know I have to do, something I should have done long ago. I should have stood up to Bradford Hawthorne. He has always been hardest on you. But that was because from the beginning you were always so perfect. Your looks. Your personality. Your success. You did everything easily."

She started to reach out to him, but her fingers only fluttered back to her side.

"When Bradford sent you out on your own," she continued, "you could have become a failure and blamed your family. Instead you became a success and credited the very man who would have ruined you if he could have. You've always tried to be better, even when you already were better than the rest." She reached out again, and this time she touched his arm. "I love Matthew and Lucas with all my heart. And each of them has their own wonderful qualities. But it was you who succeeded in the ways that Bradford wanted from the sons of his blood. Bradford Hawthorne hated you for that. And he hated you even more when Lucas disappointed him and then Matthew got tangled up in that scandal. He has ridden you relentlessly for a lifetime. But you never crumpled under the pressure. You succeeded."

He stared at her hand touching his arm. "Did you love my father?"

"In my own way, I have always loved Bradford."

"I'm talking about Smythe, my real father."

"Bradford Hawthorne is your real father, flawed and harsh, no doubt. But Richard Smythe had little to do with the wonderful man you have become."

"But he is my blood. Did you ever love him?"

The night sky beckoned, bright and sparkling with a million stars. "I don't know anymore. I thought I did. But in hindsight I'm not so sure. He appeared in my life and understood my hopes and dreams. He seemed to care about me at a time when Bradford Hawthorne cared only about the money I brought to him. I realize now that at the time I was young and alone and frightened. And I needed someone."

She looked at him helplessly, as if she understood the inadequacy of her answer.

"I needed someone to hold me," she continued, "to make me feel like someone in the world cared for me. There are times in our lives when all of us need somebody."

She looked at him, her eyes boring into him as if she willed him to understand.

"I think it is the same with Sophie," she said. She hesitated for a moment before she continued. "She has been alone and afraid many times. My heart cries for the young girl who had to deal with the death of her mother when her father took up with her mother's nurse. When I was alone and afraid, I turned to Richard. But Sophie dealt with it by running away." She shook her head. "Little Sophie. How she adored you. Do you remember the night that horrid Megan played the talking machine with Sophie's words?"

Grayson's spine straightened.

She looked at her son sadly. "I remember that night. The children all gathered around the gramophone while the parents were in the parlor down the hall. But I heard, and I remember those words. She loved you. Almost painfully, I always thought. And because of that I've never understood why, when she needed someone so desperately, she would run away instead of going to you."

The words caught him by surprise, slicing through his anger like a knife.

"Oh, but I did see where you lived!"

Sophie's words. She *had* gone to him.

She had gone to him, he realized in a blinding instant, because she had needed him.

She had lost her mother, and in all ways that counted, her father. She had come to him, but found him with

Megan. So she had turned to the only other thing in her life that gave her comfort. Her music. Late at night, alone in the Music Hall. And Niles had found her there.

Understanding nearly brought Grayson to his knees. Sophie had needed him, and though it had been unintentional, he had failed her. When Niles Prescott found her that night, he hadn't simply taken her virginity; he had then given her debut concert to someone else. He had taken her innocence; then he had taken her confidence as well.

Grayson remembered those first months in the garret, feeling lost and adrift. But he'd had Sophie's baskets and her words on a gramophone to wrap around him until he found his way.

He understood in that second that Sophie had lost herself, lost her ability to believe she had any worth. No innocence, the one thing girls were taught they had to give a husband. No talent, the one thing her mother had taught her mattered in a world that thought she was an odd, ugly duckling. And she'd had nowhere to turn but to faceless strangers who didn't already have expectations of who she was. By fleeing, she created the chance to start over. To wipe the slate clean. To become someone new, someone who wasn't that girl who, in her eyes, had failed so miserably.

And he understood in that moment that she hadn't willfully tossed her old life away. It had been taken from her.

In that second he felt free—of his past, of Sophie's. It didn't matter that Bradford would never be pleased by what he did. He could only do his best, as he always had. There was honor in that.

"But that's behind us," Emmaline continued, though Grayson hardly heard. "We all have pasts, son, and those pasts shouldn't stand in the way of the future."

Without warning, Grayson pulled his mother into a fierce hug. "I love you, Mother."

Emmaline couldn't have been more surprised. "What did I say?"

"Nothing and everything." Just as Sophie had once said. "I'll explain later. For now, I have to find Sophie."

She had hurt long enough. And he wouldn't let her hurt anymore, because yet again he hadn't been there for her when she needed him. Sophie who had saved him, Sophie who had always been there for him.

Now he would be there for her.

He would help her believe again. He would show her that someone in the world cared for her—just as she was.

Sophie stood quietly, staring at the shambles that was supposed to have been her music room. She would have smiled at the appropriateness of something that so adequately represented her life if she'd had the ability to do anything besides stand there, numb.

Deandra, Margaret, and Henry were frantic all around her. But she had blocked them from her mind. The concert was in an hour, and she stood in her robe. Her hair was done, her makeup perfect, but she couldn't seem to move herself beyond that.

She was barely aware when the front door burst open, barely heard the footsteps pounding in the foyer until she felt someone next to her.

"Sophie, you're going to be late."

Grayson's voice wrapped around her, and with effort she turned to find him there. So tall, so handsome. Her hero for as long as she could remember. Everything she had ever wanted in life. This man who had said that she would only ruin him. Why had things gone so wrong?

"Come on, Sophie," he said gently. "Let's go upstairs so you can dress."

She felt his strong fingers curl around her hand.

"You have a concert to perform."

"No." She pried herself away from him. "I can't do it."

"Of course you can, sweetheart."

A spurt of anger flared. "Don't call me that! I'm not your sweetheart. And I'm not good enough to give the concert."

He took her by the shoulders and held her firmly in front of him. "You are good enough. I've heard you play."

"And now you've read that horrid file on me and know all about my performances. I'm all about shocking people and titillating their senses. I've made a career out of the outrageous." She dashed her hand angrily across her forehead to fight back futile tears. "But tonight I wanted to do it right. Tonight I wanted to play Bach." She closed her eyes. "And I wanted them to like me. For once I wanted to fit in." As quickly as it came, the defiance seeped out of her, leaving her spent. She looked up at him through the tears that couldn't be held back any longer. "For one fleeting moment I wanted Boston's ugly duckling to play with the grace of a swan."

Grayson framed her face with his hands. "Oh, Sophie, you have always been a swan. You have always had the ability to translate people's passion into music. You have always been better than the rest of us, and that makes us uncomfortable. But that doesn't make you an ugly anything."

She looked at him, knowing she had to make him understand. "I can't play the way you want me to, Grayson, the way *I* want me to! I can't play Bach. If I try, I'll only prove that I am everything everyone ever believed. And it serves me right!"

"Why? Because you're not a virgin?" He sighed and his strong face filled with emotion. "That doesn't matter, Sophie. It doesn't, and I should have understood that all along."

"But it does matter." Her voice cracked.

"Why?"

She tried to jerk away, but he wouldn't let her go.

"Why? Damn it, tell me why."

"Because I'm the one who started it!"

The words reverberated through the room. Grayson's dark eyes flickered hot with surprise, and he stared at her. She felt sick at the look on his face, sick and dying inside, but it was too late to turn back.

"*I* kissed him." Foolishly. Stupidly. She squeezed her eyes shut. "I don't know why I did it. *Was* I trying to get back at you? Or was I lashing out at my mother for dying? At my father for locking me out of his life and turning to Patrice?" But explanations had never mattered. All that mattered was that she had kissed Niles first.

She opened her eyes and looked at him. "I never meant for it to be anything more than a kiss. Truly I didn't. I remember being so surprised that I had kissed him, surprised and repelled. But when he curled me even closer in his arms"—she felt her teeth clench—"I didn't say no. I did not say no!"

She dropped her gaze to the mother-of-pearl tacks that marched down his shirt with military precision, focusing, trying not to see the past, trying not to feel. "Afterward I was sick that it had happened, hated that it had happened, but what I hated most of all was that I had given myself away. Such an utter and disgusting waste. Because after I got over my hurt or anger or whatever it was that I was feeling, I realized I had given him the only thing I had that meant anything to you." She took a deep, shuddering breath. "You never cared about how I played, or how I looked. And though many times I have hoped differently, deep down I have always known that the only thing you ever wanted from me—needed from me—was the one thing that made me proper in society's eyes. My innocence."

Afterward, buttoning the pants he had never shed, Niles

blamed her, saying she had started it. Niles blamed her. She blamed herself. How, after learning the entire truth, could Grayson blame anyone else?

But then he spoke, the words gentle but strong. "Sweet, sweet Sophie. It doesn't matter that you kissed him. You were young and alone. And you needed to feel that someone in this world cared about you."

She looked up at him and her eyes burned.

"You needed someone to hold you, make you feel safe, and he took advantage of that. You didn't give him anything," he said, his tone unrelenting. "He *took* from you. He took your innocence. And I will see that he pays." He seemed to calm himself forcibly, and he framed her face with his hands. "But he didn't take what matters."

Confusion creased her brow.

His palms trailed down to her shoulders, and his voice was a whisper of sound. "He didn't take your heart. He couldn't have, because you had already given it to me."

"What are you talking about?"

He didn't answer, instead he laced his fingers with hers, then led her to the office, where he pulled a tiny key from his pocket and went to the small cabinet that had intrigued her since she returned. He unlocked the door, then pulled out the brass-and-wood talking machine she had thought was long gone, and set it on his desk.

"You found it," she breathed.

"I've always had it. I've saved it all these years. I've played it a thousand times."

He cranked the handle, and her voice loomed in the room, young and sweet, innocent but filled with sincerity.

"I love Grayson Hawthorne. I love him with all my heart. And one day I will be his wife."

The words faded away, and he tilted her chin until her eyes met his.

"You gave your love to me all those years ago. Your love

and your heart. I have this box to prove it. No one can take that away from us, not Niles Prescott, not Boston."

"You kept it all these years," she said in awe.

"Of course I did."

Her lips parted as she inhaled sharply. "Why?"

For the first time since arriving, his strong, confident look wavered and he glanced away. But she reached up and touched her fingers to his cheek, making him meet her eyes. "Why, Grayson?"

He bowed his head briefly, then looked back at her, his own eyes burning. "Because when those words filled the room that night, it was the first time I had ever heard anyone say they loved me. A little girl who only told the truth. A little girl who was larger than life. A little girl who was kind and good. And she loved me.

"I love you, Sophie, for that, and for who you are. With every ounce of my being. And I realize now that I always will, no matter what you do, or how you play." He kissed her forehead. "Go out there tonight and give them what you do best. Don't let Niles Prescott or your father—or even me—defeat you. Turn us on our ears; make us squirm. Give us a show we'll never forget." He smiled and pulled her to him, then whispered, "I dare you."

Chapter Twenty-five

The lights went down. The voices quieted to a buzz of anticipation. Boston's Music Hall had never been so full. Every seat was taken, and people crowded in the passageways, while hundreds of others had been turned away at the door.

Sophie stood on the stage, just behind the curtain, dark surrounding her, her black satin cape pulled tight around her gown. Her pulse skittered through her veins in expectation.

What would they think?

How would her father react?

Forcefully she pushed the thoughts away. It didn't matter what anyone thought. She understood that now. She could only play the way she knew how. And if she had learned nothing else, she had learned that she could be no one but herself.

Her thoughts shifted when the thick velvet curtain began its long, slow slide back. She stood very still, waiting in the dark, just as the crowd waited. She sensed their excitement, their eager anticipation.

She could just make out her father, in the front row next to Patrice. Bradford Hawthorne was there, sitting next to Emmaline, who looked straight ahead, her husband staring at her tightly clasped hands, as if he didn't know if he wanted to take them in his own or turn sharply away.

Then it happened. A stream of light captured Sophie

onstage. But the crowd didn't erupt; there was no sound like thunder. It was simple, pure, and true applause that washed over her. She savored each moment as she had never savored it before, because she understood that after this show, she might never hear the applause again. Oddly, she didn't care. There was only this night, a night she had been waiting for her whole life.

With that she raised her face to the light, like savoring the sun. Then she dropped the infamous cape from her shoulders, the satin pooling at her ankles, and the crowd gasped.

The sound wrapped tightly around her. But the gasp was quickly followed by the sound of awe.

She wore blue velvet, not red. Modest and respectable, a classic diamond necklace catching in the light. She was beautiful, not a spectacle, striking but not wild. And she had to force herself not to shake as she stepped back to the chair and took up her cello. No accompanist joined her onstage.

Whatever the outcome, she would play Bach. Once and for all, she would attempt the pieces that had lived in her head for more years than she could count. If she failed, it wouldn't be because she hadn't tried.

The murmurs cut off when she picked up the bow. Sitting forward in the chair, she hesitated and looked up at the blinding light. This time, however, those stolen seconds had nothing to do with luring the audience. She had to gather her thoughts, putting all else but the music from her mind.

Her heart pounded so hard it hurt. But she could do this, she told herself firmly. Then she began.

Her breath caught at the first shaky G that sounded through the hall. She could feel the crowd tense much as she tensed. G-D-B . . . A-B-D-B-D. The notes sounded like the painful bellows of a reluctant child's music lesson.

The bow felt awkward in her hand. The cello edge bit into her chest. Dread flared and she couldn't breathe. And for one flashing moment she made out Megan Robertson sitting in the first row, smiling. And Niles. Niles Prescott had the audacity to sit there as well, staring at her.

Sophie wanted to run, to set her cello aside and escape. Unable to move from the chair, she could only stumble through the first few measures of the piece. Words rushed through her head.

Yet another former child prodigy with a small, quaint sound.

But her sound wasn't even quaint. Why had she ever thought she could do this? Why had she ever thought that to have tried and failed was better than to have never tried at all?

She felt the scream well up, felt the heat of embarrassment sting her cheeks when she sensed the shuffling that grew louder in the crowd.

But then she thought of Grayson and his love for her. A true love. Regardless of how she played. Regardless of the past. And she hit a single, solitary A. Crisp and wonderful, the sound resonated against the cavernous ceiling. That one note was perfect and lovely, just like their love. And she stopped caring. About Boston, about failing or succeeding.

She lost herself to the cello in her hands and the sound she made that washed through the high-ceilinged auditorium. The audience faded away as she moved through the controlled, intense strokes of Bach. The sound was rich, the prelude perfect, before she launched into the allemande, and she could feel the searching tone of the notes. Unaware of anything besides the music, she flew through the movements, then finally came to the end of the first suite, like coming out of a trance.

Then silence, crystalline and complete, before the crowd erupted in a flurry of applause, the appreciation not trailing off until she began the second suite. After that it was much the same. She played Bach with a beauty and mastery that few artists were capable of bringing to the pieces. And when she came to the end, the crowd was hushed with stunned amazement, before one last time they erupted in applause, men and women alike standing to shout *Brava!*

With her throat tight with euphoric tears, Sophie stood, soaking in the praise much as she had always done before. But now it was different. She had proven to herself what she could do.

Looking up to the ceiling she smiled. *Thank you, Mother. Now you can be proud.*

When she glanced down, she saw Megan standing amid the applause, looking around, bewildered. Sophie felt neither triumph nor sympathy for the woman. Just freedom.

She had said she wanted freedom long ago, she hadn't wanted to be caged—by society, by Grayson. She realized that she had gained her freedom now. But it was freedom from the past that she had needed. The thought of Niles no longer held her prisoner. In that moment, she understood that she truly was free. The past could no longer defeat her.

And that was when she sat down once again.

A startled moment passed while the audience tried to understand what she was doing, but then they reseated themselves, excited for an encore.

She held the cello beside her as she waited for the guests to quiet. She waited, anticipated, drank in the moment like a fine wine. Then she pulled the instrument between her legs like a lover.

Boston gasped, but Sophie wasn't bothered. She would play as she had been playing in Europe, realizing that if this town couldn't love her for who she truly was, in all her forms, then they didn't love her at all. She launched into "A Tawdry Heart," her head thrown back, the bow flying wildly on the strings, her body filled with all the passion she felt for the music, the notes and chords surrounding each man and woman there with the intensity of a primal dance. And by the time she whipped the bow away with a flourish, her cheeks red from exertion and joy, the audience sat in shocked silence.

They hated it. She could feel it. Though it truly didn't matter. One day they were bound to learn about the way she had played in Europe. Better for it to come from her, no longer hidden in shame.

But when she stood and would have left the stage, a sole member of the audience began to clap. Just one person, the sound strong but echoing coldly against the silence. She looked through the light and her heart swelled at the sight of her father on his feet, standing alone, clapping proudly. Patrice sat in her chair, mortified. Megan looked stunned but triumphant, as if in the end she had been proved right.

It was then that Niles stood to join her father, clapping for her, acknowledging her talent.

This time it was Sophie who stood in shocked silence.

But then one more person started to clap, then another, like a slow wave gaining momentum, until the hall thundered once again. Sophie knew then that she had finally succeeded—on her own terms. She had gained the respect of the town of her birth. She hadn't pushed the past away; she had made peace with it.

Backstage there was a crush of people, voices coming at her all at once. Margaret was there. Deandra and Henry both hugged her tight. Her father told her he was proud. But as always, it was Grayson she searched for in the crowd.

Her heart sank when she couldn't find him. Had he been disgusted by what he saw?

But then he appeared, surprisingly from the other side of the stage, as always making her breath catch as his eyes bored into her.

What did he think?

Then he smiled, his dark eyes no longer obscuring emotion.

He strode across the room, taller, more powerful than anyone else. But he didn't acknowledge the people who spoke to him. He only stared at her, his gaze intense.

"You were incredible," he said, taking her hand and kissing her palm.

She gazed at him with all the love that she felt. "I had to do it. I had to see what I was made of."

He pressed her palm to his heart. "I could have told you what you are made of. Strength, honor, dedication. You are also made of a love that none of us who have experienced it will ever forget."

She laughed, a bubble of joy rising up in her. "I think for a while there you forgot."

"Perhaps," he said, his dark eyes growing serious, "but those who love you always find their way back. Like me. And like someone else."

Her eyes widened curiously. "What? Who?"

Instead of answering, he guided her back through the crowd the way he came, then pulled her to the opposite side of the stage, where he must have watched her performance. As soon as they came around the corner, Sophie stopped.

"Sweetie!"

She cried then, racing forward, her tears flowing over as she pulled the dog into a tight hug despite her jewels and elegant gown.

"Where'd you find her?" she asked.

"She found you. When I came out of Swan's Grace on my way here, she was there on the front steps with the young boy who came to retrieve her. He said Sweetie kept trying to return to you. So he brought her himself. None of us can forget you, Sophie. Not Sweetie, not the crowds. And especially not me."

He pulled her up to him, framing her face with his large hands. "I love you, Sophie Wentworth. And I will do everything in my power to make up for all that you have been through. To start with, you will never have to worry about Niles Prescott again."

"What have you done?" she gasped.

"He has been informed that he will need to search for a new position, without the benefit of recommendations."

"Oh, Grayson, you didn't have to do that. He clapped for me in the end when no one else but my father would."

"Don't try to go easy on him. The man deserves much worse," he stated coldly. Then he eased, finding a smile. "And now I am going to court you, Sophie Wentworth, truly show you how much you mean to me. I will take you on picnics, I will compliment your gowns, I will shower you with gifts and flowers—"

"Sweet, sweet Grayson," she whispered. "I don't need any of that. I just need you."

He kissed her then, long and slow. "Does that mean you will do me the honor of marrying me?"

She bit her lip. "What if I want to continue to perform?"

"Then I'll travel wherever it is you want to play."

She wrinkled her nose. "What if I want to wear low-cut dresses?"

"Then I'll have to be close at hand to keep the other men at bay."

"What if—"

"No more what-ifs." He ran his hands down her arms, then took her hands and looked at her fiercely. "I love you, Sophie, for you, any way you want to be. Just as you have loved me. Always. We are perfect together. And we will be perfect together in Swan's Grace, or another house that I will be happy to build you. We'll keep Sweetie, and you can have your ragtag group of hangers-on live with us wherever we are."

Her lips parted on a surprised intake of breath. "You mean you'd let Margaret and Deandra and Henry stay?"

"I'll convince them myself, if that is what you want. I'm in need of a good assistant, since you ran mine off." He chuckled. "Besides, I can't think of a better person than Deandra to salvage what is left of my career."

With a cry, Sophie threw her arms around his strong body. "Oh, Grayson, I love you."

"Then say you'll marry me. Say you'll never leave me again." He set her at arm's length and looked her in the eyes. "I need you, Sophie, not because you are my weakness, as I thought before, but because you are my strength."

Joy filled her soul. "We are two halves of a whole, each made complete by the other. So yes, I will marry you. And we will live in Swan's Grace. Just as I intended all those years ago."

He kissed her forehead, then pulled her close. "Good, then let's go home. We have a music room that needs finishing."

Read on for a sneak peek at
NIGHTINGALE'S GATE,
the final installment in Linda Francis Lee's
breathtaking trilogy,
coming in Summer 2001

The city sweltered.

Alice Kendall absently curled a loose tendril of white-blond hair behind her ear. It was unbearably hot in her small law office in the South End of town, but she hardly noticed.

Pulling a folded rectangle of newsprint from a file, she reread the startling headline that she hadn't been able to get out of her mind.

Prominent Son Charged in Murder

Last week she had cut the article from the paper, though she couldn't say why. She had made something of a name for herself in the short nine months she had been an attorney by defending small but difficult cases. Even though a murder charge was well beyond what she could reasonably expect to take on at this point in her career, it was just the kind of case she dreamed of defending one day. Big and important.

Tapping the newsprint in thought, she started to read.

Lucas Hawthorne, son of prominent citizen Bradford Hawthorne, has been charged with the murder of Lucille Rouge, a well-known courtesan found dead in Beckman's alleyway in the early hours of Sunday morning. After his arrest Tuesday afternoon, he was set free on a five-hundred-dollar bond.

Equally well-known as the owner of the infamous gentleman's club Nightingale's Gate, Lucas Hawthorne was unavailable for comment. The elder Hawthorne son, Grayson, emphatically declared his brother's innocence. Matthew, the middle Hawthorne son, is reportedly returning to Boston from Africa. It is to be expected that the three Hawthorne brothers would show such solidarity. What is unexpected, however, is that Bradford Hawthorne, the venerable patriarch of the clan, has refused to make any comment at all.

The article went on, but Alice sat back and barely felt the bite of hard wood pressing her whalebone corset against her. The murder had occurred nearly two weeks ago, and something had been written about the case every day since.

Even before this, Alice had heard of Lucas Hawthorne—didn't know anyone who hadn't. It was no secret he was the youngest son of a very fine family, someone who seemed to relish his black sheep image. Boston didn't take kindly to a man who laughed in the face of propriety. Neither did her father, Boston's highly successful district attorney for the Commonwealth of Massachusetts.

No one within a hundred-mile radius dared cross Walker Kendall. During his tenure as lead prosecutor for the Commonwealth, he had won far more cases than he had lost.

Alice cringed for the poor fool who would be faced with the task of defending Lucas Hawthorne. He didn't stand a chance against her father.

While she had never met any of the Hawthorne family, she felt sure that, given their name and money, not to mention the fact that Grayson Hawthorne was considered one of the finest lawyers in town, there would be a fight.

Intrigued in spite of herself, she resolved to ask her father what he knew about the case when they met for lunch at Locke-Ober's.

A sharp rap on the frosted window in the door shook her from her reverie. She blinked at the large, distorted form that stood behind the glass.

Instantly, the article was forgotten. While she had successfully defended the few cases she had gotten, she'd practically given her services away for free. As a new lawyer, not to mention as a *woman* lawyer, she didn't have clients banging down her door. Slowly, she was developing a solid reputation. She knew that. But that solidity had yet to translate into solvency. And if Alice didn't start bringing in some sizable fees soon, she'd be hard pressed to stay in business. A solid reputation alone, she was fast learning, didn't pay the bills.

"Come in," she called out in her best professional voice, quickly dabbing the sweat from her brow, before grabbing her pen and a file in hopes of looking busy just as the door swung open.

A man filled the doorway. A stranger. Her breath hissed out of her at the sight.

Despite his expensively tailored suit, he looked dangerous. He was tall with broad shoulders, seemingly unfazed by the staggering heat. His hair was dark like a raven's wing. His jaw was hard and chiseled, just like the man. And his lips. Full and masterfully carved, sensuous. The effect of such a mouth on a face so masculine was blatantly sexual.

Alice felt an odd tingle race through her, then settle low.

But it was his eyes that demanded her attention. A vivid shade of blue, they flickered over the interior of her office with quick efficiency, before settling on her—and when they did, his body went still and his eyes narrowed. His gaze was unnerving. Intense, unreadable.

Locked in his stare, she couldn't move. Her world seemed to shift and change. Minutes ticked by in some distorted facsimile of time passing. An empty, hungry feeling flared unexpectedly inside her—a feeling she could hardly fathom, much less explain.

His gaze drifted over her like an insolent caress, judging, assessing. An embarrassing sense of inadequacy spun through her. She might not know much about the affairs of men and women, but she did know that she didn't have the body to impress such a ruggedly handsome man.

Pulling up bravado like a shield, she gave him her coolest glare. "May I help you?" she asked, forcing her voice to be steady.

At the question he smiled, a slow quirk of lips making him look like a devilish schoolboy. "I think you can."

His tone made it clear that his words had nothing to do with the practice of law. He was making a pass at her. Alice couldn't have been more surprised if he had fallen to his knees and begged her to marry him. Shaking the absurd thought away, she wrote her pounding heart off to outrage.

She pushed up from her seat in a stiff rustle of taffeta skirts and the scrape of chair against hardwood floor, certain he must be lost. Hoping he was lost. Or did she? she wondered when she felt a tiny flare of that odd, breathless feeling. Her gaze drifted to his lips, which just as quickly pulled into a wider smile.

Her head jerked up, and she felt the instant burn in her face at his knowing look.

"Can I direct you somewhere?" she inquired crisply.

"I'm looking for Alice Kendall."

Her spine straightened in surprise. "For me?"

The man's indolent smile froze into a hard line. "*You* are Alice Kendall?" He glanced around the small office as if he expected to find someone else.

Her chin rose a notch, hating the fact that every time anyone met her they couldn't imagine she was old enough to practice law. This wasn't the first time someone had come into her office and assumed she was the receptionist. "Yes, I am."

His blue eyes narrowed dangerously. "What the hell?" he muttered, more to himself than to her. "I need a lawyer, not a date for an ice cream social."

She realized in that second that he was going to leave.

Instantly her brain raced, but not with thoughts of this powerful man and what he made her feel, rather with thoughts of a client. A real, live, breathing client. And if his clothes were any indication, he could actually afford to pay her.

"You're looking for a lawyer?" she burst out.

He hesitated, his gaze no longer sensual. He regarded her with disdain and an inexplicable flare of anger.

But Alice wasn't about to be put off. She thrust out her hand like any good businessman, fighting off the very real desire she felt to dash out the door. "Alice Kendall, attorney at law, at your service."

He made no attempt to shake her hand. He hung back, contempt shimmering around him like the waves of gauzy heat outside.

She tried to convince herself that he wasn't a hopelessly dangerous criminal. Truly, his clothes were nice. He shaved. His hair wasn't overly long. All right, so it was, she amended at the sight of dark hair brushing his collar. Even so, what did it matter? Didn't every man, woman, and thug deserve a lawyer?

Her heart did a little dance of excitement.

"Why do you need an attorney?" she asked, her mind spinning with thoughts of a breach of contract case, or simple mistaken identity. She'd even do a little estate planning if that was what he wanted. A client was a client.

But before he could answer, another man stepped in behind him.

This one was every bit as tall as the first, his hair as dark, though his eyes were black pools instead of blue. He looked familiar somehow, and she had the distinct impression that she should know him.

"Miss Kendall," he said, his voice smooth and polite, so different from the first man. "How nice to see you."

She tilted her head in confusion as she tried to place him, but couldn't. "Who are you?" she asked bluntly, forgetting all her hard-learned lessons in propriety. "And why are you here?"

He didn't answer at first as he noticed the article lying forgotten on her desk. Before she knew what he was doing, he picked it up and glanced at the black print. With a sigh, he handed it to her, and said, "Everyone charged with murder needs a lawyer."

"Murder?"

"Unfortunately, yes."

"You're Lucas Hawthorne?"

A brief flash of pure joy raced through her at the thought of such a client. But disappointment followed quickly on its heels. She needed a case she actually stood a chance of winning. The last thing she needed was for Lucas Hawthorne to walk into her office.

The man shook his head. "No, I'm not Lucas Hawthorne."

Relief, a resurgence of enthusiasm. Visions of solvency returned.

"He is."

Alice swung around to face the man who had taken her breath. Dark hair, vivid blue eyes. This was Lucas Hawthorne. In the flesh. More intimidating than she had heard.

So much for a nice little breach of contract case.

Damn.

"Why me?" she demanded.

"My question, exactly," Lucas Hawthorne stated, his eyes flickering over her frilly blue gown. "Aren't suffragettes supposed to be mannish and wear ties?"

"Lucas," the other man warned.

"For your information, I am not a suffragette. I'm a lawyer, and a good one, I might add," Alice snapped, her temper short as she swallowed the bitter pill that this wasn't a case she could reasonably take.

Lucas raised one black brow and looked at her in a way that was meant to intimidate.

Alice was too disappointed to care, and she glared back. "Unless rumors are mistaken—"

"I've never been one to listen to rumors."

Her smile was thin and caustic. "I'm sure that makes your mother proud. I, on the other hand, enjoy a good rumor now and again. I'm always amazed at how much information they provide. And rumor has it that you have more money than God, and a brother who's a lawyer." She jerked her head to the other man. "You're Grayson Hawthorne!"

The older brother nodded his regal head.

Stunned that two of the most well-known men in New England had showed up on her doorstep seeking her help, Alice sat down in her chair and refolded the article, then carefully straightened her already straight papers, giving herself time to think.

"So," Grayson said, "are you interested in the job?"

Her heart lurched. These weren't two run-of-the-mill thugs. They weren't lost, and they actually wanted her.

Okay, so only Grayson Hawthorne wanted her, but Grayson Hawthorne belonged to the pantheon of great lawyers as far as she was concerned.

Despite the fact that it was ludicrous to consider, blood drummed through her veins in exhilaration. This was what she had dreamed of for years. A big case. To be sought after and respected by the very lawyers who shaped the law.

But to defend a murder charge when she had only been practicing for less than a year? This was too much, too soon. Any lawyer in town would know that. At least a good one would, and Grayson Hawthorne was a good one.

Disappointment flared once again, and her eyes narrowed suspiciously. "You never answered my question," she stated, looking at the accused directly. "Why me?"

Lucas Hawthorne leaned back against the wall and glanced wryly at Grayson. "Call me naive, big brother, but shouldn't the lawyer be convincing us, rather than the other way around?"

"More than that, why aren't *you* defending him?" Alice challenged.

Grayson glanced between her and his brother.

"First of all, I deal in civil matters, not criminal. Beyond which, no jury in the land will believe that I can be objective about my own flesh and blood. We need someone from outside my firm."

"Then what about the slew of other attorneys in this very building?" she asked caustically.

"Not everyone here graduated number one in his class in law school, and not everyone aced the bar exam. You did."

A brush of pride washed over her at the words. Alice felt a slight softening in her stance despite the fact that she knew she hadn't received a single compliment from anyone except her father since she'd decided to wear her hair up at eighteen. Undoubtedly she was desperate and susceptible to the most blatant forms of flattery. But still, it felt good.

"I've also heard you were the best strategist in your class," Grayson added. "We want someone new. Someone hungry." He eyed her carefully. "And if my guess is correct, you have something to prove. A winning combination, as far as I'm concerned."

It couldn't be more obvious that Lucas Hawthorne didn't agree. In fact, he looked downright antagonistic. She bit her lip and studied him. The man was angry. Dangerous. With large hands that easily could have ended a woman's life.

A shiver of something raced down her spine, but this time it had nothing to do with feeling drawn or intrigued.

"What is the charge?" she asked Grayson, as if his brother weren't there. "Murder in the first degree? In the second? Manslaughter?"

"Murder in the first," Lucas answered for him, crossing his arms casually on his chest as if he didn't have a care in the world.

Her heart fluttered, and she tried to ignore him. "The Commonwealth must have some pretty solid evidence to go for such a charge."

Deep lines etched Grayson Hawthorne's face. "What they have is a very solid hatred for my brother and the way he has chosen to lead his life."

Unable to help herself, she turned to Lucas and studied him, took in the small, half angry, half amused smile pulling at those lips that had made her heart flutter.

"Did you do it?" she asked without thinking.

His look of bored indifference disappeared. "I thought lawyers didn't ask questions like that," he said with harsh animosity.

"This lawyer does."

He pushed away from the wall and walked toward her desk with a smooth panther's grace, as if all this time he had been holding back, containing the raw, furious power of his rage. "What do you think, Miss Kendall? Do you think I did it?"

She didn't back up, though she wanted to, and she didn't answer his question. Instead she asked, "Where were you the night of the murder?"

The air in the room seemed sparse as he stared at her. She felt the barely contained power of him, the heat of his body taking over the small space. It was all she could do to not look away.

"I was in my room at the club. In bed. Would you like to know what I was doing there?"

His voice was a deep, seductive brush of sound, and her breath hissed out of her.

"No, thank you," she managed. "But if indeed you were in . . . your room, how could anyone possibly think you did it?"

"They have an eyewitness."

Alice blinked. "An eyewitness?" she repeated, incredulous. "If someone saw you do it, you don't need a lawyer, Mr. Hawthorne, you need a miracle worker."

"That's why we came to you." Lucas drawled the last word with stinging contempt. "As Grayson said, you're smart, you're hungry." His smile returned, hard and dismissive. "And while you aren't at all what I expected, you are a woman."

"Lucas," Grayson snapped.

Her shoulders came back. "What is that supposed to mean?"

But Lucas wasn't put off. "What my dear brother has failed to mention is that he believes a woman lawyer will help my case."

"Most men would believe that a woman lawyer would do more harm than good."

Lucas shrugged, the gesture a lament. "I said as much myself. But Grayson feels that no woman would consider representing a guilty man. At least that's what he's counting on a jury believing."

She began to see where he was headed, and her stomach tightened with anger.

Grayson gave his brother a quelling look before he spoke. "The fact is, Miss Kendall, if you agree to represent Lucas, I don't believe he will ever be indicted by the grand jury, much less convicted. Yes, they have an eyewitness. But she is a woman of lesser virtue, and it will be her word against his."

"From what I hear, your brother is a *man* of lesser virtue." The words were out before Alice could stop them.

Grayson's countenance grew fierce. Lucas threw his head back and laughed.

"At least she's honest," he said. "Come on, big brother. We're wasting our time."

He headed for the door, looking pleased to be leaving.

"*Are* we wasting our time?" Grayson asked.

Alice couldn't seem to look away from Lucas. Minutes ticked by in silence as she thought about this man charged with murder, trying to understand what it was about him that drew her. He was arrogant, rude, and he had trouble written all over him. But something about him made her heart beat wildly and her knees feel weak.

It was foolish, idiotic, an insipidly female reaction. And she had always prided herself on the fact that she had never been insipid.

"I'm sorry," she said finally, still looking at Lucas instead of his brother. "But I can't take the case."

A flash of something—hurt, fear—darkened in Lucas Hawthorne's blue eyes, but was quickly covered by that wry indifference.

"Come on, let's go," he said.

Grayson pursed his lips and stared at her hard. "Just think about it, Miss Kendall," he said, his tone firm and exacting. "Lucas needs a lawyer who can counter the very reputation you mentioned." He glanced around her office with a knowing look. "And if my guess is correct, you need a client."

Then they were gone, the door closing with a rattle of glass in the wooden frame. Alice stared at the murky window, feeling shaken and angry. Though more than that, she felt a needling desire to take the case.

But to take on a man whose disreputable lifestyle could very easily have led him to commit such a crime? And even if he didn't, no court in the land would believe it.

No, she wasn't that foolish.

She pressed her hand against her heart. It raced inside her chest as Lucas Hawthorne's blue eyes flashed in her mind—the way he had looked at her, really looked for those few moments when he first entered the room, seeing her as no one else ever did.

What did he see, she wanted to ask.

Shaking her head, she scoffed at her thoughts. She wasn't going to ask Lucas Hawthorne anything, not about what he saw . . . or about what he had done. Her decision was made. She wouldn't see him again. Case closed. End of story.

If only it had ended there.